MW01229821

Within the Ambit

Book One of THE KHIMAIRA CHAIN

By K.J. Spencer

DEDICATION

To everyone that heard and believed.
For Britt.

ACKNOWLEDGMENTS

A friend who listens.
A husband who nourishes.
A boy who dreams.
A friend, wife and mother who is grateful.

All my love.

1
WITHIN THE AMBIT

I felt the cold bite my nose as I stepped onto the front porch. Before I closed the door, I turned to look at the two lumps hidden under the blankets of my bed across the room. I lingered for a moment and imagined peeling off the layers of warm clothes I'd bundled in, so that I could cuddle up once more with the two most important people in my world.

The cottage we called home wasn't much more than a large room with a two-way fireplace in the center of it. One side of the room contained a long wood table with a bench and two mismatched chairs for seating, a small stove, an ice box, and a counter space with a water basin. A wooden ladder to the right of the fireplace ascended to a small loft with a circular window and a bed for my children. The other side of the room, around the backside of the fireplace, was where my bed was pushed up against the wall. That was where they'd slept every night since he'd left.

I let them stay when I realized he was never coming back. Now I sleep in James' spot, on the edge of the bed. I moved into a lot of his spaces after that. Spaces that have always felt too big for me to fill.

Isla rolled over under the blankets and put her arm over her brother's shoulder. This gesture made me smile. It was so like her to be protective of him, even in her sleep.

She'd always been more independent and stubborn than her brother. In fact, I'm sure the only reason she still slept in my bed was to be close to him, not me.

She seemed to feel a sort of responsibility to protect him from everyone, including me. Not a single night had passed, since they were conceived, that they hadn't slept side by side. I warmed at the thought of them spooning in my womb, like they spoon now: warm, comfortable, safe.

Isla was born first, then Chasen.

That was nearly eleven years ago.

I drew in a deep breath and began pulling the door closed when the silence was broken by a frantic wheezing sound.

Chasen.

It was all too familiar a sound to me.

Not again.

I hurried to the side of the bed as my son struggled against the blankets to get up on his elbows.

It could happen just like that. One moment he was fine and the next he wasn't.

"Chasen," I said, sliding onto the end of the bed.

His throat gargled.

"Isla!" I called. She was awake and moving toward us in seconds; her instincts were quicker than mine.

It's happening, I thought.

This might be it. Please don't let this be it.

The burden of his illness sat heavy on my chest.

Any one of these attacks could be the last.

I hated the way my thoughts betrayed him.

He's strong. He's still strong. He can still fight. Tell him he must fight.

My daughter had him in her arms. She patted his back as he gasped. The color drained from his face.

A familiar panic threatened to steal what little air he was getting. I felt that same panic seep into my own breathing.

Stay calm. He needs to see that you're calm.

"Chasen, you have to breathe slowly," Isla encouraged him.

"It's too cold in here," her voice strained. "It's too cold for him." *Breathe, son,* I encouraged with my thoughts, but the words were trapped like the lump in my throat. If I forced them out, I couldn't be sure what else might follow.

"Mother!" Isla yelled. I looked up at her. "You left the door open!"

Chasen heaved, trying to find air. His hands tugged at the sheets and blankets, as though the air he needed was hidden under them.

"I--?!" I exclaimed because it was all I could muster. She pushed her brother into my arms, then whipped back the covers and jumped up. She darted across the freezing floor in bare feet, and slammed the door shut.

Chasen squeezed at the sleeve of my coat, pulling at me to do something.

"Breathe, buddy," I finally managed to spit out. "It's going to be okay," I lied.

Was it?

The episodes were getting worse. They were occurring more often, getting harder for him to overcome.

Isla collected a piece of firewood and tossed it in the fireplace. Then she retrieved a quilt from the end of the bed and laid it on the floor.

"Carry him here," she ordered.

"What?"

"Carry him over here. He needs the heat," she demanded.

"Mom?!"

I hesitated, paralyzed with fear.

Where are my instincts?

"Now!" Isla growled.

The shrill tone of her voice stirred me. I quickly lifted my son into a cradling position and carried him to the blanket by the fire.

"Chasen," Isla said with a sternness that we both recognized. "Stop panicking! You're going to be fine. Look at those flames."

Chasen knew to focus on the flames, a trick he'd taught himself to distract from the pain. Together, Isla and I each took one of his hands, placing them on our chests. We practiced slow breathing for him to emulate. The three of us sat quietly, listening for the strain in his throat to ease, waiting for the whistle of tightness to release. He was weak but his color was returning.

"He's worse," Isla said.

"No," I argued even though I knew she was right.

"Maybe Papa can come see him? He hasn't been in a while. Maybe he can—"

Isla's mention of my father reminded me where I was on my way to. "I have to go!" I gasped.

3

Quickly, I leaned down to kiss the top of Chasen's head. I shifted him from my lap to his sister's.

"You can't be serious? Mom! He needs you to stay."

"Chasen?"

His eyes opened slightly, and he looked toward me.

"There's an emergency at the clinic. A baby. Do you understand?"

He nodded slightly.

"There's an emergency *here!*" Isla scolded me.

"I'm sorry, Isla, I don't have time to argue." I wrapped my scarf around my neck again.

"I'll be back as soon as I can," I promised them.

The weight of it hurt. I didn't want to leave him anymore than she wanted me to.

Too much. It's too much to hold, I thought. *I can't hold it.*

I paused and watched as Isla pulled a blanket up over Chasen's shoulder. The burden was too much for her to be his keeper, but what choice did she have?

What choice do I have but to rely on her?

"Isla--" I started to say.

She looked up and I saw the raw disappointment in her eyes.

She hates her life here, I thought.

She hates me, I accepted.

"Close the door tight when you leave," she said coldly.

And I knew there was no point in staying to comfort her.

Pressing, gripping, strangling guilt reminded me I was needed elsewhere.

Outside of our cottage, a thick coating of snow waited for me. The footprints I'd carved out early in the morning for chores, were already filled in with fresh fluffy white flakes. Heavy snow meant heavy everything. There was a time that the pure white was quiet and made me feel hopeful, it meant newness. But now, there was nothing new about it, it nagged at my chaotic mind which was already screaming for it all to stop.

Heavy snow meant another layer of work: new footsteps to carve out, extra clothing to layer on and off. It meant a long hard walk into the clinic.

Chores were harder, temperatures were colder, the winter seemed longer. And with each day, it all threatened to take my boy away from me.

The rims of my eyelids wetted, heavy with my own sort of precipitation. Just like the clouds dropped on me when the burden was too heavy, so did my tears.

At least there are still tears, I thought.

I had felt other pieces slip away slowly as time rolled on and the harshness persisted: my instincts, my fight, my belief in anything better. All withering and yet the tears remained loyal, never evading me when I needed them. Cold, trustworthy tears.

The wind blustered and I trudged on.

Four farms on my lane, of similar size and shape to mine, passed as I counted them. Three more and I would find myself at the Mall.

Turn right toward the clinic and I'll be there, I thought. *The clinic is painted white with black shutters. My father will be there. He is six feet tall with brown skin and brown eyes.*

These were my reminders. Simple facts that were unchanging and reliable. When my emotions threatened to get the best of me, I'd learned to break the world down into pieces of truth that I could handle. The color of things, the shapes, the dimensions, the tangible qualities, and quantities that I could count on.

I'd recite them in my head, filling my thoughts with facts and observations, rather than letting my mind drown me in the inevitably sad realities of my life and existence.

"In an upside-down world, we stand upright on the truth," James would say, and I could almost hear his voice, though I wondered if it sounded the same as I remembered. My husband was gifted with words, he knew how to speak to the heart of things.

I'll admit that I didn't fully understand what he'd meant when he first said this phrase to me. Then when he disappeared, I was struck with such a sharp changing grief that holding on to shreds of truth became my means to survival. My world was turned upside down and recognizing the constants around me, stabilized me. The unchanging truth, the predictability of the simplest things, like a sunrise or a cold brutal winter, were my salvation.

The truth was that I didn't know if James was ever coming back. In my weakest moments I wondered if he'd tired of us and left. In my worst moments, I knew he was dead. But then his words would remind me. *Look for the truth.*

The truth was that he loved us. I knew that. I'd clung to that reminder for five long years, and I'd searched for the facts around me every day since. Facts that seemed like truth.

I plodded passed another farm. A neighbor-wife, Samantha, was shoveling her stoop. I heard the grinding sound of her shovel stopped as I passed. I looked up at her, letting the cold winter whip across my cheeks.

She was watching me. No expression. She seemed like she wanted to say something, but she remained silent.

"Morning," I offered to her, wishing she'd stop staring at me.

"Morning," she called back, and I noticed she'd left the 'good' off her greeting as well. We both knew few mornings in the Ambit started with 'good'.

I wondered if she felt sorry for me, trekking through the deep snow without proper shoes or a horse to carry me. I wondered if she feared she would someday be in my thinly worn shoes, single and barely tolerated by the society around her.

I wondered if she was annoyed, as many others were, that I was allowed to live as a single woman on her lane. I wondered if she, like the others, had kept her distance from me because she was worried that I'd try to steal her husband.

Since James' disappearance, I'd watched my friendships grow distant, my neighbors go quiet, my status diminish. Women in the Ambit know that having a male head of household means survival, so if I am single, they think I am a threat to their security. Not because women can't survive on their own, but because the Guiding Authority makes it nearly impossible for us to do so.

When James didn't return, I refused to move from my cottage to a lowlier lane specifically for single women. In return, they took my horse, cut our rations in half, and forbid anyone from helping us. They wanted to make an example of me. They wanted me to break down and accept a new husband, as there were a few suitors in the Ambit that'd expressed interest, but I was already married. Even if James was never coming back, I was married to my deviance.

I hurried my pace, feeling the cold seep into my boots. I heard Samantha's shovel scrape again behind me and felt relieved that she was no longer watching me struggle on my way.

Life in the Ambit is hard. The winters are cruel, the Guiding Authority is worse.

I remember the beginning, though I was very young. I remember my mother being allowed to have a horse, back when horses were in better supply, before the Guiding Authority determined that only households with men could have them.

I remember when the Three Guilts were created, before they were mandates: no medicine, no technology, no consuming meat.

Now the Three Guilts are laws and indulging in any of them means banishment. We were assured by the Guiding Authority that banishment from the Ambit, the only society most of us had ever known, is far worse than these restrictions. Yet, I watch as my son's health pales without the medicine, they say is evil, and feel sure that his escape from the Ambit will soon come without it.

Maybe they are right. Maybe medicine would only prolong his suffering here. If I were a good mother, I would welcome his release from a place such as this.

This thought stopped me in my tracks. *What was I saying?* I'd promised myself to stop thinking that way.

Keep moving, I ordered. *Two more blocks to the clinic. The clinic is white with black shutters.*

Before the Ambit existed, there was a world where medicine and technology were accepted, even encouraged. In fact, the art of science had progressed so far that medical miracles were being performed. Diseases were healed and prevented with immunizations. Technology was so advanced; humans could move through the air in planes and travel with motorized vehicles.

Communication was expansive and inclusive to civilizations across the globe, a concept that my mind could barely begin to fathom.

Freedom to move from place to place was what I was most curious about. I'd seen books with pictures of water as far as the eye could see and mountains so high, they confounded my mind. Grass so green, on rolling hills, unlike the flat earth of the Ambit and animals of all different shapes and sizes and colors.

Arrogance, I thought.

The arrogance of mankind to have so much at their fingertips and to think they could control and consume it without consequence or thought of the future. That arrogance stole our freedom.

In 2050, when medical miracles reached their peak, an annual vaccine was developed to stave off illnesses of all magnitudes.

They called it the MIL, which was short for Multifocal Immuno Lovenox. Technology of the time, spread word and use of the annual vaccine, and by 2084, nearly all the industrialized societies of earth partook of it. The immunized were known as the Meds.

In June of 2084, something went terribly wrong, and the Meds started getting sick. Very sick. Then, as though their bodies acquired all the diseases that the MIL was designed to protect against at once, the Meds started dying.

In a matter of days, they died bloody horrific deaths. Billions. Dead. Something in the vaccine turned them inside out, leaking their bodily fluids from every orifice.

As a child I had nightmares from the stories the other children told me. Our parents were the survivors.

They'd witnessed it firsthand. My father, and the others his age, saw the world go from medical miracles to disaster and disease in a matter of months.

What came next was worse, from the MIL vaccine emerged what is now known as the MIL disease, a mysterious illness from an unknown variable that the 2084 vaccine contained, with devastating results.

In the days that followed, chaos unfolded. From the bodies, more disease emerged. More death. Of the survivors, many of the ones who had received the MIL vaccine in previous years died, because their immune systems weren't strong enough to fight off the new wave of diseases.

Most people that survived 2084 were children under the age of three, because they weren't eligible to receive the MIL vaccine.

Pregnant women and incarcerated prisoners weren't given the vaccine that year either, so when the Crisis occurred, a dangerous mix of known criminals and vulnerable women and children were left behind.

In addition to the ones that didn't receive the MIL that year, was a group of people known as Naturals. Born from conservative freethinkers, they were the group that refused the MIL from the beginning.

At the time that the vaccination was developed and implemented, the United States of America was still considered "the home of the free".

Even though the government tried to mandate the vaccination at certain points in history, the American people wouldn't allow it. Naturals lived among the Meds, but not without judgement or condemnation. The Natural community was tolerated by the Meds majority, only because they represented the freedoms that the United States stood for. They all came to understand that protecting those freedoms was more important than arguing vaccination status.

After the Crisis, a group of Naturals and some converted Med-survivors removed themselves from the post-Crisis world. They hid away in the midwestern part of what was once the United States and called themselves the Ambit, which means boundary.

Now as far as the eye can see, from any direction of the Ambit, there is nothing. We are like an oasis in the desert. No other civilization, no other narrative, nowhere to go. Nothing but stories and rumors of what lies beyond.

It was to "protect us" they said. That is how they justified closing the borders of our society, cutting us off from the outside world. That was the reason they kept us in and enforced rules against the things they believed had led to mankind's destruction. Beyond the border of the Ambit, we were taught to believe there was only violence, disease, and death.

Medicine will kill you. Technology will betray you and eating meat is forgetting your place on earth. They still made our children recite this in school.

9

The clinic is white with black shutters. I reminded myself of the facts. *No use in wondering what is beyond the Ambit's border. That's a world you can only visit in your dreams.*

"Finally," Forest groaned, seeing me burst through the blizzarding doorway. He hurried around the end of his desk and started tugging my coat off my shoulders.

"Who's here?" I asked.

"Your father," he answered stupidly.

"I know that" I snipped at him. "Obviously, I know that. I meant, who is the patient?"

"That woman from the other end," he stated, trying to remove my scarf but accidentally cinching it tighter across my throat.

"I can undress myself," I demanded, pulling back from his grip.

He huffed with frustration, lifting his hands in submission.

I leaned over to remove my boots. "Which woman?" I asked again for clarification.

"The flower cart vendor," he said.

I looked up, "Elles?"

He nodded.

I quickened my pace. "She's not due for another month."

"I know," he agreed.

I quickly tossed my coat to the side and took the clean smock that Forest was holding for me. I pulled it on as I stepped to the sink to scrub my hands clean.

"This water's cold!" I exclaimed, beginning to feel the pressure of the situation.

"It was warm. If you'd gotten here sooner—"

I spun around, "It needs to be warm! I can't sanitize my hands with cold water, Forest! Put it on the fire and warm it up!"

"What? Now?"

"Yes now!"

My father appeared in the doorway, shoving a curtain to the side, "Oh good, you're here! I need you in here immediately."

Forest stood still. I yelled at him, "The water, Forest!"

My father caught on to my frustration, seeing that my hands weren't clean yet. "There's no time for that!"

My stomach dropped.

No time for clean hands?

My father had previously been in the medical profession before the Crisis. Throughout my whole life, as he'd trained me to be a midwife in the Ambit, he'd taught me of the importance of clean hands before delivering the babies.

"Now, Britt," he urged. I could sense the tension in his voice.

I darted toward him, making my way to the small examination room behind the front entry.

"Okay, Elles," I said pushing the curtain to the side. "I'm here."

"She can't hear you," my father said, rushing to the cart on the other side of the room. "She passed out moments ago."

He stripped off the buttoned-down shirt he was wearing. Rarely in my life, had I seen my father's naked arms. He kept them hidden for a reason. I stared at the small circular scars up and down both of his arms. Scars from the MIL vaccine.

Forest handed him a red smock to put on.

Red? I knew this color and smock meant there was to be blood. "What's wrong with her?"

"She's not strong enough to get the baby out, Britt. We're running out of time."

"Not strong enough?! She's one of the strongest women I know!" I said as I ran to the side of the table. "Elles," I shook her shoulders hoping my voice could reach her. "Elles, wake up!" I waited for her to respond.

"Today's the day, your little one is coming but we need you here to do it. We need your help, Elles. Can you hear me?"

"Britt..." the urgency in my father's voice calmed. He knew what needed to be done.

I touched her neck with my finger, trying to feel for a pulse. It was faint, but it was still there. I slid my hand to her belly and felt a subtle movement.

"The baby's moving," I said, looking to my father. He stood with his hands in the air, a scalpel at the ready.

"Not yet," I begged, feeling my heart race. "Elles!" I yelled. Then I reached up and felt her pulse again. "Elles, we need your help! We need you to wake up! Your baby needs you to wake up now!"

I grabbed her face and turned it toward me. Her eyes rolled back. "Sh*t, Elles!" I cried. I felt for her pulse again. I couldn't find it.

"Can't you do something?" I asked my father desperately even though I knew the answer. I felt tears rush my eyes. I pressed my thumbs into her face, pulling the thin skin on her pale cheeks, like maybe I could find her life under it.

"It has to be now," he said.

I reached down and put my hand on her belly. It moved again slightly. The baby was a fighter like its mother.

"Not yet," I cried. "I can wake her!"

"Britt," my father stepped closer to the table.

"No!" I begged, putting my hand up to stop him from getting closer to her. "Not. Yet." I pleaded. I rushed back up to Elles' face.

"Elles," I cried, "you gotta wake up. Please, friend. You gotta wake up."

Nothing.

"Britt! I need you to help me get this baby out."

"No!" I growled at him. I knew that opening Elles up would kill her. "Elles!' I focused on her face.

"Forest!" my father called.

"NO!" I yelled. "Don't you dare do it yet, she's gonna wake up."

I felt Forest's hands latch around my arms.

"Take her out," my father commanded him.

"She has to wake up!" I squirmed against Forest's grip.

"She's not!" I heard my father say. "She's gone, Britt, and if we don't move now, the baby will be too."

"No!"

"Enough!" my father slammed his hand on the cart. The tools rattled on the metal plate, startling me. He rarely lost his temper with me.

"I need your help! If you're not up for this, then get out!"

The tears leaked from my eyes. Faithful hot tears. I stared at my father. We both knew what it would mean. Without medicine, opening her up would be a death sentence. Not opening her up would mean risking them both. I closed my eyes and inhaled a deep breath to compose myself. He was right.

I shook Forest's hands off me and he stepped away.

"Get the towels," my father ordered. "Forest, get the water."

I held myself together as my father cut into my friend and retrieved the baby girl from her insides.

Elles was going to name her Abigail.
Her name would have been Abigail.
The world felt slow and cold, as I watched my father administer lifesaving motions to the baby. By the time we got to her, she'd been without her mother's breath for too long. Her lungs were too small, and so was her time in this world.

I stood stoically, as my father wrapped the child in a towel and handed her still body to Forest.

He looked at me with burning anger. "Don't you *ever* delay me again."

He stormed out of the exam room.

I felt sick, looking down over Elles' lifeless bloodied body. We'd waited too long. I'd waited too long. We'd lost them both because I hadn't wanted to lose my friend.

I put my hand over her face and closed her blank blue eyes. Then I pushed her hair back with my red hand, streaking her blood over her skin.

I fell to my knees beside the bed, sobbing silently. Regret ripped at my insides, threatening to string them all over the room, just as hers were.

"I'm so sorry," I managed to say, trying to catch my breath. "I tried to…" but my words were stuck.

What had I tried to do? Save her?
Would she have wanted that?

As a mother, I knew her wishes would have been for me to let her go, to spare her sweet girl's life. But my own selfishness wouldn't let me see it. I didn't want to lose her. She was one of the few that loved me well in the Ambit. She had an unfounded positivity and an unpopular hope. She was odd in the best ways and resourceful in the most surprising. She was like me but better. She was more than better. She was the best of us. If she couldn't survive the Ambit, how could I ever hope to?

Around her neck, there was a thin silver chain. Clasped in the middle was a charm the shape of a fish. I stared at it, thinking of her husband, Joseph. He was a fisherman in the Ambit; he fell through the ice in winter a few years back.

You can be with him now, I thought.

For a moment, I was jealous of her, and I wished to be with my James. The guilt was too heavy, the shame. The Ambit's rules killed Elles, but *I* was responsible for Abigail.

13

The clinic is white with black shutters.

Time moved slowly as I sat on the chair in the front of the clinic. I'd scrubbed my hands raw with a towel, trying to remove my friend's blood from them.

Moments too late.

If I'd moved faster through the snow, if I'd ignored Samantha on the porch, if I'd allowed my father to follow his medical instincts...

So many ifs. Regret squeezed my insides, and I was sure if there was anything left to give of myself, it would've come out now. So much grief surrounded me. It was choking me. At times, I'd convinced myself this was the way it was, and would always be but with that came this empty nothingness of inadequacy.

Do my motions in this world even matter? Had they mattered today? If I had moved quicker or been better for her in any way, could I have saved her? Or Abigail? If what I do doesn't matter, then why exist?

The front door to the clinic opened and my father stepped inside. He dusted off the snow on his shoulders and boots and then removed his coat, handing it to Forest.

"They'll be here shortly," he told us. He was referring to the Bookkeeper and carriage. The bookkeeper would tally the loss of life in the Ambit's Book of Names. The carriage would take their bodies to be burned.

"Give us a moment?" my father asked Forest. Forest nodded and then slipped into the back room of the clinic.

My father stepped around the desk and sat on the edge of it, across from me.

He was silent.

"Don't you ever get tired of it?" I asked.

He looked into me and swallowed hard. For a moment my father seemed to understand my question. Then he broke eye contact with me and said, "Death is the unfortunate ending to every story, Britt."

I sighed, shaking my head. I'd heard him say this phrase many times in my life. After my mother passed, when James didn't return, with each mother or child we lost in childbirth.

"That's just something you say to comfort yourself."

He looked up again.

"No, Britt. It's not."

14

I wiped my hands over my cheeks, trying to clear the dried streaks of tears that I'd shed.

"It's the truth," he finished.

I shook my head. "I don't understand why? What's the point of any of this if death is all that waits for us?"

He exhaled loudly. "I wish I knew."

I couldn't help but laugh. My father had never been very good at talking me through life. He seemed to be as confused by it as I was.

I stood up from the chair and looked down at him. "That's all you got, huh? No wonder I'm a mess."

"What'd I say?" he asked.

"Nothing! You don't *say* anything! You don't *do* anything!"

I retrieved my coat from the hook behind the door. I started sliding it on.

"I want to know why?!" I stopped putting my coat on. I yelled at him. "Why are we here? Why, of all the places on earth, did you and mother choose to come here?! Why would you choose to raise me in the Ambit?"

"What?" my father scowled.

"What's out there?!"

"Out where?"

I pointed beyond the imaginary borders of the Ambit. "Out there! On the Outside?" I lowered my voice, "Where James went?"

His eyes widened, hearing my husband's name. Then he hung his head. Silence. The only answer I would ever get from him. Indignantly, I shoved my other arm in my coat. He wouldn't answer me. He never did.

"What would you say to Isla, if she asked you that?"

I looked up at him, surprised.

He repeated himself, "How would you answer that question for Chasen?"

"That's different—"

"How?" he interrupted. He rose from the desk and crossed to me.

"You have to understand, the way things were after the Crisis, we needed to keep you safe…"

"From what?"

"From *all* of it."

15

"All of *what?*"

He shook his head.

"All you've done, Dad, is cage me. You've caged me my whole life and when I ask you about why, all I get are vague answers!"

He looked up. "You're an adult now, Britt. It's true, we caged you when you were young, but you can leave the Ambit now. Anytime you want--you know that."

His words scared me.

"You know I can't -- now."

He stepped in closer.

"Why?" he whispered to me.

I looked at him, he seemed serious in his curiosity. I searched his face.

Was he suggesting that I should consider leaving the Ambit?

Why after all this time, after all the years of letting the Ambit indoctrinate me into their culture, would he encourage me to think of leaving?

"I can't," I whispered, feeling my breath slip away. "I have to think of Chasen and --"

"Exactly," my father said softly. "And *we* had to think *of you*."

I looked up at him. His eyes were tender.

"The Ambit isn't keeping you here, Britt. The line is there for the crossing. You know that because James crossed it. It's the unknown that you're afraid of."

Forest stepped into the room, breaking my concentration on my father. He scowled at me. I wondered if he'd heard my father's words. If he told the Guiding Authority what my father had said, we could both be in trouble.

My father leaned forward and kissed my forehead. "Take the day," he said, squeezing my arm. "Go home and hug my grandchildren for me."

I nodded, feeling like an utter disappointment to him and myself. *What had happened to me?* I didn't understand myself any more than I understood my father.

As I left the clinic, the feelings of disappointment mixed with regret again, as flashes of Elles' body pierced my memory. I reached into my pocket and pulled her fish charm necklace into view. I clenched it in my hand.

Another loss too great to know how to reconcile it with my already depleted hope.

Death is the unfortunate ending to every story. My father's words echoed in my memory.

My mother. James. Elles.

All dead.

Chasen could be next.

Too far. Too much.

I felt the contents of my stomach rise in my throat. I hurried around the corner of the clinic and vomited in the snow. My stomach was close to empty but the bits I'd had for breakfast escaped me in violent convulsions.

Panic began to set in. *Every story ends this way.* I couldn't handle the reality of it. In the Ambit, every story would end this way. Was it crazy to think that maybe that wasn't true if we weren't in the Ambit? *What am I saying? I can't leave the Ambit.*

I threw up again.

White building. Black shutters. Come back to the truth. You can't leave.

My breathing hastened; my heart raced. Fear set in. *I can't take my children from the Ambit. What if…?*

"Are you okay?" a voice caught my attention.

I looked up from the pile of vomit I was leaned over.

A young boy stood there with his head tilted to see me.

Seeing who it was, I was still. My breath and words escaped me all at once. I plunged my hand back into my coat pocket, hiding the necklace out of view.

"Miss Britt?" the boy said again.

I nodded, acknowledging my name.

"You okay?" he asked a second time.

I quickly wiped my sleeve over the lower half of my face, hoping I'd erased any traces of getting sick.

"Seph," I managed to say.

"Yes, ma'am. You don't look so good. Can I help you inside?"

Inside? Inside the clinic. Of course, he meant inside the clinic. He was here to check on his mother.

"No!" I sputtered before I could catch myself.

Too much. Too much to hold.

"You're sure?"

I nodded, trying to force a smile.

My mind raced. Seph was only twelve years old, tall, and thin like his father had been. I thought he'd probably have been sturdier in build like his father, if his diet had been sufficient.

17

His steel blue eyes narrowed staring at me awkwardly, waiting for me to explain why I'd just been leaned over a pile of steaming vomit.

I wondered if he'd be able to guess. I hoped he wouldn't. In a matter of moments, he would know the truth that had unfolded in the hours before. He would learn of his mother and his baby sister's deaths. I simultaneously wanted to preserve this moment of unknowing for him, but also wanted to move him from the steps of the clinic before someone carelessly revealed his ruined life to him.

"What are you doing here?" I stuttered.

He pointed to the clinic, "My mother left early this morning, said she wasn't feeling well. She told me not to worry. I was just on my way to school, so I thought I'd stop to see how she's doing."

"She's sleeping," I sputtered.

His face changed.

"Sleeping?"

"Yes, she's sleeping," I lied again, desperate for anything to keep him from trying to enter the clinic.

"My father is with her, keeping an eye on her."

Seph settled back on his heels. "Can I see her?" he asked.

My mind scrambled to come up with the next lie. "Probably better to let her rest. Actually," I tried to come up with a distraction. "...you were right before. I'm not feeling well."

His eyes grew concerned.

"Would you mind helping me get home?"

"Maybe I should get your father?" He moved toward the steps of the clinic again.

Please no.

I responded quickly, "No need to bother. If you could help me home, Isla is there with Chasen, and she can..."

"Of course," Seph said, moving closer to me to take my arm over his shoulder. He wrapped his other arm around my waist and let me lean on him.

The walk home was quiet, and I was grateful to see that most of the Ambit's citizens had already made their way to their posts for the day. The children were in school, and the adults had either reported to their respective routines on the Mall or were quietly tending their farms.

As we approached my cottage, Seph asked, "Did you see my mother today?"

"No," I lied again. "I was just arriving to the clinic when I started feeling sick."

Seph stopped right before we reached the steps to my porch. "Thank you, Seph," I said, separating from him. I tried to think of the next thing to say. I wanted to invite him in, to give him a space of privacy for the news I knew I needed to share.

When I turned to say something, he was staring back down the lane toward the Mall, where we'd just come from.

His face was pale and motionless.

"Seph?"

"There's smoke."

I looked down the lane and saw the thin dark plume rising from the Mall.

He turned to me.

"You said she was sleeping?"

I swallowed hard, feeling the lump in my throat grow. This wasn't how I wanted him to find out.

"You said she was sleeping, but then you said you hadn't seen her yet because you'd only just arrived."

"Seph," I started to say.

He looked back toward the Mall at the smoke.

"Tell me, Miss Britt."

"I..." I tried. I wanted to apologize for lying to him, for keeping him from going in the clinic, for not allowing him the opportunity to see her one last time. But I knew the state of her body and wanted to protect him from it.

The smoke that rose from the Mall was for her. The Ambit required that the dead be cremated immediately, for fear of disease spreading. Seph knew that. He knew what the smoke meant. He knew it was for her.

He just stared at me, his mind racing through all the scenarios.

"Tell me?" he asked again.

I stepped forward and exhaled. I removed the necklace with the fish charm from my pocket and showed it to him.

"Your mother isn't sleeping."

His chin quivered. Red blushed his cheeks and nose. His eyes remained locked on mine.

My chest tightened, knees weakening under me, I forced my body to remain planted in place. I knew I needed to be sturdy enough for both of us.

"And the baby?" his voice squeaked as he asked. He was trying to remain calm.

I felt my voice hitch as I responded, a sudden gasp leapt from my chest. *Abigail. She is gone because I made my father wait too long. She is dead because of me. I can never tell him that.*

"I'm so sorry, Seph."

His eyes shifted from side to side, searching for something. Answers, I guessed. He was reconciling his own existence with theirs. Before his emotions could grip him, his practical mind knew to consider what this would mean for him.

"What...?" he started to ask.

I wondered how his question would finish. Did he want to know what had already happened or what would happen next? Perhaps he wondered what this would mean for him now? I guessed that was it, but I knew Seph to be too compassionate to be able to utter the question. I wanted to give him an answer. I wanted to lie to him and tell him that it was all going to be okay, but truthfully, I knew what was likely to happen now because he was an orphan.

The Guiding Authority would put him up on a stage, on a block, in front of the Ambit's citizens and offer him to be assumed into another family. They'd list his strengths and qualities, in the hopes of enticing another Ambit family to split their already limited rations with him and take him into their already limited homes. Then what? Then what would become of this poor child? What would become of my friend's son?

Death is the unfortunate ending of every story.

We'd seen it many times before.

20

The orphaned infants would get selected by women too scared to have their own children, the older strong boys would get assumed so they could help weaker families with farm chores, but Seph didn't fit either of those categories.

Who would claim this child?

"I will," I said, before I could think.

Chills rose across the surface of my skin. Even without knowing for sure the question he was asking; I was answering it.

He looked at me with helpless curiosity.

"I'll claim you, Seph," I repeated. "When there's no one left to claim you, I will. I won't let you be put on that block like cattle. I won't give them a chance. If you'll have me? If you'll live with us? I'll claim you."

I'd already cost Elles one of her children today. I would not fail them both. The hungry regret in my stomach accepted this compromise.

Seph's eyes softened.

The moment was like lightening, firing in my veins.

The Guiding Authority was not going to like that I'd added another to my roster. They were not going to approve of a single woman taking in a child that wasn't her own. Just like they did not approve of a single mother, like Elles', getting pregnant. The rebellion of it made me feel alive again, if only for a fleeting moment. Never had a child been claimed before the block.

This is a moment worth living for. I thought.

The cage door was open, and I was the bird staring at it, knowing I'd never fly. But I could still sing.

"Will you let me claim you, Seph?"

Claim. Not assume. Claim.

Seph's head nodded ever so slightly, and we both knew it would be done.

Then the air held tight in his chest exhaled.

Knowing all he needed to, sorrow washed over him from the top of his head to the bottom of his feet. I watched him give into it, letting it take him to the ground. I tried to catch him before he melted, but his weight and my own weakness let us tumble into a mess on the ground together.

He wailed, sobbing unapologetically. I envied his willingness to let his pain out so boldly.

It poured from him, straining his breathing, collapsing his muscles until his body shook with surges of sadness. His intense grief was so personal and yet I was accidentally there to catch it. And while I knew this sheering, branding pain of loss, I also knew I would never be enough to hold him through it. But all I had to be, was willing.

The door to the cottage opened and Isla was there. "Mother?" she called to me. "Is everything okay?"

I shook my head.

She came down from the porch and stood by us. "Seph?" she asked, recognizing him from school. His wails were uncontrollable and justified.

Isla looked at me, understanding the importance of her compassion in the moment. "What can I do to help?"

I felt Seph's shaking body lean into me, the cold mixed with the snow and sorrow. *Too much. Too much to hold.*

"Help me get him inside."

2
THE OUTSIDER

"This only happens here."

The sky flickered as the warm rain dropped from it. I turned to James lying next to me. We'd hidden ourselves in the tall grass of the field. In the Ambit, it was the only place to hide; it was the only place for two teenagers to be alone.

"What?" I asked.

I watched his face for an answer.

He stared up at the sky. A blanket of clouds was outlined by the dark evening behind them. Bursts of light blinked in the distance.

"The flicker," he replied, his eyes wild with amazement. "It only happens here."

I watched as the spring water droplets darkened his hair and beaded on his skin.

He couldn't take his eyes off the sky.

I couldn't take my eyes off him.

I rolled over onto my elbows, inching closer slightly. I didn't want to be too forward, but I wanted to be as close as I could to this boy that mesmerized me.

"It doesn't flicker where you come from?"

He smiled into the vastness above, like he found my ignorance amusing. Insecurity reminded me that I was just an ordinary girl trapped in a boring society, hanging on his every word.

I was dying to understand where he'd come from. Curious to hear why he'd crossed into our world. But mostly, I was wondering if he would stay.

He propped himself up on his elbows. His face was mere inches from mine now.

Did he mean to move closer to me or was that an accident?

"I don't think it flickers anywhere but here," he said.

We stared at each other. The rain dripped down our faces, rolling over our lips. I was suddenly very aware of our lips.

The sky wasn't the only thing flickering. There was something much more intriguing between the two of us.

"It's only like this when it rains," I said, breaking the silence between us but not the gaze.

His face split into a grin. He threw his head back and closed his eyes, letting the water run down his neck. With jealousy, I watched as the droplets beaded at his neckline.

Why is he so irresistible to me?

I was seventeen years old, and I'd never met a boy like James. Typically, I was running *with* the boys, not after them. The ones that were my age, the ones from the Ambit, were more like cousins to me. We'd grown up together. I couldn't remember a time that I'd had a crush on a boy. There was a time when I wondered if I was supposed to like girls, but they didn't intrigue me either. Then I met James.

Why is this boy so different? I thought.

Is it because he is from the Outside?

I looked beyond him to the single tree that stood at the Ambit Crossing. The unofficial official crossing point between us and them. He knew what was beyond it. He was one of *them*. I wanted to be one of *them* too. I wanted to be whatever he was.

"What happens when it rains, where you come from?" I asked.

He lifted his head again and I noticed that his eyes were dimmer than they were the moment before.

"They hide," he said.

I laughed, "From the rain? Why?"

"In the Outside, they hide from everything."

"But you don't?"

The corner of his mouth curled upward. He enjoyed the idea that I saw him differently from his people. I hoped he saw me differently from mine.

"No," he smiled. "I'm only interested in hiding in the grass with you now."

A clap of thunder shook the ground, startling us. We stared at each other, wild-eyed with fear. Then recognizing that we'd both reacted the same way, we burst into laughter.

A moment later, rain poured from the sky, washing the laughter away, and soaking us in seriousness. We stared at each other.

In that moment, I thought that if he would let me, I would follow him anywhere.

I didn't know falling in love would be so literal. I sank toward him, and he caught me. We kissed.

Then, something happened.

Something different than I remembered.

James' face went serious.

"James?"

He was looking for something. Then his voice changed from that of the seventeen-year-old in my memory, to how he would sound later in our life together. It was deep and protective, like he was warning me.

"There's a storm coming."

Awake.

The front door opened.

"James!?" I sat up in the dark cold corner of the cottage.

The bed was beneath me; our children were asleep beside me.

"No, ma'am," a voice called back from the dark doorframe. "It's just me."

Seph.

Not James.

James is gone.

That was a dream. A memory. All except for the last part. The warning.

A floorboard creaked as Seph stepped around the side of the fireplace. His head dipped around the stone pillar. "I was just coming in from chores. I didn't mean to startle you."

My heart sank, remembering the dream. Reliving the memory. Tears filled my eyes as the reality set in.

James will never open that door again.

25

"Miss Britt?" Seph whispered, watching me from the shadows of the fireplace. "Are you okay?"

No. I thought.

"Yes," I lied. "I just had this dream—" I started, then I caught myself.

"Are you hurt?"

I looked up at him.

Am I hurt? Why would he ask me that?

Then I realized two of my fingers were touching my lip. I'd reached out to feel for James there, but they'd returned nothing. I lowered my hand.

"No," I lied again. I was more than hurt. I was devastated.

Seph seemed to understand that I wasn't being entirely truthful.

"I'll make some tea for you," he offered. Then he quietly slipped across the floor to the water basin on the other side of the fireplace.

I searched the room around me. This reality was unwelcoming.

Chasen's throat wheezed as he slept. I watched him for signs of breathing issues and then felt the disappointment sink in.

It's not supposed to be this way. I thought. *It was never supposed to be this way.*

Some days were like that. The weight of my grief made it hard to see anything good around me without James. Even my children, who I loved dearly, didn't offer me what he had. We knew each other intimately. We'd shared the moment in the meadow and so many others that no one else knew of.

I looked around the room. This was the room we'd come home to after our wedding. This was the bed where our children were conceived, the blankets we'd shared. I remembered lying in bed watching the flickering sky through the window with him.

Regret climbed up my insides and hung in my throat.

It shouldn't be this way. He should be here. He should be lying here now.

Chasen looked like him as he slept. Soft lips, black curls rested against his forehead. His eyes were dark like mine, but his skin was like James'. His eyelashes were long and thick. I remembered James' were the same.

Chasen coughed in his sleep. I held my breath to see if it would spur him into a fit. That was another thing James would know how to ease better than me.

I am never enough. James was everything.

Chasen rolled onto his back, landing his hand on his stomach. His fist was clenched around something. Carefully, I loosened his fingers to reveal his red toy car.

Again, memories of James gutted me. The car was a gift he'd given Chasen. It was a souvenir that we kept hidden in our cottage, because the Guiding Authority would not have approved of something resembling life before the Crisis.

I reached under Chasen's pillow to retrieve its matching counterpart. It was a yellow car with a black streak of paint down one side. I squeezed them in my hands and pinched my eyes closed to conceal the tears that pooled there.

He was just here. I thought. *He was here only moments ago in my dreams. It felt so real.*

Waking up meant it'd been five years, not moments, since we'd last seen him. The fresh grief knocked my thoughts backward in time.

How did we get here?

This was a question that I asked myself regularly. It was raw today, as my dream had so cruelly tricked me into remembering what it was like before: before Chasen's illness, before James went missing, before I'd lost my mind to grief.

When I was young, I thought I would have followed James anywhere.

Then why hadn't I?

Now we were separated by something.

Was it death or misunderstanding?

Death. I thought. *He must be dead.*

He had a reason to come back. He would have come back.

Frustration layered with the disappointment and grief and began to overload my mind. This was why I shut it all out. Too many complex feelings with no way to unload them, no way to process what I couldn't understand.

Why did it turn out like this when we were so young and full of passion? How could I reconcile his absence when I didn't understand it? When my brain told me it was somehow my fault, but I didn't know what I'd done to deserve it?

The whistle of the teapot pulled my attention from my miserable thoughts. Within seconds, Seph hushed the kettle and pulled it from the fire.

I watched his movements.

He'd been with us for months now. He was the only thing about the cottage that was new since James' absence. He'd brought a calm to our home that'd been missing for years.

Gratitude.

Seph ducked his head around the corner of the fireplace. "Would you like me to bring your tea to you?"

I shook my head. "No, thanks. I'll get up."

His gentle consideration made the moment lighter.

Gratitude.

I pulled the covers back from the bed and slipped into my house shoes. I wrapped myself in a house coat, tying it in the middle. I still had Chasen's toy cars in my hand, so I leaned down and slipped them back under his pillow. He would be distraught if he woke and couldn't find them. He and Isla both kept treasures from James under their pillows. Chasen had his cars; Isla had her book.

I stood for a moment, taking them in. They were the most beautiful creatures I'd ever seen. I felt ashamed that I'd forgotten to stop and admire them more often. Too often, I'd felt sorry for myself and forgotten to enjoy them.

Grief has a way of simultaneously robbing you of beautiful moments and reminding you to see them at the same time.

Seph was putting another log on the fire, when I sat down at the table to sip the hot tea, he'd made for me.

I watched him work the embers until they embraced the new wood and caught fire.

Then he turned around and gave me a smile. Over the months since he'd come to live with us, I'd learn to recognize this exact smile. He'd offer it to me when he was unsure of what to say or when he was trying to comfort me. He would press his lips together into a thin line and then, one side would slowly curl upward.

He was a kind boy, warm and compassionate. So much like the mother that raised him.

Images of Elles' and Abigail's bodies flashed in my memory. They'd taken up residency there. I didn't mind them anymore. Better to be reminded of them, and my mistakes, than to lose them forever.

Seph leaned forward over the table, as he situated himself on the bench across from me. As he did this, the fish charm necklace fell out from under the collar of his shirt. It swung forward into view and again, I was reminded of the day I took it from his mother's neck.

I sipped my tea while stuffing the memories back into the closets of my brain.

"Do you dream of him often?" Seph asked, unexpectedly.

Him?

James.

I looked up from my teacup, surprised. I stared at him, thinking about his question.

"Sorry," he said after an extended silence. His eyes darted around the room, avoiding mine.

I took another sip of tea.

"No, I don't dream of him often," I finally answered, after the silence had rested on us for a bit.

Seph's eyes centered on me. He seemed surprised.

"Oh," he said. Then with a boldness that was uncommon for him, he pressed further. "You don't like to talk about him, do you?"

If anyone but Seph had asked, I think I would have been annoyed. He seemed to know this.

"They don't want me to talk about him," I said.

"I know," Seph replied, astounding me again.

"Then why are you asking?"

He hesitated, then offered, "I can't imagine anyone telling me that I can't talk about my mother. Or my father. Or …" I prepared myself for the word that I knew would follow. "…Abigail."

I exhaled.

He doesn't know that I was responsible for Abigail's death. My mind told me, as though somehow, I could manage to forget.

"Your mother and father were loved by many of the Ambit's citizens, Seph. You *should* talk about them. You should preserve them in memory," I encouraged, thinking I was saying what he needed to hear.

"And *you* shouldn't preserve James?" he asked cautiously.

The question stung almost as much as hearing his name did. I tried to recall the last time I'd heard someone say it to me.

My father. I remembered.

The day that Elles died my father had said his name to me. I remembered because Forest overheard us and told the Guiding Authority of our conversation. They made a point of reminding us of their position regarding my missing husband.

"They'd prefer we don't talk about him," I recited it to Seph as it had been explained to me. "They think it will remind people."

"I don't understand what's wrong with people remembering him?" Seph said. "He did amazing things for the Ambit."

"They don't want people to remember him because they think it will give them ideas," I answered.

"And if people have ideas, they may have questions," Seph said boldly. "And when they have questions, they want answers."

Answers.

What happened to James?

"So, it's better to forget," I concluded. Then I stood from the table and carried my teacup toward the water basin. It rattled on the saucer from my shaky hands. Anger mixed with hunger. It'd been almost a day since my last real meal. I steadied myself against the counter, placing both hands on the edge.

They'd prefer we don't remember him.

What do I do with that? The ones in charge of my livelihood would prefer that I forget the person I loved most in the world. The father of my children. My best friend. How can I ever reconcile that with myself?

I tucked my chin into my chest and exhaled my frustration. I was ashamed of my part in their agenda to forget my husband.

My hand smoothed over a deep gouge in the wood of the countertop. I opened my eyes, staring at it. James had built the counter for us after we were married. He didn't sand out the divot in the wood because he loved the imperfection of it. Just like he loved the Ambit, in its imperfection.

I closed my eyes and hung my head, shaking it.

Even now, I couldn't escape him. He was in every part of the room. The bed, the blankets, the toy cars, the counter. He was everywhere. How was I ever supposed to forget him? His memories were mine and I carried them alone. It was a punishment neither of us deserved.

Maybe it was the dream. Maybe it was my grief. Maybe it was that Seph was asking, and I knew I could trust him with the answers. But just this once, I wanted to indulge in my memories and share them with someone.

I turned to Seph and studied him. Why was he so interested? He was watching me from the table.

"James was from the Outside," I stated defiantly, testing how the words might sound. I decided I would start with the facts about his life, things I hadn't spoken of in years.

"He came to the Ambit when he was seventeen."

The words felt rebellious. Suddenly, I wanted to tell Seph everything. His face was curious to know more. I moved toward the table, seating myself across from him again.

"He was a bit of a rebel. He didn't care about the Ambit's rules for the Crossing," I continued, and something odd followed. A smile. It skipped across my face so fast it surprised us both. Seph's face immediately reflected it. We laughed.

Pointing toward the field with the huge tree at the Ambit Crossing, I continued. "He camped out at the tree. He was there for days, and we didn't know how he got there.

He just appeared. We didn't know if he was a threat or what he was planning to do. Finally, after a few days, he stepped over the Crossing. Made his way to the nearest person and asked who was in charge." I caught an amazed laugh as it tried to slip out.

Seph didn't catch his; he laughed at James' audacity. I laughed too, then I exhaled. It felt good to talk about James. It felt even better to laugh.

"Of course," I continued, "...the Guiding Authority was furious. No one had ever done that before. Not since the early days."

"When the Ambit first formed?"

I nodded.

"Do you remember what it was like? Before the Ambit?" he asked.

"Me? No," I said. "I was an infant when my parents came here. I was born in the middle of the Crisis. I remember that in the beginning, the Ambit was open to everyone. But then, at some point, people stopped showing up at our borders. No one came for fifteen years or so and then one day…there was James, standing at the Crossing." I smiled at the thought of it, at the thought of him.

Seph's eyebrows rose. "Why did he come here?"

I smiled. "He said he was looking for his father, but he found the Ambit instead."

"Was his father in the Ambit?"

"No." I shook my head. "He never found him."

"And what about his mother?"

I shrugged, "James didn't talk much about his family."

"Even to you?"

I exhaled with frustration, "Even to me."

Seph scowled.

I continued, "He was mysterious sometimes, but full of ideas and purpose. And he was so charismatic. He convinced the Guiding Authority to let him stay in the Ambit. And later, he persuaded them to let him teach. In some ways, I think pushing the GA's limits was fun for him."

We both smiled at that. It was a delightful thought. "He really wanted to convince them to merge with other societies, but the GA wouldn't budge."

"He'd been to other societies besides the Outside?" Seph asked.

I nodded. "He'd traveled to a few other places. He would stay for a little while to learn about their culture and then move on. He was looking for his father. I don't think he planned to stay in the Ambit forever, but…" I hesitated. "…he fell in love."

I was the reason he got trapped here. I told myself.

"And you weren't willing to leave the Ambit with him?"

I looked up. "No, I wasn't."

Stupid.

"So, what happened then?"

"When we were nineteen, we got married, and the twins were born. The GA was thrilled, overjoyed that they'd converted an Outsider to their 'good and perfect lifestyle'. That same year, he began teaching at the school. He taught about things no one else could. Things he'd learned from traveling and reading. He read every book in our library by the time the twins came along." I glanced toward my sleeping children. "He knew a lot about medicine too, and technology. But those are the things that they told him he had to keep to himself."

"When did he start going on the journeys?"

"When Chasen and Isla were three. After he'd read all the books in the Ambit library twice, he negotiated with the GA to let him go outside of the Ambit to get more teaching materials. When he came back, they were so thrilled, they sent him out again and again. He went every other month for a while."

I leaned forward and whispered, as though someone might hear me. "And no matter what people say now, the Ambitors loved him for doing it. He brought back things that some of us had never seen, like these little red candies called Sprockets," I smiled, remembering how Sprockets tasted. "...and books! So many books. They were about subjects like animals and farming, history, fairytales, anything he could get his hands on that the GA would allow. He's the reason we have the library we have now." I smiled.

"So, what happened?"

"Chasen got sick. At first, we thought it was asthma or something, but as time went on, he got worse. Several times, James made a case to the GA to reconsider their ban on basic medicines. The kind that would ease the symptoms of everyday ailments, like fever-reducers. But the GA wouldn't allow any of it."

I looked beyond Seph to where my son slept.

"The more Chasen's health declined, the more frustrated James became with his life in the Ambit. In the beginning, when the GA would send him on the journeys, he would come back within a week. He didn't want to be away from us for that long. But the older the kids grew, and the sicker Chasen became, the longer James would stay away."

I looked toward our cottage door and remembered one occasion when he returned from the Outside. The children were five years old. That was the day he gave them their most prized possessions. The treasures they kept under their pillows. It was etched in my memory.

I stared at the floorboards where he stood and imagined the three of them. I recalled the look on James' face as he demonstrated how to play with the toy cars. He said he'd had a set like them when he was little. I remember the way Isla's eyes poured over the words in the book he'd brought back for her. She could barely read at the time, but with James' encouragement, she grew to love and read that book nightly.

"Why did he stay away longer?"

I shrugged a shoulder, then I looked back from the floorboards to Seph. "I think he felt helpless. He never agreed with the GA's ban on medicine. It perplexed him. He grew impatient, disgruntled. He wanted to take us out of the Ambit, so we could get Chasen medical attention."

"Why didn't you go?"

That was the question that had haunted me for five long years.

"I ask myself that all the time. I guess I was just too afraid to leave." A tear broke free and rolled down my cheek. I didn't bother to catch it.

Seph nodded. "The GA wouldn't have allowed you to come back."

I shook my head. "Exactly, James was the only one ever allowed to go back and forth. I guess they figured if he wanted to live out there, he wouldn't have come here in the first place. And they adored James. He inspired them. They were more than happy to let him come and go, as long as he was doing what they wanted him to. But me? Or you? My children? They never would have allowed that. What would stop the rest of the Ambitors from wanting to leave? James was their experiment, and it failed."

I looked out the window and imagined a caged bird, staring at the open door. This was the way I'd seen myself since the day Elles died. I thought of it often.

"When he didn't come back, they said he was a traitor. They used him as an example of why we don't let Outsiders in, and why we shouldn't want to go out. They turned on him. Instead of honoring his memory as an admired teacher, they framed him to be a traitor that abandoned us. And that's the story they've pushed ever since."

I choked on my words.

"Then why don't you tell people the truth?" Seph asked.

I shook my head, "I've tried, but every time I would defend James, it'd push me further to the fringe of society. Eventually, I stopped talking about him because I…we…still have to be able to live here. As much as I hate it, I'm still dependent on the GA for our rations. You don't understand how difficult it is to be a single woman in the Ambit, Seph. You can't."

"Can't I?" he said. "I know I'm not a woman, but I saw how my mother was treated. Especially once they learned of her pregnancy."

He reached up and held the charm on his necklace.

"Did you know that they came to our cottage and demanded to know who Abigail's father was? They threatened to take the baby once she was born if my mother didn't tell. They wanted to punish her for getting pregnant without being married. They called her horrible names."

I shook my head. "I didn't know that," I said.

"And do you know what she told them? That if they were going to force her to reveal the father, that she'd say it was one of them."

He smiled.

"She did?" I felt my eyes widen. "I bet that made them angry."

"It did," he giggled. "But they left her alone after that."

I wondered if Seph knew who the father of Elles' baby was.

"After my mom did that," he said. "She told me that sometimes authority figures get out of line and that its our job to correct them. Maybe its time to correct the wrong that was done to James?"

I looked up.

That was the pit in my stomach. The thing I'd been holding onto. The Ambit disowned him, chose to forget him rather than send someone to see if he was alright. After all he'd done for them. For us. And I betrayed him, by letting them silence his legacy.

"I think Isla knows the truth about James," Seph said, breaking the deafening silence between us.

I looked up. "She's talked with you about him?"

He nodded. "They both talk about him…a lot, actually."

When my cheeks bloomed into a smile, the tears balancing in my eyes fell. "What do they say?"

"They defend him to the kids at school. They get called names for it." He said, "Please don't tell Isla I told you that, I know she'd be angry with me. She doesn't want you to worry about that too, but it doesn't feel right to let them get picked on."

"What do they call them?"

"What?"

"What names? What do the kids call them?"

"Weirdlings."

I looked down at my hands.

Weirdlings.

"I'm glad you told me, Seph. I'm not sure that I can do much to stop that now that Jebb is the teacher, but it's important for me to know that they're dealing with that."

"Miss Britt, can I be honest with you?"

I looked up at him. "Of course."

"Because you don't talk about James….ever. Isla thinks you believe the story that the GA has created."

My heart sunk. "She does?"

Cautiously, Seph nodded. He must have known how much his words hurt. Other than keeping their treasured trinkets, I didn't talk about James with my children. I never considered that they would think I believed he abandoned us. But what had I done to convince them otherwise?

"Mom?!"

Isla. She never called out for me.

I stood from the table. "I'm right here," I said.

She was upright in the bed, looking for me.

Her sleepy brother groaned at her.

36

"What's the matter?" I asked.

Her eyes were wild. She stared at Seph. Her chest heaved with heavy breaths, like she was afraid of something. Seeing that we were all there calmed her.

"Did you have a bad dream?" I asked.

She nodded.

"Isla?" Chasen rolled toward her. "Are you okay?"

"I'm fine," Isla said. She quickly scooted out of the bed, and past me.

"Are you sure?" I asked.

She slipped into her boots.

"Where are you going?"

Before I could finish my question, the door had already closed behind her.

"What was that all about?" I asked the boys.

Chasen and Seph shared a look.

"What's going on?" I pressed them further. Neither of them responded.

"Does this have to do with what's been going on at school?" I asked Seph.

His eyes widened. He looked at Chasen.

"We have a big project due today. I think she's nervous about it." Seph offered. "Yesterday, she was upset with me. She might still be mad at me."

"Oh."

"I'll go talk to her," Seph said, hesitantly, like he knew he was in trouble. The dynamic of their relationship was complicated. While Seph and Chasen had taken to each other like brothers, Isla was more reluctant. Seph stepped into his boots and left to find Isla.

I turned to Chasen. He'd retrieved the two toy cars from under his pillow and was driving them along the sheets and blankets on the bed, as if nothing had happened.

"Don't you have a project due today too?" I asked.

He faked a cough. "I'm not feeling so good."

"Nice try," I said.

He smiled, and I noticed that one of the toothless gaps in his smile was finally beginning to show signs of a new tooth.

"Alright," he said reluctantly tucking his cars back under his pillow.

As Chasen started to get ready for school, I sat back down at the table and considered the conversation I'd had with Seph.

Does Isla truly think that I believe James abandoned us? Does Chasen think his father abandoned him?

While Chasen ate his breakfast, I watched him. He was whittling a wooden creation. It was a hobby, that my father had taught him, to help pass the time when he was sick.

"Chasen?" I asked.

He looked up; his eyes were bright.

I wanted to say something about James to him. I wanted to tell him that his father hadn't abandoned us.

I exhaled.

"What are you making?" I deflected.

How do I begin to tell him? How can I tell him the truth?

His eyes were serious.

I nodded toward the creation in his hand because he didn't seem to know what I was referring to.

He looked down at his hands.

"Oh," he smiled his big toothy grin. "I'm making a surprise for Isla."

"Oh," I said.

He returned to his task.

I watched him.

The truth. How could I tell him the truth?

Your father is never coming home, I rehearsed in my head.

Because he's gone. He's....gone.

I don't know how or when, but I know he's not going to come back.

I know he's dead, Chasen, because when he left on his last journey, we agreed that when he came back, he was going to bring medicine for you. He'd found a way to get you exactly what you needed, and he knew what you needed because he'd read books. Studied for months trying to diagnose you. In the beginning he went on journeys for the Guiding Authority. But in the end, it was for you. He went so he could get you what we knew you needed. I wasn't willing to take you out of the Ambit, so we compromised, Chasen. We compromised.

He was going to sneak medicine in for you, Chasen. I said in my head.

We were going to risk banishment, to save you, son.

We were going to indulge in a Guilt.

And that's why I can't defend him. Because if I tell people he had this reason to return, then they'll know that I am the traitor.
We were traitors, Chasen. But not for the reasons they say.

Your dad had the best reason in the world to return to us.
He would have come back if he could.
And while I don't know what happened, I know he must be gone.
Because he would have stopped at nothing to ease your suffering.
He would have done anything for you and your sister, Chasen.
He never would have abandoned you.

Chasen looked up at me and I panicked for a moment, wondering if I'd said the words aloud on accident.

Then Chasen smiled.

"I just remembered something," he said, and I exhaled with relief.

"What?"

"Something for my project at school. I need to tell Scarlet. Can I go to school now so I can find her?"

Scarlet was his best friend at school.

School. Friends. Wooden creations and toy cars.
These were the things a young boy should be thinking about.
Not his deceased father or his mother's guilt.

"Of course," I said.

He jumped up from the table, leaving his knife and creation behind.

"If you see your sister," I added, "can you remind her that she can't wear her nightgown to school so she should probably come home now."

Chasen laughed. He quickly kissed the top of my head just like James used to.

"Love you, mom."

"I love you too, Chase," I said.

Then something odd happened. He took a moment to look at me, like he was hesitating to say something.

"It's going to be okay, mom," he said.

I looked up at him.

What did he mean by that? Did he know I was thinking of his father?

"What is?" I chuckled, trying to act as though I didn't know what he was referring to.

39

"All of it," he said. "It's going to be okay."

"I know, buddy," I said as confidently as I could.

"Now get going." I smiled at him.

He smiled back.

As soon as the door latched behind him, I felt the smile fall from my face. What did he mean? It's all going to be okay?

Chasen had always been very intuitive.

Does he feel how sad I am? How much I miss his dad?

Do my children feel the regret I feel for all these mistakes I've made? Not leaving with James? Not speaking up for him? Not telling them of his legacy in the Ambit?

Could Chasen feel that just now?

I stared at the door.

The same one I'd thought James was returning through, when I woke from my dream this morning.

The one I'd watched him exit out on the last day I saw him.

If only I had known that that was the last time I would see him alive.

If only I had known that this was the last time I would see Chasen alive.

James was right to warn me.

There was a storm coming.

3
THE RULING

My son.

When you were born, your first breath cracked the very foundation of who I thought I was and everything I thought I knew. Deep splinters seeped into the depths of me that I didn't know could exist, yet you and your twin broke me open. It hurt how much I loved you in the first moment I knew you.

Like sweet thick golden honey, the joys of watching the world unfold at your feet soothed me, dripping down into the cracks that broke me, sealing me again with the balm of your magical existence. How could someone so small and unknowing mean so very much? How could your brown eyes and smart comments hold me together?

I knew you could never fully know what that felt like until your own heart broke away from your being and walked the earth without you. I hoped that someday, you too, would understand this way of creating something and watching it in awe, afraid to lean in fully because of the fragility of it all, yet too moved not to.

I sleep listening for your next breath.

I weep knowing I'll never hear you take it again.

What is left of me?

41

Deep empty cracks. Splinters slivering into darkness where your laugh is missed, and your smile and calming presence is mourned. How did I let so many moments waste with worry, while you were still there for the holding? Why hadn't I scooped you into me every single living moment you had? Why didn't I take you away? I was so afraid to lose you, I lost us both.

Deep seething cracks, empty holes, freezing as the cruel wind of words whips through them, reminding me that you are missing, and I am empty without you. Nothing will ever fill those shattered places that you created and healed and left vacant forever. I won't allow anything to soothe me because it will be a betrayal of you. I will ache and cry and never hold back from joy or grief, because you are in it all. I will honor you with every breath I have, and only then will I rest. Until then, I will try, my boy. I will try to remember how the world ever spun without you, how music ever sounded in tune, how colors ever brightened the gray, and how seedlings ever fought the dark dirt to find the sunlight.

For you, I will try.

I will try to remember your last words to me.

You told me it would all be okay.

I don't know how that will ever be true.

But for you, I will try.

Isla, my beautiful Isla, was sitting silently across the room from me. Her gaze was blank and lost on the floor. I could tell that someone had carefully combed her fluffy brown curls into a sweeping barrette in the middle of the back of her head.

She was wearing a new dress, soft purple with white lace trim. I knew without asking her that she hated it. Her white leggings were clean and pressed, and black, shiny shoes graced her feet, which were crossed at the ankles underneath her wooden chair. Her hands were folded in her lap; she was holding the unfinished, wooden knick-knack that Chasen was sculpting for her as a surprise.

Her grandfather sat next to her. On occasion he would place his hand on her leg, reminding her of his closeness. She looked up at him when he did this, to ease his concern for her.

I could read it on her. The deep tragic grief. I wondered if she'd let me hold her now. I wondered how she'd slept without him, without me? My stomach hurt. Deep aching squeezed at me. I wanted to sweep her away. I'd run with her now, far from here, far from this. I'd start over with her if she'd let me.

Would she let me? Was it too late?

Isla was beautiful for many reasons, but her most intriguing features were her eyes: one brown, one blue, both sad.

My father explained to James and I after the twins were born, that in my womb something must have happened that hindered the pigmentation of her one eye. And so, while the left one obtained its naturally intended pigment and turned brown, the right one did not. Without the pigment, her right eye was dazzling blue.

In her early years of school, the other children teased her. They called her Weird Eye-lah.

Weird.

Weirdling.

It pained me to think of all that my daughter had been through in her short eleven years: bullying classmates, a missing father, a struggling mother, a sick brother. The responsibility of caring for her twin and now the loss of him. He was her best friend.

Regardless of what color her eyes were naturally, or how beautiful someone tried to make her look today, all I saw was sadness.

I felt responsible for it.

They believed I was.

"Good morning, Miss Britt," a soft voice said from behind where I was seated. I knew this voice was one of the only ones that would address me politely now. It was one of the few that had spoken to me at all since Chasen's death.

I twisted my body to see his warm face smiling cautiously at me. "Morning, Seph."

"Are you okay?" he asked.

Of course, I wasn't. He knew that but it was kind of him to ask anyway.

When I didn't answer he said, "I have something for you. Something I was hoping would cheer you up." He searched my face for any sign of excitement or relief. I mustered as much as I could find in me.

"I'm not sure anything can cheer me up right now, Seph," I said honestly. "What is it?"

"A gift," he said.

I scowled at him. This didn't seem like an occasion for a gift.

"Can you hold on to it for me then? Until this is over, I'm not able to open it right now," I said, lifting my hands from my lap, and showing him the thin rope wrapped around my wrists to bind me.

"Of course,," he said, stiffening at the sight of the bindings. "I'll save it for later."

I didn't respond; instead, I just nodded at him and inhaled a breath as deep as I could to keep my chin from quivering.

How could I explain to him that his gift would never offer me what I needed most in this moment?

I didn't have the energy to pretend it would.

I tightened the muscles in my face and swallowed the growing knot in my throat that threatened to break my façade of strength.

Seph reached for my shoulder, squeezing it slightly. He caught my eye and pressed his lips into that same Seph curl, to comfort me.

"I'll be right here," he said. "I'm sitting right behind you."

I nodded in appreciation that at least one person was willing to be on my side. I twisted my body back to face the front of the room.

The long table, that traversed the chair I was sitting in, had thirteen chairs more behind it. Behind them hung a chalkboard with erasers and chalk lined up immaculately on the ledge. We were in the schoolhouse, which doubled as the townhall for important meetings such as this. On either end of the chalkboard was a window overlooking the Ambit's small lake.

Behind me, I could hear the hustle and bustle of the folks that had gathered on the benches to witness the ruling.

When the thirteen representatives of the Guiding Authority entered the schoolhouse, a hush came over the cold wooden room. Each representative took his seat at the table opposite me, looking like they were carved from rock. At first, I watched their faces, trying to guess what might unfold next.

Only one made eye contact with me, Jebb. His mashed round face and thin lips snarled at me quietly. My stomach twisted. Of course, he would take this opportunity to torture me with his poisonous smile. He was the worst of them, the worst of the Ambit. An adamant adversary of my father, of James and now, of me.

Beside him, a man named Jonathon seated himself. He was opposite me directly. Of all the men of the Guiding Authority, he was my greatest ally.

More than a friend, he'd been like a favorite uncle to me growing up. He and my father worked together before the Crisis; they were best friends still to this day.

I studied his face for a second, looking for his smile, but only finding the scar that crossed over his thick, pink lips. I watched his face for a sign that he might recognize me as the little girl that he called Bitty. The one that used to bounce on his knee. I waited to see if he would wink at me, to reassure me that everything was going to be okay, as he had so many times in my life.

When he didn't so much as glance in my direction, I forced myself to look away.

Surely, he would know I did not do what they say I did!

But then again, even my own father had separated himself from me since word of Chasen's passing. Even Isla refused to come see me. In the three days and nights since, I'd been held in the back bedroom of Joylind's cottage. No compassionate words to a grieving mother were spoken to me, only unfounded accusations that I didn't understand.

They said I killed him.

They said I killed my son.

Joylind was the last member of the thirteen to sit down at the table. He was a man of few words, tall and thin, with a pointed nose and small dark eyes. He cleared his throat, and the room fell silent.

"We are ready to begin," Joylind's ragged voice announced. He continued, "As I am sure you've already heard, three days ago, the young boy, Chasen, was found deceased in his mother's arms." Only then did his eyes shift to mine, "The condition he was found in was reprehensible."

A quiet murmur rose from the room.

Joylind continued, "We haven't seen a death in this manner since..."

"She killed him!" an angry voice from the back shouted.

I felt my mouth gape open, "No!"

"Quiet!" Jebb snapped and the room silenced immediately.

"Britt," Joylind continued, "as you know, the Guiding Authority isn't accustomed to dealing with situations like this. Seeing the way your boy died, was cause for alarm and has shaken us to our core. It is for this reason, that we asked for Chasen's body to be examined, to determine the cause of his death. Aldam, please come forward."

I heard my father's chair move as he rose from it. The wooden planks of the floor creaked as he moved forward toward the table. He stood next to me.

"Have a seat," Joylind extended his hand to the chair next to mine. My father did as he was asked.

"Let me first say, I am so very sorry for your loss," Joylind said to him. "I know this must be a terribly difficult time for you and your granddaughter. We admire and appreciate your willingness to look over your grandson's body, to help us determine what has happened."

The compassion that dripped from Joylind's statements was repulsive. *I was his mother! I was the one who carried him, cared for him, held him in his last living moments and they hadn't so much as looked at me! What was going on? Why were they doing this? How could my father agree to this? He knew what kind of mother I was. He knew I would never do this!*

Joylind turned toward his counterparts at the table, "Jonathon," then he turned to my father, "Aldam, please inform us of your findings."

They'd both been a part of the investigation!?

Their betrayal burned.

I stared at the side of my father's face. He kept his eyes locked on Jonathon.

"Father?" I said quietly.

46

He turned to me. His eyes were heavy with tears, but he said nothing.

I turned to the man across the table from us. "Jonathon?" I pleaded. "You know that I would never..."

"Silence, woman!" Jebb screeched at me, slamming his hands on the table. His sudden movement startled me. I felt my face burn with embarrassment to be spoken to so cruelly. The word 'woman' etched in my brain. Jebb hated women. Ever since James' disappearance, I was the 'woman' that challenged him. I knew he would take any opportunity he had to place me back in the lowly role he felt women deserved.

I looked back and forth between my father and Jonathon, waiting for one of them to stand up for me. This was a nightmare. Both men had at one point, or another protected me in the Ambit, and now when I needed them most, they were silent.

"Jonathon?" Joylind urged. "Why don't you start by telling us why you and Aldam were asked to look at the boy's body."

Jonathon's voice quivered slightly when he began speaking. He swallowed hard. "Many of you know, Aldam and I were once licensed practitioners."

"Doctors," Joylind clarified.

Jonathon nodded hesitantly and I knew why. Naturals were opposed to medical professionals. After the Crisis, Jonathon's charisma had won him a role in the Guiding Authority, but his medical career, as well as my father's, were blemishes on their reputations. Before the Crisis, they were both admired for their professions. After the Crisis, they were judged for their role in it.

Joylind continued, "As doctors, you and Aldam both had experience with sickness, up to and including the MIL disease, correct?"

MIL disease?

Jonathon nodded.

My mind began reeling, they couldn't possibly think that I--?

"And what did you conclude?"

Jonathon looked to my father, waiting for him to speak.

"Dad?" I whispered, looking at him with confusion. This time he didn't look at me.

"The condition of my grandson..." he paused, "...was consistent with those that died during the Crisis."

A collective gasp rose from the room.

47

"MIL disease?" Jebb urged him. "He died of the MIL, didn't he?"

My father's chin dropped low into his chest.

"No, he didn't," I said. "He's been sick all of his life. You know that!"

I looked at my father, "Why would you tell them that? He was sick, he died from—"

My father looked up at me, "Britt," his eyes were overflowing now, "...you know what condition he was in. All the blood—"

"It wasn't the MIL!" I yelled. "How could it have been the MIL? He didn't get the –"

"I think it's clear that he did!" Jebb scolded me.

Then it was obvious to me that he'd been waiting for me to bring it up. The MIL disease came from the MIL vaccine. If my own father had concluded that the way Chasen had passed correlated to the others that died in the Crisis, then they suspected that the MIL vaccine had been used.

I looked over all their faces, "You think I gave him the vaccine?!"

They stared at me.

"That's impossible! How could I even--?"

"The same way you acquired the red and yellow toy cars!" Jebb blurted, like those words were burning in his mouth. He'd been waiting to spew them at me.

They'd found the cars.

"Those belong to my son! James brought them—"

"Don't you dare say that traitor's name in here!" Jebb growled.

"Traitor?!" I snarled. "My husband was not a traitor! He loved the Ambit! He wanted to help us! You know that. You were more than willing to use him for your errands to the Outside. He was the only bridge this society has ever had to the Outside. He was trying to help us merge with other societies so we could be free again!"

"There!" Jebb yelled, standing to point at me. "You heard it right there. She just admitted that her husband not only brought in items from the Outside, but she admits that his goal was to overrule us! Gentlemen, we were fools once to believe her husband, let us not be fooled again. He undermined our authority by bringing in items from the Outside and now this woman has followed in his footsteps."

48

"Undermined you?" I replied, "I didn't do *anything*!"

Joylind interrupted me, "Britt, when did you administer the MIL vaccine to your son?"

"What?! I didn't! I couldn't, and I wouldn't even if I could!"

"Forest?" Jebb called to the back of the room.

"Forest? Where are you? Come forward."

A shuffling sound prompted me to turn.

Forest rose to his feet. "Right here, sir."

"Forest," Jebb continued, "Tell them what you told me yesterday."

Forest's face blushed as he looked at me. Then his eyes narrowed, and he looked above my head to speak to the Guiding Authority.

"She doesn't agree with the Guiding Authority's ban on medicine."

"Britt doesn't?" Jebb clarified.

"Correct," Forest's snarky pale face itched with delight to spread his lies. "Several times I've heard her question her father's very honorable practices. She has implied on a number of occasions that she wishes the Ambit would allow medicine."

I looked at my father again, waiting for him to speak up.

"Father! You know I didn't give him the vaccine, why aren't you speaking?"

He stared at his lap. I turned to look at Isla. Her eyes were focused out the window. She was staring at the lake. Even she'd abandoned me.

"It's not true!" someone finally spoke up.

I turned to find Seph on his feet behind me.

"Sit down, boy!" Jebb growled.

"Miss Britt would never hurt Chasen!"

"Sit down or get out!" Jebb growled again.

"This is a misunderstanding!" Seph said.

My father turned to Seph. "Seph! Sit down."

Seph stared at him, then he looked at me.

"This isn't fair," Seph said. "I can't just sit by and let you say these things—"

"Albert!" Joylind motioned. A man named Albert moved toward Seph. Albert was bigger than the boy by at least a foot or two. Normally Albert, the Ambit's librarian, was very gentle in his giantness, but in this moment he was very intimidating.

49

"Come on, Seph," Albert spoke softly. "Don't make me carry you, son."

Seph looked at me. "I'm sorry, Miss Britt, this ain't right what they're doing. I know the truth."

The truth.

Albert took Seph under his arm and led him out of the schoolhouse.

"I think we've heard enough," Joylind's raspy voiced concluded. "Britt, the Ambit's rules against the Three Guilts have protected us for decades against the violence and disease beyond our borders. Anyone who threatens that is dangerous to us." Joylind looked around the room.

"We are not holding anyone prisoner here. The Ambit Crossing is open for all to cross, at any time. There is no secret agenda here to control you, our rules are intended to keep you safe. Anytime someone opposes them, in words, ideas or actions, we must do what is necessary to preserve the integrity of our system. It is for this reason, Britt, that we are banishing you from the Ambit."

Banishment.

"I didn't use medicine!" I cried. "It's true that we kept the toy cars that James brought back, but what harm has come from that?!"

"Don't speak his name!" Jebb yelled.

"He isn't a traitor! He only wanted –"

"Get her out of here!" Jebb shouted.

"No!" I cried. "What about my children?! Isla! Let me talk to her!"

The crowd rose to their feet and soon hands were grabbing at my arms to pull me.

"I think we've all seen what a danger you are to your children," Jebb said coldly.

"Isla!" I screamed, struggling against them to break free so I could see my daughter.

Through the cracks of people, I could see her still sitting in the wooden chair. Her eyes were set on the window as tears slid down her cheeks.

"Isla!" I screamed. "I didn't hurt Chasen! I swear!"

"Britt," my father growled at me. He was next to me, within inches of my ear.

"You did this!" I screamed, elbowing him to get away from me. "You lied to them!"

"Britt," my father moved in forcefully, against the crowd trying to get my attention. "Listen to me," he spoke sternly. "There's a woman in the Outside named Lucita. She'll meet you at the Ambit Crossing."

I stopped struggling and looked at him. "What?"

His low voice repeated what I'd thought he said, "Her name is Lucita. Wait at the Crossing for her. It may take a few days."

A few days?

The crowd pushed us apart. My father stood in one spot, watching as they pulled me from him.

How could he know that? Had he arranged that? How?

Who is Lucita?

The shock of my father's unexpected statement weakened me. Within seconds, the crowd had hauled me from the schoolhouse. Violently, they pulled me down the stairs and drug me through the center of the Mall.

The few that hadn't attended the ruling stepped out of their businesses to watch as I was carried by. They were making an example of me.

Jebb led the horde, yelling untruths about me as we went.

Some angry people shook their fists in agreement, others stood silently as we passed. I spotted Samantha, my neighbor. Her blue eyes were glassy, seeing them drag me down the lane. She seemed to feel something about the banishment, and I wondered if she cared what happened to me.

Willowby, the Bookkeeper of the Ambit's Book of Names, walked swiftly along with the crowd. The Book of Names was tucked neatly under his uptight arm. In a matter of moments, he would open it and strike my name from it. As though I never existed, just as he'd done with Chasen's, and Elles' and my mother's. I wondered if he'd already done it. If he knew the results of the ruling before I did. I wondered if my father knew, if Isla knew.

The Ambit Crossing was a distance from the lanes of houses and businesses. It was a line that circled the circumference of the society, recognizable only by the landscape that separated it from the Outside. I could see the massive tree that served as the crossing point. The crowd surged toward it, carrying me with it. Once we reached the line in the landscape, they pushed me forward toward the border. I stood staring at the line at my feet, remembering the times in my childhood that my classmates and I had dared each other to step over it. No one ever did, for fear that someone would see and banish us.

I considered turning around to plead my case again, asking for forgiveness or mercy. But what was there to forgive? These people believed I'd done something I hadn't. They'd convinced my father of it. Even my daughter seemed convinced.

Look for the truth, James' words were in my thoughts. The cool spring breeze swept over my face, and I lifted my chin to look up at the tree in front of me.

The tips of it were blooming with small pink buds.

The tree is alive. I reminded myself. *It's alone. It's outside of the Ambit, but it's alive.*

I tried to muster the courage to step forward, but fear halted me. It was against everything I'd ever been taught. Again, I considered turning around to look at the faces of the crowd. To look for my father. Had he come to see me off? To see the results of his testimony against me.

My father betrayed me.

Lucita, I remembered. *Had he betrayed me? Or was he preparing me for something?*

He'd told me that someone would come to meet me at the Ambit Crossing.

How did he know that? How could he possibly know that?

Then I remembered my conversation with him on the day that Elles' died. The day I questioned why he and my mother had raised me in the Ambit.

"You can leave this cage anytime you want," he'd said to me.

Cage. The Ambit is a cage, that is the truth. As always, the door to this cage was open. Now they wanted me to fly from it, whether I was ready or not. They did not care if I crashed to the ground.

I stepped forward.

Lifting my foot from the Ambit's soil was easier than I thought. I half expected the grass to grab me and hold me in, but it didn't. It let me go and for once, I recognized that it was only the boundaries of my mind and society that had kept me in place all these years.

I looked up again at the tree.

The tree is alone, but it's alive.

I sat my foot down on the other side. I was officially outside the Ambit. There was no going back now. They wouldn't let me.

They.

I turned around to see them. The ones that had cast me out.

Already, they'd turned from me and quietly started the trek back to the Mall. And that was it.

My whole life I'd lived within their rules. I was their neighbor, their family, their friend. Now I was nothing to them.

My stomach twisted with the realization. They were done with me. I was alone. I was alive, but I was alone.

My breathing quickened as panic began to set in.

What would happen to Isla now without me there to care for her? To Seph? Would my father assume them?

I felt the weight of unfinished business, of responsibilities left unattended. Just a few days prior, my children sat on the floor at my feet playing together.

My Chasen.

He was alive only hours ago. Alive and well. Then something went terribly wrong, something went horribly wrong, and he slipped from me, like a glass plate shattered into a million pieces on a stone floor. There's no going back. He was gone and all I wanted was to go back. I wanted a second chance to hold him, sit with him, never let him out of my sight.

What had happened?

The blood. His small body... I hit myself in the head. I did it again and again, trying to delete the images from my memory. They hurt more than anything else.

Why had they done this to me?

How could they believe I could do that to him?

I didn't understand what had happened.

One moment, I was cursing the Ambit, now I was never allowed to go back. One moment my boy was alive and well and playing, and now...

The tension built in my body, my muscles, my emotions welled up and I crumbled to the ground.

Gone. He's gone.

Isla's gone.

Seph's gone.

My home is gone.

Nothing. I have nothing.

I am nothing.

I screamed.

Anger and betrayal released from my lips in a tortured scream that I'd held onto for years. The glue I'd held myself together with melted away and I unraveled on the hard ground of the Outside. I pounded my fists on the dry grass, wailing.

Just lay here and die, I thought. *I'll just lay here and become like this grass. Would they care if my body rotted right here? Would they let me back in if I refused to leave? What if I crossed back over? What if I marched back in and demanded another chance? I could hide in the barn. Maybe someone would find me and have mercy on me?*

I looked up toward the nearest barn, but instead I found Seph standing at the Crossing. He stared at me.

I gasped, seeing him. He'd been so quiet; I didn't know he was there.

His face was stoic. I waited for the pressed curl to appear in his lips, but there was nothing. I couldn't read him. He only stared at me.

"Seph," I whispered. Struggling to find words to say goodbye, but all I could do was say his name.

He swallowed, and said, "*I* will."

I tried to understand what he meant, but before my mind could catch up with me, I spotted the strap on his shoulder. He was carrying something. A bag. A large bag.

He lifted his foot and stepped over the line.

"Seph!" I yelled, reaching my hand out to stop him from leaving the Ambit.

"*I* will," he repeated.

Calmly, he stepped over and planted his feet firmly on the ground of the Outside. His eyes were serious and set only on me.

I felt tears rush again. "No, no, no," I said, pointing to the Ambit. "Go back," I said.

He rushed to me, dropping his bag down on the ground next to me. He wrapped his arms around my shoulders.

"Seph," I cried, pushing him away. "You have to go back over, please…no one saw you cross, there's still time."

"No, Miss Britt," he whispered. Then he pulled back and looked at me in a way that dug into my deepest wounds of rejection. "When no one else will claim you, *I* will," he said. "You didn't leave me and I'm not leaving you."

"This is different," I said. "I don't have anything, I can't take care of you out here, I don't even know what —"

"Then we'll take care of each other," Seph said. He looked at me in a way that told me he would not accept any more of my rejections.

"I can't let you do that for me," I tried again.

"It's done," he said. "It's already done."

He waited for the thought to sink in. He watched my face for signs of my acceptance of his decision. He'd turned thirteen just the week before, but in this moment, he was telling me he was much older than that. He was letting me know he was a man.

He spun around and sat on his butt next to me.

For a few more silent moments, we stared at the Ambit together and cried. Our world had turned upside down in a matter of days. Chasen was gone and the pain of that alone would have been enough to change us forever. Now Isla was separated from us. And our home.

Too much, too much to hold.

"I have something for you," Seph said. He turned to his bag and dug into it. From inside, he pulled a bundle of linen, tied with a red string. He handed it to me.

"What is it?" I asked.

He nodded, "Your gift, remember? It's the thing you asked me to hold. You said you wanted to wait."

Then I did. I remembered.

Slowly, my exhausted fingers untied the red ribbon and pulled back the linen.

I gasped.

Two precious items were hidden within. One red and one yellow. Now I understood why he'd wanted to give them to me.

"Oh, Seph," I cried. "Thank you."

55

He nodded proudly, tears springing from his eyes. He knew he'd done well. I leaned toward him and put my head on his shoulder. We cried together. We were both broken and displaced. But we were together.

4
THE SHELTER TREE

I was there again, in the place called the Ambit. The place I once called home. I was gliding along my lane as if I knew where I was headed without knowing. I found the porch and the doorstep that I had many times crossed, and as I extended my hand to the knob of the door leading to my cottage, a shudder ran up and down my spine.

Don't.

My insides were screaming for me to stop my movements and turn to go, but my body forced me to turn the knob. As the door creaked open, I noticed that the usual fire was not burning to its normal height, which made the room very dark and cold. I seemed to slither across the cold wood floor until the footboard was at my feet. I looked over the perfectly made bed with confusion.

Where is the lump of child I am here for?

Instead of moving, I only turned my head from side to side to quietly search the room. It wasn't possible for me to be discovered, but I felt as though I was being sought after.

For a moment longer, I searched the corners of the small cottage room. Next to the woodpile on the other side of the two-way fireplace, I spotted one of Chasen's small wooden creations on the floor: an unfinished knick-knack that was taking on the appearance of a goat.

Upon closer examination, I found it and him lying near the woodpile. I normally craved color, and the life that it implied, but I found the brilliant red pool before me now only to mean death. His thin body was face down in a puddle of it. His hand clenched a piece of kindling I suspected that he meant to place on the fire.

I stood there frozen. Not like the first time I discovered him, when I rushed to his side, pulled him onto my lap and rocked him begging him to breathe. I didn't turn and vomit, like I had when I saw the condition he was in. I didn't press my hands against the fleshy pockets of sores that were bleeding on his face.

So much blood had poured from the corners of his mouth.

I didn't do any of that this time. This time I already knew.

He was gone.

My body couldn't move. My eyes couldn't be swayed from him. His sweet, beautiful face was marred with welts and blistering sores that hadn't been there before.

The last image I had of him was agonizing. But it was nothing compared to the truth.

My boy was dead.

Awake.

I opened my eyes to the tree branches blowing in the casual wind above my head. I blinked for a second or two trying to collect my thoughts and memories of the day's events. I wished it all to be just a nightmare, but I already knew that waking under this tree meant it wasn't. It wasn't some cruel joke of my sleeping mind. My real life was the nightmare.

I was so exhausted with emotion that I had fallen asleep accidentally and hadn't moved an inch in my slumber. My hands felt cramped, my back was sore and only one side of my body felt any sort of warmth. That was the side that Seph was laid up against, facing away from me. He must have laid down too, to nap in the sunlight that bathed us in a facade of warmth.

It was too early in the spring for there to be real warmth from the sun, but the sight of it was refreshing; just as refreshing as the sight of the small blooms on the tree above our heads, which signified life.

As I stretched my mind to remember exactly what happened that morning, I stretched my sore body: arms, back, legs. I unclenched the two small objects in my hand, one red and one yellow.

I rolled the tiny wheels of the red car back and forth with my finger. Years of play and enjoyment had left one of the wheels with a small squeak as it turned. The sound, however annoying it might seem, was a sound that brought me peace in this moment. I recalled how only a few days ago, I had peeled the car from Chasen's sleeping hand.

I exhaled.

What now?

I would have been happy to just curl up and die under this tree hours ago. My children were separated from me either by death or law, my husband was dead, and my father was something I didn't understand. I would have been perfectly content to think the world was better off without me, as the Guiding Authority had clearly demonstrated. But Seph changed all of that. Now I had no choice but to figure out something; he was depending on me to have a plan when he woke.

I studied the large bag that he used as a pillow next to me and thought about how he must have known what the outcome of the ruling would be. He had packed a bag for us.

Did everyone know what the ruling would be, but me?

I wasn't prepared. Seph had a bag packed and my father had prepared a plan for someone to meet me at the Crossing. I wondered if Isla knew that the Guiding Authority would rule against me. I wondered if she cared.

As I squeaked the wheel on the red car, it disturbed Seph in his sleep. He started churning, rolling back and forth dreaming. I thought of what his dreams must be like. He'd lost so much: his father, his mother, his baby sister, and now Chasen.

Seph rolled onto his back, and I noticed the thin silver chain around his neck. The small fish charm hung to the side.

Elles.

Abigail.

He doesn't know that I was responsible for Abigail.

Would he have followed me to the Outside if he knew I was responsible for her death?

I hushed the whisper in my head.

59

No use worrying about that now. Seph doesn't need to know about that. He's lost enough.

I was staring at the necklace. He moved slightly and it slipped down, revealing a small cut on the side of his neck. It was colored deep red. I licked the corner of my sleeve and gently dabbed at it to wipe away the dirt and crusts of blood. I knew what infection would do without medicine to prevent it.

As I dabbed at him, his eyes opened, and for a second, I thought he looked scared. In an instant, Seph's hand grasped mine. In less than the blink of an eye, he had a grip on me that frightened me. His reflexes were sharp. I'd never seen anyone respond so quickly or ferociously. A second later and the fear turned to recognition, and he retracted his hand.

"Are you okay?" I asked. "I didn't mean to scare you."

He cleared his throat and sat up.

"I must have dozed off."

"You have a cut on your neck."

He reached up, "Oh, yeah...I'm okay though."

"What happened?"

His eyes lowered with shame. "It's from the window...at Jebb's. I had to smash it to get out."

"Get out?"

"Of Jebb's cottage. He came back and I had to smash a window, so he didn't see me."

"Why were you there?"

"He took Chasen's cars from our cottage. He put them in a safe in his bedroom. Before the ruling this morning, I broke in to get them."

"A safe? Why?"

Seph shrugged a shoulder.

"How'd you get into the safe? Wasn't it locked?"

Seph's face turned red. "It was, but I have a knack for picking locks."

"You do?" I didn't know that about him.

"I'm not proud of it."

"What?"

"Breaking the window," he said. "But I guess it doesn't matter much now, does it?"

I shook my head to ease his mind. "No, it doesn't."

Seph sat up and stretched. We sat quietly.

"So," Seph looked around, "I wonder how long it'll be until this Lucita person shows up."

I shrugged. "*If* she shows up."

Seph looked at me, "You don't think she will?"

"I don't know what to believe at this point. I don't understand *any* of this."

We were quiet. Then a thought occurred to me.

"Seph, *you* know that I didn't give Chasen anything, right? I don't even have a way to get medicine." I choked.

Seph nodded, "I know, Miss Britt."

"Honestly though, Seph…." I continued, "if I could have gotten him medicine, I think I would have given it to him."

I watched Seph's face to see if he was surprised by that confession. He didn't seem to be.

"Maybe medicine would have…" I started to speculate, but then images of Chasen's tormented body flashed in my mind. "…his body, Seph. The condition of it…I've never seen anything like it. It doesn't make sense how he was so…" I was rambling, trying to make sense of it.

I thumped the side of my head with my fist. "I can't unsee him like that. I don't know how that —" I began to cry again, looking down at my hands. I remembered the blood. I stared at them, like they were still stained.

"I don't know what happen to him." I gasped for air between sobs. "I don't know what happened to my boy! How he got so….so….infected or whatever that was," I wailed.

"What's worse is that no one even asked me what happened! They all just assumed…" I sobbed. "…that I'd done something to him. I would never!" I gasped again. "…and then, they put me in a room for three days without any explanation! You were the only one that came to see me. My father…" I cried. "Isla?"

"Isla's…" Seph started to say, "—she's hurting. She doesn't know what to make of all this. She's not thinking clearly, Britt, but she loves you. She--"

"Did you talk to her?" I turned to him. "What did she say? She knows this wasn't my fault, right?"

I stared at his face. His eyes were sad.

"She misses him," he said quietly. "She can't think of much else right now."

My heart hurt to think of it. I couldn't do anything for either of them now. I buried my face in my knees.

After a few quiet moments, Seph said, "When my mom died...it felt like I lost everything. My mom, my sister, my home."

I looked at the side of his face.

"You were kind enough to let me live with you, and let's be honest, Isla tolerated it." A small smile reached his lips with that thought. "But it was Cha—It was Chasen that gave me something I'd never had before."

I felt the lump in my throat bulge. I wiped the liquid from the tip of my nose.

"I've never had a brother," Seph said.

I pinched my eyes closed to conceal the tears.

"And he –" Seph pressed his lips together in a knowing smile. "—he just always knew what to say." He wiped his face.

"I'm scared I'm going to forget what his voice sounded like," I admitted. "I've forgotten James' laugh. I don't want to forget Chasen's."

Seph nodded. "I felt like that with my mom." I don't know if Seph even realized he did it, but he reached up and held onto the fish charm when he talked about his mother.

"It's not supposed to be like this, Seph," I said. "All this loss and death. Especially for someone as young as you. It's not supposed to be something you know so intimately already."

"What's it supposed to be like then?" He asked with genuine curiosity.

I paused. Then I shook my head, "I guess I don't know."

We sat quietly, staring across the Ambit fields.

"I guess I always thought there must be something different. Or hoped at least that there was. But now that you mention it, I guess I don't even know *why* that's something I believed, when everything about our existence points to the opposite?"

Seph nodded. "I like to think that maybe there's an untold story inside of us, that can't be touched by all this pain. That maybe we are born knowing there's something more, and even in the worst of moments, and on the worst of days, we keep looking for it, because it's the only thing that doesn't change."

His theory felt very true, but then the grief rebutted.

I'd always known of Seph's crush on Isla. He saw Chasen as a brother, but Isla could never be like a sister to him. His feelings toward her were not familial. Somehow, I knew that Seph's reason for stealing the book, in the hopes that we'd someday return it to her, was of the purest intentions. It was his assurance that he'd see her again, because he knew he had to return her book to her.

"Oh, Seph, I'm so sorry I yelled…" I crouched down and put my hands over my head. Then I popped back up and went to him. I knelt in front of him, placing my hand on his knees. "I'm so sorry, you didn't deserve that."

His eyes were glassy, his breathing was quickened.

I swallowed. "I'm a mess," I said. "I have all these feelings and I'm not sure how to handle them. I saw her book and all I could think was that it was another thing that she'd lost….but I had no right to yell."

Seph swallowed and nodded.

I fell back on my bottom and let the book rest in my lap.

Laying the palm of my hand flat on the leather cover, I felt the edges of the lettering. "She was five when he gave it to her. It was the same day he gave Chasen the cars."

Seph was quiet but I could still hear the heaviness in his breathing.

I looked up, "It's just a story book, but the two of them…" I smiled slightly at the memory it produced, "…the two of them poured over these stories."

I picked the book up and flipped through the pages. Isla's sweet scent floated up and filled my senses. It smelled like our home.

"She's slept with it under her pillow every night since."

Then the thought occurred to me, and I twisted to look back over the Ambit. She wouldn't have her Bible tonight. A deep sorrow sunk into me with that thought.

"Maybe I should take it back right now?" Seph offered.

"We can't," I said. "Going back in will only make things worse. And if the Guiding Authority finds out, who knows what they'd do."

Seph looked down at his hands. He seemed to be realizing the gravity of our banishment.

"Besides," I added. "I like the thought that we will get to return it to her. We will see her again. We have to."

I turned my attention to the book. Flipping through the pages, I noticed some writing on the outer column of several of the pages. I stopped at one in a story called Romans.

The paragraph she highlighted on the page struck me. It read: "Do not conform to the pattern of this world but be transformed by the renewing of your mind."

In the margin next to this passage, she had written "Do not conform, transform."

Transform.

So much is transformed now. I thought.

I have been transformed by grief.

For the first time, the thought occurred to me that while this was the end of something, it could also be the beginning of something. Whatever happened next, I would be the transformed version of myself. Whatever happened next, I would no longer conform, as I had in the Ambit. It was like Isla had given me advice through the words on the book's margin.

Do not conform, transform.

"What's that?" Seph asked.

I looked down. In my lap a piece of paper was folded. I opened it. It was a photograph of Isla, Chasen and me. I recalled the painstaking process it had been to develop the photo years earlier. A photograph was a rare treat in the Ambit, that we were afforded only because of James' journeys.

I extended the photo toward Seph. "James took that photo. I didn't know she had it."

I looked down at the words in the margin of her book again. "Do not conform, transform."

"Have you ever read that book before?" Seph asked, extending the photo back to me. I was deep in thought over the quote.

"Who? Me?" I asked. "No, I never really got the appeal. But they did. Isla and James seemed to understand it. They bonded over it."

A scratching sound came from behind us. Seph and I both jumped up, our senses heightened by our unknown surroundings. We didn't see anything, so we waited for a moment and then heard it again. It sounded like someone scratching a chalkboard.

The base of the tree we were reclined by, was too wide to see around. Whatever was scratching was on the other side of it.

The tree was enormous, with big, beautiful branches and a thick trunk. Again, the scratching sound came. Seph and I looked at each other, keeping quiet to listen. I tilted my head and stretched my neck to see around the base of the tree. I couldn't help but let out a laugh when I spotted a goat on the other side.

I think that if it could have, it would have laughed back at the sight of me. Instead, it just chewed and stared at us.

"Look," I said to Seph. "Look at this!"

Seph came around behind me and peeked. We shared a small laugh. The little goat was white with brown and black spots. She was barely above my knee in height.

"Where did you come from?" Seph asked the goat.

I motioned to the closest farm on the nearest lane off the Ambit's Mall. "Probably down there."

The little goat worked her way around the base of the tree, eating what she could find, completely unafraid of us. We had a couple of goats on our farm that we adored for their personalities, fearlessness, but also their delicious nourishing milk.

When the goat got to Seph, she butted her head into his leg, and he laughed. He knelt in front of her, and she nudged him again, so he sat back on his bottom and opened his arms. Almost as though she'd always known him, she seated herself in his lap and curled up to snuggle. This delighted him.

"I guess she likes you," I said.

"I guess so." He scratched her and she pressed the side of her head into his hand, like a dog. "I like you too," he whispered to her.

As dusk approached, we ate some of the scraps Seph brought from our cottage. We were careful to preserve our portions because we didn't know how long it would be until we would get the chance to restock. It was easy to preserve food because we were used to doing it, but also because neither of us seemed to have much of an appetite.

Then, not knowing what level of security we had and what sorts of dangers may lurk outside the Ambit Crossing, we decided it was best to climb the giant tree to sleep for the night. We started calling it our Shelter Tree.

The branches of the tree were so big and thick; we were able to hammock the blanket Seph brought. To our surprise, the little goat decided to hang around. She knelt at the base of the tree to sleep.

When we finally climbed into the hammock in the tree, Seph rested next to me and immediately fell off to sleep.

It took me longer because my mind was stirring, trying to come up with a plan. Every day of my life, in the monotony of the Ambit, I knew what to expect. Now, I had no idea what the next day might hold for us.

My father said that someone would meet us at the Ambit Crossing, but it had been several hours, and no one had shown. I didn't know why I would have expected anything different from my father or his promises.

Lying in the hammock, I felt the quiet settle around us. I could smell the smoke from the Ambit chimneys, a familiar smell that comforted me.

I pleaded with the night air to take away the sting of betrayal that I felt all over my body. I begged the ground not to consume me, but to lend me its strength for another day. I wished for my mind to be clear as I slept and for the haunting visions of Chasen's body to be gone.

Do not conform, I thought, *transform*.

A calm settled over my tense body, and I was finally able to sleep.

In the night, a coughing sound woke me. A gagging, choking cough startled me awake. My instincts yanked my body upward as they had so many nights of my life with Chasen. For a split second, I thought I was waking up to coach him back to easy breathing.

It wasn't until I hit the hard ground with a thud that I snapped out of it and poor Seph landed next to me. My reaction had launched us both out of our hammock.

"I was wondering where you were?" a man's voice said as he approached us.

In the black of the night, all I could make out was his silhouette, which was shaded by a foreign bright light glaring from behind him. As he stepped closer, I saw his black boots were shiny with dirt crusted to the soles.

The man coughed and gagged for another second. I squinted; the spotlight behind him was so bright. I raised my hand to block the light, and then I was able to focus on the structure of his face and body. He was an older man, probably in his late fifties, wearing a red and black shirt with an unusual striped pattern on it. The buttons were shiny, and his shirt was tucked into his pants at the waist. His hips were adorned with a strip of leather, which met in the middle and had one gigantic buckle with a picture of a large horned animal on it.

His hair was dark with streaks of gray, from what I could tell, sort of long and unkempt. His face was grizzly and unshaven; from his lips hung a white stick with smoke coming from it.

Every now and then, I would see him pull the stick from his mouth, and the smoke would escape. The smell of it was something I had never experienced, like burning, but different. I figured this must be medicine for his cough.

I found my feet under me. Seph shielded his eyes with his hand, trying to keep them open in the foreign light. The little goat, who had narrowly escaped us falling on her, had already found a new spot on the ground next to Seph.

When the man noticed Seph on the ground next to me, he said, "I didn't realize you had a kid with ya. Those stupid bastards banishing kids now too?"

"Who are you?" I asked. I felt the shadow of his silhouette skip across my face as he approached. He wiped his hand on his pants and then extended it to me.

"I'm Maris. You're Britt, I reckon?"

I cautiously extended my hand to meet his, shaking it gently. His skin was warm, but his hands were as rough as sandpaper.

"Yes. Nice to meet you, Mr. Maris."

He smiled kindly. "Just call me Maris. I hope you don't mind me sayin' it, but you look just like your mother."

"My mother? You knew my mother?"

"Oh, sure. Your ma, pops, Lucy and I used to run around together a while back. Ya know, before all this," Maris nodded his head toward the Ambit.

"Lucy?" I thought for a second. "Lucita? Is she your wife?"

"Yeah, I guess you could say that," Maris said. "Not that we ever made it official. No wedding or nothin', but yeah."

"Mr. Maris, how did you know to meet us here?" I asked.

Maris puffed a cloud of smoke from his nostrils, followed by another from his lips. He pursed his lips and lifted his chin as he released it into the air. He squinted at me, looking at me sideways and then answered.

"Your father," he said. "And just call me Maris."

"But how? How did he communicate with you? How did you and Lucita know to come for me?"

Maris' face was serious. "Lucita didn't come with me."

"My father said to wait for Lucita. When will she be coming?"

"You're guess is as good as mine," Maris replied.

"My father said *she* is the one we should expect," I clarified.

"Well, he doesn't know that she's not available...." Maris cleared his throat.

"Not available? What does that mean?"

Maris' furry eyebrows lifted on his forehead; his eyes squinted again like he was sizing me up. "Truth is, Lucita's been gone for months. Just your daddy doesn't know that, I guess. He didn't mention me at all, huh?"

I shook my head.

"Figures. Well, sorry to disappoint but I'm your ride."

I stared at him, confused.

"I'm sorry, but I don't understand. How did you know to come for me?"

"This," the old man said. He reached into his back pocket and pulled out a slip of paper. I took it from him.

The words said, "Lucita, I'm calling in that favor. Pick up tomorrow night, Ambit Crossing, one woman, my daughter, Britt. My best, AL"

"This is my father's handwriting," I said, looking up at him.

"How'd you get it? Did someone deliver it to you?"

"Nah, things like that have a way of showing up," Maris said.

"What does that mean?"

Maris looked around, "Look, we can't really stand around here all night working out the details. The point is, your daddy needed someone to come get you, and I'm the someone that got the message." He looked beyond me. "What's your name, boy?"

I looked at Seph.

Seph stood up, dusted his hand off on his pants and extended it to Maris. "I'm Seph, sir."

"Why you out here, son?"

Seph looked at me, then back at Maris, "I'm an orphan, sir, and Miss Britt took me in. I'm indebted to her. Staying in the Ambit didn't make sense without her."

"That's noble kid, but you gotta know…where we're goin', life aint easy. If there's any way you can go back to the Ambit now, I'd recommend it."

Seph swallowed hard, scowling. "I appreciate that, sir."

The two stared at each other. It was clear that Seph had no intention of taking Maris' recommendation.

Maris smirked, then nodded his head in understanding. "Alright, then it's settled. Load up and I'll –"

"I'm sorry, Mr. Maris, I appreciate all the trouble you've gone through to come get us from—from wherever it is you came from." I said looking around. There was nothing for miles and miles. "But we aren't going with you."

Maris smirked and chuckled as if he thought I was joking with him." You're not, huh?" he said, with a smirk.

"No, sir," I said firmly.

"What the hell are you gonna do then?" he asked.

I didn't know how to answer, and I didn't know what 'hell' was.

"Honestly, Mr. Maris,"

"It's just Maris," he interrupted me.

"Maris," I corrected myself. "I don't know what *to* do, but I can't make sense of leaving the only place in the world that I'm familiar with, to go with a man I've never met before in my life who says he knows my dad but isn't the person my dad told me to wait for," I explained.

Maris' smile melted and he nodded in acknowledgement.

"I see," he murmured.

"No disrespect, I'm sure you're a wonderful person, I just –"

He inhaled another long billow of smoke, held his breath for several seconds and then released it again, with a choking cough. From his pocket he pulled a yellow handkerchief, which he dabbed at the corners of his mouth with.

"Your distrust will serve you well in the Outside, Britt." He laughed. "You're right not to trust me. You don't know me from Adam." I didn't know who the Adam he referred to was.

71

"And I respect that this is all new for you. I understand that your daddy probably didn't prepare you for this day, because he hoped like hell that it would never come. It's clear to me that you have no idea what kind of world you're in now, because if you knew, you'd see that no one, and I mean *no one,* will offer you help here. You'd have to walk about a hundred and fifty miles that way…" he pointed in the distance behind him, "…to find the next closest society, and believe me when I tell you that they are not as kind and inviting as the Ambit."

He chuckled, as though he knew how uninviting and cold the Ambit was and that was his point.

"So," he continued, "seems to me that you gotta choice to make. Either you and this young man here saddle up and take my offer, or you're plum 'outta luck. Truth is, I owe your pops from back in the day, and that's the *only* reason I came for you. *He* is the only reason I came tonight, and I assure you, I will not be coming back."

He dropped the remainder of his burning white stick on the ground and stepped on it.

"I'll be in the truck," he said. He looked down at the band on his wrist. "I'll give you ten minutes, then you stand here and watch me drive away if you want."

The old man turned and slowly made his way back to the bright lights behind him.

I looked at Seph. He'd sat back on the ground with the goat. She'd balled herself up in his lap again.

"What do you think?"

Seph nodded, then he leaned down to kiss the goat on the top of her head. The two of them were bonded already.

I looked back at the old man. "Mr. Maris?" I called.

He turned around. "It's just Maris!" he yelled back, annoyed.

"If we come with you, we're bringing our goat."

He laughed, shaking his head.

"Whatever gets you in the truck, Princess."

He opened the door and disappeared inside.

Princess? I hated that he called me that.

I looked over at Seph.

He'd already stood up and had the goat wrapped in his arms to carry with him. He smiled. "Well, he seems nice."

5
INSIDE THE OUTSIDE

I had never seen anything like it before; the skyline of the city formerly known as Chicago. The first bit of sunlight heralded the coming of a new day and the magnitude of the enormous structures that carried its reflection. The orange and yellow light outlined the shapes in bold blackness. I couldn't imagine a better time of day to have seen it for the first time.

In its prime, I could only imagine the sounds, lights and life that moved through its alleys and roadways. James had shared stories with me of the great stone buildings that stood side by side on the edge of the enormous lake of cold, blue water. But, even as descriptive as James was in his stories, my imagination never could have stretched to create a world this astounding. I suppose that's one of the greatest downfalls of growing up sheltered in the Ambit. My imagination could only dream as far as it had experienced.

Our journey from the Ambit to the Outside was exhausting on my mind and body. I had ridden in horse-drawn carriages that were more comfortable than Maris' truck, which donned a dented front bumper and a cracked windshield to match. From time to time a loud crack or pop sound would arise from the engine, keeping the knots in my shoulders and back nice and tight.

I found myself constantly looking back into the bed of the truck to see if Seph and the goat were still there. I was sure that some of the bumps should have sent them flying out, but each time I looked back at them, Seph would smile and give me an upward pointed thumb. His amusement with the idea of a moving vehicle was sweet. Never did a moment of fear cross his expression; he was having the time of his life, getting the ride of his life.

"There she is," Maris said, as the truck entered the city. The buildings finally blocked the sunlight from our eyes so I could get a good look at it. The roadways were covered with debris, but there was a well-worn pathway through.

"This is it? This is the Outside? The great city I've heard about all my life?" I asked. There wasn't a soul in sight.

"I don't know about 'great' but it's the one."

Birds flew low over the road, unafraid of the moving piece of tin maneuvering through the rubble of the city.

"There are a few things you need to know before you go in."

I felt my mouth gape open, as I leaned down to see the reach of the buildings toward the sky.

"Britt," Maris said, "You listening? This is important."

I sat back. "Okay?"

"First thing you need to know, is that the Ambit is a bit of an enigma to these folks here."

"Enigma? I'm sorry, Mr. Maris, I don't know what that means."

"Dammit, Britt, stop calling me Mr. Maris!" he slammed his hand on the steering wheel. It startled me.

"I'm sorry," he recanted. "But you gotta knock that sht off. You and the boy both. I ain't Mr. Maris, you ain't Miss Britt, and there are no 'sir's or 'ma'am's here. I know where you come from that's polite and all, but here, it'll be a sure sign of someone that's fresh meat."

I watched his face, insulted at first, until I understood that he was trying to protect us.

"Okay," I said quietly.

Maris seemed embarrassed to have lost his temper with me. "Enigma," he continued. "It means mystery. The Ambit is a bit of a mystery to the people here."

He leaned forward and used a handle on the inside of the truck door to roll the window down. Then from inside his shirt pocket, he pulled another white stick. He slipped it into the rim of his mouth and used a metal object to light it.

He continued, "There are a lot of rumors about it. Some even believe it's a myth of sorts." He looked at me and realized I didn't know what that word meant either. "A joke, a fake. They don't necessarily believe the Ambit even exists."

I scowled, "Really? Why?"

"Think about it, no one from the Ambit has ever made it here."

I was confused, "Well, obviously that's not true. My husband, James, came here from the Ambit. He used to go back and forth."

For the first time in all the confusion and chaos, it occurred to me that there was a small chance that James was still in the Outside.

What if I found him? What if he--? I shut down the idea immediately. James had to be dead. The idea that he might still be alive, that I might discover what happened to him, where he'd been all this time, was too much to think about. While I desperately wanted it to be true that my husband was still living, I couldn't come up with any justifiable reason for why he hadn't returned to us with medicine. If he was alive, it would mean betrayal.

"Maris, do you know James?"

Maris turned to look at me. "Yeah, Britt, I knew James."

Knew.

My heart sunk.

"How do you know him? Do you know where –"

Maris slowed the vehicle to a stop. He shifted a lever that made the truck stand still. Then he turned to me.

"Britt, all of this," he said looking beyond me toward the city out the window. "...is gonna be a lot to take in. I think with time the answers you're looking for will come, but for now, you can't worry about James."

He said that as though James was still currently something to worry about.

Current. Alive?

"I just need to know if he is still alive, Maris?"

Maris' face was solemn.

"I honestly don't know. I haven't seen James in years. Last I knew of him, he got himself mixed up with the wrong people and that's—"

"What people?"

"You're getting ahead of yourself." Maris looked at the band on his wrist. "We're sitting ducks here, so let me get this out before we go down."

Down?

Maris turned to see Seph and the goat in the back of the truck.

"Don't bring James up to anyone," he said coldly.

"What?"

"Don't mention him. Don't mention the Ambit. Don't give any information to anyone about where you came from or why, you understand?"

"No, I don't understand, wh--?"

A noise in the distance rang in my ears. It was a whistling sound. I instantly turned to Seph. He smiled at me.

"You okay?" Maris asked.

Then something that sounded like thunder in the distance rumbled. I looked out the window, there wasn't a cloud in the morning sky.

Alarmed by the rumbling sound, Maris quickly shifted the truck into gear, and it lurched forward.

"What was that?" I asked.

Maris started repeating his instructions to me, as the truck sped up.

"Don't mention James. Don't mention your kids or your father, or the Ambit. Don't tell anyone where you came from. Just say you wandered in from out of town and that should be enough. Tell the kid the same thing, keep to yourselves, you hear?"

The truck screeched to a stop.

"Maris, what was that sound?"

"Hang on," he said. Then he propped the door open, lowered his foot down to the ground and stomped three times. A loud reverberating sound clanged like metal. Maris pulled his foot back into the truck and closed the door.

Another whistling sound penetrated my ears, causing me to cover them. "What is that?" I yelled.

Maris looked at me in confusion, until the thundering boomed again. It was closer this time.

I turned to check on Seph. His eyes were wild with excitement.

"What's that sound?" I asked, beginning to panic.

Maris groaned, "C'mon," he whispered under his breath, like he was waiting for something to happen.

"C'mon, son, where are you?"

On the walls of the buildings ahead a dark shadow moved.

"Sht," Maris growled. "Stay calm," he said to me.

"What is *that!?*"

Maris propped his door open again, lowered his foot, and stomped just as he'd done before. As he closed the door, the ground below the truck began to quake.

"What is that?!" I said, placing my hands on the dashboard to steady myself.

Maris turned around to look at Seph, I did too. Seph's face was pale as he stared off in the distance ahead of the truck. I twisted to see what he saw.

"Hang on," Maris groaned. The truck began lowering below the ground.

"What is —" I started. "Maris!"

In the roadway in front of us, as we were lowering below the ground, I could make out the shape of something black and massive rounding the corner toward us. I didn't have words to describe what I was seeing.

"Seph, get down!" I yelled, turning to see his face was frozen with fear, seeing what I saw.

"One more second," Maris said, as the last bit of the truck lowered below the ground and the metal door above us covered the opening we'd just entered through. A shadow slipped across the opening.

Darkness fell over us as the door closed.

Blackness. Silence. All I could hear was the beating of my own heartbeat in my ears and the panting of my breath.

"Seph?!" I called into the darkness.

"What was that?!" Seph's voice returned with a cry in it. "It had a tail!"

A light turned on in the distance and a voice called out, "Maris!?"

"Yeah!" Maris responded with a shout.

"What was that?" I said, feeling fear release its hold on my body, allowing me to panic fully. "There was something up there! What was—"

Quietly, the old man whispered, "There's one more thing you need to know, Britt—"

"*One* more thing?" I said panting.

"Are you listening to me?" Maris asked.

The man who had called out to us was approaching from the darkness. I could hear his footsteps.

I turned to Maris. He was staring at me, waiting for me to give him my attention. "Britt!" he snapped at me to get me to focus.

"What?"

"Don't trust *him*," he nodded toward the man approaching.

"Who is he?"

"Don't trust *him* or anyone else, you hear me?"

I looked at the man that was approaching. My breath caught in my throat. He was significantly younger than Maris, tall and well built. It'd been years since I'd seen someone that so distinctively resembled James, but I knew it wasn't him.

"Who is he?" I repeated. But it was too late. The younger man was already too close, and Maris was already exiting the truck.

"Too close, Zale," Maris scolded. "Too damn close, what the hell were you doing?"

"Power surge. Good thing your old ticker's still working, huh, old man?" Zale said with a sly smile, like he was proud of himself.

"Lucky for you, it is," Maris sighed.

Zale looked up from the old man to me. He seemed surprised to find someone else in the truck.

"I thought you said you were picking up supplies?"

"I was. Found these two wandering, thought I better bring 'em in before—" he shrugged. "—you know."

"I'm Zale," the younger man said, extending his hand just as the older man had.

"Zale, this is Britt," Maris said, then he moved between us interrupting the opportunity for a handshake.

Zale's face went from jovial to serious. He looked down at my dress and boots. "Where'd you come from?"

"I—" I stuttered; I hadn't had enough time to prepare a lie. Maris had only just told me not to share the truth.

"Britt," Maris said, "this is my son."

His son!? He told me not to trust his son?

Seph sat up in the back of the bed of the truck.

"Seph?" I said, rushing to the side of the truck. "You okay?"

"I think so," Seph said, still stunned by what we'd just seen.

"What was that thing?" he asked me quietly. "Did you see it? It had a tail?!"

I turned to see Zale and Maris were whispering. I leaned toward Seph's ear. "Don't reveal anything about who we are or where we've come from, just follow my lead."

Seph scowled at me.

"Do you hear me?" I asked him.

"Yes, but Miss Britt?" he uttered quickly.

"Don't call me Miss Britt. Drop the manners, they'll give us away. Do you understand?"

He nodded.

"Britt?" he tested it without the formal title. "Where *are* we?"

"Honestly, I don't know."

We stared at each other.

"You ready?" Maris asked us.

Seph handed me our bag. Then he lowered the goat out of the bed of the truck. She trailed him, like she'd been trained to stay with him.

"I'll be damned," Zale laughed, seeing the goat. "You must've come from a long way off."

"Yeah," Maris said, "Where was it you said you were coming from again? The Majestic Isles?"

Majestic Isles.

"Yes," I lied.

Transform, I told myself. *Don't talk about the Ambit.*

I remembered James talking about the Majestic Isles. It was a society in the middle of the country, known for training their citizens to fight. They had a reputation for being brutal and strong.

Zale looked up from the goat to me. "Really?"

I nodded, doing my best to embody the strength that I was claiming to have.

Transform.

"Really."

Zale smiled. "So, you must be good hunters then?"

Hunting. Animals. To eat. My stomach turned.

"She's the best," Seph said quickly, trying to help.

"Really?" Zale said, crossing his arms and looking at me. He was studying my build. I did not look like a hunter. I didn't even have the body of someone who ate meat, let alone someone who could kill for it.

Maris took our bag from my arms, "Don't mind him, come with me. I'll show you the Floor."

Zale watched me as I walked by him to follow Maris. He had a smirk on his face, like he wasn't believing anything we were saying.

As we walked, Zale said, "Brokers will want to know about that goat."

"I know," Maris called over his shoulder.

"Brokers?" I asked.

Zale waited for Maris to answer. He didn't.

"Brokers run things down here. In the meantime, you probably want to carry the goat. It'll get you some good chits, but not if anyone gets to her first," Zale said.

"What?" Seph stopped and turned around. "Get to her? You don't mean they'd want to *eat* her?!"

Maris stopped walking in front of us and turned.

"You're not planning to eat her?" Zale laughed.

"Of course not, she's my pet," Seph said.

"Your pet?" Zale turned to me. "Really?"

"What's it to you?" I snapped at him, trying to embody the Majestic Islander I was supposed to be.

Zale raised his hands in the air in submission, smiling.

"Nothing, I guess."

Seph and I followed Maris through the platform full of vehicles parked under signs that were numbered. We'd parked the truck in the one labeled, "MCC Guard 37."

When we reached a door, Maris held it open. On the other side bright flashing lights and bustling noise awaited us. The door led to a long cement walkway, lined with metal railing. We stepped up to the railing and overlooked the massive space below. It was an underground city.

"Welcome to the Outside," Zale said to us.

I turned to him. "*This* is the Outside?" I looked back in disbelief.

"This is it," Maris said, "The outside city that isn't actually outside at all."

"Pretty damn disappointing, isn't it?" Zale chuckled.

I looked at him and wondered if he had any idea how true his statement was.

This was the great city?

In the distance there were gigantic screens that flashed lights and colors, pictures, and sounds. The walls had smaller versions that were flashing with photographs of people, with the word 'WANTED' written above the pictures. One picture caught my attention because it was terrifying. It was of a person with a black hooded coat and a mask covering his face. I assumed it was a man, but it may have been a woman; the mask made it hard to tell. It had yellow eyes painted on it. The rest of it was mostly white but faded into black at the chin. The nose and mouth of the mask reminded me of a cat, but not one I'd ever seen before. Under the picture was a caption that read, "REWARD".

The movement of the screens, with the lights and flashing was so overwhelming, I had to close my eyes to let my brain rest. I knew without asking that they were using the technology that the Ambit frowned upon.

When I reopened my eyes, I saw people, hordes of them, walking in all different directions below. Their clothes were colorful, but dirty. Some of the men had long greasy hair, while some had shaved their heads completely. Both the men and women had drawings on their skin, mostly their faces and necks.

Suddenly the lights went dim and started flashing.

"What's going on?" I asked, on edge.

After another second, they brightened again, and the motion below resumed.

"Power surge," Zale said. "The city is run off solar-powered wind turbines that are above ground. You'll get used to the flickering."

Flickering. I thought of James. Suddenly I understood why the sky of the Ambit mesmerized him when it rained. This is where he'd come from. He said people from the Outside hid. Now I understood what he meant.

No wonder he never wanted to talk about it.

Looking around, I recognized that the platforms and tunnels underneath the former city of Chicago, were the same ones that I had read about in the books from the Ambit. They had once been used by the city folk for traveling by train. I had read about the underground railroad tracks and the trains that zoomed through the stations. Now trains didn't race down the tracks because the railroad gutters had been flooded with water. Instead of trains, people traveled on small narrow boats. While we watched, I'd seen at least a dozen of the gondolas. A few of them stopped to drop off or pick up passengers, and then they continued and disappeared down the dark corridor.

"This is called the Floor," Maris said, watching us take it all in.

"Where does that go?" I asked, motioning to the disappearing boats.

Maris turned to see what I was pointing to. He smiled at my ignorance. "The canals lead to the other platforms, where there are living quarters and other platforms like this one. But the Floor is the main terminal."

"Down that hall there," Zale pointed, "…there's a set of elevators that we use to go above ground to farm for resources."

"Elevators?" I asked.

"What? You don't have elevators in the Isles?" Zale smiled like he already knew it was all a lie.

I shot a look at Maris. His face winced.

"Look," Zale finally said, "You don't want us to know where you came from, that's fine, but the dress gives you away. Majestic Islanders wouldn't be caught dead in that." He looked at Seph, "…and they'd eat the goat."

He was on to us already. I was a terrible liar.

"But what's it to me anyway, right?" he winked, reminding me of my own statement from a moment earlier.

"One thing is for sure though, Pops." Zale said to Maris, as he began walking away from us. "She needs a good cover story." He looked at me and then said, "A woman like *that* won't go unnoticed."

Woman like that? What did he mean?

I would have asked, but he'd already disappeared through another door.

I turned to Maris, "So, that's your son? You must be proud." I said sarcastically.

"Yeah," Maris sighed. Then he turned and rested his elbows on the metal railing overlooking the Floor.

"...you told me not to trust him?" I said, "Why?"

Maris watched the people below for a second.

"See there," he pointed down to a young man, probably only a few years older than Seph. "Watch his hands."

The boy was moving quickly through the crowds below. He slipped in between the cracks of people with grace and ease.

"Wait for it," Maris said.

Just as Maris finished his statement, it happened. The young man ripped a bag from the hands of a woman and took off running. Within seconds of the theft, a different man that was walking beside the woman, who had witnessed the act, took off after the boy. Seeing that the man was chasing him, the boy ran faster, but he was no match. The bigger man violently snatched him up by the fabric on the back of his coat and took him to the ground with one quick motion. The bigger man's fists landed on the boy over and over until the boy was motionless on the ground.

I knew that the theft was wrong, but the punishment from the full-grown man was brutal. Seeming proud of his brutality, he then took the bag from the boy's hands and turned to find the woman next to him. She smiled at her hero with gratitude. But instead of returning the bag to her, the man slipped it over his shoulder, across his chest and then he walked away.

The woman cussed at him.

"He didn't give it back to her!?"

Maris laughed, "No favors. No one does anything for nothing. You hear that, Seph?"

I turned to Seph. He was still staring at the bloodied boy his age that hadn't moved since the attack.

"Seph?" Maris called, waiting for him to respond.

Seph looked up and I saw tears balanced in his eyes.

"Nobody does nothing for nothing, kid, you got that?"

Seph nodded.

"Don't take what ain't yours. If you value something keep it close to you." He looked down at the goat.

Maris spit on the ground next to his boot.

"This place is a hellhole," Maris groaned. "You'll be missing the Ambit, but you'll get used to it."

"So, what do we do now?" I asked.

Maris sighed. "You'll come stay with me until we can get you some sort of work. What can you do?"

"In the Ambit, I helped deliver babies."

Maris' eyebrows rose on his forehead, "Well, that won't be helpful down here."

"Why?"

He motioned to the Floor, "How many kids do you see?"

I looked again. I didn't see any.

"I don't understand. How can a society like this survive without children?"

Maris scowled, "Who said we're surviving?"

A chill trickled down me.

"We can farm," Seph said.

Maris nodded, "That word doesn't mean the same thing here as it does where you come from, kid."

Seph and I shared a look.

"Are you strong?" Maris asked.

I waited for Seph to answer. Then I realized Maris wasn't asking him, he was asking me.

"Me?"

Maris rose his eyebrows, "Yeah, you, Princess."

I scowled. "Please don't call me that."

Maris laughed, "Well, if you ain't strong, at least pretend you are."

"She's stronger than she gives herself credit for," Seph said.

"She'll be alright."

I forced a smile for Seph. It was sweet of him to try to reassure me.

I looked at Maris, he was still waiting for me to answer.

Am I strong?

If you ain't strong, at least pretend you are.

"I'll pretend," I said.

Transform.

6
PRETENDER

Two months ago, Seph and I were banished from the only home that either of us had ever known. Left without options or understanding of the world beyond the border of the Ambit, we relied on an old man and his beat-up truck to guide us to a new life in the Outside. Since that time, I'd learned more about the way the world worked than I ever wanted to know. And now I desperately craved the society that I once hated.

In the Ambit, there was order, there were rules and standards, but there was peace. In the Ambit, there was numbness and disregard for life, but there was safety. In the Ambit, I was considered weak merely because I was a woman, but at least I knew where I stood.

In the Outside, there is violence and poverty, there is take without give, there is kill or be killed. The Outside is a dark hole in the ground, where humans don't live, they merely exist. Joy is as hard to find as natural light. Life is concealed, confused with the temporary highs that medicine and alcohol, violence and lust provide.

Since we had arrived, I'd been mugged twice and threatened more times than I could count. Seph had been jumped several times. They stole his shoes and his belt. One time, he'd been beaten so badly, I didn't let him out of our living unit for a week. Since then, Zale and Maris had taught him a few things about how to defend himself. He did exercises daily to build his muscles.

When we first arrived, I thought that the inhabitants of the Outside were even more pathetic than the Ambit's citizens, weakened by their circumstances and too afraid to do anything about it. Who would choose to live below ground, when the city formerly known as Chicago was abundant and bountiful right above their heads?

But I realize now that it wasn't their ignorance and sloth, or an unwillingness to help themselves, that kept them trapped in this literal pit of despair, it is something far, far worse.

I'd spent countless hours wondering why James had never told me the truth about the Outside and its monsters, but deep down I knew the answer was simple. He knew that if he told me, there was no chance I would ever leave the Ambit.

Stay down. I heard a voice say.
Stay down, don't get up.

I looked around for the man whose voice I'd heard. There was no one, nothing but fire.

You're down. Stay down.

I looked again, reaching up to feel my head. I was dizzy, confused.

Where was the voice coming from?

I looked up toward the buildings.

Where was I? Where was I supposed to be?

Down the roadway, a massive building with three sides skyrocketed into the blackness above. That was the building I needed to get to. That was where the elevator to the Outside was. That was where I'd gotten separated from Zale.

Get up! My mind commanded.

A stream of warm liquid slid down my face. I could taste the metallic tang of blood in my mouth; I forced myself to swallow before the realization set in that I was hurt.

Stay down, the man's voice came again. It was a whisper.

I looked up to the triangular building and thought I saw a yellow sliver of light. I rubbed my eyes, looking again.

How is there light coming from inside the building?

The light disappeared. The side of the building was black again. *How?*

Then a high-pitched whistling sound cut through the noise. It was the same sound I'd heard the first time we entered the city. I winced from the pitch. I had to move.

Get up! I told myself.

I tried to collect my thoughts, to remember what had knocked me out, but my mind didn't allow me to; it only ordered me to move. My body sprang into action, searching the ground for something to defend myself with. A shrill scream tore through the sky and I looked up, expecting to see a shadow zoom overhead again. There was nothing. I panned the area around me, finding only smoke and fire, burning red and orange and yellow all around. It seemed like only seconds ago that it was pitch black.

I fought off the urge to curl up in a ball and cower in the corner of what was remaining of the brick wall I had just sheltered myself with.

Reminders. I thought.

The building has three sides. It's shaped like a triangle. The triangle-shaped building has the elevator. The elevator will take me to safety.

With more clarity, I felt around on the ground below me looking for my weapon. An object pricked my finger. Seeing what I'd found, I closed my hand around it. My leather satchel was still strapped across my chest. I quickly shoved the object inside.

With one last pan of the surrounding area and fire, I took a deep breath and remembered Zale's advice to me, "Fear will only affect you if you let it. Keep your head about you and don't get cornered. Keep moving."

I closed my eyes and counted to three. Then all in one motion I jumped up and bolted toward the place that I had last seen Zale.

With as much focus as I could muster, I ran - heart pounding, fists sweating, jaw clenched - toward the rendezvous point. I told myself not to turn to see if my predator was following, but instead to concentrate on getting back to where the elevator was, to where I would be able to descend back into the hole known as the Outside.

If it hadn't been for my own clumsiness, I may have made it too. My feet were my nemesis, and I fell hard to the ground with a thud.

Stay down. I heard the whisper again.

Again, the fear welled up, but this time I fought it off with a loud scream of agony. It was as if my fear had been personified and yelling at it could scare it off. I didn't mean to yell and instantly knew that it was the worst thing I could have done.

I couldn't stop here; I had to keep moving.

Up ahead in the distance, a shadow grazed the brick wall that I was running toward. Just as quickly as it caught my eye, it disappeared. Those things could move fast.

My best option at this point was to find cover and hold out until I knew the coast was clear. I ducked into the doorframe of a small building. I would have gone in but there wasn't any room to enter; it was covered with broken furniture and debris. Other than the heaving of my chest, I was silent. Listening.

I'm going to get myself killed, I thought.

Reminders.

The triangle-shaped building has the elevator. The elevator will take me to safety.

I stuck my head out of the doorway just a little bit to scan the path between me and our checkpoint. It was clear. Clear of immediate threats but also clear of help. *Where's Zale?*

"Britt," a whisper broke the silence. "Britt, over here."

I searched the openings in the wall across the path from me.

"Where are you?" I whispered into the dark.

"Look up."

I looked up and found Zale standing above me on the roof of the little building.

"What do I do?" I asked, trying to conceal the fear in my voice.

He looked around from his vantage point.

"Sit tight, I'll—"

A whistle cut through the air. Zale looked up, wincing. I covered my ears.

"They're coming," Zale said, then he disappeared.

"Zale?!" I shouted. *Did he just abandon me?*

I felt the ground shake slightly under me. In the distance an explosion burst in the darkness, lighting the sky. With the fire, I could see again.

"Sht."

I decided to stay still, partially because I hoped Zale would come for me, but also because I was too terrified to move.

"Stick with me," he had ordered before we left the elevator. I meant to; I really did. But when I saw the great beast for the first time, I lost all conscious thought and ran. Like a child, I ran for cover, forgetting all the training he had given me over the past two months. No amount of training could have prepared me to find myself centered in front of a beast so massive and horrifying.

An anguished scream in the distance, jolted me to reality as I ducked back in the doorway, flattening my back against the wall. It was the kind of sound that was both intriguing and repulsive. I wanted to see the monster that produced it, but knew I needed to run for my life every time I heard it.

Sht. Sht, sht. Where is he?

A reply scream came from a closer proximity. There was more than one and they were communicating, howling like hungry wolves would call to their packs. Fear choked me as I realized they were hungering for us.

I listened closely, trying to hear Zale's approach. Several minutes had passed since he disappeared on the roof, and I began to plan my next move if he didn't show up soon.

Then the whistle came again. It was so piercing; I pulled my hands to my ears. When it stopped, I dropped my hands and heard a pattering sound closing in on me. I felt my heartbeat speed up and hot blood swarm my legs and arms.

"Run!" Zale screamed at me.

I wanted to, but I couldn't tell where he was or in which direction I was supposed to be running.

From around the corner of the little building, Zale bolted. A flash of hot light followed him.

"Britt, run!" he screamed again.

My feet obeyed before my mind could register the order. I sprinted in front of Zale in the direction of our rendezvous point, the triangular building. It was still fifty yards away, a distance that felt like a thousand steps to me, but less than twenty to the enormous monster that followed.

I could hear Zale's feet pacing mine. "Faster!"

As we ran, I felt the earth shake under our feet. A striking, clanging sound came from behind us, prompting Zale to shove me to the side, into a wall. He covered me with his body as a blaze of bright light flashed down the trail we were running. Zale cried out as the flames grazed his back. When they dissipated, he grabbed me by the hand and yanked me behind him. We were only steps from the charred black doorway of the rendezvous point building.

Zale whipped around the corner, with me in tow, tossing me into the wall as he turned. I accidentally tore my hand from his so

I could catch myself from running into the wall. The heat from the flamed cement blocks scalded my hand. I gasped, stopping for a moment to look at my palm. That moment of distraction was only broken as I looked up to see one of the beasts face-to-face for the first time.

Black. Reptilian. Beast.

They called them monitors. They believed them to be a breed of dragon. It was so large I wouldn't have believed it, if my own eyes weren't widening at the sight of it in that very second. It was just as terrifying as they'd said, with a massive jaw full of teeth, and a long lizard-like body that moved at an unimaginable speed. It outsized me by ten times as much at least. I screamed. Zale yanked my arm violently, pulling me out of its path, before it reared back and threw another stream of scalding flames toward me.

Triangle building. Triangle building.

Using our size to our advantage, we hid in the building, ducking, and crawling around debris. The monitor paced on the opposite side of the wall; sniffing the spaces he was too big to follow in, with his long, blue, slithering tongue. He screeched out in frustration at not being able to get to us.

"There!" Zale yelled above the squeal. Within seconds we were far enough into the interior of the building that the monitor could no longer find us. Zale led me to the elevator and smacked the button. When it finally rang and the doors slid open, we poured inside. Neither of us exhaled until the doors were shut completely.

Once inside, he turned to me.

"You're hurt?!"

He took my face in his hands, turning my head to the side to examine the source of the blood.

"I'm sor—" I started to say, feeling dizzy.

"Turn around," he demanded, turning me.

"Where does it hurt?!"

"I don't—" I tried to say.

How do I explain it to him?

"Where's all this blood coming from?"

"I'm not hurt," I said, turning back to face him.

Seeing that I was telling the truth, the concern in his eyes turned to furious anger. He separated from me. When he turned around, I got a look at the burn on his back. My stomach dropped.

He was the one that was hurt.

"Dammit!" Zale shouted, slamming his hand into the metal wall. His outburst startled me, and I felt like crumbling into a wailing pitiful mess on the floor. I knew better though, I had to keep it together. "Even if you're not strong, pretend you are. Not brave? Pretend you are. Basically, anything you aren't, pretend you are, if you want to survive," Maris had told me.

Do not conform, transform.

The back of Zale's shirt was charred and gaping open, his flesh was pink and swollen. I reached into my satchel and found the tube of ointment that I carried with me, knowing full-well that we might come across a flame-thrower when we farmed. I squeezed a dollop of the cream on the palm of my hand and smoothed it over the burn that I'd sustained from the wall. I moved toward Zale, hoping to do the same for his back.

"I'm fine!" He yelled, "I don't need that." He was fuming mad at me. I wanted to apologize and beg his forgiveness, but that might appear as weakness.

Zale walked to the panel of buttons on the interior of the elevator and punched the button labeled STOP. The elevator did as the button commanded. Then he turned around and glared at me.

"Stick together! Didn't I say, 'stick with me'? Maris was right! He said you weren't cut out for this. But you said you could handle it! You almost got us both killed, you know that?" He paced back and forth in the tiny metal box.

I swallowed the lump in my throat. I wanted to cry, but I didn't show it. Instead, I moved in on him again, so that I could apply the ointment that I knew he needed.

He whipped around and locked eyes with me. I could see the rage in them. He seemed like he was trying to contain it but wasn't doing a very good job.

"There are two kinds of people, Britt. There are people who run toward danger and people who run *from* it. Which one are you?"

His question caught me off guard. It wasn't rhetorical; he wanted me to answer him.

I run. I thought. *That's which one I was. I run from danger.*

I rested back on my heels. "It's not that black and white, Zale."

He closed in on me, getting only a foot from my face. He

91

pointed toward the door of the elevator. "When you're out there, it is."

He turned away from me again. I thought about whether I should try applying the ointment or not. Part of me didn't want to anymore.

Zale was shaking his head and mumbling to himself. He seemed like he was trying to self-soothe and I would have been perfectly fine to let him, until I heard him mumble, "I'm as crazy as my old man, there's a reason why women shouldn't be up there."

"What'd you say?" I asked, feeling the apologetic lump in my throat disappear completely.

Zale turned, "I said 'there is a reason why no one will train a woman to farm for resources'. You can't handle it. I should have listened to Maris, but you had me convinced."

I'd had enough of his tantrum. "*I* had *you* convinced? This was your idea! I didn't coerce you. You have as much to gain for taking me up there as I do." I scowled back at him. I knew, just as well as he did, that the only reason he agreed to train me to farm for resources was because if I *did* happen to be successful, it would gain him recognition at the Rally. And the better he looked at the Rally, the better his reputation in the Outside would be.

Zale paced back and forth on the opposite side of the elevator.

I pressed him further, "I know you took a risk taking me up there. But don't pretend like you're not getting anything out of this! You need me, just as much as I need you."

"Let's get something straight," he scolded me, "I don't need you. I was doing fine on my own." Something about the way he said that last part made me wonder if he was really referring to the farming missions, or if he was meaning something else.

"You do too! Ya know why?"

He scowled at me again, assuming that I would tell him whether he answered or not. "Because you're stupid."

His eyebrows rose in surprise and then furled again in offense.

"There are two kinds of people, Zale. People who will let someone treat their wounds when they're hurt, and people who refuse help and let the wound fester, until it kills them. Which one are you?"

Zale's face softened as he pondered my question, then the corner of his mouth turned up into a smirk. He got it. He had guts, but I had sense. There was a reason why Zale didn't have a farming partner. He was too stubborn and preferred to be alone. And while it was true that he'd managed to garner a worthy reputation in the Outside working by himself, adding me to his resume, would make us both untouchable. He was already one of the best farmers in the Outside but having me by his side would make him legendary. Whether he liked it or not, he needed my help. His angry gaze finally broke, and he said, "Then stick with me next time."

I kept a straight face on the outside, but inside I reveled at the feeling of winning the argument. Each time I chose to push back when I was told I wasn't enough, I learned to trust myself. Every bit of trust fueled me further. I was beginning to see that I was more capable than I ever imagined. I hoped that someday I could stop pretending to be all the things they required of me, and just know that I was enough.

"Are you gonna turn around or not?" I asked him, steadying my eyes on his. He looked down at the tube of ointment in my hand, then back up at me. His eyes narrowed. Then with an indignant sigh, he turned around.

His skin was swollen from the burn. I pulled the pocketknife from my belt and switched the blade open. Carefully, I cut back the strips of his shirt that were still covering the burn. His muscles tensed as I delicately peeled back the threads that were stuck in his tender flesh.

"Almost done," I said.

I put ointment on my hands then as gently as I could, I lathered the lotion over the wound. The heat under his skin warmed my fingertips, charging them. It felt electric.

In my mind, I replayed the moment in the alley when he'd pushed me against the wall to block me from the flames. Shame washed over me. He was hurt because of me. He had every right to be upset.

With as much clarity as I could manage with my shaky voice, I whispered, "I'm sorry."

He turned around when I said it, curious about my sudden change in tone.

I stepped back and turned my attention to replacing the cap on the ointment in my hands.

"For what it's worth," I said. "I'm sorry. I'll do better next time."

His eyes transitioned from confusion to understanding. He nodded.

Then he reached up and pulled the STOP button out from the panel, shifting the elevator back into motion.

When the elevator doors pulled back, and the crowd saw both Zale and I returned in one piece, a commotion erupted. I buried my chin in my chest, trying not to be seen.

"Britt, Britt, Britt…" the crowd chanted.

Zale took my hand and raised it above my head, like I was some sort of champion of something. I felt like anything but. I let him hold my hand there for only a second before retracting it. I forced a little smile at the crowd, then pushed forward.

"She's a natural," Zale lied to them. There was no way for them to know otherwise. I turned around to look at him. He was smiling for the crowd, playing the politics, putting on a show.

"Were there monitors?" someone from the crowd yelled.

Zale turned around and showed them the wound on his back, "What do you think?" he laughed.

A gaggle of women swarmed him, cooing over his wound. That was when I stopped watching.

I found Seph waiting on the fringe of the crowd. He was anything but excited. He came forward and wrapped his arms around my neck.

"Are you okay?!"

I nodded, taking the canteen of water from his hand, and gulping down half of it.

"You're bleeding," Seph said, pointing to the mess of red down my shirt. "Your clothes are burnt!"

"I'm okay," I panted, then I gulped down the other half of the water.

I looked around, "Where's Maris? You aren't alone down here, are you?"

Seph nodded toward Maris. He was leaned against the wall across the corridor from us. A white stick balanced from his lips; he was watching his son indulge in the attention our return had won him. When he saw me looking at him, he pushed off the wall and made his way over to us. "He's always been a showoff."

I looked back at Zale. A forced smile was plastered to his face in front of his supporters. He was getting the attention he'd hoped.

"Well, you did it, Princess." Maris stared at me. "Your first mission and you didn't die. Had enough yet?"

I didn't answer. I knew Maris wasn't happy with me for going through with it. I didn't want to engage in another debate about whether it was appropriate for a woman to farm. I was tired of being told what was appropriate.

In the Outside your reputation is everything. If you're someone of importance, someone of value, then you live longer and better. You're less likely to be made a victim and I was tired of being a victim.

Reputation is currency. It's a meal ticket. It's protection. The closer to the top of the food chain you are, the more food there is. That's the reason I volunteered to farm above ground in the first place. As the only female farmer, I could guarantee Seph and myself some safety and decent comfort in the Outside.

Farming for resources above ground was important to the survival of the Outsiders. But it was also like a sport. If I provided, if I entertained, I could make a living. If I was admired, we would be left alone. Of course, if I died, no one would mourn me but Seph. They'd just move on, but surviving the farming missions was a means to surviving the Outside.

This is why I had to pretend. Pretend to be strong, tough, brave. Everything a farmer was supposed to be. Everything a man was supposed to be. I had to pretend to be it all, no matter how small or weak I felt underneath. I had to transform so that I could make my own way. Isla's book had taught me that.

I watched as a woman hung on Zale's arm. I tried to ignore the jealousy that sprouted against my will. I didn't have real feelings for Zale, but I did feel possessive of him. I was depending on him to train me, so I felt like my survival and his were closely intertwined. Since he was the only one willing to teach me, I didn't want him to get distracted.

"There are some very unhappy gamblers down here today," Maris said, seeing a group of men staring at me from down the corridor. "Don't go off on your own, ya hear?"

The way the men looked at me made my skin crawl. They

expected me to die on my first mission. They bet their food chits that I would. It's a weird feeling knowing someone mere feet from you would rather you be dead than alive. My survival had cost them.

I pulled Seph closer to my side.

"I wish he'd hurry up," Maris groaned, as we waited for Zale to finish lobbying with his supporters.

"Me too," I mumbled, keeping my eye trained on the men staring at me. Zale had taught me not to avert my eyes. He told me to keep my eyes locked on anyone that was trying to intimidate me. "Don't let them see you sweat," he'd taught me.

But I knew the risk. If I didn't look away, I was inviting confrontation. I wondered if they could see the fear behind my eyes when I refused to shift my gaze.

Pretend, I told myself. *Pretend you aren't afraid of them.*

Then it happened. One of the men took a long swig off the canteen in his hand and then broke away from his gang and started toward me.

"What are you lookin' at, btch?"

I didn't flinch.

Pretend.

"You think it's funny?" he asked me.

He was moving toward me. Seph stepped in closer. Maris turned around to see who was approaching.

"Now, now," Maris put his hand on the man's chest. "You're drunk, Finneas."

The man called Finneas stopped walking and looked down at Maris' hand.

"Hands off, old man," he warned. "I don't answer to you no more."

While he'd broken eye contact with me, I exhaled the air in my lungs and then quickly sucked in another strong breath.

Maris removed his hand as Finneas demanded.

"You lost some chits today," Maris acknowledged. "No one can blame you for being angry 'bout that, but it ain't *her* fault."

"Like hell it ain't," Finneas said, glaring at me again. "I'd say she owes me."

The man stepped toward me. This time Maris let him, and I knew why. He and Zale had prepared me for this.

Dark alleys.

Empty passageways.

Opportunities for them, meant I had to be prepared to be attacked at any moment.

Seph began to shift his weight in front of me and I knew this was my moment to do as they'd trained me.

Pretend.

I put my hand on Seph's arm and gently pulled him back. Then I stepped forward, my eyes locked on Finneas.

"What exactly do you think I owe you?"

We all knew what he was implying. I am a woman, and just like all men throughout history, he thought it his duty to let me know he could conquer me if he wanted.

The last thing I wanted to do was tempt him into seeing me as a challenge he needed to conquer. My intelligence was my most powerful defense. If I could confuse him, it would turn him off.

Finneas' smile crept over his face. His eyes dropped and crept over my body. He licked his thin chapped lips and his eyes flickered with delight. The disgusting smell of his breath dusted my face as he asked, "You offerin' ?"

I kept my shoulders back and my chin high.

"You have really pretty eyes," I said.

Finneas' eyes slid to the side, like he was searching his brain for clarity. He looked back at me. His face contorted. "What?"

"You have really pretty eyes," I repeated.

He was thrown off by my compliment.

"All my life I wished I had eyelashes like yours," I added.

Finneas stepped back half a step and broke eye contact with me. It made him uncomfortable to think that I was looking at how pretty his eyes were now. He couldn't reconcile if I was being nice or if I was poking fun at him. I was doing the latter. I wondered how it made him feel to be thought of as nothing more than pretty.

I glanced at Maris over Finneas' shoulder. The old man rolled his lips inward to contain the smile that I knew wanted to crack his face wide open. He diverted his eyes from me so he could contain it.

Finneas looked back up at me, completely deflated and unsure how to proceed with his flat attempts to threaten me.

"Finneas?" Zale called.

Finneas turned.

"You gotta problem over here?" Zale asked him. Finneas floundered even more in Zale's presence.

It was clear that Finneas wanted to back out of the situation but didn't know how.

"Finneas was just expressing his regret for not betting in my favor today," I told Zale.

His eyebrows curled down in disbelief.

"Maybe next time he'll consider it," I said, turning to look at Finneas. His eyes caught mine, then they dropped to the ground.

He averted his eyes from *mine.*

Bobbing his head, he said. "Btch." Then he backed away.

"What was that about?" Zale asked, watching the man shrink back to his cronies.

"Nothing she couldn't handle," Maris assured him.

Zale looked at me inquisitively.

I smiled shyly, trying to calm my nerves.

"Let's go," I said.

I stepped inside the dingy unit we called home and let the door close behind me. I leaned against it. I had only a few minutes of reprieve before Zale and Maris expected me to emerge again, refreshed, and ready for the Rally.

The goat, that Seph had named Nanny, was standing on the back of the small couch in our unit. As soon as Seph and I came through the door, she bellowed her frustration at us. We hadn't let her out of the unit in weeks.

"I know, I know," Seph said, the exhaustion weighing down his tone. He extended his hands to her. She'd gotten thin. We both regretted bringing her to the Outside with us. Keeping her in our unit was the only way to keep her safe. Taking her out attracted too much attention and we worried someone would snag her. Taking her above ground to free her was most definitely a death sentence, so we kept her locked in.

The goat bleated at him a few more times, letting him know how hungry and depleted she was. After a few more moments, she finally let him put his forehead to hers. That quieted them both.

I knew the guilt he felt for keeping her. I felt the same way about allowing him to come to the Outside with me. He was thin and depleted too. We spent most of our time scared. I looked over his body, seeing how thin he was, even though he had put on muscle from working out. The idea that we should solve one problem with another, had occurred to me. Nanny couldn't last much longer in the Outside behind closed doors without sunlight or proper nutrition, but she could feed Seph. But then I watched the two of them together and knew that her headstrong but comforting presence was the only thing keeping him sane.

With that thought, a flood of tears started seeping from me. I slid down the door, burying my face in the palm of my hands and sobbed.

The day.

The mission.

The threats.

The hunger.

The fear.

The constant pretending.

Behind closed doors, with only Seph to see me, I could let my pent-up emotions release. I'd gotten better over the months. Now, I'd give myself two minutes to cry and then I'd wash my face and step back out.

Seeing me cry as soon as I crossed the threshold of our unit was not new for Seph, yet he always responded the same way.

He moved toward the couch and pulled Isla's book out from under his pillow. He opened to a random page and began reading, "Let thy hand be upon the man of thy righthand, upon the son of man whom thou madest strong for thyself. So will not we go back from thee; quicken us, and we will call upon thy name. Turn us again, O Lord God of hosts, cause thy face to shine; and we shall be saved."

We didn't know what the words he read meant, just that they reminded us of Isla.

He continued, "Sing aloud unto God our strength; make a joyful noise unto God of Jacob. Take a…"

A loud thundering pounded on the door behind me, and I jumped.

"Britt?" Zale's voice called. "We gotta go."

I closed my eyes and took a deep breath.

When I opened them again, Seph was looking at me. He pressed his lips into that same Seph smile and the familiarity of it soothed me. Seph's smile and Isla's book. Moments of what once was.

Reminders.

Look for the truth.

Seph is safe in this unit. I told myself, grasping for anything that resembled the reassuring truth I needed.

Seph is safe in this unit and Isla is safe in the Ambit.

And that was enough for the moment.

I took another deep breath and then opened the door.

Zale was waiting for me. He'd changed his shirt from the torn burnt one to a green intact one. I wished I had time to change out of my blood-soaked clothes, but I'd wasted it crying on the floor.

"You ready?" he asked with a gentleness I didn't expect.

I wondered if he knew what happened on the other side of the door when I disappeared behind it.

I patted the satchel attached to my hip. "As I'll ever be."

7
THE RALLY

At the Canal Passage, Maris, Zale, and I boarded a gondola. Within seconds, Zale held out his hand to me.

"What's this?" I asked, allowing him to drop four small metal tubes into my hand.

"That's your bounty for today," he said. Then he looked up again, "I'm assuming you didn't manage to farm anything up there today, right?"

I considered telling him about the object I'd found on the ground after we got separated.

"I—"

"You can't go in empty-handed, so keep these close," he interrupted. "The Rally is dangerous and the pickpockets are pros. They'll cut your pockets, they'll rip your bag off your arm, and even if your arm is still attached, they'll take that too. You *need* to stick with me. If you lose your bounty, you're nothing but a pretty face, and that's not what you're selling, right?"

I cocked my head to the side. "I can handle it."

I secured the metal tubes in the small pocket of my satchel.

"Who are you selling to?" Maris asked.

"The Caller," I answered as they'd taught me.

Maris nodded his approval.

"Who are you not selling to?" he rehearsed.

"Anyone else."

He nodded again.

"What if the Caller doesn't accept my bounty? Then what?"

101

Maris smiled. "Not to worry. You'll get his attention just fine."

I groaned. I hated how they both implied my "bounty" was more than what was in my satchel.

"But what about the others, what do they do, if they aren't chosen?"

"Then they sell to the Brokers, or they sell them on the black market," Zale answered.

"I thought the Brokers were the ones who police things on the Floor?"

"They are, but they're also street sellers."

"They're thieves," Maris growled. "They'll take your resource and trade it on the Floor for double."

"And they take that role very seriously," Zale continued. "They're territorial and violent about street sales, so you need to do everything you can to sell to the Caller. Steer clear of the Brokers."

"How do I know who's who?"

Maris pointed to the lapel of his coat, "They wear badges shaped like eyes. The Caller's eye is black. The Brokers wear red."

"The black market?" I asked, "That's when the Outsiders trade in secret on their own?"

Zale nodded, "Yes, and the Underground doesn't take kindly to getting cut out so stay away from the black marketeers."

The Underground.

The invisible puppeteers of the Outside. All I knew about them is that they could be anywhere, anytime and they could be anyone. The Caller and the Brokers answered to the Underground. Maris and Zale told me that the Underground stayed anonymous to avoid uprising. If the Outsiders don't know who exactly is pulling their strings, they're less likely to try to cut them.

As we came to the end of the gondola passage, I spotted a WANTED screen with the picture of a masked person on it. I remembered the same picture from my first day in the Outside. Over the months since we'd arrived, the other pictures had changed, but this one remained. I stared at the mask, wondering what it was meant to represent.

Someone had vandalized the screen. Where the word REWARD was, they'd crossed off the RE and D. Under it, the vandal had painted the word STORIAN.

"War Storian?" I read aloud.

Zale twisted to see the moving poster on the wall.

"Do you know about Storian?"

I shook my head.

"That's probably for the better," Zale said.

"Why? What is it?"

Zale looked at Maris, hesitantly.

Maris answered, "The Underground likes to have control of what information moves in and out of the Outside. The Storian thinks information should be free and accessible, so they smuggle it."

Zale nodded toward the poster, "War Storian is the face of their faction. The Underground will reward anyone that turns them in."

"What kind of information do they smuggle?"

"The kind that the Underground doesn't want shared," Zale said.

"Like what?" I asked.

Zale's eyes focused. He glanced at the gondola driver and then he leaned forward and whispered, "It would be better if you didn't ask those kinds of questions, Britt."

"Why?"

Zale shook his head, "Because just like anyone can be an Undergrounder down here, anyone can be Storian. And that's a war you don't want to stumble into the middle of. Trust me."

I looked at Maris. He nodded.

"A war? For information? Are the Storian the good guys or the bad guys?"

I looked back and forth between the men, but it was clear that neither of them wanted to answer.

"They're both trouble," Zale said. "All you need to know is that they're dangerous."

Dangerous? More dangerous than the Underground?

Why did Zale seem so hesitant to answer?

Didn't he know it just made me more curious?

"But--?" I started.

"Drop it," Zale said, flatly. His eyes floated toward the gondola driver. He was listening to us. "Please," Zale added, seeing how I didn't like him commanding me.

I sat with my curiosity, resolved to ask again when we were alone. What kind of information would the Underground want to keep hidden? What kind of information would warrant a war?

The gondola was closing in on the light at the next platform. In the distance, I could see a single large black eye had been painted onto the wall at the exit. Zale leaned in, "See the eye? That's to remind us that the Underground is always watching."

A roar of voices grew louder. The gondola broke into the light as we approached the Rally platform; it was bustling with activity. We waited in a long line of other boats, with men climbing out, clinging to various items. When it was our turn to unload, Zale climbed out first and then extended his hand to me. I noticed people were watching us. Their looks questioned what a woman was doing at the Rally. Women had a very specific reason for being at the Rally, and I didn't fit that category. I wanted them to see me as their equal, so I refused Zale's hand and climbed out on my own.

"Good luck, kid," Maris said, remaining in the gondola.

"You're not coming?" I asked.

He shook his head, then exhaled. "I think you can handle it without me." He and Zale shared a knowing look, then Zale turned and greeted the other farmers around us.

"Just be careful," Maris whispered to me. "I'd tell you to lay low, but I think we both know you can't do that now. I just hope your daddy doesn't kill me for not stopping you from doing this."

"How will he ever know?" I asked rhetorically.

Maris shrugged his shoulder. "Just be careful," he repeated.

"I'll lay as low as I can," I assured him.

He nodded, as the gondola driver pushed the boat back out into the water.

I turned and took in the commotion of the Rally platform.

Remembering the warnings Zale had given me, I slid my hand inside my satchel and clenched the metal tubes he'd given me to claim as my bounty. With a quick movement, I turned away from the crowd and faced Zale, stuffing the contents of my hand into my bra under my shirt. Zale's eyebrows rose with surprise.

"What? You said the pickpockets are pros."

Zale laughed. "They would have to be pretty stealthy to get them from there, I guess."

I nodded, "Exactly."

The platform where the Rally took place was the same size as all the others in the Outside. The only noticeable difference was the large, windowed box that overlooked the entire space. I could see that it was an office of some sort. In the window a man stood with his arms crossed, watching us.

Puppeteer, I thought. *He's the one I need to impress.*
Do not conform, transform.

"C'mon," Zale said, grabbing my hand. I took it back from him.

He turned to look at me. "I need to do this on my own," I said. Then with my eyes I motioned up to the man in the box watching us. Zale didn't have to look to know what I was referring to.

"Okay," he said. "Just stick with me this time, would ya?"

I nodded.

As we pushed further into the platform, I noticed a large stage in the center, with a brass bell suspended by cables from the ceiling. Around the edges Zale showed me the four quadrants, each representing an important resource. They were labeled: Food, Medicine, Luxuries and Necessities.

At the base of each Quadrant, stood a Broker. I saw the red eye patches on their lapels, just as Maris and Zale had described.

Just looking at them gave me chills. They were large and muscular, with square jaws clenched tight. They scanned the crowds as the Outsiders pushed inward to get close to the stage where the Caller would be.

Many of the farmers in attendance at the Rally, were new like me. Over time, they'll either die off or gain attention, fame and eventually retire. They ranged in age from sixteen to mid-sixties. They were probably brothers, sons, husbands, fathers, and grandfathers. I wondered how many of them were there to feed their families and how many of them were going to end up feeding the monitors instead. Some farmers sign up for the glory of the hunt, but most new farmers go out of sheer desperation to provide protection for their families. It's sad to me that these are the farmers that usually end up dying first. It's even more unfortunate that I'm one of these farmers.

Other than the farmers, there were a few dozen women who stood off to the side of the Luxury Quadrant. I recognized a few of them to be some of the women who were so attentive to Zale at the elevator. This was the capacity for which women would attend the Rally. Not to sell bounties from the farming field, like me, but to sell their services. They were prostitutes. They were considered luxuries, items, objects to be sold.

"We're over here," Zale pointed to the busiest quadrant, the one labeled Necessities.

As I followed him through the crowd of burly, smelly, men he stopped every few strides to see if I was still behind him.

"Britt, hurry up!" Zale yelled back to me.

I growled under my breath as I bounced back and forth off the shoulders, backs and bellies of my counterparts. At one point, someone managed to grab my rear end, but by the time I turned to sucker punch whoever it was, a fight had broken out and I couldn't tell who'd done it. When I turned back again to follow Zale, he'd completely disappeared in the chaos.

A circle of men closed in around me. One of them noticed me and smiled. Stupidly, I smiled back, forgetting that a smile in the Outside is never actually a smile. Then something slithered across his face, and I began to feel uneasy. He wasn't smiling at me to be nice; he was smiling at me because he wanted something from me.

Recognizing my position in the crowd, I turned around to move away from him. My breathing hastened as I realized how unsafe I was, even though I was surrounded by people. From the band at my waist, I carefully pulled my switchblade. I kept it closed but tightened my hands around it in case I needed it.

"Hey!" the man called. I twisted around. He was following me, trying to catch up to me. I moved faster.

When I turned around, I bumped into a wall of a man. His skin was darker than my father's, the darkest I'd ever seen. His head was bald, and the lights reflected from it. He towered over me. I shrunk back from him, looking up into his face. His dark eyes were set on me. He looked like he wanted to smile, then he looked up and saw the man that was following me. His face turned serious.

"Shouldn't you be in the Medicine Quadrant, Gus?!" he asked firmly. An accent I'd never heard before thickened his words. I turned to look at the man called Gus. He stared at me. I stared back at him, feeling less afraid since the bigger man had stepped in.

Gus backed down, keeping his eyes trained on mine. Once he

disappeared in the crowd, I turned to the man that'd stopped him.

"Thank you," I managed to say. Then I noticed the red eye patch on his lapel. He was a Broker.

"Are you hurt?" he asked, the accent weighed down his question. I'd never heard someone that sounded like him.

Hurt? The blood.

"No," I shook my head.

"Okay, ya'll…" a voice came across the loudspeaker to address the tiring crowd. I pushed up on my tippy toes to see where the voice was coming from. "We're gonna get started here in just a few minutes. Find your quadrant."

"Britt?!" Zale yelled over the noise.

I turned.

Zale came to rest next to me, across from the Broker that'd helped me. Zale took a moment to look from one of us to the other.

"Everything okay?" he asked.

I nodded, feeling too embarrassed to tell him what'd happened.

Then Zale turned to the Broker, "Eamon," he said with a nod.

The Broker nodded back respectfully, "Zale."

Then Zale turned to me. Only then did he seem to recognize the gravity of the situation. He noticed the men standing around us, staring at me.

"Let's get you to a safer spot, shall we?" he asked.

I nodded.

I looked up at the Broker named Eamon. He was statuesque. His dark eyes set on me. "Thanks," I said sheepishly, not fully knowing if he'd protected me from Gus or if he'd had other motives.

When he nodded his head in response, I felt confident it was not the latter.

"They're about to start," Zale said. This time when he extended his hand to me to hold, I didn't hesitate. I took it.

As he pulled me away, I turned one last time to look at Eamon. He watched me for a moment, then moved toward the stage.

Was he a friend or another threat?

Zale led me to a wooden crate against the back wall.

"This should be good," Zale said.

I stepped onto the crate and smiled. I could see the whole platform.

"Thank you," I said.

I spied Eamon at the edge of the stage. He noticed me on the crate. I smiled at him.

He diverted his eyes from me.

Not a friend. I guessed.

"They're gonna start soon," Zale instructed me. "You have to make yourself heard. Got it?"

I nodded, looking back over the sea of competition. I studied the faces of the men.

They couldn't all be bad, I thought.

Surely some men in the Outside still had good hearts, like Maris and Zale.

I looked down at Zale.

Does he have a good heart? I'd like to think he does, but Maris said not to trust him.

I looked back toward Eamon and caught him looking at me. This time his lips did curl upward into a small shy smile.

I hesitated at first and then I smiled back.

Eamon is a Broker. You can't trust him either.

Even if he does have a nice smile.

"Okay, ya'll…" the same voice as before called our attention back to him. The Caller stood on the stage above where Eamon stood.

He was a tall thin man that appeared to be aged into his sixties. His long face had a dented chin, worn skin and dark eyes. I guessed his hair had once been a dark color, but now it was salt and peppered, and thinning. I got the feeling that he commanded respect with his presence, not because he was intimidating, but because he was seasoned. Like nothing could get past him, he already knew all the tricks and thoughts of the men in the room. Like he'd always been one of them, and nothing could ever catch him by surprise. I wondered if *I* might surprise him.

"It's time to get started. Please remember, gentlemen…" he noticed me across the room standing on my box before he continued, "and lady…any pushing, shoving, fighting or otherwise, will not be tolerated. You will be removed immediately."

As he finished his warning, most of the heads in front of me turned to see who the 'lady' was. A catcall and a whistle chimed out of the crowd. I ignored it. I wasn't here to be a woman. I was here to be a farmer, just like the rest of them.

"MMmm...kay. When the bell rings, ya'll are good to go. When the bell rings a second time, we're done."

He held up a small metal tool. When he clanged it on the large brass bell, he casually said, "Begin."

Immediately, a flurry of activity started. The Caller spoke so fast I could hardly make out what resource he was asking for. Farmers were waving their hands in the air and yelling back. When he got the resource he needed, he pointed to the Broker who would then immediately start chanting and chattering like the Caller. Farmers would call and wave back at him and he would write it down. Then the Caller would turn to the next quadrant and the farmers waiting there would start yelling. It was madness.

I looked down at Zale, suddenly reconsidering the whole thing. I didn't know how I was going to hear my resource called, let alone how I was going to call back in time.

"What do I do?" I yelled to Zale.

"You have to get his attention!" Zale yelled back. Then he leaned against the wall and crossed his arms. He was waiting for me to make my move. Determined, I turned my attention back to the Caller.

I focused my eyes and my ears to hear his voice.

"Bushkets?" What are bushkets? Did he say blankets or baskets or bushes? "Lernins?" Is that a book or a kind of food?

I was going to miss the whole Rally.

The Caller was turned toward the Luxuries Quadrant, which meant the Necessities Quadrant was next. I had only a moment until the chaos would erupt in my quadrant again. I needed to get closer.

Finally, I'd had enough. I never imagined that the Rally would have been harder than the farming.

Well, if I can handle a monitor I can handle a bunch of testosterone-driven, smelly, hairy, azz-grabbin' men!

And with that notion, I jumped off my wooden crate, picked it up with both hands and held it in front of my stomach. I took a deep breath. Then, using it as a sort of mover, I stormed forward toward the stage. I had no shame in jabbing the others in their backs and sides to get by. I worried for half a second that they might boot me for being abrasive, but then I remembered no one could see me for all these man beasts that towered over me.

I finally found my way to the front of the platform, placed my box back on the floor and stepped up on it triumphantly. I puffed out my chest and clenched my jaw to look as intimidating as I could possibly muster.

Eamon the Broker was only a few feet from me now. He watched me with interest. Knowing he was there; I wasn't afraid of the other men. Maybe I was naïve to think he'd look out for me again, but it was a feeling I had about him that I trusted.

When the Caller turned to our quadrant, he stopped for a second to raise his eyebrows at me, seeing how I'd moved. Then he continued.

Now I could hear him, and I was just in time.

"Who's got batteries?" the Caller yelled.

"I do!" I screamed and jumped because I actually did. I couldn't believe my luck. "I've got your batteries right here!!" I reached into my bra and pulled them out. The man next to me made a comment about hoping they were a size double DD, but I blocked him out.

"What size batteries do you have, young lady?" the Caller asked, amused by my enthusiasm.

"I have 4, size Double A."

He pointed to me and yelled, "Her!" Then he pointed to Eamon, directing him to accept my bounty. My heart leapt in my chest. I'd done it. I'd sold my bounty. That was going to make Zale very happy with me.

Eamon accepted the direction from the Caller. When he looked at me this time, the shy smile he'd shared with me before had turned into a full-blown grin. Seeing his face open so beautifully took me by surprise. He seemed like he might be kind. Kindness was an even rarer find in the Outside than batteries.

"What else you got?" the Caller broke my concentration.

I was shocked that he was giving me another chance to sell my bounty.

"Um," I stammered, wishing I had something more to sell him. Then I remembered, I did have something else. I wasn't sure if it would mean anything, but it was something. I opened my satchel to find it, hoping it hadn't been snatched by stealthy hands in the busyness of the platform. It was right where I'd left it.

"I've got a tooth!"

"A what?" the Caller yelled back, cupping his ear to hear me better.

"A tooth! I have a monitor's tooth!"

The Caller and almost everyone within hearing range of me stopped what they were doing.

I looked around at them.

Why did they stop?

"A monitor tooth?" the Caller repeated. "Lemme see!"

I pulled it into view and held it up for him to see. It was almost the size of my hand, curved like a fang, and sharp enough to shred through flesh.

His face was stoic as he stared at it.

"That ain't no regular monitor tooth, girl," he called back to me. "That came from the Cinder Dragon."

Everyone on the entire platform stopped when he said those words. I looked around. They were all staring at me. Every set of eyes was on me.

Then the lights flickered, and the power went out from another power surge.

The Cinder Dragon?

I knew that Cinder was the name the Outsiders had given the only known female monitor because of the ash and soot she left in her path. Sightings of her were rare.

"The only one that can fly," Zale had told me in my trainings.

Then a flashback loaded my memory. It was the flying dragon. The one I'd seen while I laid in the rubble of the fire. The only one.

I'd seen *her.* I'd seen the Cinder Dragon.

The only female.

In an odd way, though I knew her intention would have been to destroy me, I felt a likeness to her.

I, too, was the rare female.

I ran my fingers over the tooth, feeling the sharp point on the end of it. *Had she tried to shred me with it?*

The power surge ended, bringing the lights into full beam again.

When I looked up the Caller was still staring at me. His face hadn't changed at all in the moment of darkness. He seemed deep in thought. Then he broke the line of sight he had on me, so he could ring the metal bell again.

111

"Rally's over," he said. The crowd groaned with disappointment.

I looked around, feeling responsible.

"Young Miss," the Caller asked for my attention. He pointed to the windowed box above the crowd. "Care to have a chat in my office?"

I looked up into the box. The Caller was the man I'd seen in the window.

I turned to find Zale through the crowd. He was at full attention, watching me. His eyes were curious with anticipation.

His head ducked slightly, as if to tell me to agree. I looked down at the object in my hand again and closed my fingers around it.

The Cinder Dragon's tooth would definitely earn me something.

I looked up at the Caller and nodded, "Okay."

So much for trying to lie low.

8
THE TOOTH

The Caller's office was small, with one wall made entirely of windows overlooking the Rally platform. I stood in the window staring down as the platform slowly cleared out. A few men were haggling with the women in the Luxury Quadrant. I couldn't stand to watch as the women sold themselves, so I turned my back and looked over the rest of the room. A desk and chair sat in the center with two more chairs on the opposite side. Behind it, on the wall overlooking the room, someone had painted a giant eyeball. The iris was black.

It matched the painting of the black eye on the cement wall of the platform below.

The eye.

Creepy.

"A reminder that someone is always watching," Zale had told me.

As I waited, I explored the office, looking for anything to distract my nervous mind. It'd been almost a half an hour since the Caller asked for a chat, but he had yet to meet with me.

I found my reflection in the long oval mirror on the wall. Now I could understand why they were concerned. I was covered with dried blood. My face, shoulders, hair. I remembered the smock I'd put on was blue. Now it was burnt and torn and brown from blood.

I leaned into the mirror.

113

My eyes were a paler brown than they used to be. Sadder. Tired.

I was exhausted. I felt like I hadn't really slept in eleven years.

Chasen. I thought.

Then I pushed him to the back of my mind.

I looked at my hair in the mirror. That morning, I'd tied it back into a ponytail. Now it was a mess, with thick black curls popping out of my head like wildflowers. I reached up and tried to tame a few of them, but it was no use trying with my shaky hands.

I dropped my hands down and held them together, trying to control the shake. I fiddled with the wedding ring on my left hand and remembered Zale's recommendation to leave it behind while we were farming. Asking me to do that was like asking me to leave James behind, but he didn't know about James. No one did.

James.

I looked again at the mirror and studied my face. *Would he even recognize me now?* I looked at the reflection of the platform below. *If he was down there looking up through the window, would he recognize me?*

I looked at my eyes again.

I'm not sure I recognize myself.

I pressed my hands against my cheeks and pushed the skin backward, trying to remember what I looked like. Maris said I looked like my mother, but I couldn't find her in my reflection.

I pulled the collar of my smock upward and wiped my face. Streaks of dirt and ash remained, revealing my true skin color between the cracks. My mother was white and my father black, so my skin was a blend of the two, but my skin had darkened with age.

I leaned into the mirror. I'd aged since coming to the Outside; in fact, I'm sure my smile lines were the only wrinkles on my face that hadn't deepened.

I noticed all the dried blood that had turned my smock from blue to brown. It was all over the side of my face too. I turned my head, pulling the loose curls back to see just how much blood there was. My ear was completely brown from the dried blood. I wondered if my eardrum had burst from the explosions above ground. But I could hear fine.

After a minute or two of searching, I couldn't locate a wound. I noticed myself scowling in the mirror from uncertainty. I assumed that my body was in shock from the injury and that was why I hadn't felt it, but now I wasn't sure if I had been hurt at all. I looked at my hands, my torso, my legs, and feet, using the mirror to examine my back side, but there was no injury.

I released my hair from my ponytail and felt my scalp for cuts. Still, I produced nothing, but crusts of dried blood and debris from the rubble and fire. I pulled my hair back into a ponytail again, and inspected my neck and ears, no cuts, just dried blood.

I exhaled a frustrated breath. I didn't understand.

If I'm not hurt, then why was I bleeding?

And if I wasn't bleeding, who was?

I jumped a little when the door opened behind me. I spun around in surprise. Zale was there, clean-shaven and dressed in a fresh set of clothes. He looked like he may have even attempted to put a comb through his shaggy dark hair.

Now that his face was free of stubble and scruff, I could see his facial structure better. His jawbone was sharp when he wasn't talking. I had never seen him so clean-cut and found that his freshness softened my approach to him.

"Still waiting?" he asked.

I nodded, trying not to seem impressed by his appearance.

"You clean up nice."

I cringed at how silly that must have sounded.

"Yeah, you and your tooth got us noticed now it's my turn to impress," Zale teased.

I rolled my eyes.

"How come you didn't tell me you'd found the tooth?" he asked.

My hand rested over the lump in the satchel at my hip.

"I didn't know if it was worth anything," I said. "I guess I figured they probably already have some monitor teeth."

"Monitor, yes, I'm sure they do, but Cinder…those are a little harder to come by." Zale came to stand in front of me. "Can I see it?"

"Uh," I stammered, "sure."

I took it from the pocket of my satchel and handed it to him.

He ran his hands over it. Then he slipped it between his knuckles like it was a claw and swiped it through the air.

115

"She must be massive," he said. "Did you get a good look at her?"

"No," I said, taking the tooth back from him. I put it back into the pocket. "I was…" I looked up at him, "…knocked out or something? When I came to, I think I saw her fly overhead."

"Maybe you got hit with something?" he asked. "That would explain the blood."

"Would it?"

He scowled at me.

"I don't know," I said. "I mean, it makes sense, except…"

"What?"

"I can't find anywhere on me that's injured." I turned and looked at myself in the mirror again.

"Really?" He crossed over to stand behind me. He was tall enough to see over me. "Here, let me see." He spun me around to face him.

Then he reached for my hair and carefully released my ponytail. He delicately examined my hairline.

At first, I could feel my body tighten as he touched me. When he noticed the tension in my demeanor, his eyes moved from my hair to meet my eyes.

I gave him a small, embarrassed smile to break the awkwardness of my nerves. He didn't seem nervous at all to be in proximity of me. But I was very conscious that we were sharing the same air, and with that thought, I controlled my breathing so that I wouldn't breathe on him.

When I inhaled again, the smell of his cleanliness consumed me. I felt my blood rush as warmth spread through my body. Tingling ran down my spine. I hated that my body was feeling beyond my mind's control.

For the first time, in a long time, I felt a connection. I suddenly became very aware of his caress on my hair and skin as he moved my chin from side to side examining my face. His eyes locked with mine. They were brown but now they looked greener.

"I don't see anything either," he said, matter-of-factly.

Then something odd happened. He didn't move. He didn't back up. He didn't break eye contact.

I closed my eyes to break the gaze between us. I took a deep breath and without my consent a tear dropped from beneath my eyelid. A lump swelled in my throat, and I suddenly became overwhelmed with emotion.

I hadn't been touched by anyone so sweetly in years. I knew what a pathetic creature I must have appeared to be in that moment, but for some reason I was allowing it. Suddenly, I welcomed the feeling of attraction, of attention; I welcomed anything that wasn't sorrow, regret, or sadness.

"Are *you* okay?" Zale's quiet tone oozed into me.

My chin dropped to my chest. I opened my eyes to see that his body hadn't moved an inch from me. I felt the interest between us, and I wanted to lean into it, but it paralyzed me at the same time. I sniffed and sheepishly raised my face and eyes to let him see the tears that balanced in them.

I decided not to hide them from him. I didn't know if there was anything there for him, but if I wanted to find out, I would have to stop pretending. Even just for a moment.

He reached up and wiped the one loose tear from my cheek.

"You know," he said softly, "sometimes I get the feeling that you've lived a whole life that I don't know about."

I looked up at him.

"You don't have to carry it all by yourself, you know?"

I looked away before I dissolved into a mess of tears.

Then he pulled me toward him, and I let him hold me.

I buried my face in his chest and cried. He stroked my hair as he hugged me. I could feel his cheek on the top of my head.

Then I heard Zale whisper, "I knew you were in there somewhere."

I looked up at him.

I was sure that if he inhaled deeply enough, he could pull me into a kiss, and I wouldn't do anything to stop him.

Is that what he wanted? To kiss a bloody mess of a woman with a past she wouldn't speak of?

A loud pop shattered the moment. Both of our bodies jolted in response.

"What the hell?!" Zale exclaimed, looking up and moving toward the window of the office.

A piece of food, something that looked like a tomato, streaked down the window. Someone from the Rally platform had thrown it at us.

I'd completely forgotten about the window.

Were they watching us? Embarrassment flooded me.

Did they see me cry? Did they see him hold me?

Weak.

"Sht!" I said, wiping my face and rushing to the other side of the room. "Sht!"

"Britt?" Zale started to cross toward me, but the door to the office opened before he could reach me. We stared at each other, knowing that the moment had passed.

Stupid.

"Sorry we've kept you waiting," the Caller said, as he entered. A string of people followed him. First was an even older man with a weathered unpleasant face, followed by a young man that looked like he'd never missed a meal. Last to enter was a young woman, with gorgeous pale skin and dark red hair. She smiled at me, instantly putting me at ease with her presence. Men grossly outnumbered women in the Outside, so it was refreshing to have another female in the room.

All four of them were acquainted with Zale. I wasn't surprised by this at all. They either nodded in a mutual expression of acknowledgement of each other, or they merely grunted each other's names. Each one, that is, except for the woman. She greeted Zale with her full smile and said his name with noticeable inflection.

The Caller sat a set of glasses down on the desk with a bottle of brown liquid. He uncapped the bottle.

"Miss Britt? Is it?" the Caller started. I nodded.

"I understand you've had quite the day," he smiled with a wink. "I thought you might appreciate a drink?"

He poured a small portion of the alcohol into each glass.

"Thank you," I nodded, accepting the glass he offered me. I looked at Zale to see if I should drink. With a quick look, he approved. I guessed it was an honor of some sort to have a drink with the Caller of the Outside.

"I'm Rutherford," the Caller introduced himself. A hint of a southern drawl laced his words. I'd only ever known one other person with a southern drawl like his. Chester, a man from the Ambit, known for the sweet rolls he'd bake for the summer holiday, was from the southern states before the Crisis occurred.

"This here," Rutherford gestured toward the older man, who'd taken up the corner of the room with his presence. "...is Gunnar."

Gunnar had to have been in his late sixties or seventies. It was evident from the deep wrinkles and scars on his overly tanned skin, that he'd lived a life of action and violence. He wore a tight t-shirt against the muscles that defined his arms. Tattoos illustrating pictures of knives and half-naked women climbed up his skin on both sides. At his hips, a belt full of different metal objects clung to him. I noticed the handgun first, then the knives. I didn't recognize the rest, but it was obvious that they were devices of ill-intent.

I tipped the glass of brown liquid back to take a sip. It burned in my mouth. I felt my eyes water as I forced myself to swallow. It was awful.

Zale took his alcohol down in one quick shot and I thought that seemed like a good idea, so I did the same. We put our glasses back down on the desk and Rutherford refilled them.

Sht.

"This is my son, Buckley," Rutherford continued. Buckley couldn't have been more than a head taller than me. Still speckled with pimples or the scars that were once pimples, I guessed him to be in his early twenties. Overconfidence oozed from his movements, as he bounded forward to sit on the front edge of Rutherford's desk.

He had dark eyes and a mess of strawberry blond hair that matched the fuzz attempting to grow on his chin and top lip. He crossed his arms like he was trying to be as intimidating as Gunnar, but he failed miserably. He sneered at Zale.

"And I'm Fairchild," the young woman stepped forward and extended her hand to me. I guessed her to also be in her early twenties, still sweet with an excitement for life. She smiled again, like she was trying to break up the tension of all the testosterone in the room.

I met her hand and shook it. "Nice to meet you, Fairchild."

"May I…" Fairchild looked to Rutherford, to see if he would stop her from jumping ahead, "…see the tooth?"

"Of course," I said. I pulled it from my bag and offered it to her. She used a pressed white handkerchief to accept it from me. Then from her satchel at her hip, she retrieved a small round tool with glass. She placed the tool against her eye to examine the object.

"This is remarkable," she said. She looked up at us, smiling. "It's definitely one of Cinder's." She waited for the rest of us to return her enthusiasm, but no one did. "I'll examine it closer, of course," she said to Rutherford, "…I'm hoping that it has traces of her DNA still on it. How did you get it?"

"I found it," I said.

Fairchild looked at Rutherford. He was looking at me. "Can't help but notice all the blood on you. Did she injure you?"

"No," I said. "I'm okay."

Fairchild looked across the room at Zale. "Are you sure?"

I scowled, looking at her.

"It's just that—" she continued. "The male monitors have poison in their saliva, it's not usually fatal, but causes decay of the flesh."

"Okay?" I said. "That doesn't sound good."

"Exactly," she continued. "We don't know if Cinder's saliva does the same. If there's any chance that she injured you, we would want to catch it early. Do you mind if I do a quick scan to see if you're infected?"

"Infected?"

"It's rare but contact with Cinder has been known to cause people to hallucinate and have some confusion. We call it Delirium."

I scowled.

"I feel fine," I said. "I have all this blood on me from something, I'm not sure what, but it's not mine. I'm not injured, I promise."

"She's not," Zale added. "I've looked her over too."

Rutherford's eyes narrowed on Zale when he said that, and I wondered if Zale's statement may have come across wrong.

"Still –" Fairchild started to say.

"I'm sure she would know if Cinder had hurt her," Rutherford interrupted. "If she has any symptoms, I'm sure she'll let you know. Am I correct, Miss Britt?"

I nodded.

Fairchild looked uncomfortable with his determination.

"What are you hoping to do with the tooth?" I asked him.

"I'm glad you asked," Rutherford said. "As Fairchild said, she'll analyze it and see if she can get any of Cinder's DNA from it. For years, we've been limited in what we can do because of the monitors. The more we know about them, the better our chances are of exterminating them before they exterminate us."

"On occasion, we have a farmer that manages to kill one," Fairchild walked behind Zale's chair. She slid her hand over his arm and shoulder.

He looked at me.

"How many have you killed, Zale?" she asked.

"Three."

"I think that's the record," Fairchild said.

Buckley piped in, "Nah, I think Coya killed four."

"Coya said he killed four," Fairchild corrected him. "We only found one."

Rutherford continued, "The point is that we've learned a lot about them. They're all males, except for Cinder. From what we can tell, she's the only one with the anatomy to both fly and breathe fire."

"She's their mother," Fairchild said.

I sat forward and took the glass off Rutherford's desk. I threw the liquid back and swallowed hard. The second round didn't burn as bad as the first. I sat the glass down and he refilled it again.

"Having her tooth will help us tremendously in understanding her, but getting her blood, that'll be a game changer," Fairchild finished.

"Why do I sense a question coming?" Zale asked.

Rutherford looked him over. Then he turned to me. "Fairchild here is one of the Outside's most promising minds. She and her team think they've narrowed down the location of the Cinder Dragon's nest."

"No sht," Zale said.

121

"Yes sht," Buckley replied. I was beginning to get the idea that he had some sort of grudge against Zale. He offered a snide rebuttal each time Zale spoke.

"Buckley," his father said, "get the map."

Buckley stood from the edge of the desk. From the corner of the room, he retrieved a long tube. He unlatched the end of it and slid a roll of paper from it.

Rutherford moved the alcohol and glasses from the desk, so Buckley had space to unroll it. Everyone except Gunnar gathered around to get a closer look at it.

The map showed the layout of the city of Chicago. In the corner was the word "BioRev". Of all the words I didn't understand in the Outside, this was one I knew. BioRev was the name of the pharmaceutical company that produced the MIL vaccine.

"BioRev?" I said.

"Yes," Rutherford replied. "Of all they took from us, at least they gave us good maps."

"Where'd you get this?" Zale asked.

"Wouldn't you like to know," Buckley grunted.

"This is us here," Fairchild pointed to a red circle on the map, over a building labeled "MCC".

"This is where we think the nest is," she said. She pointed to a green circle on the other side of the city.

"How do you know?" Zale asked.

"Wouldn't you like to know?" Buckley said for the second time.

Rutherford groaned at his son's attempts to instigate an argument with Zale.

Zale stood up straight. He outsized Buckley by an embarrassing amount. "Do we have a problem, Buck?"

"You know we do, Zale," Buckley responded, also standing up as straight as he could.

"Buckley," Rutherford said, "I don't have time for your sht right now, so cool it, or get out."

Buckley looked at his dad, defeated by the undermining.

"Yeah, cool it, Buck," Zale added.

"Why are you showing this to us?" I asked, starting to feel a little woozy from the brown burning liquid.

Rutherford gestured to the map. "This is where the wind-turbines are. The ones that are faltering, causing the power surges." He made two black Xs near the green circle, that indicated the nest. "We're sending out a team of engineers to see if they can fix the turbines. Fairchild and her team are going along, to investigate."

"Safety in numbers," Fairchild added.

"Or dinner bell for monitors?" Zale scoffed.

Rutherford continued, "We have a team of six, including Fairchild, Buckley and Gunnar. We could use a few more guns to escort them if you're interested?"

"And another female would be nice too," Fairchild said to me directly. "I would rather have you escort me to the latrine than one of *them*." She nodded her head toward Buckley and Gunnar.

"What exactly are you investigating?" Zale asked.

"If we're right, if that is where the nest is, then we're going to try to collect samples," Fairchild said.

"Of what?" I asked.

"Ideally? Her blood."

"Well, sht." Zale was holding his glass of brown liquid. He tossed it back with one swig. Rutherford refilled it. I followed suit, noting how the burning was completely gone with the third shot.

"What's in it for us?" I asked, feeling courageous because of the alcohol.

Rutherford stood up straight and smiled.

"That depends." He rolled the map back up and replaced it in the tube.

"On?" I asked.

"What the outcome is."

"The outcome is likely to be a lot less than good, if we don't go," Zale said. "Clearly you're desperate if you've asked me to help you."

Rutherford's eyes narrowed on him. "We're hoping that was water under the bridge by now."

I looked at Zale, unsure of what they were referencing. I didn't know the history, nor did I care. I saw my opportunity.

"I'm not going without something upfront," I said.

Rutherford looked at me. He smiled. "Well, you can't blame me for trying, right?"

He opened the drawer to his desk and pulled out two badges. He slid them across the table. They were eye-shaped, just like what he and the others wore, except the iris of the eye was blue.

"You can't be serious?!" Buckley objected. "You're giving him one of those?"

"Well, sht," Zale said. He picked his up and examined it.

"What does the blue eye mean?" I asked, looking at mine.

"It means no one will touch you," Rutherford said. "You or anyone else you run with."

I thought of Seph.

I tossed the badge back on the table. "It's not enough," I dared. "I need living arrangements for my kid. Better ones."

I knew the likelihood was that I wouldn't make it back from the mission. My badge wouldn't do anything to protect Seph if I was gone.

"Okay," Rutherford said, "Where are you staying now?"

"Quarter S," I answered. Quarter S was close to the worst section of the Outside.

"Buckley, get them moved to Quarter B," Rutherford ordered. "Anything else?"

Zale looked at me then back at the old man.

"Lupio Injections," he replied.

Rutherford scowled at him. "Those are hard to come by."

Zale nodded. "No sht."

"You know someone that's got the Crud?" Rutherford asked.

Zale nodded, "My old man."

I turned to him. I didn't know Maris was sick. In the Outside they called it the Crud, but in the Ambit, we called it cancer.

Rutherford nodded, surprised. "Okay. We'll see what we can do."

"He's going to need the first injection before I go anywhere," Zale demanded. Rutherford stared at him.

"Done," Fairchild said. "What else?"

Zale smiled at her. "That's good enough for me. When do we leave?"

"Three days," Gunnar finally spoke. "Get your affairs in order and meet us on the dock at 9pm on Tuesday. You familiar with launchers and grenades?" he asked me.

I gulped.

"I'll make sure she knows what she needs to," Zale stated.

I looked at my shot glass and felt grateful that Rutherford had stopped refilling it.

"That's it then?" Rutherford looked at me.

"No, I need one more thing," I remembered, feeling the brown liquid's full effects.

"Name it," Fairchild said.

"Grass."

They looked at me with confusion.

"I'm gonna need some grass....for my goat."

9
A MISSION FOR BLOOD

It'd been three days since I accidentally got drunk in the Caller's office and demanded grass for my goat.

To my surprise, the Caller made good on his promises. Three large slips of grass were left on the stoop of our new unit in Quarter B. When Nanny goat ate, I saw Seph smile the first real smile I'd seen in months.

The eye badge had worked too, warding off the thugs and creeps. Seph was safe for the moment and while we were gone, Maris agreed to keep him that way.

They'd made good on their promises, now it was my turn to make good on mine.

As the gondola approached the Floor, Seph squeezed my hand. Light and noise grew.

"Blood, blood, blood…" I could hear them chanting. A crowd of Outsiders waited for us on the Floor.

Word of the mission had gotten out and hope had sprung up in the gutters of the underground city. A mission for blood, might mean liberation from the monitor monsters and that little shred of hope was the only thing anyone could talk about.

I stared at Zale, sitting across from me in the gondola. He stared at me. We both knew this was a terrible idea.

I'd pretended enough to get on the mission, but now all my fears and weaknesses were about to be exposed. I'd run from the monitors the first time I saw them a few days ago. He and I were the only ones that knew that. There was no way I was ready for this.

I wasn't from the Majestic Isles. All the fighting I'd ever learned in my life, came from the one punch I'd thrown at a snotty girl in my fourth year when she told me my skin was the color of dirt. Beyond that, I'd only ever used my words to fight. I wasn't tough. I was only brave and stupid enough to let them believe I was.

I swallowed hard.

"Look at all of them," Seph whispered.

Faces lined the edge of the platform. Some of them were waiting there to see the so-called heroes that were going above ground to finally fight back. Others were there to place bets about whether we'd succeed.

"Pretend," Maris leaned in to say.

I turned to him, searching his face for help, "Then what?"

"One step at a time. Right now, they need to know you're ready for this."

The gondola came to rest at the platform and the crowd parted to make room for us to exit. Zale stepped out first and Maris handed him two large bags, filled to the brim with equipment and supplies.

I let go of Seph's hand and reached for Zale's.

As he pulled me from the gondola, an even louder cheer erupted. The gondola carrying Gunnar, Buckley, Fairchild, and the others, emerged from the tunnel behind us.

"Blood, blood, blood…" the chant grew louder.

Did they want the Cinder Dragon's blood or ours?

I was relieved that the crowd's attention shifted to the rest of the team.

Zale hoisted my rucksack onto my back, and we pushed our way through the crowded platform, seizing the opportunity while the crowd was distracted with the newcomers. Still, hands brushed my shoulders as we made our way through. Words of encouragement were hurled upon us, pressuring us to deliver.

Zale had hardly said a word all day. I wondered if he was as frightened as I was.

We climbed the stairs to the cement pathway that guided us to the garage where our vehicles were waiting. Seph and Maris followed behind closely.

Once we reached the higher level, the crowds turned back to welcome the rest of the crew on deck. We slipped through the door to the garage and let it separate us from the commotion.

This would be our last opportunity to say good-bye to our loved ones with any sort of privacy.

I turned to Seph. His eyes were as terrified as mine.

I tried to think of what it would be like to return to him safely, imagining all the credit a mission like this would give us for the future.

"We could leave this place," Seph said. "You don't have to go. We could get Nanny and –"

"Seph," I stopped him with my word.

He obeyed.

"Even if it hurts," I said "…this is worth doing." I nodded toward the crowd. "You saw their faces just now. They're trapped down here. If I can do anything to help them live above ground again, then I'm going to do it."

His eyes flooded. I pulled him close and put my forehead to his.

"I'm scared you won't come back," he whispered.

"Me too."

I pulled him into a hug.

Seph held on for a long moment before he let me go. I turned to Maris and whispered, "If I don't come back, promise me that you'll take him and Nanny back to the Ambit."

Zale's eyes widened, hearing me finally admit where I was from.

"We can't—" Seph started.

"Tell my father what happened to me, and he will find a way to get him back in, I'm sure of it. He may be able to get you in too, it's been done before." I finished, giving him a knowing look.

Maris nodded, understanding my meaning.

"Wait, *you* know where the Ambit is?" Zale asked.

Maris nodded, "Your old man still has some tricks up his sleeve."

He pulled Zale into a hug.

"I'll tell you all about it when you come back to me," Maris suggested. Then he patted his son on the back twice.

The door pushed open, and the crowd's chants filled the air again.

"Blood, blood, blood…" Buckley chanted gleefully with the crowd. He was enjoying every moment of his campaign for attention and glory.

Fairchild settled in front of me after handing her rucksack to Zale and Gunnar to load in the vehicle. She had a small metal box attached to her hand. She patted it, showing me. "These are the vials."

Vials?

"There are six of them, but we only need one to make it back," she said solemnly. She propped the box open and revealed six empty glass vials. She gestured toward the crowd, "This is what they're cheering for."

I nodded. "Okay."

She removed one and handed it to me with a needle. Then she demonstrated. "This is the strongest needle we have. You put it in, pull the plunger up and then whatever you collect, you seal in the vial. Got it?"

I nodded.

"Everyone on our team will have one and then there's one extra. They're glass so we have to be careful."

I nodded again.

Collect dragon blood with needle, seal it in vial. Don't break the vial while running from pissed off dragon. Sounds easy enough.

I tucked the vial and needle into the satchel on my hip.

"Keep the vial on you at all times, you never know when you may get the opportunity. Got it?" Fairchild asked.

I nodded for a third time.

My face must have shown how uneasy I was with the whole idea.

"It's okay that you're scared," she said.

I must not have been doing a very good job of pretending.

She smiled at me, and it put me at ease.

"I am too," she said. "But ya know what makes me feel better?"

"What?"

She leaned in, "Knowing I'm not the only woman on the mission." She winked. "That and knowing that this is so much bigger than us. If we don't come back, at least we were willing to do something, right?"

Do something.

I felt an odd sense of purpose in those words. Doing something was better than doing nothing. And nothing is what I'd always done.

Do not conform, transform.

"Right," I said.

"You should ride with me," Fairchild suggested.

"I think Gunnar assigned me to Buckley's vehicle, Zale is escorting you in yours."

"Oh," she said, not seeming disappointed by that at all.

"Hey! Have you met Jordan?" Fairchild asked. She pulled a young man from the group next to us. He was tall and thin, but muscular. He had black glasses, a blond buzz cut and pale blue eyes. It was obvious that he hadn't spent much time above ground, judging by the paleness of his skin.

"Hi," he said nervously.

"Jordan's an engineer. He and his pops," she nodded toward an older man standing with Gunnar, "they're going to work on the turbines to see if they can fix these stupid power surges we've been having."

Jordan nodded in agreement. He seemed uncomfortable with Fairchild.

"What do you think is wrong with the turbines?" I asked.

Jordan shrugged, "Could be a lot of things. We won't know until we get there."

I got the feeling that Jordan didn't talk to women very often.

"You're Britt?" Jordan's father approached.

"I am," I said, extending my hand to him.

"Conrad," he introduced himself, taking my hand. "Thanks for agreeing to come along. Makes me feel better knowing we have more escorts."

I nodded.

No pressure.

"And this," Fairchild interrupted, "...is Coya."

The third team member turned around. His head was shaved bald and replaced with tattoos. When he smiled at me, I noticed that most of his teeth were gold or silver or missing.

Coya looked me up and down.

I didn't bother extending my hand to him, I could tell he wasn't the friendly type.

Rutherford appeared through the door. He had a woman with him.

"Alright, listen up," Rutherford clapped his hands together as he called to us. We all broke away from our huddles and turned to give him our attention. "Gunnar is leading the mission. That's a direct order from the top."

The top? The Underground.

"He's calling the shots. Coya is his second. When you get to the other side of the city, you'll split. Coya will go with Conrad and Jordan to the wind farm to see what's going on with the turbines. We don't expect much resistance there." Rutherford nodded toward the rest of us, "Gunnar, Buckley, Britt and Zale, you'll escort Fairchild to the nest. Both teams will be in touch with the communicators, you should be set to Channel 9. Check them now."

I looked at Zale. He handed me a communication device. Then he showed me how to turn it on and set the channel to number nine. He helped me attach the device to my hip with all the other gadgets he'd introduced me to over the last three days.

Rutherford continued, "You have two days, then you should rendezvous at whatever location Gunnar determines once he sees the lay of the land. Any questions?"

No one said anything.

"Gunnar," Rutherford said, "they're all yours."

Gunnar stepped forward, "Coya, Jordan and Conrad, you're in vehicle one." He pointed to a green vehicle they called a jeep.

"Britt and Buckley, you'll take vehicle two," he pointed to another vehicle identical to the first.

"Zale, Fairchild and me....we'll take up the rear, in the truck," he pointed to a large black truck. It had a cab that could fit two or three people. On the bed of the truck, a large gun was mounted. From the side of the gun, a long belt of ammunition hung. "I'll be on the gun."

No surprise there.

"Keep your comms open. We estimate it'll take us about five hours, depending on the debris and how much we have to clear to get through the city. Any questions?" Gunnar looked around. I don't think anyone would have dared to ask him a question, he didn't seem like he had any patience for that. He looked down at his watch and then added, "Good, then, we head out in fifteen."

I exhaled.

Rutherford and the woman he'd brought with him approached us. "We had a deal," Rutherford said to Zale, gesturing to the case in the woman's hand.

"Indeed, we did," Zale said. He called to Maris, "Hey, Pops, come here for a second, would ya?"

Maris and Seph came over. Maris adjusted his waistband nervously. "Yeah?" He noticed Rutherford standing there.

"Rutherford," he nodded respectfully. "What can I do for ya?"

"Not what you can do for me, but what we can do for you?" Rutherford gestured to the woman with the case. She put it on the hood of the closest vehicle as we watched. From inside, she pulled a needle. An injection.

"I'll be damned," Maris said, swiping his hand over the lower half of his face in disbelief. He looked at Zale, "That what I think it is?"

"Your boy said you got the Crud?" Rutherford asked.

Maris was near tears. He looked at Zale, then at me. Then he nodded.

"Are you familiar with Lupio?" the woman asked.

Maris was choked up but managed to answer. "I am."

"Then you're aware of the risks?"

Maris nodded again. "Yes, ma'am, I am."

"You're going to feel sick, really sick for the next few days, but that's just your body getting rid of the Crud," she stated. "You understand?"

"I do," Maris replied. "What I don't understand is how you got your hands on it. My wife's been out looking for this stuff for months."

"It *is* hard to find, impossible even." Rutherford said, "...but Zale drives a hard bargain. Said he wouldn't go without it. And what do you know, a box of injections just happened to show up." Rutherford scoffed.

I looked closer at the case. The BioRev logo was on the side of it.

"I'll need you to pull your shirt off your shoulder," the woman said, readying the injection.

Maris did as he was asked. From what I could count, he had a dozen MIL vaccine scars on his skin. Given his age, I was surprised there weren't more.

He winced when the woman injected him with the serum.

"Take it easy for the next 24 hours," she ordered. "Depending on how far along the Crud is, you'll need at least six more of these."

"Those other five injections are gonna just 'show up' too, right?" Zale asked Rutherford.

Rutherford gestured to the woman. She closed the case and handed it to Maris.

"There's six more in there. Take one a week, not sooner," she said. "And I'd be careful with that, if I were you."

Maris nodded. "Understood."

Zale smiled.

Rutherford and the woman parted from us.

Maris looked at Zale. "You got these for me?" He motioned to the case in his hand. He was in disbelief.

Zale nodded slightly. "Got tired of hearing you cough."

Without another word, Maris pulled Zale into a long hug. They finished their embrace with two firm pats on each other's backs.

I turned to Seph, "You two take care of each other, okay?"

Seph agreed.

I took the blue-eyed patch from my jacket and gave it to him.

"Load up!" Gunnar ordered the group.

I turned to Seph one more time and hugged him.

"I'll be back in a few days," I said.

"Okay."

I turned to Maris, "Take it easy."

"Don't worry, Princess, I'll lie low," he winked at me.

Then the two of them moved to the side of the garage and waited by the wall. When I turned to go to my vehicle, Zale was there.

"You ready?" he said.

I looked beyond him to see if anyone else was within earshot. When I saw that they weren't, I replied, "No."

Zale smiled and I found it refreshing.

"Listen," he leaned in. "If anything goes down, just –" His instruction trailed off. He didn't seem to know what to say.

"I know you're not trying to tell me to run," I smirked, attempting to lighten the space between us.

His eyes smoldered at me. "These people," he leaned in further, "…they won't die for you."

I rested back on my heels. I'm sure he was right, but I hadn't considered it until now.

He continued, "…so don't get yourself killed for them either."

I nodded, understanding his point.

"What about you?" I asked.

He was confused.

"Should I get myself killed for you?"

He smirked.

"Let's just make sure we get back here together, okay?"

Together. I liked the way that sounded.

"Let's go!" Gunnar yelled at us.

Reluctantly, I took my seat in the passenger side of the jeep that Buckley and I were assigned. I watched Seph and Maris stand to the side while they cleared and opened the overhead door.

Then one at a time, starting with Coya's vehicle, each car was lifted from the dark underworld to the dark city above.

I listened to the rumble of the metal lift as it hoisted us upward.

When it stopped, Buckley shifted the jeep into motion.

"Here we go," he murmured. "Let's hope we don't die."

10
NIGHT ONE

The first six hours of the Blood Mission went exactly according to plan. We left the Outside around midnight in three vehicles: Coya's crew led us, Buckley and I followed, while Zale, Gunnar, and Fairchild took up the rear of the convoy.

Monitors have poor eyesight, so they require as much light as possible when they are hunting prey. They only eat every few days and mid-afternoons are usually when the hungry ones hunt. This is why we farm for resources at night. It's not often that farmers run into monitors at night, but occasionally, as I'd discovered, desperate hunters will come scavenging. I was just unlucky enough to stumble across one on my very first farming excursion.

The primary goal of the first day of the Blood Mission was to arrive safely on the other side of the city. There Gunnar would identify our rendezvous point and Coya's team would head for the wind farm. The rest of us planned to have a safety perimeter established by sunrise.

We'd traveled for six hours without any stops to the far side of the city formerly known as Chicago. Travel was slow because of the overgrown vegetation and debris on the roadways. Most of the trip was made off-road for this reason.

My brain had gone nearly numb from the shallow conversations Buckley insisted on having with me. He passed the time by talking in circles about his past experiences hunting and his previous relationship with Fairchild. I was shocked to learn that they'd once been romantically involved, and it was clear that he still had feelings for her.

"What happened?" I asked. "Why'd she break it off?"

He groaned, "Why do you assume *she* broke it off?" He seemed offended, then he answered, "She's too committed to her work, didn't have time for a relationship and she's got some stuff she needs to work through."

She's definitely the one that broke it off. Not only was she way out of his league, but those excuses sounded exactly like what someone would say when they weren't into the relationship anymore.

Beyond that story, which I found amusing, pretty much anything Buckley talked about bored me out of my mind. To keep the peace, I chose to tolerate him. I never shared any details about my life, but Buckley didn't seem to mind. In fact, I'm not sure he even noticed. I got the feeling that he was more interested in talking to himself than me anyway.

I was so desperate for something to do; I searched my satchel to stimulate my mind. Upon opening it, I came across an unexpected gift. I instantly knew who had put it there and why, and I was grateful. I opened the brown leather book and flipped through the pages. The wafting smell of Isla and Seph filled my nostrils. Isla's Bible.

I found Isla's picture of us tucked in the front cover and I welcomed the image of her. I wondered if she missed it, or knew who had taken it from her bed, and if she resented its absence. It occurred to me that she may have found consolation in it, the way Seph and I did. And if she did, what did she do to find the peace it had once provided her? This thought saddened me.

I dwelled on that thought for a while. I hadn't allowed myself the pain of thinking of what her life was like in the Ambit without me. In the hours after my banishment, I was convinced that she would be happier without me there with her. But upon finding her Bible in Seph's possession, the picture of us and the passage she had highlighted in the book of Romans, I felt like I couldn't fairly assume her thoughts at all.

136

I opened the book and started reading the first page, in a book called Genesis. It read: "In the beginning, God created the Heavens and the Earth." God was a character in the book, I knew that much because Isla had spoken of him on several occasions.

As I read, I did not fully understand what it meant, but welcomed the escape it provided me. I found myself both consumed and confused by it. There were many words that I had never heard before and didn't understand. I wondered how Isla had felt so connected to it.

I couldn't tell for sure if it was supposed to be factual or fictional. I had a hard time believing that there was a snake that spoke to the woman named Eve and convinced her to eat an apple from the Tree of Good and Evil, and that God then banished her and Adam from the Garden of Eden, just as I had been banished from the Ambit. That didn't seem fair to me, and it put a bad taste in my mouth. It didn't seem believable.

If someone had told me that only thirty years ago, everyone drove cars and flew on planes, I'm not sure I would have believed that either. Yet, I knew that was true, so maybe this was too.

The jolt of the stopping vehicle was the only thing that broke my concentration on the book. My body shifted into defense mode, and I instantly recalled where I was. Buckley unbuckled quickly and hopped out of the car.

"What's going on?" I asked quietly, unsure if we had arrived or if we were in danger.

Coya's jeep was in front of us. I looked in the mirror and saw that Zale's vehicle was still with us. On the back of the black truck, Gunnar was poised with the massive gun. He used the scope to surveil our surroundings. After a moment, he turned to Buckley and made a gesture. Buckley turned and passed the gesture to Coya.

"All clear," Coya yelled.

We unloaded into a street that had been devastated by something. It looked different from the part of Chicago that we were from. Other than the destruction that the monitors had caused, many of the buildings on our side of the city were intact. The area we stood in looked like a bomb had gone off. Most of the buildings were destroyed. Chunks of walls were missing and there was rubble everywhere.

"Are we here?" I asked Buckley.

He shrugged.

Zale came up beside me, "How'd that go?" He motioned to Buckley. "Did he talk your ear off?"

I nodded, rolling my eyes.

"How about you?" I looked beyond him at Fairchild. She had a tool in her hand. She was scanning the rubble.

He turned to look at her, then back at me. "She's a good kid," he said. "Unbelievably smart."

"Did *you* know she and Buckley dated?"

Zale's eyes went wide with surprise. He turned to look at her again. "Okay, maybe not so smart."

I laughed.

"Alright, listen up," Gunnar addressed us. "We're in the center zone. Perfectly equidistant between the wind farm and the nest. Coya, you and your team will head that way." Gunnar pointed to the southwest. "We'll be heading this way." He pointed in the opposite direction.

"We will meet up in 42 hours right back here. Midnight. That'll give us enough time to make it back to the other side before sunlight."

We all looked at each other. Gunnar said what the rest of us were thinking, "If you're the first to arrive, you wait for the other team to rendezvous for two hours. If no one shows by 0200, assume they're dead and head back. Don't wait around. There's no cover here. Got it?"

We nodded.

Coya and Gunnar stepped aside to make plans while Buckley disappeared to pee somewhere.

"Hey, guys, there's a BioRev pharmacy here," Fairchild came up and whispered to us. She pointed to a destroyed building in the distance.

"Pharmacy?" I asked.

Fairchild scowled at me. "I know, right? They're super rare. Once people started using the MIL, pharmacies faded out."

"I find it odd that BioRev manufactured the MIL, but also had pharmacies," Zale said.

"People think the MIL had stuff in it that made people sick, instead of healing them, like it was supposed to. And when people got sick, they'd have to buy more meds to treat their symptoms," Fairchild said.

"And where did they go for those meds?" Zale said.

"The BioRev pharmacy, of course," Fairchild laughed, pointing toward the building with the BioRev logo above the door.

The two of them laughed, like it was some sort of an inside joke that I was on the outside of.

"Wait," I said, trying to catch up, "So BioRev developed a vaccine that was supposed to prevent all illnesses, but they also had pharmacies to sell meds for the illnesses their vaccine didn't prevent?"

Fairchild shook her head, "Pretty eff'd up, isn't it?"

Then she asked Zale, "I want to go check it out. You wanna come with me?"

"We're supposed to stick with the team," I said.

Fairchild looked at Zale, then at me. "There might be medicine in there," she said. "Stuff that people in the Outside need."

"Still—" I said.

"It'll only take a minute. C'mon, Zale, there might be Lupio injections," Fairchild tempted him. I didn't like the way she was acting with him.

Zale looked at me. "We could go quickly, I'm sure they won't even notice we're gone."

I scowled at him, shaking my head.

The two of them turned to go toward the building.

I hesitated for a moment and then I followed.

The interior of the pharmacy was wrecked. Years of vegetation and overgrowth climbed the walls, growing in between cracks. Zale had his gun drawn, as we moved through the aisles, scanning our surroundings.

A bird fluttered up from the mess to get out of our path. Fairchild and I both jumped in surprise.

"This place is trashed," Zale whispered.

"I bet the good stuff's in there," Fairchild nodded toward a set of closed metal doors behind a counter with a shattered glass partition. We moved around the counter toward the back. Next to the door was a keypad.

"Hold up." Zale pulled a flat metal object from his belt loop. He peeled something off one side of it and then stuck it to the keypad. Then he fired his weapon at it.

A flock of birds startled us as they lifted from various parts of the room and escaped through the large hole in the roof.

We heard a lock adjust.

"Step back," Zale said.

We did as he commanded. He kicked the door and it swung open.

The small room was dark. Zale gestured for us to stay still, as he disappeared inside. My hand was on my hip, near my gun, just in case.

Soon, Zale reappeared in the door smiling. "Jackpot," he said.

Fairchild, who was biting her nails in anticipation, scrambled past him. She cracked a blue light stick and placed it on the floor in the center of the room. It cast enough of a blue glow over the interior that we could see the shelves.

When I stepped into the room, I was amazed at how well-preserved it was. The shelves, although layered with dust, were just as I imagined they were meant to be, lined with hundreds of organized boxes and bottles.

"We better move quick," Fairchild said. She found some large black bags hanging behind the door. She handed us each one.

"How do we know what to take?" I asked.

"Let's just get as much as we can," Zale said. "We'll sort it out later. If you see Lupio, make sure you grab it."

Zale moved toward one of the middle sections labeled with an L. I stepped forward toward the section to the left of him, which was labeled with an A. Fairchild intercepted me.

"Start over there," she said, pointing to the opposite side. "See those boxes, those are Z-packs."

She stared at me like I was supposed to know what those were for. "What are Zpacks?"

She scowled like I should know.

"Antibiotics. Used for infections like pneumonia."

Pneumonia. I knew this word.

My father had said it to me many times over the years.

Chasen.

"Oh," I said. "Right."

I took a Zpack off the shelf and looked at it. Chasen needed this medicine. My father suspected that he'd had pneumonia several times over the years. This one box had enough medication in it for five days.

That's all it would have taken?
This tiny box was all that James had to bring back for him?

Then I remembered what Chasen's body looked like when he died and knew that it wasn't pneumonia that killed him. They said it was the MIL disease.

"Do you think there are MIL vaccines in here?" I asked.

Zale stopped and looked at me inquisitively.

"Maybe," he said. "I'm sure this pharmacy administered them."

"Wouldn't matter," Fairchild said. Her back was to us as she studied the names of the drugs on the shelves. I noticed that she wasn't swiping them off the shelves into her bag, like Zale was. She seemed to be looking for something. She continued, "The MIL vaccine needed to be kept cool. Even if there were some here, they'd be dead."

"Dead?" I asked.

She turned to me, scowling again. "Dead. The vaccinations had to be kept at a certain temperature. If they got too warm, then it would kill the live virus in it and the vaccine would be useless."

Zale didn't miss a beat, "Some would say they *were* useless, considering they killed billions."

"I guess it depends on your definition of useless," Fairchild retorted.

Zale and I looked at each other.

Was she implying that the vaccines had served a purpose by killing people? That was a dark thought.

"Fairchild!" we heard Gunnar yell.

"Sht," she said.

"We're in here," Zale called back.

I grabbed the Zpacks off the shelf and anything else I could fit into my black bag. When I was done, I zipped it and threw it over my shoulder. When I turned around, I noticed that Fairchild still hadn't packed anything in her bag. She was frantically looking for something on the shelves. Then she seemed to find what she was looking for. She snatched it from the shelf and read the label.

We could hear Gunnar approaching. He cussed as he made his way toward us. He was furious.

Before he got to the door, Fairchild took all the bottles matching the ones she'd been looking for from the shelf and stored them in her satchel at her hip. Then she started shoving handfuls of the other bottles and boxes into the black bag.

141

"What the fck are you thinking?!" Gunnar burst through the door, with Buckley on his tail.

"We were just –" Fairchild started to say, but Gunnar snatched her by the throat and pushed her up against the wall.

"Hey!" Buckley and Zale yelled simultaneously. Both men lunged at him, but Gunnar's reflexes were quick. He held them at gunpoint before they could get any closer.

"Easy!" Zale said, raising his hands in the air.

"Let her go!" Buckley stepped forward again.

Fairchild's face was beet red, as he pinched off her air.

"Let her go," I screamed at him. "That's not necessary."

Gunnar released her. Fairchild's hands found her throat, as she gasped for air.

"What the hell, man?!" Zale screamed at him.

"We were just getting medicine to take back," I yelled.

Gunnar looked down at the packed duffle bags on the floor. "I'm in charge here!" he yelled. "You wanna fck with me?!" he yelled at Zale.

Zale puffed his chest out. "Yeah, I think I do!"

"No! Stop!" Fairchild moved forward between them. "This is my fault. It was my idea to come here, not theirs. I'm sorry, Gunnar."

Gunnar and Zale stared at each other, waiting for the other to make a move.

"You don't need to apologize," Buckley said. "He had no right to lay hands on you."

Gunnar turned to Buckley, "Like hell I don't! She's the reason we're all here! She gets herself killed and this is all for nothing."

"You're right," Fairchild conceded like she was afraid of him. "I shouldn't have gone off without telling you. Can we go now?"

I didn't want to go anywhere with Gunnar. I hadn't been naïve enough to imagine he was a good guy, but I certainly didn't expect him to turn on us so quickly. We hadn't even encountered any monitors and I was already afraid for our lives.

"Everything alright in there?" Coya yelled to us.

Gunnar still had his gun pointed at Zale and Buckley. Fairchild was in the middle between them. I was behind Zale.

"Is everything alright in here?" Zale asked Gunnar.

Gunnar put his gun down, "She doesn't leave my sight again, you understand?"

Zale nodded.

I looked at Fairchild, wondering how she felt about two men deciding what she was allowed to do. I know I didn't like it. I decided then that I was going to look out for her, for more reasons than just the blood.

After Coya and the engineers parted ways with us, our team moved further into the city, until we found a small park. Within an hour, we'd secured the perimeter of the park, setting traps and snares. We harnessed two hammocks about thirty feet from the ground, camouflaged in the brush of the largest tree at the center of the park.

As daylight began cracking the dark sky open, we ate from vacuum packed dinner pouches and then settled in to sleep. Gunnar and Buckley agreed to take four-hour shifts, while the rest of us slept the day away.

As I settled into my hammock, I shivered uncontrollably. Even though it was the end of summer, it's always coldest before the sun dawns. I was also nervous, which contributed to my shaking. I'd been foolish enough to think the monitors were our only enemy out here, but Gunnar had proven otherwise. Fairchild seemed afraid of him, which meant I needed to be too.

I was curious to hear what Zale would have to say about it, but we hadn't had a moment alone to talk since we'd left the Outside.

I sat up in the hammock looking for him. To my surprise, he was in Fairchild's hammock on the other side of the tree.

Embarrassment turned to humiliation, then to denial, as my mind told me what he was doing there.

He's protecting her, I thought.

Maybe he did see how afraid she was of Gunnar. Maybe he didn't want to leave her alone while Gunnar was around.

I heard her laugh.

That was not the laugh of a scared woman. I thought. I knew exactly what kind of laugh that was.

I laid back in the hammock, turning my back to them. I couldn't make out what he was saying to her, but I could hear the tone. She giggled.

Gross. He'd called her a good kid. Kid. What was he—?

The hammock shifted. I turned.

"Hey," Zale said.

"Hey."

"Fairchild's cold, can I steal this blanket?" He reached for the extra blanket on my feet.

No! I thought.

"Sure," I said, keeping my tone under control.

He took the blanket. I shivered for more reasons than the cold.

I pulled my blanket up over my head, trying to block out their voices. Fairchild's voice sounded vapid and giggly, which did not seem like her personality at all.

Quiet. We were supposed to be quiet. If the monitors heard us and came after us because of her giggling --

The voices stopped.

Good.

Now it was too quiet.

Sht.

I imagined them kissing or worse.

I pinched my eyes shut, trying to unsee the images that my imagination cruelly projected in my mind.

This is not the time or place for that. That would be wildly inappropriate. And dangerous. It would be dangerous and inappropriate for them to be doing that out here. Make it stop. I'm gonna say something. I--

My hammock swayed again bouncing me upright. Frustrated, I sat up and turned. "I don't have any more blankets!" I snipped at Zale.

He seemed surprised. "I know." He laughed at me.

I watched as he moved closer to me in the hammock. He acted like he was going to try to lay with me.

"What are you doing?"

He smirked. "There are only two hammocks, Britt, did you expect me to sleep on the ground?"

"I thought you were going to sleep with---" I reconsidered my phrasing. "I thought you were going to sleep *in* with Fairchild."

He scowled.

"Would you rather me do that?"

"No," I said. "I just thought –"

"You're my partner, Britt, not her."

Partner.

I stared at him.

"We got ourselves into this mess together," he said. "I thought we should probably stay in it together too."

Together. There was that word again. I wasn't sure he meant it the way I wanted him to, but I appreciated the sentiment. I appreciated that he'd chosen my hammock over hers.

I lifted the edge of my blanket for him, as a gesture of truce. He slid under it and immediately the temperature between us rose. There was something very comfortable about it, like we both knew this was how it was supposed to be. The two of us together. Like it was natural. We'd spent months together training for farming missions. In that time, we'd learned to be close like this without awkwardness.

I rolled over, putting my backside up against him. I hadn't taken gravity into account, as the angle of the hammock pressed us together. Something shifted between us.

As he was trying to get comfortable, he reached up and moved my hair from the side of my neck, so it wasn't in his face. His subtle movement against my skin caught me by surprise and I gasped. I didn't mean to but as soon as I did, it seemed to unleash something primal between us.

He pulled in closer to me, letting gravity bring our bodies closer still. Then I felt his breath on my neck. He inhaled next to my skin, and I reacted by instinct, arching my neck away from him. I inhaled sharply. Then his hand was at my hip, squeezing me and I couldn't think straight. The movement shifted the hammock, rocking it slightly.

My breathing quickened, as his did behind me. Something subtle but animalistic kicked in between us. Almost instinctually, I put my hand over his on my hip and pressed my fingers between his. He squeezed our hands shut together. Then he paused and pulled away from me.

I held completely still, unsure of what I was feeling: relief or disappointment.

Sht.

I pinched my eyes closed, wishing that hadn't happened at all, if it wasn't going to go further.

Finally, I rolled over. Zale was on his back with his hands tucked behind his head. He was staring upward, trying to calm his breathing.

"I'm sorry," I said.

His jaw clenched. He exhaled in frustration, then looked at me with concern. "Why are you sorry?"

"I shouldn't have—" I stopped myself.

Shouldn't have what? Enjoyed the way that felt? To be held.

Had I always been taught to feel ashamed for feeling? For being fully female?

"Actually," I recanted. "I'm not sorry."

He looked at me.

"Good," he said. "Because I'm the one that crossed the line. You have nothing to apologize for."

"Crossed the line?" I scoffed. "That felt like you were right *on* the line."

His eyes shifted to me again. They were flirtatious. "Don't say that," he lowered his voice in a way that I could only describe as growling, "I'm trying to be a gentleman here."

I smiled. I could appreciate that, even if I didn't necessarily want him to be a gentleman. And I didn't necessarily want to be a lady. Yet I knew he was right. This wasn't the time or place.

"Okay," I readjusted moving closer to him. "Well, how about this…" I said, laying back down next to him. "I'll lie here like this," I pulled his arm around me. "You know, just so I can stay warm." We both knew I was no longer cold.

"Uh huh," he agreed.

"And you stay like that," I gestured to him staying on his back. "So that your hands don't….cross the line."

He laughed.

"Okay, partner?" I said looking up at him from where I was laying against his shoulder.

"Okay," he said, recognizing that I was teasing him.

Carefully and respectfully, I kept my hands close to my own body. I truly didn't want to tempt him any further. I thought about the Caller's office and how I'd felt about him since that day. Finishing what we'd just started felt inevitable, the idea of which terrified and thrilled me.

Still, we had a long two days in front of us. Survival had to be our primary objective. I tried to refocus on the mission, on what had happened between Gunnar and Fairchild, on the fact that we were sleeping in a tree with monitors lurking nearby. But my imagination kept running back to the Outside and what would happen when Zale and I returned…together.

11
NIGHT TWO

A hand covered my mouth, waking me. I struggled against whoever was holding me down, trying to catch my bearings. For a moment I'd forgotten where I was. It wasn't until I found my face pressed firmly against the hammock netting under me, and I saw the monitor below me, that I lurched with panic.

"Shhhh...." Zale hushed me. I turned to look at him. His finger was over his lips. I nodded and he let go of my mouth. I looked down at the monitor.

Daylight was fading, but the pink glow of sunset offered enough light to see the hunter below. He was circling the tree, tasting the air, feeling for vibrations on the ground.

I slowed my breathing; we didn't move.

His long blue tongue stretched out to taste the air around him and I wondered if he could sense us. I thought of how Zale smelled to me and how his scent filled me as I slept next to him. I wondered if the monitor could smell him too, or me, or the others.

I couldn't take my eyes off the creature. If it spotted us in the tree, it wouldn't be able to get to us, but we would be trapped. I wondered if it could take the tree down with a few hard shoves.

Where are Gunnar and Buckley? I thought they were keeping watch.

Why hadn't the traps gone off and warned us?

Surely, if they'd seen the monitor coming there would have been some sort of commotion to wake me.

147

From a bird's eye view, I studied the monitor, recognizing that it was an uncommon privilege to get to see one so close without dying. I tried to memorize what I saw, hoping I could draw it later for the others.

The monitor had a wide head and long neck, with a pointed nose, like an alligator. His body was covered with thick black scales, which formed an impenetrable armor over every part of its body, even its eyelids. He had one eye on each side of his head, which made me wonder if he could see directly in front of his nose. As he searched the perimeter of the tree, he wiggled from side to side to scan the area visually. I knew his eyesight wouldn't be enough to detect us because he couldn't look up, but also because monitors relied on their sense of taste and smell to hunt.

The monitor must have picked up on something in the air because all the sudden he shifted his weight back to his hind legs and propped up on his tale end.

I held my breath.

He leaned on the tree with is two front feet, scratching at the tree bark. His long-forked tongue tasted the exposed wound in the wood. He was thoroughly processing the area.

We held perfectly still; I hoped that the hammock nets blended in with the foliage of the tree enough to conceal us.

In an instant, the monitor dropped his two front feet back to the ground and turned his head as though he'd heard something. He listened carefully and with a burst of energy he bolted away from the tree. Monitors could run faster than what seemed physically possible.

For the first time in moments, I took a deep breath.

The monitor was gone.

"We gotta move!" Zale whispered, as he rocked the hammock with his hurried movements. He quickly strapped on his boots, wadded up the blanket and put it in his bag.

I searched his face for some indication of what to do. I was dazed as I started to put my boots on and tie them up. My fingers fumbled.

Breathe.

The blood was still rushing through my body as my 'flight or fight' demanded blood be diverted to my legs, rather than my brain.

Calm down and breathe. I demanded.

After getting my shoes on, I went to check on Fairchild. Her hammock was empty. I immediately thought of Gunnar and Buckley. *Where were they?*

"Fairchild?" I exclaimed. "Where's Fairchild?"

"Down there." Zale quickly checked the clip on his gun to make sure it was loaded fully. "Let's go." He threw his satchel over his shoulder and started cautiously climbing down the trunk of the tree.

"Down where?" I followed his lead descending.

Zale scanned the area below our tree with his gun before he dropped his feet to the ground. As I shimmied down behind him, I took note of the horrific depth that the monitor had dug into the tree trunk just a few minutes before.

I stepped lightly next to Zale, unholstering the handgun strapped to my side.

"This way," he whispered and gestured for me to stick close. I followed him to the vehicles, both of which were still parked where we'd left them.

Zale leaned into the back of the jeep and grabbed a second pump-action shotgun, which he checked for ammo and then handed to me. He pulled a long dark green metal case up onto the hood of the car, flipped the locks on it and slid the lid open.

I watched him with one eye and kept watch for more monitors with the other. Upon opening the case, a variety of explosives came into view. Zale grabbed a couple of grenades and tucked them into his pockets on his belt. He handed several to me, and I stored them on my belt as he'd trained me.

"Where'd they go?" I asked, trying not to panic.

"Gunnar and Buckley went with Fairchild, she had to pee."

"You let her go with Gunnar?"

Zale looked at me, "Buckley was with them."

"Why didn't you wake me?"

"They said they'd be right back," Zale said. "Does it really matter now?"

"No."

He continued to strap extra weapons to our bodies.

"Which way did they go? How far do you think they are?"

"They went that way," Zale said looking in the same direction the monitor had bolted.

Then a shot rang out from a distance not too far away. A man's voice yelled and then a huge explosion lit up the pink evening sky.

"Come on!" Zale jumped into the seat of the vehicle. I ran around the other side and hopped in. He had already started it up and with a mighty blow to the gas pedal, we zoomed in the direction of the explosion.

Gunfire filled the air as we approached. The element of surprise was one of our best defenses and we had to use that to our advantage, even if it meant not being able to offer support to the others immediately.

Zale parked the vehicle behind the remains of an old building, jumped out and scanned the area and then nodded to me. I climbed out of the vehicle, holstering my handgun at my hip once again. I opted to use the shotgun if necessary. It had more stopping power.

Before moving away from the vehicle, Zale turned to me and warned me, "Britt, I swear, if you do not stick with me —"

"I will," I interrupted him.

We crept slowly up on the rocks and rubble that shielded our vehicle from sight. As we broached the top of the rubble pile to examine what was on the other side, a hunting call rang out.

"Damn," Zale exclaimed. "We have to move fast."

Below us we could see that three monitors had surrounded two of our crew. Fairchild and Gunnar had taken a stand on the top of a pile of cement blocks, which probably belonged to a building at one time. The monitors circled around them like sharks.

"Where's Buckley?" Zale asked. "Do you have eyes on Buckley?"

I scanned the scene between the smoke, the monitors and the gunfire.

"I don't see him," I replied.

Zale cursed Buckley. "Gunnar's holding 'em off, but with the hunting call, more will be along shortly."

A burst of flames flew at our backs just as Zale finished his sentence. I spotted a monitor behind him and forced his head down to shield it from the flame-thrower.

When the stream of hot fire ceased, Zale jumped up, grabbed my hand, and made a run for it. I grabbed a salt bomb from his belt loop and tossed it toward our predator. Salt in the air would confuse the monitor, which might be enough of a distraction to give us time to hide.

We stood side by side with our backs against the wall of the building that separated us from where Fairchild and Gunnar were surrounded. I was shocked that they hadn't been killed yet.

Zale took a grenade from his belt, and I took one from mine. The shotgun that was strapped across my chest had bounced to my back while we were running.

I looked at Zale to make sure he was ready to move, he nodded. I pulled the pin on my grenade and tossed it around the corner of the building that shielded us. In one motion, I flipped the shotgun around from my back to my front, placed my finger on the trigger and my other hand on the pump. I cocked my first shot and fired it at the dark shadow standing in our way.

The kick-back from the shot threw me off balance ever so slightly. I pumped the gun a second time and fired again. This time I planted myself firmly, so I could keep my balance. Zale was right there, pacing me, scouring the tops of the nearby buildings. I pumped my gun a third time and fired again. All three rounds were at the same figure in front of me. Finally, it moved, disappearing down an alley between buildings.

Fairchild screamed off in the distance, and Zale called for her.

Fairchild yelled back, "Zale! Over here! Zale!" She sounded terrified.

Back-to-back, we moved toward her voice. The smoke was thick and the light fading. The only light we had left was that of the burning fires around us.

Zale continued to yell commands to Gunnar. "Gunnar, we're on your six! Don't shoot!"

Finally in the shadowy billows of smoke, we could make out two human silhouettes. We broke into sprints to get to them. Then together, the four of us battled.

We fought back the monitors for what seemed like forever. We didn't have a moment to breathe and the fires around us were burning hotter and hotter.

This part of the city formerly known as Chicago had been all but charred to the ground by these evil things.

I had already used all my ammo from my shotgun and was now relying on my handgun, which did little more than sting the beasts. Both of my hand grenades were gone and all I had left was one salt bomb, but those typically were put to better use as a distraction than as a deterrent.

As long as the salt bomb was attached to me, I felt we still had a chance. I fell back behind Zale and Gunnar. They were both much better shots.

Fairchild was out of ammo too. She was between Gunnar and me. I noticed that she was bleeding fast and furious from her arm, which she was holding with her other hand. Horror came over me at the sight of her blood. I don't know how I had imagined we would all make it out of this unscathed, but I did. Her blood reminded me how grim our situation was and that out of all of us, *she* was the most valuable.

If she couldn't finish the mission, we were done for.

I had some medical knowledge from my training with my father, but not enough to reattach her dangling limb. As Gunnar and Zale covered us, I pulled Fairchild back up against the brick wall of a nearby structure and sat her on the ground. Her eyes were dazed. She was starting to black out.

"Fairchild, can you look at me?" I asked her, to keep her attention. I pulled my belt off and used it as a tourniquet to slow the bleeding. Her blood covered my hands as they trembled.

"Look at that," Fairchild whispered. "She's so beautiful."

She was no longer making sense.

I looked behind me in the air to see what she was referring to. A board was high in the air propped up on top of the building across from where we were battling. It was a picture of a woman smiling. I figured it must have been an advertisement, but with the aging and damage from years of neglect, I couldn't read what product was being touted.

"Isn't she beautiful, Britt?"

I put my hand on Fairchild's face and turned her to look in my eyes.

"Yes, she is, Fairchild. Can you tell me more about her?" All I could think was that I needed to keep her conscious until we could get help. I wondered if there would be help.

I pulled my communication device from my hip. "Hello?" I said. "Anyone there? We need help!" The device returned nothing but static.

Realizing we were cornered, miles from safety, running out of defenses, and now with an injured crew member, I started to panic.

I stared at Fairchild's face, blood in her frazzled hair, her eyes no longer glowing with excitement. I didn't know what to do. I allowed myself a second to close my eyes to collect my thoughts.

I swallowed, opened my eyes and without any other options, I started begging anything that would listen.

"Help us. Someone please, help us."

"Are you talking to her?" Fairchild asked. The poor thing was so delirious from the blood loss, she was still rambling on about the woman on the billboard.

"No, I'm not talking to the billboard, Fairchild."

Her eyes focused on me, and she scowled in offense. "Not the billboard, Britt. Her." She looked past me again, into the air and added, "Cinder."

"Cinder?" I turned quickly and before I could turn all the way around a terrible screeching sound found our ears.

All of us shuddered at the sound and without thinking about it, we all dropped what we were doing to cover our ears. I could have sworn that my ear drums had burst.

I looked behind me to see a magnificent creature lower herself between us and our predators.

"Don't shoot her!" Fairchild managed to yell. "That's her! That's the Cinder Dragon!"

Zale and Gunnar obeyed; they backed up to stand directly in front of Fairchild and me.

The Cinder Dragon was the most amazing thing I'd ever seen. She outsized the other monitors by twice as much. She must have been forty feet long at least. Her head was huge. No one had ever seen the Cinder Dragon this close before and lived to tell about it. Her tail was long and graceful as it swayed behind her ominously.

She landed on her hind legs with her mighty wings spread behind her. There was no doubt that this was the Cinder Dragon, her massive wings made us sure of it. She dropped to all four feet, folding her wings behind her as she paced the space between us and the other monitors. She hissed at them. They howled at her.

"I think she's claiming us as her territory," Fairchild murmured.

The Cinder Dragon seemed to draw an imaginary line that the other monitors weren't allowed to cross. Once the others had backed down; she turned her attention to us. We froze.

First, she approached Zale. My chest tightened as she came within feet of him. Her long orange tongue slithered out to taste him. Zale stood like a statue. His chest was puffed up, his gun in his hand, but he held perfectly still.

Next the Cinder Dragon analyzed Gunnar. She didn't take nearly as long to examine him. With a swooping motion, she turned to her minion monitors behind her and screeched again.

With the proximity of her powerful lungs, we all forced our hands to our ears, causing Gunnar and Zale to drop their guns. Before I could even open my eyes to see why the Cinder Dragon had squealed, I heard Fairchild scream.

"No, no, no, no, no!" Zale shouted. Cinder turned and hissed at him, keeping him in his place. She then stepped back to allow one of the monitors to come closer to us.

Gunnar started to panic. He reached into his pocket.

"Hold still!" Zale yelled at him. "Don't move!"

Gunnar didn't listen. From his pocket, he pulled a long slender object made of silver.

"Hold still, dammit!" Zale yelled.

Gunnar put the end of the object in his mouth and blew into it. It was a whistle.

A high-pitched sound cut into our ears. I'd heard it before but didn't know what it was from.

It was the whistle.

Zale and I winced, covering our ears, but Fairchild was unaffected by the sound. The monitors responded by backing away.

How did Gunnar know how to do that?

Cinder seemed to be thinking the same thing I was.

"How 'bout that?!" Gunnar yelled at Cinder. "Your btches are my btches now. How do you like that?!"

He blew into the whistle again. A different pitch this time and the monitors reacted by turning toward Cinder. One lunged at her and she knocked him back with her tail. She hissed at them as they closed in. They were surrounding her.

"They're turning on her!" I belted.

How was he controlling them?

He blew the whistle again and again. "Do it now motherfu—"

Before he could finish, a familiar sound echoed through the courtyard.

I looked up in the direction it came from.

"Gunnar," Zale said, starting to move toward the old man.

"No," Fairchild said faintly, grabbing at Zale's hand. "Don't."

She seemed to know what would happen next and was right to keep Zale back.

Gunnar dropped the whistle in the dirt. His hand went to his chest.

He looked down as a red stain leaked through his shirt. Then he looked up in the direction of the gunshot. There was no one in sight.

Cinder screeched at the monitors, and they stopped advancing on her.

She was communicating with them. They turned back toward Gunnar.

By this time, he was hunched on a pile of shattered cement blocks. I could see the red puddle forming on the blocks below him. His breathing was shallow. Still his eyes were focused on the lines of the buildings surrounding us. He was searching for the shooter.

"Get down," I yelled to Zale, worried there might be another shot fired. Zale lowered himself to the ground next to us, covering us with his frame.

"Where'd that shot come from?" Zale asked in the confusion.

As if we didn't have enough to worry about with the monitors, now we had to worry about getting shot?!

"Gunnar!" Zale yelled a warning, as the monitors closed in on him.

But it was too late, the first monitor to get to Gunnar, snatched him up in his mouth and crunched down until we heard a crack. Gunnar's body went limp.

"Sht!" Zale backed up closer to us.

The subordinate monitors each grabbed one of Gunnar's limbs and tore him apart as we watched. They threw their heads back and swallowed their portions whole. I watched as the lumps in their necks bulged as his remains moved down their throats.

Fairchild's head bobbed.

"Fairchild!" I yelled at her. "Stay with us!"

"Britt!" Zale shouted.

I looked up. The Cinder Dragon was stalking us again. This time she set her sights on me.

Zale held the ground in front of me, even as she approached. Soon, her large head moved toward us, her orange tongue reaching in front of it. It was tasting for me. I pinched my eyes shut while she decided what flavor fate I deserved.

Behind her the inferior monitors were growing impatient. They squawked, pacing. They'd had a taste of our blood and they wanted more. They were waiting for her to give them permission to attack. She turned and hissed.

She returned to me. After another excruciating moment of examination, she shifted her attention to Fairchild.

Fairchild's eyes were going blank.

Cinder's tongue tasted for her, just as it had me and Zale. We could do nothing but watch.

Without another second of consideration, Cinder backed away and screeched. This roused Fairchild from her blackout. She panicked and started flailing.

The monitors started moving toward us.

"No!" I screamed at them. "Stay back!"

"Britt?!" Fairchild floundered, pulling me in front of her.

"No, she isn't going to hurt you!" I pleaded with Cinder, like I knew she could understand me.

Cinder watched from behind the enclosing monitors.

Zale and I crouched down in front of Fairchild, putting our hands up to stop them, foolishly thinking we could hold them off after what we'd seen them do to Gunnar.

Fairchild did all she could to shield herself from the dragon's sight, using Zale and I as her cover.

"She's already hurt!" I pulled free of Fairchild's frantic grasp and stepped forward. "Don't let them hurt her!" I commanded Cinder.

The Cinder Dragon hissed from behind the other monitors. They were getting closer to me. Instinctively I put my hands up.

"Britt, get back!" Zale yelled.

"You can't have her!" I yelled at them.

She hissed again, but they kept creeping closer. Finally, Cinder swooped in between me and her young. Then she turned to me. She knocked me off my feet with her nose, like she was trying to separate me from Zale and Fairchild.

"No!" I growled and jumped up between them again.

I shook as I stood in her presence. "She's with -- with us," I said. "She's one of us."

The Cinder Dragon stared down at me, breathing heavily for what felt like a full minute. Finally, she grunted at the other monitors and they howled in contempt. She hissed again, knocking a few of them back with her tail. After a tense moment or two, they retreated reluctantly, leaving us alone with their female.

She came to me again, lowering her head to look at me closely. "Thank you," I said, stupidly. I didn't know what else to say. She'd had mercy on us.

Then the female dragon reared back and bellowed.

When she dropped down to her feet again, she twisted to her own tail and sunk her teeth into her own flesh.

"What the hell--?" Zale asked.

After she inflicted the wound, Cinder let out a wail. It was the most pitiful sound I've ever heard an animal make. She was hurt.

Why would she do that?

Why did I feel bad for her?

Then, as though she was performing some sort of animalistic ritual for the wounded, she let the blood from her tail gush over Fairchild.

Fairchild had passed out again. It was probably for the better, as the warm red liquid washed over her.

"I don't know what she's doing, but we need to get Fairchild out of here," Zale whispered. "She's fading fast."

"Just wait," I replied, watching Cinder finish whatever it was that she was doing. "This feels important."

When Cinder was done, she came face to face with me and Zale for the last time. There seemed to be some sort of understanding between us, but I wasn't sure what it was. She hadn't hurt us. Maybe she expected that we wouldn't hurt her now either?

The dragon was weak from her own loss of blood. She tried to expand her wings to fly off, but instead, she stumbled and landed in a lump on the ground.

"Let's go," Zale whispered to me. "Help me get her up," he commanded. I did as he suggested, gently hoisting Fairchild up off the ground, until he had her in a cradling position in his arms.

I looked back at Cinder. She was still laying on the ground.

"What's wrong with her?"

"I don't know," Zale said. "But we can't wait around to find out. If the monitors come back, while she's down..."

I nodded. He was right. I scooped up our satchels and we headed for cover as quickly and quietly as we could.

We managed to carry a completely unconscious Fairchild and our belongings to a living unit on the third floor of one of the few remaining buildings. We wanted to be as far away from the ground as we could, so we could avoid more surprises. We needed to collect ourselves and start again, this time two men down.

Gunnar was dead, someone had shot him. Buckley was MIA and the most likely suspect. But why would he kill Gunnar? He didn't seem like the type.

We hoped that if Fairchild regained consciousness, she might be able to shed some light on where Buckley disappeared to. But until then, we had no choice but to sit and wait.

The condition of the hideout was shabby at best, but it offered us two rooms, one with a bed, where we laid Fairchild. I used antibacterial cleaner from the pharmacy bounty to clean her wounds.

When I removed my belt which I had applied earlier, I was surprised to see the bleeding had almost completely stopped. I wondered how she'd gotten injured in the first place. Her arm had almost been completely torn from her body. Yet somehow, she was stable.

As I washed away the blood on her face and in her hair, I thought of how our bounty for this mission was now dried on poor Fairchild's body.

I was sitting here with the Cinder Dragon's blood dried on me and I knew that would not serve our mission's purpose.

We were so close to getting what we needed and now had no choice but to turn back. Survival was our mission now.

As I dressed her wounds, Fairchild moaned and tossed her head from side to side. She must have been reliving it all; her face twisted with anguish and fear.

"No! I don't want to! No!" Fairchild moaned in her sleep, and I noticed a tear dripping from the corner of her eye. Her mind had her trapped in some terror-induced nightmare.

I stroked the hair off her forehead and whispered to her, "Shhh…it's okay. It's okay."

Fairchild rustled for a few more seconds and then returned to her comatose state. I left her to rest.

On my way out the door, I spotted Fairchild's satchel on the chair and remembered the meds she'd stashed there. I looked back at her to make sure she was still sleeping, then I peeked inside the bag to see what was important enough for her to hide.

The medicine was called Ambiex. The label told me it was a narcotic, a painkiller. Altogether, she'd stowed somewhere around 300 pills in her bag.

I looked back at her and wondered what kind of pain she was trying to kill. I didn't have to stretch my imagination too far to guess. I knew that the meds were highly addictive and wondered if they were for her or if she'd planned to sell them on the black market when we got back to the Outside.

I closed the door behind me as I stepped out into the main part of the living quarters.

While I tended to Fairchild, Zale started a small fire in the fireplace in the main part of the apartment. The warmth of it was refreshing.

Zale sat with his back to me, facing the fire. He was reloading the guns we'd retrieved from the jeep after the confrontation with the monitors.

"Buckley better show in the next few hours or we're leaving him here," Zale said begrudgingly. "They lied to us. This mission is not what we think it is."

I wasn't sure if Zale was talking to me or himself. He didn't look up at me. I could tell he was furious with the results of the night. I was too, so I didn't say anything.

I crossed the room behind him.

The monitors turned on Cinder. The whistle that Gunnar used, seemed to communicate with them. Did someone shoot Gunnar to protect Cinder or was there a reason someone wanted him dead?

I didn't know what to think. I retrieved some water from my satchel to clean up with. I was covered in blood, both Fairchild's and Cinder's. I looked around for a cloth or towel. When I couldn't find one, I stripped off my outer shirt and turned it inside out. I wet it down and wiped my face.

I found a mirror on the wall in the main room and swiped it clear of dust, so I could see myself as I washed up. I couldn't help but cry quietly, as I replayed Gunnar's murder and mutilation in my mind. My hands trembled as I reached up to my face with the damp shirt and wiped away the blood and dirt.

Out of desperation, I hyper-focused on a stain of blood on my cheek. I wanted it off my skin. I convinced myself that I could smell death on my hands, and it made me nauseous. I knew the blood wasn't my own and the thought of its true owner, made me shiver.

As I stared in the mirror, my mind started racing with memories of this same thought that had mystified me days prior. The night I found the tooth, I had blood on me and didn't know the source.

My mind flashed back to the images of my reflection with the blood stains on my face, and my burnt and torn clothes. In the days since, I had tried to remember what had happened while I was on my farming mission, but I couldn't remember anything beyond running from the monitor and then waking up in the fire.

A flash came to me of the Cinder Dragon's tail showering Fairchild with blood. A thought struck me.

"Zale?"

He turned, "Yeah?"

"How long were we out there?"

"Out where?"

"In the field. The farming mission, three days ago. How long were we separated in the field?"

"I don't know, a couple hours, maybe?"

"Hours!?"

It felt like only moments to me.

"Yeah, hours. I couldn't find you. It was at least an hour before I found you. Why?"

A burst of energy shot through my body, and I rushed back to the room where Fairchild was sleeping.

"Britt?"

I hurried to the side of Fairchild's bed and quickly started unraveling the dressing on her wounds that I had just set in place.

"What are you doing?"

When I finished unwrapping them, I sat back in astonishment. "Look!"

He came along side of me and looked down on Fairchild. Her wound was already closed. She was healing.

"I don't understand. How is that possible?"

"It is possible." I reached up and felt my scalp. Before, when I was searching for a reason for the blood, I was looking for an open wound, not a scar.

"Look at me," I said, opening my bare arms wide. "Do you see any scars?"

Zale looked confused. "No?"

I lowered the straps on my tank-top, so my shoulders were bare. "Anything?"

He shook his head no.

I spun around so he could see my backside.

"Sht," Zale said.

"What?" I looked over my shoulder at him.

"Where'd you get that?!"

"Get what?"

He ran his finger from the back of my shoulder to the middle of my back in a line about six inches long. "This."

"What is it?"

I bolted past him to the mirror in the living room. I lowered the shoulder of my tank-top and twisted to see my back in the mirror. Just as he said, there was a massive scar.

"You don't know where that came from?"

"I do now," I said. "How big is it?"

Zale came closer and touched the streak of flesh across my shoulder.

"You didn't feel that when it happened?"

I shook my head. "No."

Pain. That'll be a story for another day.

I turned around, "But I think I know how it healed."

Zale and I paced quietly in the main room of the hideout. We passed each other as we alternated back and forth, on a path that I was sure we would burn into the floor.

We were furiously working our tired minds to put the puzzle pieces together.

Finally, Zale broke the silence, "Okay, so Cinder's blood heals. And she healed you in the farming field and now she's healed Fairchild. But why would she do that?"

"I don't know. Why would she spare some of us, and not others?"

We continued pacing.

"Maybe she could sense something about us?" Zale offered. "Maybe she could sense something about them?"

"Gunnar *was* sketchy," I said. "And he had that whistle…."

We turned and crossed the room again.

"The whistle," Zale shook his head. "I'd sure like to know what that was about. Was he protecting himself with it or was he trying to…..control them?"

I stopped, "Maybe both. Maybe she *could* sense his intentions were to hurt her…? Do you think that's possible?"

"Dogs can sense that kind of stuff, why not dragons?"

"Then why was she going after Fairchild? Fairchild doesn't want to hurt her."

"Do we know that for sure?" Zale said. "What do we really know about Fairchild? Or Buckley? What did we know about Gunnar? I'm getting the feeling that you and I are in the dark here. I'm starting to wonder what they really brought us out here for."

I nodded. "I'm wondering that too."

We passed each other again.

"If Cinder sensed something was off with Fairchild, why would she heal her?"

Zale stopped and turned to look at me. "Because of you."

I stopped pacing. "Me?"

"Yes, you spoke to Cinder, begged her and she…seemed like she listened." He shrugged a shoulder. We both knew how crazy that sounded.

"You think she could understand me?"

"How the hell would I know?" he scoffed. "I'm just guessing, same as you, but there was a shift when you stood your ground. Cinder didn't like it, but she yielded."

The Cinder Dragon yielded to me?

We continued pacing.

"Maybe," Zale speculated, "...maybe Cinder remembers you from the farming field. Maybe she saved you there for a reason. Like she recognized you? Did you feel like she recognized you?"

"Kind of," I replied, "I mean, I know that sounds crazy but there was something very familiar about her. Do you think that's weird?"

"No," he shook his head. "When she was examining me, I felt that too." We stared at each other wondering what that meant.

We heard a noise come from the next room. Fairchild was having another nightmare. She squealed in her sleep, but we couldn't make out what she was saying.

"When she wakes, I'm gonna find out what she knows. I'm betting that it's more than she's letting on," Zale said.

Exhaustion set in from pacing and postulating. I sat down on the couch. "I can't get the image of Gunnar out of my head." I replayed the scene over and over. I shook my head, "That shot came from somewhere high, but who?"

"I have a pretty good guess," Zale said, slumping down on the couch next to me.

"You think it was Buckley?"

"I'd bet my life on it. Unless someone else is out here. But if that's the case, why wouldn't they take us all out?"

"What about Coya?" I said.

Zale scowled at me, "Coya is Gunnar's recruit. He's the reason Coya has a spot in the Underground's food chain at all. I seriously doubt he'd take him out. And he isn't anywhere near here."

"Could it be War Storian?"

Zale looked up.

"The Storian isn't usually violent. I doubt they'd kill an unarmed man, that's not their style. And I definitely don't think they'd be on this side of the city. No," he shook his head, "it's gotta be Buckley."

"Why would Buckley do it?"

"I don't know, but if that little weasel turns up, I'm sure as hell going to find out."

I rested my head on the back of the couch and closed my eyes. I thought of all that had happened. If I was being honest, I was grateful that we no longer had to worry about Gunnar.

He was a wild card, one moment he was protecting us, then next he was threatening our lives. I felt relieved for Fairchild especially. Gunnar demonstrated especially vicious behavior toward her.

If it was true that he had control of the monitors, that was a far scarier reality to me, than Cinder having control of them. In a world where the MIL disease and monitors existed, it seemed crazy to me that I would be more afraid of humans than dragons. But at least with the monitors, we could explain and predict their behaviors. It was the humans that were unpredictable. Humans were clearly the most dangerous animals of all.

I sat up with a start.

"You're safe," Zale said immediately. I'd dozed off on the couch by the fire. I exhaled and looked at him. "I fell asleep?"

"Yeah. It's okay. I'm not surprised."

"How long was I out?"

"Just twenty minutes or so."

"Is she okay?" I sat up and looked to the room where I'd left Fairchild to sleep.

He nodded. "I think so. I haven't heard her in a while, I think she's finally sleeping."

"Okay," I said. I let my head fall backward onto the back of the couch and closed my eyes again.

"Britt?"

"Yeah?"

"Who's Isla?"

The mere mention of her name woke me completely. I lifted my head to study his face.

"Isla?"

"Yeah," he said, turning to look at me. I noticed the genuine curiosity in his eyes. I considered lying. I considered denying that I knew who he was talking about.

"You said her name just now," he said. "…in your sleep."

"I did?" I turned to look at the fire. I thought of the fires in our fireplace at home in the Ambit. I remembered Chasen's trick, letting the flames calm him during a difficult breathing episode.

"Nevermind," Zale said. "Sorry, it's none of my business."

I looked at him for a moment in silence. Then I stood and walked over to the table where I'd placed my satchel and recovered the Bible from it. I took a minute to be sure I was prepared to trust him with details from my life before the Outside. Maris had warned me not to share them with anyone, even Zale.

Things are changed now. Aren't they?

All that we'd been through together? Together.

I thought of the hammock.

We're partners, I thought. *We're in this mess together.*

What would Maris say now if he knew?

I thought of Zale getting Maris the Lupio injections and wondered if Maris would still choose to be untrusting of him.

I turned around, still clutching the Bible at my chest.

"Isla is my daughter."

I pulled the picture of us out from inside the book and gazed at it. Zale got up from the couch and came toward me.

"Is that a photo of her? Can I see?"

I handed him the picture. He examined it. "She looks like you."

I smiled, tearfully.

"And the boy?"

"My son, Chasen."

Dead. They think you killed him. The old voices reminded me.

"Where are they now?"

Images of Chasen's lifeless body answered.

"In the Ambit, with their grandfather," I lied. Any other answer and I would have to explain more than I was prepared to.

I reached out to retrieve the picture from his hand, but as I did so, Zale caught my hand in his.

"And what about this?" he asked. His finger smoothed over the band on my left ring finger. My wedding band. I remembered Zale holding that hand in the hammock.

Is that why he'd stopped crossing the line with me? My ring?

"Is he in the Ambit too?" Zale asked.

I'd almost forgotten that my wedding band was on. I remembered refusing to remove it before the first farming mission.

"No," I said, then I pulled my hand back.

"Did I upset you?" He handed me the picture.

"No," I reassured him. "You just reminded me."

I folded the photo in half and tucked it back into the Bible.

165

"My past is complicated, Zale," I finished. "It's painful and messed up and..."

I put the book back in my bag and turned to him.

"No one is supposed to know where we're from," I said.

He came in closer to me.

"You can't tell anyone. Maris says it's dangerous for anyone in the Outside to know, which I don't understand because --"

"I'm not going to tell anyone." He stepped even closer.

I stepped back to look at his face. I wanted to make sure he knew how serious I was.

"I promise," he said, stepping closer again.

Did he mean to be closing in on me like this?

"So, I talk in my sleep, huh?"

"You do," he smiled.

"No one's ever told me that before."

He stepped closer still.

"Well, how many bedmates have you had?"

My eyes widened at his implication.

"Hardly," I said, blushing. "Not nearly as many as you, I'm sure."

Zale's smile widened, "You think you got me figured out, huh?"

"You're not that hard to figure out."

"I'm a gentleman, remember?"

I smiled. "So, what'd I say...in my sleep?"

"Well, let's just say Isla isn't the only one you dream about."

He was teasing me, but I sort of panicked to think of all the other things I may have discussed while unconscious. "Really?"

"Really. You talked while you were sleeping in the hammock," Zale was being coy with me. "I quite enjoyed listening to you actually."

"What did I say?" I smiled, I only noticed because it felt so foreign to my face.

"Well, I don't want to embarrass you, but you seem like you have a little crush..."

"A crush?" I repeated.

Obviously, I have a crush.

"Really?" I said sarcastically.

"You do...and apparently, it's on Buckley," he teased.

"What?" I laughed. "Yeah, right!"

166

"Oh, what?" Zale taunted me. "You aren't a fan of Buckley? You sure seemed to be a fan of Buckley in your sleep!"

I scowled at him.

He moaned and mocked me, "Buckley…Oh, Buckley!"

"Stop it!" I laughed. "What's wrong with you?!"

He continued, "Buuuuckley."

I pushed him playfully to stop. It felt refreshing to laugh.

"Yeah? Well, there was some obvious flirtation happening between you and that *child* in there?" I pointed toward Fairchild. "What about that?"

"Child?" Zale repeated. "She's twenty-two. Hardly a child."

"Gross," I said.

"Why? Do you think she's interested in me?"

I scowled at him.

He laughed. "Come on, *she's* not my type."

"Why? Too smart for you?"

"No, she's too nice." Zale's voice lowered when he said that. It was that growl again, the one that I'd heard in the hammock. He closed in on me, placing his hands on my hips.

"I'm nice," I said, catching his meaning.

"No, you're not," he growled and one of his eyebrows lifted.

I smiled.

He came closer until his face was at my neck. He inhaled. My skin tingled with flushness.

"Britt?" Zale whispered at my ear.

"Yeah?" I closed my eyes, trying to keep my knees from buckling.

"You weren't talking about Buckley in your sleep."

I turned to smile at him, lifting my chin slightly. We were inches from each other.

"I knew it," I replied.

"It was *my* name you were calling out," he smoldered.

What? Had I really--?

He was serious, staring directly into me, waiting for me to remember my dream. Then I did. He was right, I'd had a dream of him in the hammock.

He leaned forward. "May I…?" he whispered. His eyes dropped to my lips.

"Cross the line?" I smiled at him, biting my lip.

"And this?" he laced his fingers with mine and held them up. I saw the ring on my hand. He wanted to be sure I wasn't going to regret anything.

"I won't ever take it off," I whispered truthfully. "But the man that put it there is gone."

He stared at me, waiting for me to signal him. I thought of how letting Zale kiss me for the first time, would mean losing the kiss that James gave me the last time.

I hated the thought of that.

But I wanted Zale to kiss me, because he was the first man since James that I wanted to be with.

With that notion, I looked up at him. I bit my lip to signal him. He pulled me forward and my eyes went closed. Exhilaration flooded my thoughts and senses; I leaned into him for more. Primal instincts took over as our hands moved. Then panting, he broke free from me, only inches between us and stopped to ask, "Is this the first time since…?"

I exhaled, trying not to let my emotions get the best of me. He wanted to know if there had been another since my husband. It pained me and thrilled me to answer. He was the first and only since James. I nodded as if to say yes. And with a small sexy growl, Zale inhaled me.

Then taking my hands and placing them on his chest, he pulled away. Breathing hard, he placed his forehead on mine. He was giving me time to think and rethink it. He gave me ample opportunities to change my mind, even though I knew he didn't want me to. I had no doubt of what I wanted. We caught our breath, panting with anticipation. I whined at him for leaving my lips. He didn't have to hold back anymore. I was not interested in his manners. He got the message and he answered by breathing me in again …and again…and again.

12

MIDDLE-NIGHT

Gunnar's death wasn't a nightmare.
Sleeping with Zale wasn't a dream.
Both events happened. It was all real.

Maybe it was the chaos of Gunnar's violent ending that catapulted Zale and I toward each other. Maybe it was pent-up pressure and stress that we needed to release.

Or maybe it was real. Maybe it was inevitable. Or maybe we had both seen our feeble mortality staring back at us, in the face of a dragon and knew there was no more time to be wasted.

Whatever it was, I welcomed it.

"I don't know," Fairchild growled. Zale had already asked her the same question three or four times. She sipped from her water bottle, looking awful and hungover. "He just left us there."

"And he didn't give you any indication of where he was going?" Zale interrogated her.

"I've already told you this. I went behind the building to use the bathroom and when I came back Buckley had left me alone with Gunnar," she said. She was peaked, almost green. Her wound had completely closed but she wasn't fully recovered.

"Did he take anything with him?" Zale asked.

Fairchild scowled. "He had his bag."

"His satchel?"

"Yes, his satchel and his duffle bag. I remember thinking it was weird that he took that with us when I only needed to use the bathroom."

Zale looked at me.

"So, what do you want to do?" I asked Zale.

"What do *I* want to do?" he scoffed. "I want to high-tail it back to the Outside and let that little sht figure out how to get back on his own..."

Fairchild scowled at him.

"...*if* he's still alive," Zale added.

"We can't just leave him out here," Fairchild said. "I know you and he have history, Zale, but he's a good man."

Zale rolled his eyes.

"And he's not a coward," Fairchild added. "Look, I'm not too happy about him running off either, but there must be some explanation. I don't know what happened to Gunnar, but even if he would do that to Gunnar, he wouldn't do it to me."

Fairchild had a good point.

"I think she's right," I said. Zale glared at me. "The whole ride here, he talked about her non-stop."

"He did?" she asked.

"Yes, it's obvious that he cares about you. I don't think he would have abandoned you, if he'd known what was going to happen down there."

I looked at Zale and finished, "Maybe he's back at the park?"

"Or maybe he got himself eaten," Zale said.

"Either way," Fairchild interjected, "We can't go back without some explanation. His dad is the freaking Caller. He'd have our heads."

Zale swiped his hand over his face. "Okay, so clearly you two overrule me. What do *you* want to do?"

Fairchild and I shared a look.

"Let's go back to the park and see if he's there. At the very least, we need to get the supplies out of the other truck before we can head back," I said.

Zale looked at his watch, "It's 5am, which means we have nineteen hours to figure out what happened to Buckley before we're supposed to rendezvous with Coya's team."

"Sun-up is two hours from now," Fairchild said. "So, we better get moving."

She got up from the couch and slowly made her way to the table. I was happy to see her upright again. I watched as she unzipped her satchel and got some of the Ambiex out. She popped two pills into her mouth and guzzled down the remainder of our water.

"What are those?" I asked like I didn't already know.

Fairchild looked at me and then down at the pill bottle. "Pain pills," she said. "Ambiex." She didn't lie to me.

"Are you in pain?" I asked.

She looked at me like the answer to my question should have been obvious. "Are you *not*?"

We cautiously crossed the street in front of our hideout. We ducked behind corners and walls to carefully trace our way back toward the jeep that Zale and I had parked nearby hours before.

I helped Fairchild get into the passenger seat and then I jumped into the back. Zale slowly maneuvered the jeep back to where we'd left our camp in the park.

The hammocks were still strung up in the tree and the black truck sat untouched. Buckley was nowhere to be found.

"Sht," Zale said.

Being out in the open without Gunnar or Buckley, and with an injured team member, made us feel very vulnerable. We had only an hour left until daylight.

"Should we hide in the hammocks?" I asked Zale.

He shook his head. "After our close encounter yesterday, I'm not sure that's a good idea. I don't think we are as safe up there as we thought we were."

He looked around. "These buildings are riddled with holes big enough to fit the monitors. We can't hide in there. I don't know," he said, running his hand threw his hair nervously. "I'm thinking we should head back to the rendezvous point and wait it out there. Maybe Buckley's there?"

Fairchild scowled, "Buckley has a terrible sense of direction. If he couldn't find his way back here, he definitely couldn't find his way back there."

"I don't know then, Fairchild," Zale threw his hands up in the air. "But I know waiting around out here is a terrible idea."

Zale got out of the jeep. He went to the back of the black truck and began moving supplies. He seemed to have his mind made up that we were leaving without Buckley.

I looked up to make sure Zale was no longer within earshot of us.

"Fairchild," I whispered. "Did Buckley have a reason to hurt Gunnar?"

Her face went serious.

"Did something happen when you three left the tree?"

Her big green eyes filled with tears.

"Buckley knows that—" she sniffed "—Gunnar's not a good person, Britt. He *wasn't* a good person and ---"

"What happened?"

Fairchild reached up and held her wounded shoulder.

I gasped, "Fairchild, did Gunnar do that to you? Is that how you got hurt?"

She looked at me. The look she gave me was enough to answer the question.

"Why?"

She looked down at her lap. "I'm really not supposed to –"

"I'm not going to tell anyone."

She was silent.

"He shoved me and I fell into something sharp. I think the monitors could smell my blood," she said.

"Why did he shove you?"

She was quiet.

"Does this have anything to do with the Ambiex you stole from the pharmacy yesterday?"

Fairchild looked back up at me.

"Are you addicted to it?"

"I didn't know you saw that," she said. Tears streamed down her face. "I just wanted to have my own stash instead of relying on them—"

"Them who?"

Her eyes cleared. "The Underground."

"Fairchild, do you know who runs the Underground?"

"Not exactly, but Gunnar—" she hesitated. "He's been my handler since I was little."

Handler. My stomach turned.

"What does that mean? Handler?"

"He makes me do stuff… in order to get my fix. He thought he owned me."

"So, you wanted your own stash…"

"…so I could get away from him."

"Did Buckley know that?"

She nodded slowly.

"Fairchild, you stay here. I'll be right back, okay?" I told her.

"Please don't tell Zale!" Her eyes widened with fear.

"Why?"

"He'll tell on Buckley and the Underground might come after him."

"Okay," I said. "I won't tell him."

I hopped out of the jeep and walked to the black truck.

Zale was pulling ammo out of the green metal case on the tailgate of the truck. He was loading it into various weapons.

"I think we should go back," I said.

"I know. I do too," he replied without looking up.

"No, I mean, I think we should go back to where everything happened last night…where Gunnar died."

He stopped and looked at me with confusion. "Why?"

"It's a feeling I have. Buckley's gotta be there, or near there or something. I think it's worth checking out, don't you?"

Zale looked in Fairchild's direction, "I don't know if she's up for going back over there. She's a wreck already, and there's no telling how she might react. And that place was crawling with monitors."

"I know, but I just need you to trust me. I think there's something over there. Think about it. If Buckley killed Gunnar, he must have a good reason. Otherwise, why would he kill one of our strongest allies against the monitors?"

"Because he's dumb," Zale snapped.

"I'm serious, Zale. Buckley may know about the whistle. And I'm positive he wouldn't have left Fairchild in danger if it weren't for a good reason."

Zale rolled his eyes. "I think you're giving the kid more credit than he deserves. He probably saw something shiny and went toward it."

"I don't think you're giving him *enough* credit. I don't know what you two have against each other, but it's not enough to justify leaving him behind."

Zale stared at me.

"Is it?"

He rolled his eyes. "I don't know that he'd stay for us, Britt. You really want to risk your life, and mine, and Fairchild's, for some spoiled Caller kid that may have murdered one of our team?"

"I do, Zale. We need answers and Buckley might have them."

He exhaled, closing his eyes. "Okay, but if we're gonna go, it's now or never." He looked at his watch. "Sun's coming up in less than an hour."

Freshly armed and hydrated, we loaded ourselves and the remainder of the supplies into the jeep and made our way back toward where Fairchild had last seen Buckley.

The sky started to lighten somewhat, and while we had been there only hours earlier, the scenery already looked very different.

Fairchild walked cautiously around the rubble, searching for signs of Buckley. She seemed to be getting her energy back. I wondered if the Ambiex had anything to do with that.

Zale and I had the same idea. We started searching the area where Gunnar had been shot. The pile of smashed cement was splattered with his blood. We searched the ground for the whistle.

"Look!" Fairchild yelled, running toward something in the distance.

Zale and I took off after her, trying to catch up.

"Fairchild, wait!" Zale hollered after her. He was trying to keep his voice low, so we didn't draw the attention of any unwanted predators. She was too focused on whatever had caught her eye to hear him anyway.

She stopped and stared down at the ground below her. Zale caught up to her first, stopping alongside of her.

My heart sunk. Why weren't they doing anything?

Had they found Buckley?

"What is it?" I came up beside them. To my relief, it wasn't a body.

Zale knelt and reached for the object in the dirt. He picked it up and examined it. "It's a Glock."

Buckley had a Glock.

The gun was covered in blood.

"Is it Buckley's?" I asked.

Zale smoothed his hand over it to wipe it clean enough to read. The name *GUNNAR* was etched in the side of it.

"It was Gunnar's." Zale stood back up.

He opened the clip on the weapon to reveal a few remaining bullets. He shoved the clip back in and then stuck the barrel of the gun into his belt.

Fairchild exhaled and then resumed her search without a word. She didn't seem too upset about Gunnar's death. After seeing what he did to her in the pharmacy, I could understand why.

I studied the ground with my flashlight. It was covered with dust and soot and burnt debris. In all the blackness, anything with color stood out.

I spotted a sliver of white on the outside of one of the cement structures. Looking up, it appeared as though half of the building had been wiped out by something. The other half was in decent shape. The building was huge, several stories high and a few blocks wide.

I stepped closer to the white piece. It was a metal sign. I wiped it with my sleeve so I could see the entire message written on it.

It said EMERGENCY in bright red lettering.

"Emergency?" I said to Zale. "What was the emergency?"

The arrow on the sign pointed to the right.

Zale looked up at the structure in front of us.

"Emergency *Room*," he said. "This is a hospital."

Emergency felt like such an appropriate word. I looked at Fairchild and Zale's faces as we all tried to comprehend the building's significance to our quest. I could guess that we all had the same notion as to what our next move should be, but Zale was the first to say it.

"This way," he said, walking in the direction the red arrow on the emergency sign was pointing. Fairchild didn't hesitate to follow him. I followed behind her.

We made our way along the outer wall, climbing over rubble and moving debris out of our path. We scanned the area for the next indicator of where to go.

Knowing now what the building was, I found myself with a clearer idea of what the hospital must have looked like over three decades ago, when I was sure it was last cared for.

It was the windows that set the building apart from the others. The hospital must have had a lot of natural light for its patients.

Zale searched the outer walls of the hospital in a strategic fashion, hunting for more signs. He ran his hand along the surfaces of any place that seemed fitting. Finally, his search paid off, and we located one.

As Fairchild and I closed in on Zale and his discovery, confusion turned to triumph and then back to confusion. The words on the sign read *Memorial Hospital*, but that's not what confused us. What confused us was that the words were already visible.

Unlike the emergency sign we had discovered, this sign was uncovered. And it was obvious that a human hand had wiped it clean. Someone else had cleaned it off and read it before us. Someone who was on the same track that we were now.

Buckley.

Fairchild gasped at the realization that another human had recently stood in this spot to read this sign. We assumed that we were the only living souls, with hands and the ability to read, within range of the hospital.

That meant our missing crew member was not only alive, but that Buckley was indeed onto something that steered him away from the rest of the team.

"Buckley," Fairchild whispered under her breath.

She seemed relieved, assuming that Buckley had not run out of fear, as Zale would have liked her to believe. He must have discovered the hospital sign and trudged off without us, out of curiosity and duty to the mission.

"Well, if that is Buckley's handprint, then he can't be too far from us now," Zale admitted.

Zale started moving, shifting piles of rocks and rubble out of the way of the door to the hospital. Fairchild's visible relief and refreshed energy were noticeable. She practically stepped on Zale's heels, helping him move the debris.

I took another look at the sign. While I was happy to see the hand swipe of clarity on it, something struck me as odd.

I squinted, wiping my eyes with my dirty hands to clear them of the smoke and dust that had been agitating them. I turned my head to the side and studied the sign again.

I stepped closer to it, and with my own hand this time, I wiped away the remaining layers of dirt to reveal the sign in its entirety.

As I suspected, there was something we'd missed. The sign didn't just read, *Memorial Hospital.* It read *Children's Memorial Hospital* and under the words, there was a logo. The same one that seemed to follow us wherever we went.

BioRev.

"BioRev owned this hospital too," I stated.

"BioRev practically owned Chicago, everyone knows that," Fairchild said.

"*I* didn't know that," I said, following them, as they cleared debris from the door to the hospital.

Fairchild stopped and looked at me, "You're serious?"

I nodded.

She laughed, "Where are you from?"

Sht. What had I said to give away that I wasn't from around here? Would she believe me if I said I'd lived under a rock for thirty years? That's what it felt like coming from the Ambit.

"She's from Los Les," Zale said.

Fairchild's eyes narrowed. She seemed like she was trying to decide if she believed him or not.

I put my head down and kept working, grateful that Zale had kept his promise to keep the Ambit a secret.

"You're a long way from Los Les," she said.

I nodded. "Tell me about it."

Los Les? I'd never even heard of that place.

"Well," Fairchild continued, "The BioRev manufacturing plant is just outside Chicago. The MIL was invented here in this great and cursed city."

I stopped what I was doing and looked up. "Here? In Chicago?"

She nodded. "What's left of it."

The MIL came from here?

That was something the Guiding Authority had left out of their indoctrination. *Why was I surprised?*

We'd almost completely cleared the door of the clutter and were starting to pull it open now.

Fairchild asked Zale, "Do you think Buckley went this way? I don't think he could have gotten through this door if we can't."

177

Suddenly, a tremendous crash shook the ground. Fairchild let out a shrill squeal and then clamped her hands over her mouth. Zale took aim with his shotgun and scanned our surroundings. I did the same, stepping in front of Fairchild.

"Inside," Zale whispered as he quietly tip-toed over the remaining rubble and then nodded to us, gesturing for us to enter through the door to the hospital. "Get inside."

I entered first, then Fairchild and Zale. Once inside, Zale hid around the corner of the door to watch outside for movement. Fairchild and I stood behind him, with our backs against the wall.

Inside the building, my lungs filled with the dust that we unsettled with our movements. I focused on the interior of the hallway. It gave me the creeps. There was no way of knowing what threats may have been waiting there for us.

My flashlight barely lit enough for us to see in the shadows of the hallway we took shelter in. I scanned the walls looking for the next place we could escape to.

"The walls are black," I whispered to Zale.

He didn't respond. He turned his flashlight to the walls and joined his light with mine. Now with both lights illuminating together, we could see that it wasn't the darkness that made the walls black; it was that they were charred from top to bottom. It looked like a fire had swept through the hospital hallways scorching them but did not burn long enough to weaken the structure.

"Fire-breather," Zale whispered.

I instantly regretted my suggestion to return to this place in search of Buckley. I'd led us directly into the belly of the beast, with no escape now. We didn't have a choice but to continue into the interior of the hospital. As the sun was coming up, our chances were better inside, than out in the open.

Another rustling sound came from outside the hospital doors. All three of us flattened ourselves against the walls to blend in. A shadow wandered slowly past the door window.

"Move," Zale whispered, gesturing to a charred door frame about five feet down the hall.

I swallowed and then quickly slipped across and down the hall as he directed. I peeked around the corner of the doorway to scout out our escape.

There was nothing in the room but more black walls. I showered the area with the little light I had, then waved to Fairchild to join me. She obeyed.

In the room, there were objects that looked like they had once been chairs and tables; they were charred, like the walls.

It was large and open. Fairchild and I stepped through the space, dodging the obstacles in our path, working our way to the other side.

We were so careful and quiet, and yet, I'd failed to realize that the entire outer wall of the room had once been made up completely of windows. The glass was no longer there; just open holes in the wall. On the other side of it, a big black monitor watched our every careful, quiet step. I saw it first and froze. He was enormous. Behind him, not one but two tails rose and pointed at us like a scorpion.

He has two tails?!

My memory came flooding back. I'd seen him before. He stared at me like he remembered me too.

The farming mission.

I remembered the two tails were forked, merged into one at his body. Each tail seemed to have a mind of its own. They were whipping around wildly.

One body, two tails.

I remembered what it felt like when the creature whipped me across the farming field before I blacked out.

That's what happened. That's how I was hurt!

Seeing him now, I knew exactly why I'd run.

Fairchild screamed at the sight of the beast.

Zale nearly tripped as he hurried around the corner and stopped in his tracks next to us. "Sht."

Fairchild and I were frozen, paralyzed.

I didn't move, I was waiting for him to lunge at me.

Zale opened fire and unloaded his shotgun, which did nothing but anger the beast. Then he reared back, and I heard the clanging sound that meant he was igniting his throat.

"Run!" Zale yelled.

My mind told my feet to move, but they didn't answer.

Zale grabbed the strap of my satchel as he ran by and pulled me toward the stairwell.

Fairchild bolted behind, slamming into us. A billow of fire surged toward us, as we pushed the metal door closed to shield ourselves from it.

"Up!" Zale yelled and we started climbing the stairs. In the process, Fairchild's boot slipped off.

"My boot!" she yelled and went back down to retrieve it.

"Forget the boot!" Zale yelled.

"I need it!" She screamed back.

"Keep going!" Zale yelled at me, but he didn't need to. I was already up to the second floor.

After frantically climbing stair after stair, I stopped on the last landing. It was the sixth floor. We all panted from exhaustion. The stairwell was silent behind us.

Fairchild tried to utter words between breaths. Pointing to the sign, she said, "Look….Buckley…?" The sign for the sixth floor had been wiped clean like the other.

Zale looked at me. "Are you okay?"

"That thing…" I tried to catch my breath. "…had two tails. Did you see it?"

He nodded, laughing slightly, "I definitely saw it."

"That….was…." I panted. "…what hurt me in the farm."

His eyes widened. "That thing?! That's what you saw that night?!"

I nodded. "I don't know how I could ever forget now," I said. "He whipped me with his tail …his tails…and threw me. That's the last thing I remember before waking up in the fire--"

Zale moved toward me and scooped my face in his hands. He kissed me. When he was done, I asked, "What was that for?"

"I owe you an apology," he said.

"For what?"

He pointed down to where we'd left the fire-breathing two-tailed monitor below. "Britt, you were right to run."

I felt an unsure smile cross my face. "You were right to run," he repeated himself with a laugh. "You're an absolute badazz, do you know that?"

His affirmation stunned me. *Badazz?*

Had I moved from pretending to be tough, to becoming it?

I thought about all that I'd done over the last two days: thrown grenades, fired weapons, battled monitors, patched Fairchild's mangled arm, stood up to Cinder…

180

I realized then that I was no longer pretending.
I had transformed.

Fairchild finished lacing up her boot and got to her feet. "I'm going to see if Buckley's in there," she said, reaching for the doorknob to floor six.

Zale caught her before she could open it. "Let me go first. You two stay here."

She looked at me, hesitant.

"We don't know what's in there," I agreed with Zale.

She backed away from the door.

Zale took Gunnar's gun from his belt loop and handed it to me.

"If you see anything come up those stairs, kill it."

I nodded.

Badazz.

Before he went through the door, Fairchild put her hand on it. "If you find him, don't hurt him…please."

Zale laughed. Pulling the door open against her hand, he said, "I'm not making any promises." He winked at me and then disappeared.

Fairchild leaned over the railing of the stairwell, checking the lower levels to see if there was any movement. Then she joined me sitting up against the wall.

"That was crazy," she said, trying to fill the air between us. "That thing had two tails." She pulled her water bottle from her satchel and gulped down a bunch of it. Then she offered it to me. I refused with a wave of my hand.

I was still in shock of what had just taken place. I didn't understand why the monitor hadn't leapt at us or released a hunting call or something.

"It doesn't make sense," I whispered. Fairchild stopped drinking and turned her attention to me as though I had more to say.

"I know. Everything we've ever been taught is that if you come that close to one, you won't live to tell about it." She responded, "I guess we were wrong about them."

She was right. We had been so wrong about them. I studied her face from the side. I was inspired by her sudden bravery and how she had stepped up under pressure. I doubt that she expected our mission to turn out like this.

"I mean, look at this." She pulled at the bloody scraps of cloth that had once made up a shirt sleeve on her right shoulder. The jagged scar was the only evidence left of her near amputation. She flexed her right hand and arm to demonstrate its perfect recovery.

"How could we have ever known?" she said in amazement. "With Cinder's blood, we could do so much good. We wouldn't need BioRev's drugs anymore."

I wondered if she meant the Ambiex.

"I don't think Cinder is going to give up her blood that easy," I said. Fairchild looked at me. "I know," she said. "Let's just hope we don't have to put her down to get it."

"Put her down?!"

The door burst open, startling us. Our missing teammate was there, wild-eyed and panicked.

Not Zale, but Buckley.

"Buckley!" Fairchild exclaimed. She threw her arms around his neck.

"What the…?" Buckley grunted. I couldn't tell what confused him more, finding the two of us in the stairwell or Fairchild's loving reaction to him. "Where the hell did you two come from?"

Fairchild dropped her arms from around his neck and stepped back, looking to me to explain what had happened.

"Didn't you see Zale in there?" I asked, suddenly concerned.

"In where? In there?" He motioned to floor six.

I bolted past him, threw the door open and entered. I looked both ways, left then right. I listened closely for noises and squinted to see if there was any light coming through any of the openings.

"Zale?!" I called out quietly. I searched both directions with my flashlight.

Buckley and Fairchild stood behind me. I turned to Buckley, "Which way did you come from?"

"That way." Buckley motioned to the right. "But he can't be up here, Britt. I've been here for hours and haven't seen him."

I started heading down the hall to the left, opposite of where Buckley had come from. "It's a big building."

"Is there anything up here?" Fairchild asked.

182

"Yeah, clean air," Buckley said sarcastically.

For the first time, since we had climbed the stairs in the stairwell, I realized I could take a deep breath without coughing. Thanks to the missing section of the building, there was a subtle breeze coming down the hall. It was a refreshing change from the heat and ash that the rest of the building seemed to be consumed with.

We moved further down the corridor. Buckley didn't have a weapon drawn, but I did.

"You don,' need those up here," he pointed out.

I stopped and turned to look at him. "What?"

"You don't need weapons up here. There's nothing up here."

"Call me untrusting, but you also said Zale wasn't up here, and I know for a fact he is," I whispered, continuing with the gun in hand.

"Hey," Buckley pointed at my hands, "where'd you get the Glock. That looks like Gunnar's gun."

"That's cause it is," I said.

Fairchild was quiet.

"How'd you get Francine?"

Francine?

"What?"

"Gunnar's gun? He loves that thing. Calls it Francine."

"Well not anymore, Buckley" I whispered, continuing down the hall. "Gunnar's dead, remember?"

"What!? How?"

Zale's voice came from the corridor behind us, "I'll give you one guess."

We all turned around. I exhaled, seeing that Zale was safe.

"You killed him?" Buckley guessed.

Zale hung his head and then said, "Okay, I'll give you two guesses."

We knew then. It was not what we had assumed.

Buckley did not kill Gunnar.

13
FLOOR 6

We spent the next several minutes explaining to Buckley the events of the hours since he had been separated from the group. I don't think he would have believed us about the Cinder Dragon's blood healing Fairchild's severed arm, if she hadn't been there to personally convince him.

Buckley explained that he had gone off to pee, when he found the *Memorial Hospital* sign and ventured off to see what was inside the building. When he returned, we were all gone, so he opted to hide out at the hospital. It turns out that he hadn't gotten much sleep because he had spent much of the night searching the medical offices and supply rooms for resources to take back to the Outside. This thought pleased Fairchild to the core.

It was clear to us that he did not know what had happened with Gunnar.

"So, someone just shot him?" Buckley said. "And then the monitors ate him?"

Fairchild nodded.

I watched the two of them together. I couldn't tell if she was concerned about who had killed Gunnar if Buckley wasn't the one who did it. Either way, she'd been freed of him and her feelings for Buckley seemed to have been rekindled in the process.

Buckley went on and on to Fairchild about the items he had recovered, and how he had managed to survive alone for the night.

I can't pretend to understand Fairchild's sudden infatuation with Buckley and his story, but I did think it was kind of sweet how she relished his every word. Her fear for his safety must have changed her perspective of him and their relationship.

"I need to talk to you," Zale whispered in my ear from behind. He nodded for me to follow him.

I turned to tell Fairchild and Buckley that we would come back shortly, but they were deep in conversation and infatuation, so I let them be. I followed Zale down the hall, stopping in front of an office door.

"I wanted you to see this." He tapped on the small sign outside the office. It read, *Dr. A. Laden, M.D.* I shook my head because I failed to see the significance. Zale beamed as though it was an important discovery, and I was supposed to know what it meant.

"You don't know who Alexander Laden is?"

"No," I said, confused. Zale seemed stunned by my answer. "Who is he?"

"I forget you're an Ambit girl," Zale said quietly. "Dr. Alexander Laden was one of the original founders of the MIL immunization. There were six founders. They all lived right here in Chicago. I can't believe you didn't know that."

"Really?" I said, scowling at him. "I don't know much about the MIL immunization at all really. They didn't teach us that stuff. Just that it was unethical and evil."

"The MIL wasn't evil," he said. "It was flawed, but for twenty-five years before the Crisis, it saved countless lives. Evil? Of course, they would say that. Damn Naturals."

"Hey," I corrected him. "That's not a term we take lightly. No one there calls your people Meds. All of that is years in the past."

"Is it?" Zale laughed.

I scowled at him.

He put his hands up into a submissive position. "I'm just saying, the Naturals thought they knew better than everyone. They still do. That's why they keep to themselves. No one even knows where the Ambit's located and that's how they want it. No one else is good enough to join their pure and *Natural* society."

"Were they wrong?!" I snapped.

"You tell me?" he replied.

"They're not pure, that's for sure, but they weren't wrong about the MIL," I said. "Now that I've seen what the Outside is like, I can see why they were always so protective."

Now Zale seemed offended. "The Outside is —"

I waited for him to finish. He seemed stuck on his words.

"—they are how they are, through no fault of their own. The rest of the world turned their backs on us because we are BioRev's city. Our city was mighty and strong because of what BioRev developed here, but after the Crisis, *we* became the virus."

"You could leave—" I said.

Zale whipped around to stare at me. "To go where?!"

I knew I'd struck a nerve with that statement.

Zale scoffed, "Not to the Ambit! The Ambit doesn't want us. And neither do the other societies. Outsiders are scum to your people. They're rotting in a hole in the ground, with monitors hunting them and who has come to help?"

"Zale, I'm—"

"But when you or others come to us, we take you in. We trained you, we gave you a place to hide--"

"Now hold on," I interrupted. "Your people also mugged us, beat Seph within an inch of his life and —"

"Welcome to the Outside, Britt! That's how it's been for all of us, all our lives! I was six years old the first time I was pulled into an alley and assaulted—" Zale's face went dark.

His breathing was heavy.

"—I grew up in that tunnel. Imagine not having clean air to breathe or sunshine. I started farming resources with my Pops when I was twelve just to get out of the hole. I figured out long ago that the worst things in the Outside are not the monitors."

It was obvious to me now that this was not a debate between the two of us, or our people.

"I was envious of the kids whose parents sent them to the Collective. Do you know what that is?"

I nodded. "The society for children, run by children. I've heard of it."

James told me of the haven where desperate parents could take their children and leave them, but they couldn't get them back. The children either grew up and aged out of the Collective or they had to decide to leave on their own.

"Not my parents though—no," Zale shook his head. "My old man has some deep-seeded sense of loyalty to the Outside. Wouldn't even leave to go find Lupio to save his life. My mother left months ago to find some, and we haven't heard from her since." His eyes were wet now. "Our people are dying of the Crud because medicine is 'hard to come by' when the truth is that it's not. We're sitting on a BioRev gold mine of meds. There are no shortages of meds, only people. So, you tell me why we can't get what we need?!"

His eyes were round with anger and emotion. "I've seen what else is out there. I've done my share of traveling. The other societies don't want people like us contaminating them. So, I came back."

He stared at me.

"I would have come on this mission even if they didn't get the Lupio for my dad," he said, looking deep into me. "Because it ain't right to know you can make a difference and not do it. If getting Cinder's blood helps turn the tide, and gives my people a chance to live above ground, how can I say no to that?"

"You can't," I said, shrugging a shoulder.

He nodded.

"The monitors are the first problem," he added. "But they aren't the only problem. Someone is calling the shots in the Outside. Someone is controlling the meds, controlling everything, keeping us under their thumbs."

I stared at him.

The Underground.

"And everyone knows it. We just don't know what to do about it," he finished.

"Isn't War Storian trying to do something about it?"

Zale laughed, "All War Storian is doing is spreading rumors about things they claimed happened before the Crisis. That doesn't give people what they need to survive and it definitely doesn't stop the monitor problem."

"Well, then maybe," I whispered, stepping closer to him, "*we* get Cinder's blood." I put my hands on his midsection and inched closer, "Then maybe *we* take it back to the Outside..." I leaned toward him. "...and *we* work our way up that Underground ladder."

His eyes softened.

"Then," I continued leaning in, "together, maybe *we* climb into the Underground's belly and *we* gut it."

He smiled.

Something about that felt right. This mission was about so much more than blood and monitors. It was about freedom.

He leaned forward and kissed me.

I turned to look at Dr. Laden's office. "Is it locked?"

"Yup."

"Is that going to stop us from going in?"

"Nope."

We looked at each other and smiled.

Zale fired his weapon at the knob of the door and stepped inside the office. I followed.

"This seems like a small office for someone with such a large reputation," I said. I ran my finger along the edge of the doctor's desk. Thirty years of dust gathered on my fingertip and formed a furry ball. I exhaled on it and watched it float to the floor.

"I doubt this was his only office," Zale said, as he looked over the books on the bookshelf. He pulled one off the shelf and blew the dust off the cover.

"Why?"

"I'm sure the BioRev plant had offices too, but that place is like a fortress."

"How do you know that?"

He turned to me and one of his eyebrows lifted, "I told you I've done my share of traveling."

"Really?" I said, intrigued by his posture.

"And what did you find in all your travel, good sir?"

"A whole lot of electric fences."

I scowled. "Electric? And they still work?"

"They're probably solar powered or linked to a wind farm."

"So, they're trying to keep people out? Even after all these years?"

Zale nodded, "It appears that way."

How could BioRev still be operational after all these years? Who was operating it?

Zale tapped on the doctor's desk and something blue flickered in the space above the desk.

"The computer dock is dead."

"What's a computer dock?"

Zale shook his head, "No technology, right. Computers were the basis of all technology." He pointed to a button on the desk. "If it was working, I would be able to push this button and a screen would pop up here."

"What would be on it?"

Zale shrugged, "Files. Patient Information. Maybe even the formula for the MIL." He was being sarcastic.

We both knew there was no way that the most important formula in mankind's existence would've been that accessible.

"Is there a way to turn it on?"

Zale knelt to look under the desk.

"No, the whole system's been ripped out. Someone definitely did not want this turned on."

"I wonder who."

"Maybe old Alex himself," Zale shrugged.

"Alex?"

"Alexander," Zale said. "Alex is the shorter version of Alexander."

"Why?"

He laughed. "I don't know. I guess because it's easier to say. Isn't Britt short for something?"

I was confused.

"Like Brittany or ---"

I stared at him.

"Okay, clearly it's not."

"My name is just Britt. Why would my parents name me one thing and then call me something else?"

"I don't know," Zale shrugged. "It happens a lot though."

"Is Zale short for something?"

Zale shook his head. "No, my name's just Zale Farmer."

"See," I said. "...that's another thing that's odd to me. Second names."

Zale stared at me, "Wait, you don't have a last name?"

I looked up at him. "No, I only have one name. Britt."

"So how do they tell you apart in the Ambit?"

"Tell us apart? That's why we have names!"

"But what if you have two people with the same name? How do you tell them apart?"

"We don't have more than one person with a name. The Bookkeeper makes sure of it."

"The Bookkeeper?"

I nodded. "The Ambit has a Book of Names. The Bookkeeper keeps track of every name and person that's ever lived in the Ambit. We don't duplicate names, ever."

"That's so weird."

"Not as weird has having your last name be your occupation, Zale Farmer."

"How do you think last names used to be assigned?"

"I don't know. I just know that in the Ambit, they aren't," I shrugged.

In the moments that passed, I thought about Isla's Bible and how the characters in there only had one name: God, Moses, David, and so on.

"Wait, so you really don't have a last name?" He asked again, intrigued.

"No," I laughed.

"Not even an occupational last name?"

"Nope."

"What was your occupation?"

"I helped deliver newborns."

"So, then you'd be Britt Baby Doctor?" Zale smiled.

"Sure," I laughed. "…and that's exactly why we don't have last names."

It felt good to laugh. It was something I hadn't done enough of in my life.

We resumed our investigation of the office.

I turned my attention to the bookshelf. There were quite a few books about the MIL immunization. I wondered if they could help me understand Chasen's fatal diagnosis.

"Do you think I can take this?" I asked Zale, holding up a book called "The MIL Generation", which was written by someone named Motley Roberts.

"I don't see why not. Not like Alex will be needing it back."

"Alexander," I corrected him with a smile.

"Alexander Vaccine Inventor," he corrected me.

We smiled together at the ridiculousness of it.

I put the book in my satchel.

"What do you think happened to him?"

Zale stepped back and thought for a second, "I guess, he probably died of what everyone else did."

"His own creation," I stated.

He nodded, "Isn't that the saddest thing you've ever heard? Man creates medicine to save mankind but kills mankind and self in the process."

"Zale, look at this."

The office window overlooked the courtyard where we'd had our encounter with the monitors and Cinder. Below us, the two-tailed monitor was pacing outside the building in the same spot we'd seen him earlier.

He never entered the building.

Zale looked at me, scowling and searching my face for an indication of what I thought the monitor was doing.

"What's he doing?"

"Looks like he's waiting for us," I replied.

"He could easily fit through that hole in the wall, why didn't he come into the building?"

"I don't know."

"I'm gonna go get Fairchild. She might know why he's doing that." Zale disappeared out of the office door, returning a few minutes later with Buckley and Fairchild.

"I've never seen anything like that before," Fairchild said.

"I have," Buckley announced. "All last night they did that. I told you, you didn't have to have those guns in here. They won't come in."

Zale, Fairchild, and I were silent, waiting for more of an explanation. Buckley didn't seem to pick up on that.

"And?" Zale said expressing his agitation.

"Oh, and so that's why I hid here. I don't know what else you want me to say?" Buckley snapped back at Zale.

"Okay, so we can use that to our advantage," Zale said. "We can sleep here while it's daylight. Then tonight, we'll collect some samples and get the hell out of here."

Fairchild's eyes widened. "I thought we were aborting the mission?"

Zale looked at me, then said, "We came all this way looking for blood. They got some of ours, I think it's only fair that we get some of theirs."

Secretly, Zale and I knew that returning without the blood, meant we couldn't infiltrate the Underground. We couldn't go back empty-handed.

"I'm rested," Buckley offered. "I can take first watch, so you three can rest. You all look like hell."

Even Zale seemed appreciative of his offer.

"I'll stay up with you," Fairchild replied. "I'm not sure I can sleep anyway, after all that –" she gestured toward the courtyard.

"Okay, then its settled," Zale said. "You two take first watch, while we sleep and then we'll switch."

Fairchild and Buckley left Zale and me to make a bed on the floor of Dr. Laden's office.

"Zale?" I whispered, once we'd settled in.

We were staring up at the ceiling.

"Yeah?"

"What do you think they'll do when they find out Cinder's blood heals?"

He turned his head to look at me. I looked at him.

"Healing blood or not, Britt, I think they're going to try to kill her."

Kill her?

"And we're going to let them?"

"Killing her means killing her young. I don't like it but if it's the only way to get rid of the monitors…"

"She saved us," I said.

He turned his attention back to the ceiling.

"Don't you think that mean's something?" I pressed.

He kept his eyes forward, as though he'd already made up his mind on the subject.

"She's different from the other monitors," I said. "I can feel it. Can't you?"

"She's different alright," he agreed, looking at me again. "But we humans have a long history of killing things we don't understand, killing things that are different."

He turned to look back at the ceiling.

"Especially when they kill us first."

14

DRIP DROP

Drip Drop. Drip Drop.
Drip Drop. Drip Drop.

Awake.

In my slumber I could hear the slightest sounds, as they echoed through the hallways of the sixth floor.

Drip Drop.

When I opened my eyes, I strained my mind to decide if the sound was in my imagination or if it was real. I squinted, as the blazing pink and yellow sunshine illuminated Dr. Laden's office. It was mid-day. I rubbed my eyes.

Sitting up, I focused my senses on the silence that sat tranquil around us. Zale was next to me. A smile spread across my face as I noticed that he had covered me with his blanket. I fought my smile back with a conscious effort only briefly, and then I released it once more to fully light up my face. No one was around to see it anyway, and I allowed myself a moment of selfish pleasure in the thoughtful gesture of Zale.

Looking at him, he inhaled and exhaled softly as he slept hard and fast. His eyes fluttered and rolled underneath his eyelids, but besides that and his inflating and deflating chest, he didn't move.

Drip Drop.

I was so focused on Zale's breathing that I had almost forgotten what I was thinking about. The sound, that I was sure was real now, came again. It was faint yet pronounced. My imagination struggled to understand its origin.

Drip Drop.

I thought for a second about whether I should wake Zale, but I decided against it. He was sleeping peacefully, and I didn't feel the need for his protection from a simple sound down the corridor.

I tip-toed as quietly as I could out of Dr. Laden's office, pulling the door closed behind me. I was back in the main hallway of the sixth floor.

It seemed that the further I ventured into the interior of the hospital, the darker it became. I was getting further from the natural light that glared through the windows on the exterior walls of the building.

Standing in the hallway, even the shadows that fell across the length of it were a welcomed breath of fresh air, compared to the pitch black of the hours before.

A cool breeze blew through the hallway, catching me off guard for a moment. I inhaled through my nose, noticing hints of smoke and dirt, but welcoming the fact that the air was moving and not stale.

I continued down the hallway a bit, and found Buckley and Fairchild around the corner, fast asleep.

I fought back the urge to kick Buckley's leg, waking him violently. Fairchild was next to him, with her head delicately lying on his shoulder. They sat in a perfect ray of sunshine, that I'm sure had provided them with the warmth and temptation to rest their eyes.

If Zale had been with me, he would not have resisted the urge to kick Buckley. But in a way, I found their position innocent and sweet as they tried to stay awake together. In so many ways, they were like children, caught up in this craziness.

This thought reminded me of Isla and Chasen, sleeping like warm little lumps under the covers of my bed. Sweet and innocent, like Buckley and Fairchild. Jealousy filled me. I wished to have an ounce of that kind of innocence once again.

I dismissed the memory of my children immediately, trying to focus on the dripping sound. Buckley and Fairchild seemed unaffected by it, and so like Zale, I decided to let them sleep.

Before inspecting the sixth floor any further, I decided to arm myself with more than Gunnar's Glock, Francine. I needed something bigger. Something like Buckley's shotgun, which balanced on his lap.

I stepped closer to Buckley to remove the gun from his sleepy death grip. I struggled for a moment, trying to unclench his fingers from around the barrel.

In the process, I twisted my body to yank the barrel from his hands, which accidently released my satchel off my hip. The satchel swung down in full force and plowed Buckley right square in the face. I gasped, instantly feeling guilty. But I soon realized that he hadn't been roused at all by the blow.

In fact, it worked in my favor because he released the barrel of the shotgun, so that he could reach up to his nose, wiggle it, wipe it, and then doze back off to sleep. He never opened his eyes, and he never realized I was a mere foot from his face.

I struggled not to burst into laughter at the entire situation.

Some watchmen you turned out to be, I thought. I'd smacked the poor sucker dead in the face with my satchel and he didn't even feel it.

Oh, Buckley, good thing it was me and not Zale that found you like this. Zale would have hit you so hard; you would have felt it in your dreams.

I inspected the shotgun, checking it for ammo, before continuing down the corridor toward the dripping sound. The further I got down the hall, the more natural light brightened it. I knew I must be approaching the side of the building that appeared to be blown off the foundation.

Drip Drop.

The sound continued to intrigue me as I proceeded in the direction of the light. The breeze came a little stronger; it cooled my cheeks and pushed backwards the few curls that had fallen on my face.

The closer I got to the light, the stronger the breeze became. Soon the breeze was a wind and its subtle touch on my face became a whipping current. The further I progressed, the harder it became for me to see because my eyelids were having trouble staying open in the force of the wind.

My other senses were compensating for the disabled ones. I smelled a stench that the wind carried: rotten fish and curdled milk.

The floor was wet.

Rain? No, the sky was clear.

Curiosity nudged me and so I trudged on into the puddle.

I was now on the opposite side of floor six from where my counterparts were. In a few strides, I would be at the turn in the hallway.

As I rounded the corner, I finally understood the source for the light and the water and the wind. As I rounded the corner, the realization set in: I should have woken Zale up after all.

Halfway down the hall, a huge hole in the ceiling exposed the blue sky above it. It was almost the entire length of the hallway, and I was amazed that the structure was still standing despite it. The hole had left piles of blocks and rubble in the hallway. I was able to quickly hide behind one of the larger pieces, as I studied the source from which the dripping sound originated.

On the edge of the hole, in the ceiling above me, a long, pointed appendage dangled.

A tail.

Unlike the scaly black back of the monitor I had tried to memorize back at the hammock tree, this one's tail was a dark plum color. It would have looked completely black, but I could see in the sunlight that it had a dark purple hue to it.

The tail was shiny and reflected the sunlight so intensely, that when it would sway back and forth, certain angles of sunlight would shine in my eyes and blind me temporarily.

Back and forth, back and forth the tail swayed.

Drip Drop, Drip Drop.

From the very tip of the tail, large droplets of water slid down, one after another.

Drip Drop.

He must be soaked from head to toe, to have this much water flowing from him. I ducked, as the movement of the appendage, and the enormous body that it was attached to, shuffled its positioning on the roof above my head.

I cursed under my breath, fearful that he had sensed my presence. But seconds later, the tail went limp again and the dripping continued.

At this point, I wasn't sure what to do next. Curiosity wanted me to step closer, to get a better look at him, but my nerves urged me to run back to wake the others. We were wrong. The monitors *were* in the building and I had to alert them of the imminent danger that rested above our heads.

How many were up on the roof?

I was terrified, but I compromised with myself. I would not run back to the others for fear of alerting the monitor of our presence.

If they are all sleeping quietly, then they are less likely to be discovered.

Curiosity won me over. I thought about trying to get a vial of blood from the tail. I considered that I could tell them it was Cinder's blood and then we would get the credit for the mission, but Cinder's secret would be safe.

I removed the glass vial from my satchel, along with the thick needle, that I hoped would be enough to penetrate the monitor's scales.

The purplish, black tail swayed back and forth, back, and forth. I used the sound it created to camouflage the sound of my approach. I stepped carefully toward the beast.

When I got less than five feet from the tail, still hiding in the shadows, I stared intently at the appendage. I stepped closer. The tail swayed.

Drip Drop. Drip Drop.

I was three feet from it now. I leaned in with heightened instincts and reflexes, preparing to dodge any movement it made.

I slowed my breathing, wondering if it could feel me breathing on it. I swallowed, waiting for the downswing toward me, where I would have the opportunity to test the sensitivity of the tail.

It swung close to me; I blew on it. Nothing happened. The tail swung away, it swung back and this time I blew on it with more force. Nothing happened.

The tail swung away and back, this time when it approached, I touched it slightly with my finger. Still nothing.

Again, I touched it, applying more pressure. The tail didn't seem to have any feeling at all.

That settled it. I was going to do it.

Badazz. I remembered Zale saying.

I readied the needle in my trembling hand, while I held the vial in the other.

Poke the tail, pull the plunger, extract the needle, and then seal blood sample in the vial. Easy enough. I remembered Fairchild's instructions.

I took a deep breath as the tail swung away and then started its descent toward the needle.

It was less than a foot away when the tail stopped mid-swing. It pointed straight to the floor, no motion whatsoever. I froze. I gulped the air in my lungs back down, not allowing even a breath to escape me.

The creature shuffled above my head; its tail swished from side to side with the movement. In the readjustment, the monitor's tail flipped over, revealing the vulnerable underbelly to me.

Even better. I knew the needle could pierce it there.

After a second, the swaying resumed. I exhaled the breath I had held hostage.

He's sunbathing. He may not even notice me. I lied to myself.

As the appendage approached, I saw a huge, jagged scar on the pale underbelly of the tail. Then I spotted another and another. There were several, but one stood out to me. It was pink and raw and fresh.

That's when I knew.

This isn't a monitor's tail. This tail belongs to Cinder!

Drip Drop.

The water droplets continued to fall, slower now.

Drip, Drop.

I knew in a matter of minutes the sound that had lured me here and covered me as I approached, would cease, leaving me in silence with Cinder. I had a small window of opportunity to get what we came for and get out.

With one quick motion, I stabbed the needle into the belly of her tail. She screeched, whipping her tail to the side, just as I pulled the plunger back, sucking her precious blood into the syringe. Her enormous body shifted. She looked down at me through the hole in the ceiling with her big yellow eyes.

She whipped her tail from me while the needle was still stuck in it. I looked up at her, then back down at her tail. I lunged at it, extracting the needle as I crossed under the opening below where she was laying. I was careful to run away from where I knew my friends were.

I swung my body around the corner, catching myself in a sliding fall from my wet shoes. I found a room with an open door. It was a laboratory.

Closing myself in, I pushed anything large and mobile in front of the door. I panted with exhilaration and stupidity. Then I looked at the needle. I'd managed to get half a vial of her blood.

Please let that be enough.

I emptied the syringe into a glass vial with a purple cap. Then I carefully put it in my satchel.

The hall was silent. She hadn't chased me as I expected.

After a few more quiet moments, a horrible thought occurred to me.

What if she went looking for me, but found my team instead?

I'd taken Buckley's shotgun.

Zale!

I lunged forward at the thought of it, abandoning my hiding spot and cautiously darting across the lab toward the hallway.

Before opening the door, I flipped the shotgun around from my back to my front and pumped it. I opened the door to the lab and stepped into the hall. The barrel of Buckley's handgun found my forehead.

Upon recognizing me, he lowered his gun. He was scouting out the hallway. Behind him, Fairchild tip-toed and behind her Zale brought up the rear, scanning the walls carefully. His back was to me.

"Cinder's here," I whispered to Buckley.

"Yeah, we know," Buckley scowled at me. Then he gestured to the shotgun in my hands and then pointed to himself. He seemed to be taking the time to express his frustration about me taking his gun from him while he slept.

I was thankful that silence was of the utmost importance in this moment, because otherwise I'm sure I would have gotten an earful from him about his stupid gun. Instead, he tried to intimidate me with his angry gestures. I removed the shotgun from around my torso and handed it to him.

I then made a gesture to him to let him know how much I didn't care if he was upset. He pinched his lips together in disapproval of my hand gesture and then nudged me to get behind him. I fell in line behind Fairchild, in front of Zale.

Once Zale turned to notice me in front of him, he too, did his best to express how displeased he was with me, without speaking. I'd worried him. I reached into my satchel and pulled the vial out. Once I saw the worry fade from his face, I tucked the vial back in my bag before the other two saw it.

Behind me, Zale leaned forward and whispered, "Britt Badazz. That's your new last name." He winked at me, and I smiled.

Then the four of us, in single file, stepped lightly in the direction of the hospital floor that we'd had yet to explore. It was separated from the rest of the building by large cutouts in the walls. At one point, we had to shimmy along a narrow ledge while stepping over exposed rebar, to gain access to the unexplored section.

On the open side of the building there was a dark corner where the walls were mostly intact. As we ventured deeper, it got darker.

Something crackled under our feet. It was a crunching sound, like we were walking on dried leaves.

"What is that?" Buckley asked. We kept moving.

"Yeah, this looks promising," Zale said sarcastically. He gestured toward a set of dented double metal doors that were hanging off their hinges in the hall in front of us. The sign read, *Authorized Personnel Only.*

We moved forward.

Beyond the doors, we could only see darkness. There weren't any windows. I could barely make out the metal tables and shelves that lined the room. Some shelves leaned up against the wall while some were toppled over on the floor. The only light in the entire room was that which followed us in.

Once inside, roughly half of the room became visible to us. The furthest points were pitching black. A clicking sound rattled in the distance.

"Uh, Zale?" I whispered.

"What is that?" Buckley moved forward.

A gust of hot humid air came from the other side of the room. We froze. We'd found her.

Again, a puff of air came at us, a hot humid musk. Like a bull, exhaling puffs of furious air, Cinder was there in the shadows, laying and waiting for us.

Buckley yelped, "What the--!" He lifted his gun and took aim at Cinder.

"No!" Fairchild screamed at him and grabbed his arms. "Don't shoot her!"

Zale grabbed my hand as I started to step toward Buckley and Fairchild. I looked at him, and he gave me a stern look, recommending that I stay where I was. I heeded his warning.

Cinder, from beneath the shadows, ducked her head into view. First, her long orange tongue slithered out. Then she revealed her flaring nostrils on the top of her long narrow face. The scales on her muzzle were blackish purple, like the rest of her body, as they heaved in and out with every breath. She puffed at us anxiously. Again, the hot humid stench touched our faces and turned our stomachs.

Cinder's yellow eyes glowed in the shadows. I could tell she was resting, like a cat on her side. I focused my eyes to the rest of her body trying to make out the outline of her torso, legs, and enormous tail.

Fairchild gently touched the barrel of Buckley's gun and forced it down.

"It's okay. We aren't going to hurt you," Fairchild spoke to Cinder like a toddler hiding in the corner.

"Like hell we ain't," Buckley whispered indignantly.

Cinder's eyes flared and again she puffed hot air, this time directing it at Buckley. Buckley jumped a little and then stepped back a few steps. He maintained eye contact with her as he retreated slowly.

In the process, Buckley bumped into Zale, who didn't budge. Buckley grunted, Zale stood still and firm like a statue, and when Buckley turned to see what he had run into, Zale just stared down at him. Buckley casually stepped behind Zale, trying not to look scared.

"What's Fairchild doing?" Zale whispered to me.

Fairchild seemed to be the bravest of us, like she knew something we didn't. She slowly approached Cinder talking to her lovingly.

"Are you hurt, girl?" Fairchild asked Cinder, as though Cinder would answer.

Fairchild extended her arm out in front of her as she closed in on Cinder's head. Her gigantic jaws could surely kill Fairchild in an instant, but as she approached, Cinder remained calm and silent.

"See that, Buckley?" Zale teased. "She's braver than you."

Buckley groaned.

I remembered the flashlight in my satchel and reached in to find it. After fumbling for a second, I pulled it out and flipped it on.

The batteries were wearing down, but it still produced enough light to help. I stepped closer to Fairchild and Cinder, focusing the beam of light on Cinder's face.

"I can't believe this," Fairchild said aloud to us. "She's so incredible."

I used my ball of light to travel down Cinder's body, examining her for the wounds that Fairchild suggested she had. I wondered if she was hurt because of me.

Had I injured her when I got the blood sample?

Then I saw something and knew that wasn't it at all.

"Fairchild, back up," I said sternly.

"What, why?" Fairchild asked.

"Back up," I repeated, "Now."

Just as Fairchild turned to question me again, Cinder lunged at her. Before Fairchild could react, Cinder's mammoth jaws were open and coming toward her.

There was nothing she could do to move fast enough. If Cinder had wanted to eat her, she would've been gone. She didn't even have time to scream or squeal. Instead of eating her, Cinder's massive gaping mouth hissed at Fairchild like a cat. I noticed that the dragon was missing several teeth and I knew where one of them had gone.

Fairchild stumbled in reverse trying to get out of the way of the hot steam that showered her. She scurried backward like a crab, joining Buckley behind Zale.

"Are you okay?" Buckley asked.

Fairchild nodded, trying to act as though she was.

Cinder followed Fairchild with her eyes. And then the Cinder Dragon lowered herself once more and slid back into the shadows. She returned to her resting place.

"What was *that* all about?" Zale asked.

"I know what we were walking on now," I referenced the crunching sound from a moment prior.

"What?" Zale whispered, keeping an eye on Cinder in the corner.

"Her skin."

He was silent. I pulled the light back and showed them how the floor of the room was covered with it.

"This is where she sheds."

Long pieces of white, translucent, and dry skin shed covered the floor. It wrapped into a circle under where Cinder was laying.

I wondered if she was sunbathing her new skin when I interrupted her on the roof. Perhaps she'd dipped in water to help it heal and that's why she was dripping wet.

"Gross," Buckley whispered.

"It's not gross," Fairchild said. "It's incredible."

"And so are they," I said. I used the light to show them that underneath Cinder's hind leg there were three large green eggs.

"We're in her nest."

15
THE ENEMY

Cinder is not the enemy.

This thought played on repeat in my mind.

I pulled the blood vial from my bag and studied it. I hadn't given it to Fairchild yet because I didn't know if I wanted to.

"Let's just hope we don't have to put her down to get it," I remembered Fairchild saying, when I said I didn't think Cinder would give up her blood that easily.

If I hand the blood over, then Cinder's secret will be out.

What will happen then?

Will they come after her?

They will want more of her blood.

I knew humans were too curious to just let her be.

I remembered the moment after Cinder spared Fairchild's life when she came face to face with us. It felt like we made an agreement. She didn't hurt us, and in exchange, I felt like we weren't supposed to hurt her.

I tucked the blood vial into the bottom of one of my socks and wrapped the sock around it to protect the glass.

A glass vial. I shook my head.

Please don't break, I thought, tucking the sock bundle deep into my satchel.

Of all the medical equipment that BioRev had left behind after the Crisis, you'd think we could have found a more durable storage container for such precious cargo.

Fairchild had explained to me that glass was preferred because we wouldn't risk contaminating the sample.

Maybe the sample would have a better chance of making it back at all, if Fairchild had it. It's probably safer with her, in her metal case with the other vials, than in my clumsy hands.

"When are you going to tell Fairchild you got a sample?" Zale asked.

I looked up.

"I don't know," I said. "You think I should give it to her?"

"Isn't that why we came?"

"It is, but that was before we knew what Cinder's blood could do."

"What difference does it make? I thought we agreed that we'd get her blood and take it back, so we could get in good with the Underground?"

"I'm just having second thoughts, is all."

"Zale?" the communication device in Zale's hand chirped.

It was Buckley's voice. We were sitting in the vehicles at the rendezvous point waiting for Coya and his team.

"This kid is relentless," Zale said to me. Then he put the device to his mouth. "Yes, Buckley, what?"

"It's ten after two."

"I know, I can tell time," Zale looked at his watch.

"We should go," Buckley's voice reiterated. "Gunnar told us to leave by 0200 if they didn't show. We should go now. We need time to get back before daylight. Over."

"I'm aware of that," Zale growled into the device. "Get off the channel and I'll try one more time. If there's no answer, then we'll go."

"Okay. Over," Buckley responded.

Zale rolled his eyes, "He doesn't have to say 'over' every damn time."

The device went quiet.

"Coya," Zale called over the communicator, "...if you can hear this, we are pressed on time. It's after two, we're going to head out soon. Give us some indication that you're comin' and we'll wait."

Buckley's voice came through the comm again, "You forgot to say 'over'. Over."

"Buckley!" Zale said. "Stay off the damn comm!"

KJ. SPENCER

We listened to empty static on the device for a few moments. There was no response.

I stared at the back of the black truck parked in front of us. We agreed that Buckley and Fairchild would lead the convoy back to the Outside, while Zale and I followed in the jeep.

Buckley's voice came through the device. "I don't think their coming back," he said.

Zale looked at me. "Is it me or does he seem like he doesn't want them to come back?"

"Over," Buckley added. "Can you hear me, Zale? I don't think they're coming back. Over."

"I know, I heard you," he replied to Buckley. "Okay, let's go ahead and —"

Before Zale could finish his sentence, the taillights on the black truck illuminated and Buckley shifted the truck into gear and started pulling out.

Zale cussed under his breath.

"He really wants to get out of here," I said. "What if they come after we leave?"

Zale shrugged, "They're on their own, I guess."

"Do you think they're okay? We haven't heard anything from them since we separated."

"I guess we'll find out when we get back," Zale sighed.

We rode in the quiet for a few moments. My mind wandered back to the blood vial in my bag.

"I'm going to give Fairchild the blood, like we said," I concluded. "I know it'll help. Either they'll use it to learn about the monitors and that'll be good, or maybe they'll find a way to use the blood to help people, like Maris, who can't get Lupio."

Chasen.

I wondered if Cinder's blood could have helped him.

Then I remembered the book in my bag that I'd taken from Dr. Laden's office. I pulled it out.

"The MIL Generation," I read the title. "By Dr. Motley K. Roberts."

I looked at Zale, "Should we see what Dr. Roberts has to say about the MIL?"

Zale glanced at me, "I'm sure she has a lot to say," he said.

She?

"You know who she is?" I asked.

206

He nodded, "Motley and her husband, Rodrigo Roberts, were two of the other inventors."

I looked at the picture on the back of the book. It was a picture of Dr. Motley Roberts. I read the biography written on the back:

"Motley Karen Roberts was born to Nina and Sebastian Baker on April 14, 2023, in Chicago, Illinois. She attended an all-girls private Catholic school, where she earned the President's Award for Educational Excellence at the age of eight. In high school, she led her mathematics team to national victory and worked as a delivery driver for her family's pharmacy. After high school, she attended Cornell University's Medical College, where she became a physician-scientist and immunologist. In 2048, she spent time working abroad with a nonprofit medical program that served third world regions. By the age of thirty, Motley Roberts was one of the most recognizable names in the world, because of her important contribution to the life-saving Multifocal Immuno Lovenox vaccine, known as the MIL…"

"What is he doing?!" Zale interrupted.

I looked up from the book. "What?"

"Buckley," Zale said. "He's all over the place."

In front of us the black truck seemed to be speeding up. Buckley was swerving back and forth sporadically.

"He's gonna flip the truck!"

"Maybe he's trying to show off?"

Zale put the communicator to his mouth, "Buckley, what the hell are you doing? You need to slow down."

There was no response.

"Buckley, slow down! You're going too fast, you're going to—"

Out of nowhere, in a flash, a huge black shadow rolled across the path in front of us and when the dust cleared, the truck was gone.

I gasped. Zale slammed on the brakes, screeching the car to a halt. The dim lights of our vehicle, which had been on Buckley and Fairchild's truck only seconds before, now fell onto nothingness. The truck had disappeared; Buckley and Fairchild were gone.

"What just happened?" I whispered.

We couldn't see anything around us. All we could hear was the sound of rolling crushing metal and then, a terrifying screech.

"Cinder?"

Zale threw the gear of the vehicle into reverse and backed up. Again, he slammed on the brakes, violently forced the shifter into drive and then turned the steering wheel until the headlights spotted Cinder.

Buckley and Fairchild's vehicle was upside down, rolled onto its roof. Cinder paced around the outside of it, kneeling to peek into the shattered windows. She reminded me of my old barn cat, trying to locate a mouse under an overturned crate.

Cinder's tongue slid in and out of her mouth, she tasted the air for something. She seemed completely unaffected by Zale and me watching her.

We didn't speak. We weren't sure what was going on. We just watched her search under the car.

I trusted that Cinder didn't really want to hurt us, because she had had ample opportunities to do it before now. Finally, she lunged toward something in the vehicle and in a matter of seconds she'd retrieved Buckley from the interior.

Blood was pouring from his forehead, as he kicked and screamed. Cinder carried him by his shirt, like a mother cat carries her kitten by the back of its neck.

Cinder disappeared with Buckley into the shadows, outside of the spotlight that our headlights provided us.

"Where's she going?" Zale sputtered.

A crashing sound came from the vehicle again. The passenger door popped open next, and Fairchild tumbled out, rolling onto her back. She looked frightened but unharmed.

She reached back into the window for something and in an instant, she bolted out of the light in the same direction Cinder had carried Buckley.

"Where's *she* going?" Zale sputtered again, this time referring to Fairchild.

Zale threw our vehicle into reverse again, backing up and turning the wheel until the light centered on Cinder's enormous body. I unbuckled myself and threw the door open. I panicked; worried that Fairchild had grabbed a gun and was going after Cinder.

Zale yelled after me to stop. I didn't listen.

As I approached, Cinder had pinned Buckley under her huge front feet and claws. Her head and tongue dangled over him. She was mere feet from his face, staring intently at him.

Every time he would scream from the agony of her weight on his tiny body, she would hiss at him. Drool from her enormous jaws dribbled onto his head. Buckley's eyes were closed; tears poured from them.

His face was red. He floundered under her weight, punching her feet with his fists, fighting to release himself.

"Stop! Stop!" Fairchild screamed at Cinder. I could tell that Fairchild was scared to get too close. "Britt, do something!" Fairchild cried to me.

I didn't understand what was going on. I didn't know what I *could* do. Somewhere inside of me, I found myself rooting for Cinder.

I turned to see Zale was standing behind me. He stood motionless, like he shared my feeling. Of course, he did, he hated Buckley.

Fairchild began crying hysterically. "Stop! You're hurting him! He doesn't have them!"

Cinder stopped and turned to Fairchild and started closing in on her instead. Fairchild lifted the black case that she had retrieved from the crumpled metal vehicle. She squeezed her eyes shut and held it out at arm's length.

Cinder puffed air at her, blowing Fairchild's hair back and dampening her face.

Zale and I watched. Buckley coughed and gagged, while crying and panting, laying in the same spot that he had been tackled. Fairchild knelt on the ground, opened the case, revealing Cinder's three eggs tucked safely in a padded cocoon inside the box.

"What the hell!?" Zale cursed at her.

Fairchild sat the eggs down on the ground and crawled away with the case. She was hysterical, curled up into a ball, rocking herself. "That was so stupid, I'm so sorry."

Cinder scooped the eggs up gently in her mouth, and before she vanished, she turned and glared at Zale and me. We didn't do or say anything. Then, just as quickly as she appeared, she vanished into the darkness.

Fairchild sniffed, as her red face and puffy eyes searched me for some sort of patience with her behavior. I remained as stoic as I could, to not relieve her but to intimidate her further.

209

"It was stupid," she sputtered between whimpers. "I just thought that if I could get it back to the Outside, that we would be able to…"

Fairchild was sitting on the ground hugging her knees at her chest. She was visibly shaken and frantic. Buckley sat next to her. He was quiet for once, listening to her try to explain away her stupidity. He had a cloth that he was dabbing his bloodied forehead with.

The light flashed across Fairchild's face, as I paced back and forth in front of her, trying to decide what to do or say. When my body blocked the light from the headlights, her face would disappear in the shadow, only to reappear once I had passed.

Zale was out of earshot now. He couldn't stand the sight of either of them in that moment, and I had encouraged him to step away to contain himself. He was scavenging the shattered black truck for weapons and resources.

I interrupted Fairchild by saying, "You do realize, that you gave her all the reason that she needed to rip all of us to shreds, right?"

"That's not going to happen," Buckley finally spoke.

"How do you know?!" I yelled back at him.

Fairchild's face crumbled and she sobbed quietly at the thought of it. Buckley didn't say anything; he just looked at her, then at me. His eyes searched the ground in front of him; I could tell he was deep in thought. Or as deep in thought as Buckley was capable of being.

After a few more minutes of listening to Fairchild cry, I felt my blood cool. The tension in my neck and back began to give and my breathing slowed.

I knelt in front of Fairchild, placing my hands on hers. Her cold fingers were folded together over her knees. I felt the dampness on them, from the tears she had wiped away.

"Fairchild, why would you do that? You must have known she would come for them. You put us all at risk."

"What do you want her to say?" Buckley snipped at me. "She already told you she was sorry and that it was stupid. Cinder didn't rip us to shreds, so stop makin' her feel worse," he added.

I glared at him. Again, my blood boiled, and my heart started pounding because of his ignorance. "Stay out of this, Buckley."

I wish he had listened to me, but instead he fired right back at me. "Stay out of what? You stay out of it. Who do you think you are? You're just Zale's little princess, that's what you are. You don't know anything about anything, and you ain't got no right to…"

Out of nowhere, the light on Buckley's face turned to shadow. Before I could see what had caused it, Zale pummeled him. They rolled one over the other in the dirt, kicking up dust.

Zale pinned Buckley, almost exactly as Cinder had moments prior. He held him by the collar of his shirt, with his body holding Buckley's down.

Fairchild began crying again, burying her head in her knees. She refused to look at the skirmish that ensued behind her. I didn't bother to try and help Buckley either.

Zale released Buckley's collar only long enough to punch him square in the face. Buckley moaned and kicked his legs trying to get free. Blood streamed from his nose.

"Don't you dare try it!" Zale warned Buckley as he tried to shift his attacker off him.

I stood up and walked over to them. I didn't say anything to Zale. This eruption between the two of them was a long time coming. I thought they probably needed to get it out of their systems.

"Get him off of me!" Buckley screamed at me, as though I would have been able to do it.

I placed my hands on my hips and glared at Buckley.

"I'm going to ask you this one time, Buckley. Do you hear me?" Zale threatened him, and then continued, "Was it you?"

Fairchild lifted her face and turned to us. She seemed just as interested in the answer to the question as Zale. I was the only one that didn't know what Zale was referring to.

"Was it?!" Zale shook Buckley violently.

Buckley spit out blood.

"You're crazy," he said to Zale's question.

Zale smacked him in the face. I could see Buckley's ego and dignity diminish by the second. He turned his head back and forth, trying to escape Zale's childish slapping. "Tell me!" Zale demanded.

"Buckley?" Fairchild whimpered.

Buckley looked over at her; he tried to see her through the blinding light that was behind where she sat.

"I can go all night," Zale said after another moment with no answer. He lifted Buckley by his collar and slammed him into the hard ground.

Buckley muttered obscenities and grumbled.

"What do you want?" He finally screamed back at Zale.

"I already told you it was me!" Fairchild yelled at Zale. "He didn't even know about it. I'm the one that stole Cinder's eggs. I'm sorry. Please stop hurting him!"

"Not the eggs, this!" Zale yelled at Buckley. He was holding Gunnar's whistle. "Where'd you get this?!"

I gasped.

"What do you care?" Buckley gargled the blood that was caught in his throat.

"Where did you get it?" Zale demanded.

"I found it, okay?!"

Zale relented a little, but kept Buckley pinned. "Found it where you shot Gunnar?! You killed him, didn't you?!"

"What does it matter to you?" Buckley hollered. "You don't know him like I do!"

"Zale!" I said. "Let him go."

Zale looked at me, confused.

"Let him go," I said.

Zale backed off Buckley.

"Did you know it was him?" he asked me.

"Not for sure until this moment, no," I said. I looked at Fairchild.

Buckley got up off his back and rolled over onto his side. He spit up blood and a tooth.

"You knocked my tooth out!"

Zale growled, "You've got a lot more I can take care of for you too, if you don't start explaining right now!"

Buckley moved toward Zale, "I am so sick of azzholes like you picking on me!"

"Is that why you killed him? Huh? Did Gunnar hurt your feelings?"

"Zale," I said.

"No, I wanna know…what did you think was going to happen when you shot him, Buck? Did you even consider that the monitors may have turned on us then?!"

Buckley's face was blank. Clearly, he hadn't thought through his plan.

"See, you're a moron, Buckley!" Zale said, shoving Buckley backward.

"Don't touch me," Buckley said in a low tone.

"Why? Cause you might shoot me too? When I'm unarmed and busy fighting monitors?" Zale shoved him again.

"Zale, stop!" Fairchild yelled.

"Don't touch me!" Buckley screamed at him.

"You good-for-nothing little—"

"You were next!" Buckley yelled.

Zale's face went serious. "What'd you say?"

"You were next, Zale! Next on the list."

"Who's list?"

"Mine," Buckley said under his breath.

"Buckley?" Fairchild said.

"What list?" I asked for clarification.

"I had you in my sights," Buckley said, closing in on Zale. "Good for nothing?" Buckley nearly spit when he spoke because he was so angry. "Ya know what I'm good at, Zale?"

Zale was silent.

"Shootin'." Buckley stepped back. "I'm good at sharp-shootin' and following orders."

Buckley was nearly in tears. "Gunnar was easy," he said. "He's been hitting Fairchild," Buckley looked at Fairchild. She listened quietly. "…for as long as I've known her. I've been dying to get my shot at him. Yeah, I shot him from a distance because I knew I couldn't take him up close and I'm a good shot. And they said to make sure he didn't come back, and honestly, I relished it. Every second of it, because he deserved it."

Buckley's face was red. "…and because it was an order."

We listened.

"But you…" he said to Zale. "I saw the way you covered her." Buckley started to cry. "I saw that you were trying to protect them from Cinder…and the monitors…and then, I couldn't do it."

"Buckley?" Fairchild moved closer to him.

I looked at Zale, his face was honest and hurt.

"You have a kill list?" I asked Buckley.

He nodded.

"From whom?"

"Who do you think?"

Rutherford.

"Water under the bridge, my azz," Zale scoffed. "I'm out here doing honest work! I don't do that sht anymore. All that went away with Winnie."

Winnie?

Buckley stepped up to him again, "You got people killed, Zale. You don't get to just come back from that! You don't get to just say you're sorry. Your sorries don't matter to the families of the people who died because of you."

In the distance, an explosion erupted in the direction of the hospital. The sky lit up as it boomed on the horizon.

"What the—" Zale cursed.

We could feel the ground rumble under us from the magnitude of it. The sky was orange and black from the fire and smoke.

"How?" I started to ask.

"Was that the hospital?!" Fairchild exclaimed.

"We need to go," Buckley said, looking at the sky. "It's not safe here."

Zale turned to him. "What'd you do?!"

"No wonder you were in such a hurry to leave, you little weasel!" I yelled.

"Buckley?!" Fairchild cried. "Did you do that?"

"Yeah, you bet I did." Buckley said, picking up his things off the road by the overturned black truck. "We need to go, I'll explain on the way."

Cinder.

The nest.

"You blew her up?!" I cried, pacing back and forth.

"Explain now!" Zale shouted. "Or we'll leave you here on the side of the road and let the monitors deal with you."

"We don't have time," Buckley yelled, "We need to get back to the other side. We're not safe out here."

"Just tell us," Fairchild cried. "Did you blow up the hospital? The nest? Did you?"

Buckley's face went serious. "I was following orders!"

"You idiot!" Zale shoved him. "You don't get to use that as an excuse all the time! You have to think for yourself."

"Push me again, Zale," Buckley said, lifting his gun toward Zale. "Push me again and then tell me how I shouldn't follow orders. You're alive because I didn't follow orders, don't you get that?"

"Put the gun down, you idiot!" Fairchild yelled at him. She was furious. "You have no idea what you just did! You just killed Cinder!" she growled. I'd never seen her so angry.

"Yes! I killed the mother dragon!" he smiled. Then he put his hands up in the air and spun in a circle. "No mother, no babies." He turned to us and pointed to himself. "I killed her so that she will stop bringing monitors into *our* world. Stop killing *our* people. What's so hard to understand about that?" His chest heaved with exhilaration and frustration, "I knew if I told you that I set the charges that you'd try to disarm them," he told her.

"You're right, I would have," Fairchild said. "Because we need to understand her! We don't know conclusively that there aren't other mothers out here somewhere or that the monitors aren't reproducing asexually. What you *did* is kill the one dragon that didn't kill us! The one dragon with healing blood!"

Cinder was not the enemy.

215

16
POWER SURGE

Cinder was dead.
The nest was destroyed.
Gunnar was dead.
Coya, Jordan and Conrad were MIA.
Nothing had gone as expected.

I looked down at the blood vial in my hand.
What did it matter now? It was all that was left of Cinder, of our mission.
I turned to Fairchild in the backseat of the jeep. She and Buckley hadn't spoken a word since we'd gotten back in the car.

"Here," I said, holding the vial out.

She turned from the window. Her eyes lit up at the sight of the blood. "Is that--?"

"Yes," I said. "I got it at the hospital."

"How?"

"While you all were sleeping, before we found the nest. I'm sorry that I didn't give it to you sooner. I didn't know if I would because I didn't want Cinder to get hurt."

I looked at Buckley, "But that doesn't really matter now, does it?"

Buckley looked away.

I continued, "Maybe you can still use it for something, but there's only half a vial."

She took it from my hand. "I can't believe you managed to get this. Thank you."

"Well," I said, "at least we have something good to take back with us."

I turned back to look out the window. The rest of the trip was quiet, other than a brief stop to use the bathroom, we made quick time getting back to the Outside.

In the hours of travel, I pondered how my brain and body hurt, my clothes were torn, burnt and bloody. I was out of water and hadn't eaten a meal that wasn't freeze-dried in days. I longed for the comfort and warmth of a bed.

I wanted nothing more than to see Seph, then bathe, eat and sleep. I figured once I had recovered some, I would be ready to begin unraveling the web of information that floated in my head.

At one point, I drifted off to sleep, but I kept having disturbing dreams with churning and twisting thoughts. Nightmares. After waking up in a sweat from one, I gave up on trying to sleep at all.

I had dreamt of a goat and a snake coexisting, sharing the same piece of grass without attacking each other or showing fear. I watched the animals from afar, in amazement of their relationship. The snake lied in the sun as the goat grazed peacefully.

Moments later a rat the color of blood approached. I thought that the hungry snake would surely unhinge its jaw to eat it, but it didn't.

Instead, the snake acknowledged the rat without attacking it, and the rat crept in closer and closer to the other two creatures. The goat ignored the rat, sharing its grassy green dinner. And for a time, the three coexisted harmoniously.

However, the more that the red rat ate, the larger it grew. The goat and snake didn't seem to notice or care. Eventually the rat was large enough to take advantage of the snake's vulnerability and attacked it. The rat sank its yellow teeth into the back of the snake's neck, and then violently shook it back and forth, trying to kill it. The goat watched as the rat shook the life out of the snake. Then with one motion, the goat stomped on top of the rat. The rat fell to the ground, releasing the injured snake. Without hesitation, the goat stomped on the rat repeatedly.

I tried to wake up, but before I could the goat had completely crushed the rat, leaving nothing but blood and gore on the ground.

When the red rat was killed, the snake and goat returned to their grassy meals. And once again, the snake lied in the sun as the goat grazed. Then I woke up.

The nightmare was just another thing that I didn't understand and couldn't possibly begin to contemplate with my exhausted mind.

As we drew closer to the Outside, I felt anticipation grow in my belly to be home safe: away from dragons, away from the untrustworthy members of my team, away from danger.

Before too long, we found ourselves at the camouflaged slice of ground that slid open and revealed a ramp for us to enter through the parking platform of the Outside.

Zale put the jeep in park. We'd hardly spoken for the drive, but now it was time to ask the questions that were on all our minds.

"What are we gonna tell them?" Zale asked us.

Another question to think about. My brain hurt.

"The truth," Buckley spouted off first.

"You think that's a good idea?" Zale pointed his question to me.

"I don't know," I couldn't think anymore.

"I don't think we should tell or give them anything until we get some answers," Zale replied.

I thought about how nice that sounded, *answers*. I nodded in agreement. "There's just one problem with that." I motioned toward Buckley, who sat arms-crossed in the backseat.

Zale and I both turned and glared at him.

"Well?" Zale asked Buckley.

"Well, what?"

"What are you going to tell them?" Zale managed to sound somewhat interested in Buckley's opinion.

"I already told you. The truth." Buckley added, "I don't have any reason to tell them otherwise."

"Buckley, you can't deny that there's something going on," I said, trying to negotiate with him. "They sent you with orders to kill Zale and Gunnar and to blow up the nest. That doesn't make sense. Gunnar works for them, why would they want him dead?"

"At this point," Buckley said, "I don't really care what you two think about any of it." He looked around the exterior of the car. "I just want to get out of here. It's daylight. We need to get below ground."

"And what about me?" Fairchild asked Buckley.

Buckley settled in his seat and turned to her. "What about *you*?"

"Do you care about me? About protecting *me*?" Fairchild asked him sincerely.

"You're kidding me, right? I shot that old man outta protection for you. I don't *got* to protect you from my dad. You didn't do nothing wrong."

"You're right. I didn't. But is he going to see it that way?" She looked at all of us. "We all know things now that they may not want us to. We know about Cinder's blood, and the whistle, and the kill list. We all know what the Underground does to people that have information they don't want shared. Like what they do to the Storian?"

I stared at her. I didn't know what she was referring to exactly, but I could guess.

"She's right, Buck. We're all in danger for what we know, including her," Zale said.

"You ain't done nothing to make 'em not trust you," Buckley told Fairchild. He looked at Zale, "You, on the other hand, don't go gettin' it twisted. My dad doesn't trust you as far as he can throw you, and neither do I. Just cuz I didn't off you, doesn't mean that I think you deserve to live. I just don't want you on my conscience. You're not even worth that to me."

"What about me?" I asked.

"I don't even know you!" Buckley yelled. "A week ago, I didn't know your name. For all I know you're from the Ambit or some imaginary place like that!"

Sht. How'd he know that? I kept my face still. *Don't react.*

Fairchild scowled at me.

Buckley continued. "Why should I have loyalty to *you* over my own family?"

"It's not loyalty," Zale replied, "it's blind stupidity if you think they're not gonna put your name on a list someday too."

"I don't have to listen to this," Buckley growled. "And I don't have to sit out here anymore either."

He propped the door to the car open, "C'mon, Fair, let's go."

Buckley extended his hand out for Fairchild.

"No, Buckley," she said timidly.

"What?" Buckley seemed surprised.

"No," Fairchild said louder and lifted her face so that she could look at him directly. "I'm not going with you. I can't. I appreciate what you did for me, taking care of Gunnar, but if I go back in there with you, they're just going to assign me to another handler. Don't you see that?"

Buckley's face turned red from the embarrassment of her rejection. Fairchild reached into her bag and pulled the vial of Cinder's blood from it. She extended her hand to lay it in Buckley's hand. "If you give this to them, then maybe they won't come looking for me."

"Looking for you?" Buckley asked.

Before Fairchild could successfully hand over the vial, Zale snatched it from her. "Actually, I'm going to hold onto this. We worked too damn hard to get it, and we're not going to just let you hand it over until we have answers." Zale took the vial and tucked it inside of his jacket pocket.

Buckley scowled at Zale. "I don't want it anyway. I don't want anything to do with the damn thing. It's not worth it. Damn Cinder Dragon's dead anyway."

Fairchild didn't say anything. A few tears streamed down her face. After a moment, she turned her body away from Buckley and looked out the window.

"Fine," And with that he slammed the door to the vehicle, threw his pack over his shoulder and stormed off. Silence fell on us.

"What now?" I asked.

Zale turned to Fairchild, "What'd you mean, they'll just assign you to another handler?"

Fairchild looked at me and then at Zale. "I think you know exactly what that means, Zale."

Zale's face sobered, "You mean Gunnar was--?"

"That's why Buckley did what he did," I started to say.

Zale nodded his head, "Yeah, I get it now."

"So, what do we do?" I asked.

Zale started, "Well, I don't know about you two, but apparently I'm on a hit list. If I go back in there, it's just a matter of time before someone does what Buckley didn't. I need to lie low. I'm thinking maybe we let things cool off before we go back down."

I nodded.

"We can go to Los Les," Fairchild said, looking at me. "You must have connections there."

I glanced at Zale, "That's an option," I said, trying to cover that I didn't know where Los Les was, let alone who was there.

"Before we go anywhere, I need to go get my pops. He's not going to want to leave but I think we need to get him out too, at least for a little while."

"So, we're running?" I asked.

Fairchild looked at us with interest.

"We got all those BioRev meds from the pharmacy. We can use those to bargain our way in somewhere," Fairchild offered.

I shook my head. "Okay, I'm in, I just need to get Seph and Nanny first."

"Nanny?" Fairchild asked.

"You and that damn goat," Zale shook his head with a smile

"It's a long story," I said.

Zale put the jeep into motion.

"Wait, we're not going in through the garage?" Fairchild asked.

"No, that's where they'll expect us, once we're in, we may not be able to get the jeep back out. We'll take the elevator down."

Ten minutes later, we'd hid the jeep in the brush next to the triangular skyscraper that we used as our rendezvous point when farming. We armed ourselves with the few remaining weapons and made our way to the elevator.

Once inside, Zale went over the plan. "If we get separated, we all know where to go, right?'

Fairchild and I nodded.

"Fairchild'll get food and ammo, while Britt and I get my dad and Seph…then we'll meet back up top." He looked at his watch. "I'd guess we have fifteen minutes before they come looking for us."

The elevator settled on the lowest floor of the Outside and the doors parted.

Zale was wrong.

We didn't even have one minute before they'd found us.

Rutherford and a group of his cronies were waiting for us on the other side of the doors.

"Welcome back," the Caller said. Buckley was behind him.

I looked down at the gun in Rutherford's hand. "Ya'll come with me nicely and things won't have to get messy out here."

We followed Rutherford and his men down the hallway toward the Floor. There were three men walking in front of us, including Rutherford, and four men following closely behind, including Buckley. Each of them had an eye patch on the outside of their jackets.

As we approached the Floor, I noticed that the WANTED poster had changed. War Storian was still occupying the main slide, but the face on the next slide was new.

"Seph?"

Seph is wanted? For what?!

The picture they had of him was from some security camera footage. It was a black and white close-up of his face.

I nudged Zale and he looked up at the moving poster.

"What the—?"

"Keep moving," the man behind us ordered.

Zale stopped.

My mind ran through scenarios in which Seph could possibly have been wanted by the Underground. Had he gotten in trouble somehow while we were gone? Not Seph. He was anything but a troublemaker.

"I said 'keep moving'!" the man jabbed Zale in the ribs with the butt of his gun.

Was Seph missing? Or were they looking for him because of me?

Then a thousand thoughts turned into one, and I realized why Zale had stopped in the middle of the Floor. I understood why he refused to move.

If Seph is wanted, then where is Maris? Why wasn't he also on the WANTED screen?

"Where's my dad?" Zale growled at Rutherford in a low tone.

Rutherford and his men turned around and came back. The Caller settled in front of Zale.

"Remember Winnie?" he asked Zale.

Zale's eyes widened. He knew something then.

Rutherford leaned toward him. "Remember how I said then that someday you'd have hell to pay for that?"

"You son-of-a-btch," Zale said shaking his head. "My dad's got nothing to do with that. He —" Zale's eyes were wet.

"Yeah, but he had your dirt on him, didn't he?"

Had?

"Where is he?"

Rutherford smiled slightly, "Turns out that Lupio injections are hard to come by after all, but you know what's not?"

"If you hurt him, I'm going to ---" Zale growled at him.

"Cosmos injections," Rutherford finished.

"What?" Fairchild exclaimed. "That's not—"

"What is that? What does that mean?!" I asked, beginning to panic.

Was he implying that Maris was dead?

Had they given Maris something to hurt him instead of healing him?

Zale lunged at Rutherford, but Rutherford's men caught him before he could reach the old man.

"Zale!?" I asked. "What does that mean?"

Rutherford turned his attention to me. "It's a real shame that you hitched your wagon to the wrong stud, young miss. Now his dirt is on you too."

Rutherford nodded to the men, and they nudged us forward.

Zale's face went red, and he threw his weight into the man next to him, throwing him over. Another man approached to assist, but Zale, took him to the ground before he could get the gun from his hip. I moved forward but someone held me back before I could get to where Zale was fighting the others.

"Let me go!" I yelled, trying to make a scene on the Floor. No one seemed to notice or care. The people, who did look up, immediately diverted their eyes as soon as they saw the Caller and the other badges.

"Help!" I screamed to the passers-by, but they did nothing. All our fame and recognition for the Blood Mission had disappeared. *What happened while we were gone?*

Exhausted from our efforts, Rutherford finally retrieved a black handled mechanism from his belt and pointed it at Zale. Zale didn't stop fighting, so Rutherford pulled the trigger. From the end of the black gadget a blue rope with electrical currents shot out and attached to Zale, dropping him in convulsions to the floor.

I went to move toward him, but the man holding me tightened his grip on me.

"Buckley, do something!" Fairchild yelled at him. She was also being forcefully removed from helping Zale.

Buckley backed away from the skirmish.

"Where are you going?!" Fairchild yelled at him. "Coward!" She screamed, as he disappeared into the crowd of the Floor.

Zale rolled on the ground for a few more moments before he finally came to rest, heaving from the pain.

"May we?" Rutherford asked him. Zale moaned and Rutherford's men lifted him from the ground and drug him with us.

Rutherford and two of his other men led us across the Floor. We followed them down the tunnel shaft to a platform I'd never seen before.

Once on the platform, we went through a door, which led to another door. I turned to see if we were all still together and saw that Fairchild was behind me, followed by the men who practically carried Zale.

At the end of the hall, Rutherford used a key to unlock a door. He opened it and then held the door as the rest of us passed through.

"Jones, you and Scalin can escort Zale to that room down there." Rutherford motioned down another long hallway to a closed door.

Then Rutherford turned to the man holding my arm, "Put her in the closet until he's ready for her."

The closet? Until who's ready?!

Rutherford pointed out a doorway on the opposite end of the hall from where Jones and Scalin were headed.

"Loust, you stay with Fairchild down there," Rutherford pointed to the last door.

As we passed each other, I caught Zale's eyes. I searched his face for an indication of what I should do, but there was nothing. His face was vacant and pale.

"Zale?!"

I squirmed against the man holding me. He threw me into a dark closet and slammed the door closed.

"No!" I screamed, pounding my fists on it. "Let me out!"

I heard Fairchild screaming in the distance.

"Fairchild!"

I turned around and surveyed the room. There were shelves lining the walls of the small closet.

There must be something in here that I can protect myself with.

224

I remembered my switchblade at my hip and felt for it. It was gone, they'd swiped it from me.

Francine.

I remembered storing Gunnar's Glock in my ankle holster. I knelt and pulled my pant leg up. Francine was still there. I checked the clip.

Two bullets.

It wouldn't get me far, but it was better than nothing.

Am I ready to kill someone to get out of here?

Seph.

I was ready to kill for Seph.

I heard the doorknob rattle. Quickly, I tucked Francine back into my ankle holster. I stood up and turned around with my hands in the air. As soon as the light from the hallway landed on my face, I offered, "I'll cooperate." I kept my hands up, I didn't want to give them a reason to search me for more weapons. "Just tell me what you want."

"Let's go," the man grunted at me.

He clasped his hand around my arm, so I lowered it.

"Where are we going?"

He didn't speak.

"Where are my friends?"

Silence.

At the end of the hall, he tossed me into a bare room. There was nothing but a table and two chairs in it. Sitting at the table was a man I recognized.

Eamon the Broker.

The door latched behind me.

I stared at the man I remembered from the Rally.

He helped me there. Maybe he will help me here.

He stared back at me.

"Where's Zale?" I asked. "Where's Fairchild?"

"Have a seat," he said with the accent I'd forgotten he had. He nodded toward a bottle of water on the table. "That's for you."

"Why is my kid on the WANTED screen?" I growled.

He waited.

"I'm not sitting until I know they're okay."

"I give you my word that they're okay."

"How do I know you're telling me the truth?"

"The truth?" Eamon laughed. "I guess you don't."

225

I thought about that. I had no reason to trust him other than the smile he'd given me at the Rally. Eamon was wearing a yellow shirt with a spot of red on the sleeve. *Blood?*

Cautiously, I moved toward the table and sat down across from him.

"My name is Eamon," he said.

"I know, I remember you."

"Good," he said. "Cause I'm here to help you."

"Like you guys said you were helping Maris?" my eyes narrowed on him.

He exhaled. "Maris? Zale's old man?"

I nodded.

"He was sick," Eamon replied.

Was.

"I was there, ya know? I was there when Maris got the injections. They were supposed to give him Lupio. That was the deal. We kept our end of the deal, but your people--"

"Lupio is impossible to find."

"That's what they told us too, but then when they said they had it, and we watched them inject him, we trusted that they were telling the truth."

"Ah, there it is again. The truth," Eamon said.

"This was all a set up! We went on this mission in good faith, trusting that we all wanted the same thing. We were trying to help!"

Eamon's eyes narrowed. "What do you know of faith?"

"What?"

"You said you went in good faith."

I scowled.

"We went in believing that your people would do as they said."

"Belief," Eamon said slowly.

I stopped, unsure of what his point was.

"What do you know of belief?" he asked.

I scoffed. He wasn't making sense to me.

"Your kid," Eamon said. "Do you know where he is?"

"No! Obviously, I don't. I just got back from the Blood Mission. And even if I did, I wouldn't tell you!"

"The kid, is he your son?"

"Why?"

"So, he's not."

"I didn't say that."

"But you like to tell the truth. That's why you deflected with another question. You didn't want to lie and say he is your son because he's not."

"He *is* my son."

Elles.

Eamon smiled and his grin cracked his face wide. His teeth were beautiful and white.

"So, he's adopted?"

How did he know that?

"Not exactly."

Eamon's eyes understood something I didn't mean for them to.

"Ah," he said. "So, you assumed him?"

My skin twitched with chills.

He stared into me.

"Assumed" is an Ambit word.

Does he know I'm from the Ambit? Did I just give it away?

I stared at him, afraid to say anything more.

"*I'm* adopted," Eamon offered, tilting his head to the side in a friendly way.

"I don't care," I stated flatly.

He smiled again.

"Yes, you do."

I squirmed uncomfortably in my chair.

How was he doing that?

"Why are they looking for Seph? He's just a kid," I said, giving in a little. What was the point of trying to hide information now? Clearly, Eamon had a knack for seeing through my guard.

Eamon reached up and pointed to the space where his pale, yellow shirt laid against his dark thick neck. "The boy is wearing something here. A necklace. Do you know it?"

I scowled. "Yes."

"Where is it from?"

I thought carefully. Why would Seph's necklace, of all things, matter right now?

"It was his mother's."

Elles. Abigail.

I'm responsible for Abigail.

Eamon's eyebrows rose and his head tilted back, like he understood.

"He wears it to remember her?"

I nodded. Eamon was quiet for a long moment. Then he continued, "What do you know of War Storian?"

War Storian? The other face from the WANTED screen.

"I don't."

He analyzed me. Then seeing that I was telling the truth, he said, "War Storian is a problem down here."

"I don't know him."

"Him?"

"Or her...I don't know War Storian."

Eamon smirked. "Tell me about Storian?"

I recognized the trick he was trying to play on me.

"I don't know anyone that's Storian."

"I didn't ask you if you knew anyone. I asked you to tell me what you know *about* them."

I scowled. "I've been advised to stay away from them."

"By whom?"

"Zale."

Eamon processed what I'd told him before he continued his line of questioning. "The Storian has been a problem for the Underground for years. Every time a group gets snuffed out; a new group rears its head. Every time they think they've found War Storian, he...." he paused, then continued, "...or she...pops back up."

Is he implying that he thinks I'm War Storian?

"I don't know anything about that," I said.

He stopped and smiled. "You already said that."

I was confused.

He continued, "That's why I'm telling you. Seeing that you're not from around here..."

Sht.

"...I thought you should know."

I sat quietly.

"While you were away, an order came down and a sweep was done."

"Sweep?"

"A clean out...of Storian."

He stared at me. That's why all the people on the Floor seemed too afraid to help us when Rutherford and his goons were dragging us away.

"That doesn't have anything to do with me, so I'm not sure—"

"Your kid, the boy you *assumed*—" Eamon seemed to draw that word out like he was saying something more without saying exactly what he wanted to.

Is he referencing the Ambit without saying it?

"—the necklace he is wearing is a Storian symbol."

What?

Elles?

" I assure you that he doesn't know that—" I said quickly. "It must be a coincidence. We barely know how to survive down here, let alone get messed up with—"

A knock at the door startled me.

Eamon rose from the table and went to the door.

Someone was there whispering something to him.

He turned around and said, "I'll be right back."

Did they find Seph?

"Eamon?!" I almost shouted in desperation.

Eamon turned around.

"Seph doesn't know anything about anyone down here. If he's mixed up in something, it has to be an accident."

Eamon turned and left the room.

I stood up from the table and began pacing back and forth.

I scooped the water bottle from the table and guzzled it down.

My hands were shaking. *What is going on?*

Somehow, we'd gotten mixed up in something even deeper than the Blood Mission. More than anything, I wanted to find Seph and my friends and get out of here. If I could get away from the Outside, I swore to myself that I would never come back.

How badly do I want to get out?

Am I willing to use Francine?

Am I willing to use Francine against Eamon if necessary?

Something about him intrigued me. He didn't seem like he wanted to hurt me. *Am I willing to hurt him?*

For Seph, I was.

I am responsible for Abigail.

229

I took my seat back at the table, facing the door. Carefully, I reached down and pulled Francine from my ankle holster. I switched the safety off and sat the gun on my lap. I covered it with my shirt. My hands were so shaky, I didn't know if I would be able to handle the gun, let alone pull the trigger.

The door opened and Eamon entered.

"Did they find Seph?"

"No," he said.

I exhaled. Under my shirt, on my lap, I carefully fumbled with Francine to turn the safety back on.

"Britt," he said, and I found myself surprised that he knew my name.

"...where's the blood?"

The blood. They knew we had it.

"What blood?" I asked blankly.

Eamon's eyes dug into me with examination.

"The dragon's blood."

"We didn't get any," I said. "We failed the mission."

Damn Buckley.

"Who has it?" he pressed, ignoring my obvious lie.

"I don't know what you're talking about," I pinched my lips. I was not going to budge on this.

Eamon's voice lowered and he leaned in, "I need you to tell me who has it. I can't help you if I don't know who—"

Another knock at the door interrupted us.

Eamon dropped his head down and exhaled in frustration. Reluctantly, he rose from the table again to answer the door. This time when he opened it, his hands immediately went up into the air.

"Back up," I heard Zale's voice say.

Eamon took a step back.

Zale was in the doorway, behind him Fairchild cowered.

Relief washed over me to see them.

Zale lifted a finger to his lips, so I knew to remain quiet. I did as he gestured. Then I pulled Francine from my lap and pointed it at Eamon too.

Eamon backed into the corner of the room quietly. He stared at me.

"We aren't Storian," I said to Eamon. "That's not what this is. We're just people that got mixed up with something and we want out."

Eamon was staring at the gun in my hand.

"Where'd you get that gun?" he asked me, and I felt like it was a silly question given the situation.

I turned the gun to the side and showed him the name etched in the side of it.

"Guess," I said.

He didn't know that Gunnar hadn't returned with us.

Suddenly the lights went down. It was a power surge.

In the dark, I heard Zale whisper, "I guess that means Coya and his team didn't make it back."

If they hadn't fixed the power surges, they must have met a similar fate to Gunnar's.

The lights came back up. Eamon was still standing in the corner with his hands in the air. He didn't even try to move. His eyes were on Zale.

"Can we go?" Fairchild whispered. I looked at her. She lowered her eyes, and I noticed her cheek was red. Someone had hit her.

Zale nodded to me, "Come on."

I stepped into the hall with him.

"I have to find Seph—" I started to say, stopping when I saw who was in the hall with us.

"Buckley?" He was watching down the hall in case someone surprised us. I turned to Zale, "What's he—?" I asked.

"He's the one breaking us out," Zale said. "No time for questions. Let's just get the hell out of here."

I nodded.

"This way," Buckley led us down the hall.

Within moments we were back on the Floor. Patterns of people moved without noticing us. The ones that did, ignored us just as they had before. I understood them differently now. They wouldn't help us when we were in the grasp of the Underground because they were afraid. But they wouldn't stop us to assist the Underground either.

I followed Buckley and the others, trying to keep my head down. I turned to see if Eamon was trailing us. He wasn't.

Seph.

"We can't go without Seph," I called to the others.

No one answered.

Buckley led us down the corridor toward the elevator we'd arrived on. He called the transport with the push of a button.

"What about Seph?" I asked, waiting for someone to acknowledge me.

The elevator opened. Buckley and Fairchild hurried inside.

"I'm not leaving without Seph!" I yelled.

They stopped and looked at me.

"Where is he?" Zale asked.

"I don't know," I cried. "We have to go back and find him!"

Zale looked over my head down the corridor. No one was following us.

The elevator doors began closing. Buckley huffed and leaned forward to catch them. "Got on!" he yelled.

Then behind us we could hear a commotion stirring.

"Britt—" Zale started.

"I'm not leaving here without him, Zale."

Buckley growled. "Get on the fcking elevator so I can take you to him!"

I examined Buckley. "You know where he is?!"

The commotion behind us grew louder.

"Just get on and trust me!" Buckley growled, looking above my head.

Zale was waiting for me. He wasn't going to get on the elevator if I didn't.

"They're coming!" Fairchild cried.

Zale stood motionless, waiting for me to decide.

Can we trust Buckley?

Hadn't he just turned us over to them?

Why the sudden change?

I turned around. The movement of the crowds surged, like something was about to break through. I rushed past Zale onto the elevator, and he followed.

Once the doors closed, I slammed my hand on the button labeled STOP. The elevator rattled to a halt.

"Trust you?!" I shoved Buckley into the wall.

Buckley's face was still. "You turned us in!" I yelled.

"You got Maris killed!"

"Britt!" Fairchild yelled to stop me.

"Where's Seph?!"

Something was different about Buckley. He didn't try to defend himself. He didn't fight back. He was accepting my rage.

"I didn't know, okay?!" he sputtered. His face turned beet red and his eyes glassed over when he looked up at us.

He was grief-stricken.

"I didn't know what they were doing while we were gone. I didn't know!"

I stepped back.

Buckley looked from me to Zale. "Your dad. I didn't know that they were gonna—"

We all stared at him.

Then he looked at me, "I know where they put your kid. I'm trying to take you there. I'm trying to fix this, okay?! Let me try to fix this!"

I looked at Zale. His jaw clenched.

"We don't have time for this right now. We need to get out of here!" Fairchild scurried to the elevator panel and released the elevator back into motion.

No one stopped her. Instead, we were quiet while we waited for the elevator to deliver us to the upper level. Buckley stared at the metal doors while I tried to decide if he was telling the truth.

He'd convinced us that he didn't kill Gunnar. But he did.

He'd also blown up the hospital and killed Cinder.

The elevator rang. Buckley looked at the door as it slid back. His eyes were low, then he looked up at us.

The three of us examined at each other, trying to decide if he could be trusted. Fairchild didn't hesitate, she stepped off first. Zale went next. Buckley stared at me.

What choice do I have?

I stepped off the elevator with the others.

Buckley was close behind me. Then without a word, he started walking down the hall closest to the exit.

"Where's Seph?" I asked.

Buckley didn't respond because he knew I'd see soon enough.

I looked at Zale. His eyes were as curious and cautious as mine.

We followed Buckley to a door. It was thick and metal. The sign on it hung at a slant. It read, "MCC Custodian".

"He's in a closet?!" I exclaimed.

From inside his pocket, Buckley retrieved a key. He unlocked the door and with a strong tug, he popped the door open. Then he stood back.

The inside of the closet was black and silent.

A putrid stench wafted over my face and my heart dropped.

"Seph?" I managed to whisper through cracking emotion.

The smell turned my stomach.

Seph.

It smelled like a farm.

Then I heard her bellow.

Nanny.

"Miss Britt?" I heard Seph whisper from the dark.

A shuffling sound, then he was there. Stepping into the light with his goat wrapped in his arms. They were filthy and fragile, but they were alive.

END OF PART ONE

Part One - Bonus Chapter
THE MAN

A man does not become a man simply
by age or change of shape.
A man becomes a man in moments
when choices are made.

The Crisis was upon him in his fourth year of life. He lost his
mother to it, a woman with a kind-heart and a tender touch. For
his whole life, he remembered her wearing the charm around her
neck that she said meant life, but after her death, it was forbidden.

In his littleness and loneliness, a family took him in and raised
him in the belly of the city his mother had died in.
Years went by and the undercity became violent and desperate,
with monsters creeping both above ground and below it.

The boy was taught to fight, taught to steal, taught to hold his
own space, and taught to make himself known. The father, who'd
raised him, a man accustomed to fighting well before the Crisis,
did well for his family below the surface. Soon, the family, which
was torn apart by Crisis and seamed together by fate, took their
place of power among the dwellers of the undercity.

Beyond the bloodshed, there was a burning inside the boy. A
need to be known and to understand where he'd come from. A
longing for laying in the grass in the sunshine and heat. A longing
for answers. Without a mother to tell him who he was, he learned
to bury his questions of identity and truth. Trading them instead,
for weapons and wars waged on truth-tellers and identity-shifters.
But the wondering didn't cease, it only quieted in the dark hours
of violence and power.

Until a voice came. A different kind of whisper. From the
darkness of an alley, he heard his name as his
mother had said it to him. "Lion"

235

He stopped. Again, he heard it. "Lion"
Knowing only what he did of this nickname given from his
mother, he drew closer to the voice.

The Lion boy followed the voice into the darkness.

The voice belonged to a man, wounded, and dying on the cold
pavement of the corridor that no one traversed.

"Help me," the man gargled.
The Lion boy knelt in the puddle, unafraid of the blood, as he'd
seen it so many times before, yet he knew this time was different.
He saw the red life escape from the dying man's middle.

"What's happened to you?" Lion asked. "Who shot you?"
But the man didn't have time for those answers. He knew he
had something more important to give.
From under his jacket, the man struggled to pull something.
"Here," he said to the boy.
"What is it?" Lion asked.
"Take it," the dying man begged.
"What is it?" Lion asked again.
The man fumbled but managed to pull it into view. It was a red
book.
The bullet had pierced it. Blood had soaked the cover.
"A book?" the boy said.
The man stared at him.
"You're a lion, aren't you?" he asked.
Confused, the boy nodded, wondering how the man knew of
his mother's nickname for him.
"Then this is for you now."
"I don't understand," the Lion boy said. "You don't know me,
why would you give this to me--?"

The dying man coughed, and blood dribbled from the corner
of his mouth.
"This is everything I have to leave her," he said.
"Leave who?"
The man's eyes rolled backward, and the boy moved closer,
feeling a sense of kinship. He hoisted the man onto his lap.

"Who?"

"Francine," the man said.

The boy knew Francine. It was not the name of a woman, but of a gun. Then the boy knew who'd shot the man.

"Gunnar?"

The man nodded, slightly.

"Tell her for me, will you?" the man coughed again, fading.

"Tell who?"

The man's eyes went blank, and his breathing hitched.

He was gone.

The Lion boy knew he had a choice then.
He took the book from the dead man's hands.
The bullet hole was still warm.
He knew it was a significant moment. It was a calling.
He needed only to decide if he would answer it.
He stood up with the book in his hands.
The boy stood up as a man.

He opened the book's cover and stared at the handwritten words on the first page. It read:

Within the Ambit, there's a woman named Britt.
She'll be wondering what happened to me.

Part Two

17
THE GUARDIAN

"Where are you taking us?" Fairchild asked.

She was in the front seat with Buckley.

"I know a place where we can hold up," he reached for her hand, but she withheld it from him.

"Where?" Zale asked.

"My grandparents had a farm outside of the city."

I looked at Seph. He'd just finished scarfing down the food we'd given him. He was staring out the window. The goat was balled up in his arms asleep. "Are you okay?"

He turned to look at me, tears balanced in his eyes. I waited for the small smile to press his lips together for me, but they didn't.

He was not okay.

What the hell happened?

We all fell quiet.

"It's okay if you don't want to talk," I said. "You're safe now. Why don't you try to get some sleep?"

He nodded and then turned back to the window.

My mind nagged at me. I wanted to know what he knew. I wanted to understand how he and Maris had been separated and how he'd ended up in a closet above ground.

I knew he needed time before he would speak, but as soon as I got a chance alone with Buckley, I had every intention of discovering how he knew where Seph was hidden.

On hour passed and Seph fell off to sleep, before anyone spoke. Zale whispered, "What'd he tell you?"

"Who?"

"Eamon," he replied.

"He wanted to know if I knew who War Storian was."

"What'd you tell 'em?" Buckley asked.

I looked at him in the rearview mirror. "The truth."

Buckley waited.

"I don't know who War Storian is," I clarified.

Buckley looked at Zale in the mirror.

I turned to Zale. "Wait, do *you* know who he is?"

Zale shook his head, then turned to look out the window.

Is Zale War Storian? I realized there was so much about him that I didn't know, it may have been possible.

"Who's Winnie?" I asked.

Zale looked back at me, then forward toward Buckley.

I looked at Buckley in the rearview mirror, then at Fairchild. She'd fallen asleep against the window.

Zale's eyes searched my face.

"Winnie was my sister," Buckley answered first.

Was?

I looked up, then back at Zale.

"She was my partner," he said. "When I worked for *them*."

"Them?"

He nodded toward Buckley.

"You worked for Rutherford?"

"Basically, except I answered to Gunnar, just like she did."

He nodded toward Fairchild.

"Was he *your* handler?"

Zale shook his head. "No, it wasn't like that."

"What'd you do for them then?"

"I was a Broker." He looked ashamed.

Zale the Broker.

"Winnie and I worked the same platform."

He kept his eyes out the window, "We did shakedowns, broke up black market operations, enforced whatever needed enforcing."

"What happened to her?" I looked at Buckley. His eyes were on the road.

"She was Storian," Zale said. Then he carefully lifted his eyes to look at Buckley in the mirror.

"You *thought* she was Storian," Buckley corrected him.

"I was just a kid," Zale explained. "And Gunnar was like this badazz macho man that I wanted to impress. He gave me orders to keep an eye on Winnie and I did whatever he said. That's when I learned you can't just follow orders blindly," he directed that last part toward Buckley.

"You turned her in? To Gunnar?" I asked.

Zale nodded. "Gunnar hated Storian more than anything. He didn't even give her a chance to explain before he---"

"He killed her," Buckley said. "Her and everyone on the list."

"What list?" I asked, scowling.

Another freaking list.

"She had a set of names on her when she died," Zale said.

"More Storian?"

He nodded.

"People she suspected were a part of it," Buckley said. "She was investigating them for my dad. She had the brains to not turn someone in without being sure."

Zale and I both caught the dig Buckley made with that comment.

"Your dad knows Gunnar killed her?"

Buckley nodded.

"Isn't your dad in charge down there? Why didn't he have Gunnar punished for that?"

Buckley laughed. "You don't get it."

"Get what?"

"Gunnar ran things. Gunnar answered to someone up the pipeline. My dad is the Caller, but he doesn't know any more than the rest of us."

"Is *that* why he wanted you to kill Gunnar? So, he could move up the food chain?" Zale asked.

"My dad had a lot of reasons to want Gunnar dead. And so did I," Buckley clarified. "Years of reasons." I noticed that Buckley glanced toward Fairchild when he said that.

I felt like I was beginning to understand him. He had a deep need for justice.

"After I realized what Gunnar did to Winnie and the others, I turned my badge in," Zale said. "I didn't want to be a part of their organization anymore. Which made life in the Outside even worse. All the people that I pushed around came calling for me and my folks. So, I left."

"But you came back?"

"After a couple years away, it became obvious that Outsiders aren't welcome anywhere else."

Buckley scowled at him. "Only reason they didn't kill him when he came back was because of his old man."

Maris.

We all shared a moment of quiet for Maris.

"After Zale sht the bed with the Underground, his folks got lumped in with him. Your mom was smart to distance herself from you. Your dad shoulda disowned you when you got back."

"I know," Zale said sadly.

"Maybe if your old man had, he'd still be alive," Buckley said coldly. It was cruel to say, but there seemed to be truth to it.

"Your mom disowned you?"

Zale looked at his hands, "Yeah."

I couldn't imagine anything turning me against my children. "Where is she now?"

He exhaled. "She went out months ago looking for Lupio. I thought maybe if I could get some for him, that she'd come back and see what I'd done, then maybe it'd make a difference to her."

"What will happen now, when she goes back?"

Zale looked at me, shaking his head. "I don't know but when she finds out that I'm the reason they poisoned Maris…." He exhaled. "She won't care if I'm dead."

I took Zale's hand from his leg and held it. I could relate to all the guilt he felt. He didn't directly cause any of those things to happen, but I knew from experience that that would never ease the burden of carrying the shame for them.

I have Abigail.
He has Winnie.
I have Chasen.
He has Maris.
Shame.

243

"We're here," Buckley announced. I looked out the window. We were turning into a long driveway, off the main road in the country. From a post hung a sign that read, "Zember".

The drive and fields that surrounded it were lined with aged, white horse fencing. It reminded me of the Ambit.

The jeep jolted to a stop in front of a huge farmhouse. Fairchild and Seph woke with the stop. Nanny let out a frustrated grunt as the quick halt of the vehicle tossed her into the seat in front of her.

"Where are we?" Fairchild asked, rubbing her eyes.

"Zember Farms," Buckley answered. "This old place belonged to my grandparents, once upon a time."

"Have you been here before?" Zale asked.

"No."

"Are there monitors out here?" I asked.

"Not sure but I doubt it. We're probably a hundred miles from where the nest was," Buckley replied.

"We better act like there are, just in case," Zale said.

The men went about unloading the duffle bags that were strapped to the roof of the jeep.

When Buckley handed Fairchild hers, she didn't seem grateful at all. He said something to her quietly, but she stormed off. He looked up at me. "She needs time," he said.

I didn't blame her for being upset with him. He'd turned us in to his father. His sudden attack of conscience only came when he heard what they'd done to Maris and saw what they planned to do with Fairchild.

Seph released Nanny to a patch of grass near the base of the porch. She was delighted to be out in the open country again.

"Stay close, okay?" I advised him.

He nodded, without a word or smile.

Before too long, we had set up camp. Buckley built a fire inside the fireplace of the farmhouse, while Zale patrolled the perimeter of it. Fairchild and I brought blankets and bedding from the bedrooms and made up some beds on the floor. We prepared freeze-dried meals for our hungry bellies.

"Looks like we'll be eating these again for a while," Fairchild complained. She'd been in a terrible mood since we'd gotten out of the Outside.

244

Zale secured the perimeter of the property and set some traps around the camp to make sure that if anything crossed them, we would know. Then the five of us and the goat, sat down on the floor of the farmhouse living room and ate by the fire.

We were all relatively quiet, other than a few lighthearted comments. At one point, I even took a deep breath and exhaled with relief. We were out of the Outside, and away from monitors. I felt safe for the moment. But it was short lived.

Half an hour later, we heard one of Zale's perimeter traps go off. Zale hopped up and ran to the table where his shotgun was.

"What's that!?" Seph asked. It was the first thing he'd said in hours. I went to stand next to him. He picked Nanny up as she bleated her annoyance with being held.

"Shut that goat up!" Zale growled.

Fairchild helped herself to a weapon from the arsenal we had on the table. She loaded a handgun and tucked it into her belt loop and then she slung a rifle over her shoulder.

She went to the window and pushed the curtain back.

Around the corner of the curtain, Fairchild lined her rifle up and looked through the scope of it.

"There's a truck," she whispered.

"At least it's not monitors," Buckley quipped. I noticed that he was the only one still sitting by the fireplace. He was still eating.

"Buckley?" I asked.

"Someone's getting out," Fairchild said. She shifted a latch on the rifle and lined it up.

"Well, don't shoot him," Buckley laughed.

"Shoot who?" Zale asked.

"My brother."

"Sht," Zale said.

"It's Eamon," Fairchild confirmed, putting her weapon down. Zale and I shared a look.

"What the hell is he doing here?" Zale asked.

"I admit that I'm pretty incredible," Buckley gloated. "...but I didn't get you out of the Outside by myself."

"He's on the porch," Fairchild updated us.

"Why's he--?" Zale started to say but was interrupted by the knock at the door.

We all stared at each other.

"Are you gonna let him in?" Buckley asked me. "Or are you gonna stand there with your ungrateful jaw on the floor?"

I looked at Fairchild. She seemed as confused as I was.

I stepped forward to pull the door open. Neither Zale nor Fairchild set their weapons down.

Eamon stood there, in the same pale, yellow shirt that he was wearing hours ago when we'd left him in the Outside. No wonder he didn't yell for help or fight back when the power surge gave him a perfect opportunity. I was sure he was large enough to take us all on at once, if he wanted to.

"Hello, Britt," Eamon smiled.

"Hi."

I stepped back and let him in the room.

The color drained from Seph's face when he saw Eamon step through the door.

"Are you okay?" I asked Seph, returning to his side.

"He – he's the one that locked me in the closet," Seph whispered.

Zale lifted the barrel of his gun to point at Eamon.

Eamon put his hands up in the air. "That's true," he said to Seph. "…and I apologize for scaring you. I didn't have time to explain or introduce myself before."

"Then do it now," I growled.

"There's a lot to explain—"

"Just do it," Fairchild snapped.

Eamon stared at her, then he turned to me, "Two days ago, just after you all left on the Blood Mission, a list came from the Underground. That's how it happens. They send a list and we're just supposed to do what they say. Well, this time it was a list of Storian, and we were supposed to sweep them."

"Kill them?" I asked.

"Murder them," Zale confirmed.

Eamon continued. "We haven't had an order this big in years." He nodded toward Seph, "The kid's name was on the list."

"What?! Why?" I exclaimed.

Eamon looked at Zale. "And so was Maris'."

"Why? He wasn't part of the Storian," Zale scowled.

Eamon's face told another story.

"What?" Zale narrowed his eyes. "He wasn't. I would have known."

246

"Zale," Eamon started.

"He wasn't a part of it. He stayed out of that sht."

Eamon moved toward Zale. "What happened to your dad," Eamon said, "wasn't right. We didn't know—"

"You didn't know?!" Zale stepped up to him. "How could you not know? You work for them!"

"Your dad and mine knew each other for a long time," Eamon said. "Did you know that?"

Zale nodded, "Yeah, my old man mentioned it. So?"

"So?" Eamon repeated, "My dad kept your dad's name off the list for years. He protected him as long as he could. I can personally confirm that. The Underground was on to Maris for a long time, but my dad kept covering for him, and as many of the Storian, as he could."

"Wait, so you're telling me…" Zale moved forward again, "that you two," he looked at Eamon and then Buckley, "are a part of Storian?!"

Eamon's face was still.

"Hell yeah, we are," Buckley said proudly. "Ever since the Underground swept our sister!"

"Winnie?" Fairchild repeated. "That was years ago."

"I know," Buckley said, crossing to her. She seemed hurt that she didn't know this about him. "I wanted to tell you, Fair, I really did, but our father was adamant that no one know. If Gunnar ever found out, I didn't want to put you at risk of ending up on a list."

"Is that why you broke up with me?"

He broke up with her?!

Buckley looked down at his hands.

"You could have been killed!" she scolded him. "Gunnar would have—" she cried. He moved toward her.

"Well, that's not something we have to worry about now, remember?" She hugged him. She squeezed her eyes closed and held him tight.

"So, what are you telling us?" Zale asked, trying to contain his anger. "That your old man and mine were working undercover against the Underground for all these years and my dad never told me?"

"Why would he…" Buckley asked, "after what you did to Winnie?"

Zale's jaw clenched. Buckley's words were cold but true.

247

"The injections they gave Maris weren't Lupio," Eamon said.

"No sht," Zale said.

Eamon sighed, trying to maintain his composure with Zale's aggressions. He continued, "They were Cosmos. But my dad didn't have anything to do with that. He's just keeping up the act, playing along, like he knew the whole time. But believe me," Eamon said to Zale, "he never would have hurt your old man."

Zale's face was skeptical. He lifted the barrel of his gun upward again toward Eamon.

"Yeah, or maybe this is all a damn trap..."

"A trap?!" Buckley laughed. "We risked our azzes getting you out of there! We're completely exposed now. And our dad is still there trying to evacuate the other Storian."

Zale turned his gun toward Buckley, and said, "Yeah, but to what end? Just a few hours ago you told me you were supposed to make sure I didn't come back from the Blood Mission. Now you're telling me that my father was murdered and Seph was supposed to be killed...."

I looked at Seph. His face was red.

"...and you think you're going to waltz in and we're all going to sing campfire songs or something?"

"Zale," I said, moving toward him to keep him calm.

"The Underground wanted you dead," Buckley said. "The Underground put orders out on you. My dad is the one that told me to make sure Gunnar didn't come back. Honestly? I didn't care if either of you came back, but then things changed while we were on the mission, and I—"

"I want answers!" Zale slammed his hand down. He was furious.

"We're giving them to you!" Eamon growled back, stepping forward toward Zale. " Aren't you listening?! We're telling you what happened. We're telling you what's been happening under your nose for the last six years, while you were off being a glory hog, farming for resources or whatever it is you do, while the rest of us were trying to help people. We were trying to expose the Underground."

"And where did that get you?!" Zale stepped forward. "You still don't know sht and the people of the Outside are still trapped under the thumb of whoever the Underground is. How is that helping them? Your story doesn't line up!

You can't be a Broker one day, harassing the poor people of the Outside, shaking 'em down for whatever your dad tells you, and then tell me in the next second that you did it for the Storian cause!"

Eamon's face was furious. He clenched his fists at his sides.

"Can someone please tell me what Storian really is?" I asked, trying to break the tension between the two men before it came to blows.

"The Storian is only interested in mutiny," Zale said, staring directly at Eamon. "*They* want to remove the Underground from control so they can take over."

Eamon shook his head and laughed.

Zale continued, "They're radicals and the more people they win to their agenda, the more people get killed. People like my father!"

"What agenda?" Buckley asked. "The Underground has the agenda, not us. All we want is for people to know the truth."

"Which is what exactly?" I asked.

Buckley looked at me, "Have you ever heard the saying that 'he who controls the past controls the future'?"

I shook my head.

"George Orwell said that. Do you know who he is?"

I shook my head again.

"He was an author in the 1900s. He is one of many authors that they've concealed from us. When the Crisis happened, the book files were erased, libraries were burned to the ground. Have you ever heard of the Holocaust?"

"No," I said.

"Exactly. That's because they don't want you to know."

"Who?" I asked, shaking my head. "The Underground?"

Buckley seemed annoyed with how little I understood.

"Not just the Underground," Eamon said. "Many of the societies we know of, that formed after the Crisis, have adopted these exclusions from history. They called it the Purge. They purged things like art, religion, languages, geography, anything they don't want passed on. We know because we have connections with Storian in most societies. People risk their lives to share this information."

"Why?"

"Because the ones who control the information, control the narrative," Eamon said. "Whatever it is that they're trying to hide from our history, it's worth killing a lot of people. Since many of the books were burned, people started retelling the stories orally. But if no one is left to talk, then—"

I thought of the Ambit and how Eamon's theory seemed to be true.

"You really want to know what Storian is?" Buckley asked me.

I nodded.

"It's a school."

A school?!

"The Storian are teachers and students," he said, with a laugh. "That's all they are."

"A school?" Seph repeated in disbelief.

"I don't understand," I said. "Why would the Underground hunt them then?"

"Because they don't want anything taught that they don't have control over. And they want to control the truth about everything."

"Everything?"

"Everything that happened before the Crisis," Buckley clarified. "Storian teachers hold the history of our world."

"The unedited version anyway," Eamon added.

Storian teachers?

I thought of James.

Was he Storian?

I remembered how passionate he was about bringing books into the Ambit. How he wanted to introduce new ideas to us. How he wanted to educate us about what happened in the world beyond our borders.

I watched as Zale slid down into a chair in the corner of the room. He seemed to recognize the truth in what they were telling us.

"Did you know?" I asked him. "Did you know that Storian's a school?"

He shook his head. "I've never heard it described like that, no."

He wiped his hand over his face. "All the Underground ever told us is that Storian is like a disease, spreading lies about what happened to create chaos and mutiny."

"Chaos? Mutiny?" Eamon growled. "Storian aren't violent. Never have been. Most of them are elderly or children."

"What did Maris say Storian was?" I asked Zale.

"He talked lot about the way things used to be before the Crisis," Zale said. "I didn't know he was trying to teach me. He wanted me to know, but I..." Zale stopped and thought for a second. "I never had much use for it."

"Maris," Eamon replied, "hid books after the Crisis...once he knew they were burning 'em. He and Lucita would teach children in the early years. The ones that were left behind after the Crisis, the ones without parents. Most of those kids are still there," Eamon said. "They're grown, of course, but they're still there. Maris knew them from the time they were little."

Zale's face was red and swollen.

"Did you know *that?*"

He nodded. "I knew he always had a soft spot for the outcasts," Zale said. "They named me after one of them. That's why he never wanted to leave and why people from the Outside didn't mess with him much. He was like—"

"—everyone's favorite uncle," Buckley said.

Zale looked up at Buckley with surprise. Buckley's remorse for Maris' death was genuine.

We were all quiet for a moment, remembering Maris.

"I wasn't with him when he died," Seph blurted, like the words were burning in his mouth.

Zale looked up.

"I wasn't with him," Seph's chin quivered.

I moved toward him, but he remained planted in place, staring at Zale, as if he owed him an explanation.

"He got really sick," Seph's voice cracked as tears slid down his cheeks "...from the injections. He asked me to get the Caller."

Seph turned to look at Eamon, "Rutherford. Your dad," he said with disdain.

Then he looked back to Zale, "Rutherford told me to go back to the unit, to stay with Maris until someone came and I did. I thought they were going to send help."

"We—" Eamon started to say.

"Let him talk," Zale growled.

Seph blinked, looking between the men. His eyelashes were weighed down with tears. His blue eyes were tired and bloodshot with the burden of the memory.

"When Rutherford came, Eamon was with him." He sniffed. "They talked to Maris alone for a bit and I thought they were going to give him more medicine, something to help him."

Zale's face was stoic. I watched his fist clench on his lap.

"The next thing I knew," Seph cried, then looked at Eamon, "….he was carrying me away."

"I—" Eamon wanted to explain but stopped himself.

"I tried to stay with him, Zale. I screamed and kicked and bit him," Seph cried. "But I wasn't strong enough," he sobbed.

I scowled at Eamon. His eyes dropped to the floor. Then I recognized that the blood on the shoulder of his yellow shirt must have been from where Seph bit him. I felt a little better that Seph had managed to put up some sort of a fight.

"He locked me in closet!" Seph nearly spit in Eamon's direction when he said it.

"Seph, I did it to protect you," Eamon said softly.

"I had no choice!" Seph screamed at him. "I would have stayed with him. I never would have chosen to hide like coward in a closet, Zale!"

Zale stood and crossed to Seph. He wrapped his arms around him and Seph sobbed.

There was something in that moment between the men. A question of honor or dignity. Something I could feel but couldn't understand.

Zale pulled away from Seph and took his face in his hands, "That's why Eamon did what he did."

Seph's sobs calmed as he listened.

"Your honor would've gotten you killed, Seph, and Eamon knew that. He wasn't right to force you, but he wasn't wrong to keep you safe. Do you understand the difference?"

Seph sniffed. He shook his head slightly.

"My dad woulda wanted you safe, kid," Zale shook his head. "More than anything, he would have wanted you safe."

Eamon added. "He asked me to get you out, Seph, and I promised him I would."

Seph nodded, understanding. Zale let go of his face and Seph wiped the liquid from it. Then he straightened his shoulders and looked around at the rest of us. He seemed embarrassed but he had no reason to be. We all understood. I pressed my lips together to reassure him, as he'd always done for me.

After a moment of quiet, I asked, "Why was Seph on the list in the first place?"

Eamon sat defeated in the corner. He looked up, "It was his necklace."

I scowled. Seph looked at him.

I remembered Eamon asking me about it when he was questioning me in the Outside.

"What necklace?" Fairchild asked.

Seph reached under his shirt and pulled the necklace with the fish charm into view.

"It's a fish, so what?" she asked.

"It's not just a fish," Eamon said. "It's a symbol."

"Of what?"

"Another piece of history they want erased," Eamon explained.

"Which is?"

"Religion," Buckley said. When most of us failed to recognize that word, he clarified. "Faith."

"Faith? In what--?" I scowled, "--fish?"

He laughed, "No."

"Then what?"

Eamon answered, "God."

God?

The character in Isla's book?

"God's a myth," Fairchild was quick to say.

"Well, that's what many believe," Eamon said. "Because information about Him is limited." Eamon turned to Seph. "There was a time that God's people used fish symbols just like that one to signal to each other."

"To signal what?" I asked.

"That they believed."

"In God?"

"Why would they need to use a symbol to do that?"

"Because," Buckley explained, "back then people were murdered for their beliefs."

"That sounds familiar," Zale said.

"Exactly," Buckley replied. "History repeats itself when we don't learn from it. That's exactly what Storian wants to change."

"So, they saw that Seph had a necklace with that symbol and assumed what? That he was Storian?" I asked.

Eamon shook his head.

"But he's a kid!"

"There are Storian children," Eamon said. "There are probably more children than adults actually. They're the students."

"And they kill them, sweep them, too?"

Eamon closed his eyes and shook his head in shame. "How many children have you seen in the Outside?"

My stomach turned.

"A few years ago," Eamon said, "Someone started sneaking the children out and taking them to the Collective. There's an unspoken understanding between all the societies, that the Collective is off limits for adults. No one is allowed to mess with them. It's the one thing all the societies seem to agree on."

"Who moved them?" I asked.

Eamon looked at Buckley.

Buckley looked at Fairchild.

"War Storian?" I asked, understanding the looks they were sharing. It was so obvious. That's why he was the Underground's number one enemy.

They nodded.

"So, he's wanted by the Underground for taking the children?"

Eamon laughed, "That and he's the one that moves the books between societies."

"What books?"

"Teaching materials. Anything he can get his hands on. Anything rare or limited or censored. Anything *they* tried to hide," Eamon explained.

Teaching materials.

The journeys.

James went on the journeys to bring back teaching materials to the Ambit.

Maybe that was why James came to the Ambit in the first place? To teach. But the Ambit was closed. No one else could have moved in and out unnoticed. James was the only one. Becoming a part of the Ambit is the only way he could have moved materials.

Was James Storian?

Was he War Storian?

My heart raced. Could that explain where he's been all this time? Why he never returned? Maybe he saw that there was a greater need than what we---?

Would he have abandoned us, abandoned Chasen, for Storian's cause? To save other children? To teach?

"So, who is he?" Zale spoke up for the first time in moments.

Buckley shrugged, "No one knows, but that's not the point. The point is that as long as War Storian is moving books and information between societies, people are getting wiser. The wiser they get, the more they realize just how controlled they've been and that terrifies the Underground."

"Because they're hiding something?" I asked.

"Because they're hiding something," Eamon repeated.

James.

"So, is it you?" Zale asked Eamon.

I looked at Eamon.

"You snuck Seph out to protect him," Zale said. "So, is it you? Are you War Storian?"

Eamon shook his head, "No, I'm not. I snuck Seph out because it was the right thing to do. War Storian set the example, I just followed it."

Zale was quiet.

"You must know who he is?" Fairchild pressed.

"War Storian doesn't reveal himself to anyone. Even to Storian. It could be more than one person for all we know," Buckley said. "The Underground thinks it might be. He moves so quickly and gets in and out of places that are impossible to access. It could be a whole team of people!"

"But you're not a part of it?" Zale asked Eamon again, suspicious.

"No, I'm not." Eamon's eyes burned at him.

"And it doesn't matter anyway, because it's what War Storian represents that matters," Eamon added. "That's the point of the mask. Anyone can wear it and keep the movement going."

"So, you just blindly follow someone, when you don't even know who he is? You haven't even seen his face!?"

"I wouldn't be the first to follow someone without seeing their face," Eamon said, referring to Zale's time working for the Underground.

"The difference is that War Storian puts information in the hands of Storian and lets people decide for themselves."

"All the information, except his identity," Zale griped.

"What kind of information?" Seph asked. We all stopped and looked at him. I'd almost forgotten he was there listening.

Eamon smiled, "History books, maps, encyclopedias…"

"Bibles?" Seph asked.

Eamon's smile grew even larger. "Those are very rare, but yes."

Seph and I shared a look.

James.

"A Bible?" Zale asked.

"A book that tells the history of God," Seph said.

Fairchild looked at him, "How'd you know that?"

"I've seen one," Seph smiled.

Eamon continued, "All these years, War Storian has been arming people with knowledge. And the more it spreads, the more powerful the people become."

"You mean, the more powerful War Storian becomes," Zale growled.

Eamon pushed his fist into his hand. "People are realizing that education is a weapon that can free them. Every person that picks up and reads a book someone else has tried to hide from them, becomes Storian and it spreads. The more people know, the more they grow and make their own decisions. If they can do that, then they can move out of their societies and--"

"…get eaten by monitors." Fairchild interrupted coldly. "None of this matters as long as monitors are eating people."

"Exactly, Fair," Buckley said, taking her face in his hands. "Now you understand why I had to blow up the nest. The Underground wants to understand the monitors, that's why they sent us on the Blood Mission. At no point was the plan to kill Cinder, it was to collect her blood, so they could learn about her! What's there to learn if she's just going to breed killers?"

Eamon added, "They wanted her blood so they can learn how to control her."

"She was different, Buckley," she replied, pulling her face from his hands. "She didn't kill us. She can't help her instinct to breed, but she didn't kill us. We may have killed off an entire species of dragon, just because we didn't understand them."

"What's there to understand?" Buckley asked. "They were eating our people!"

"See, you're thinking isn't all that different from the Underground's," Fairchild said. "Make sure you're at the top of the food chain. Kill anything that gets in your way and never…" her eyes narrowed on him, "…never lose control."

She had a good point.

"How do we know that War Storian is sharing the information freely? That he isn't just moving information that helps his cause, and radicalizes people to rally under *him*? Maybe there's a reason the Underground has kept things from us? Maybe it's for our own good?!"

"You, of all people, know the Underground is not in place for our good," Buckley said gently.

"What I know," Fairchild's eyes welled up, "…is that if War Storian was sneaking out children, to protect them, then he forgot about me."

We were all silent.

I looked at Zale. I knew he felt the same as Fairchild, but there was something about Eamon and Buckley's explanation of everything that made sense to me.

"He's not a hero," she said. "He's just like every other man in history. He has an agenda and will only move information that moves him up…and you…" she looked at Buckley, "…became a part of it."

"How could you think –?"

"Isn't it obvious?" Zale cut in, "Your family wants to be on top. Top of the food chain, top of the information train. That's the only thing Rutherford cares about. That's why he's playing both sides. Whoever moves him up first, gets his loyalty. It drives him crazy that he hasn't been called up by the Underground, after how many years?" Zale said. "This War Storian character has offered him a position and he has jumped at the opportunity and you two have jumped in with him."

"The truth will come out," Eamon said quietly, shaking his head.

"What truth!?" Fairchild asked. "No one is keeping anything from you, that's just something you say to make yourself feel important. To give yourself some imaginary war to fight. In the meantime, you really are causing disorder and people are dying for it."

"Fairchild," Buckley started to say.

"They're lying to you, Buckley!" she yelled. "All of them! The Underground and Storian. Don't be an idiot!"

Buckley's face went serious. "Don't call me that."

Eamon was calm, "None of this changes the fact that Seph's name was on that list. They wanted us to sweep a child because of a charm around his neck. A charm that symbolizes a religion that they don't want us to know existed. Think about that! Why does it matter to them if we believe in something they think is a lie? Why would they care?! Unless there was truth to it?"

Zale sat back in his chair and sighed.

Then Eamon said, "In an upside-down world, we have to stand upright on the truth."

I looked up.

Did he just say what I thought he did?

Eamon was staring at me.

Those words belonged to James.

He knew those words meant something to me.

"What'd you just say?" I asked.

"The truth is all we have," Eamon said.

Zale looked back and forth between us, as we stared at each other, understanding something that Zale did not.

"Britt, can we have a word in private?" Eamon asked.

Zale scowled, then started to answer for me, "I don't think that' such a good—"

"Yes," I said.

18
THE BOOK

I followed Eamon outside to a fire pit in the front yard of the farmhouse. We took a few minutes to find kindling and logs in the overgrown mess of brush and grass, then put a flame to the wood, so that we could get warm.

"You know who I am, don't you?" I asked, after the silence between us sat for too long. Not only did Eamon quote James to me but he seemed to know I was from the Ambit too. He'd hinted at it during his line of questioning in the Outside.

I watched the crackling fire reflect off his face. He stared at it intently. He seemed nervous all the sudden.

"I do," he said.

"Who else knows?"

"Only Maris."

"What do you know about me?"

He looked at me. "You're from the Ambit. You're the daughter to Aldam and Genevieve. Mother of Isla and Chasen…" he looked at the farmhouse, "…and now Seph."

"…and?"

I pressed him. If he knew all of that he must know the rest too.

"…and…wife to James."

I released the air that was hostage in my lungs. After years of not knowing, I could feel that this would be the moment with answers.

"You know my husband?"

He nodded.

I swallowed.

"How?"

"James was wanted in the Outside."

He is War Storian!

"Is that why he came to the Ambit? To hide from the Underground?"

"He went to the Ambit to --"

I looked down at my hands, they were shaking.

Things were starting to become clear to me. My adrenaline was kicking in after such a long day, but at least I was getting answers.

"He's Storian, isn't he?"

Eamon seemed relieved that I understood. He nodded his head.

"Where is he now?"

Eamon was quiet.

"Is he War Storian?"

Eamon looked up. His eyebrows crinkled.

"No, Britt, he's not."

"Then where is he? Is he back in the Outside?"

Eamon's eyes were heavy.

"Eamon?"

He looked down and reached into his bag. He pulled a book from it and handed it to me. By the light of the fire, I could see that it was red. The corners of the book were rolled and damaged from wear and I could feel that the cover was crusted with something.

"What's this?" I asked.

Eamon swallowed hard and then said, "That was his book."

Was.

I opened the front cover of the book.

"His story," Eamon clarified.

"His story?" I repeated, looking up again. Then I angled the book in the firelight to read the inscription on the inside of the book.

> "Within the Ambit, there's a woman named Britt.
> She'll be wondering what happened to me."

I looked up.

He knew I'd be left behind. That I'd want to know why he didn't come home.

"I don't understand," I said. "Did he abandon us?" My throat tightened.

"No," Eamon shook his head thoughtfully.

"Then what happ--?"

Eamon pulled the book upward and a beam of light pierced it. There was a hole that went all the way through the book.

It was a bullet hole.

I gasped, dropping the book onto my lap.

"Is that?"

Eamon's dark eyes lifted to search mine.

"Is he?"

Eamon closed his eyes and exhaled.

"He's dead?"

He didn't want to say the words any more than I wanted to hear them.

Slowly Eamon reached over and tapped on the cover of the book. "These words are where he lives now."

A gasp tore itself from my lips and my hands covered my mouth. I felt like I'd been holding that breath for all the years I'd missed him. Now it was cracking me open, escaping every way it could.

The crusted substance on the book is dried blood.
His blood.

My chest felt heavy. I couldn't breathe. Tears came faster and heavier and soon I was hyperventilating. Years of pent-up hope and grief allowed itself to burst from me, against my wishes.

It was over.

I had my answer.

James...is...dead.

I simultaneously wished I didn't know and felt relief for knowing.

How could this be true? It can't be.

He is War Storian. I was sure of it.

He must still be alive.

I sat back up, uncovered my face, and decided it wasn't true.

"Are you okay?" Eamon asked.

261

I didn't answer. I couldn't.

Eamon took the book from my lap and sat it on his.

"It's been five years," he said.

I looked at him and then melted in emotion all over again.

He was telling me James was dead. He knew how long it'd been.

It felt so final. It felt surreal. It felt wrong, but it also felt true.

I gasped and gulped for air between sobs. Eamon tried to reach out and place his hand on my shoulder, but I jerked my body away from him. I turned away so that he couldn't see my face, but I knew the convulsions of my body would give me away.

I didn't want to be touched. For so many years, I had no one to touch and hold me when I cried over James. I couldn't expect my children to do that for me, that wasn't their responsibility, it was my job to do that for them. As a result, I would only allow myself to wake up in the night to mourn him, in silence and solitude.

I looked at the book on Eamon's lap. "How did you get it?"

Eamon looked down. "I found him." He hesitated, "…in the Outside, in an alley off the Floor. He was shot."

"Why would someone—?"

"He was still alive when I found him. The book was in his jacket when --"

I whimpered, wiping my face with the sleeve of my shirt.

Eamon pulled a handkerchief from his bag and handed it to me.

"Why did he give it to you?"

"I've asked myself that same question for years," Eamon said.

I stared at him.

"Maybe because I was the only one there. Because I was his only option."

I looked down.

"But…" he continued, "It was odd because I was walking past the alley where he'd been shot and I---I was so used to bodies and the violence of the Underground, I'm not sure I would have stopped, but --But James called to me."

"So, he knew who you were?"

"No," Eamon said. "That's why it was odd. I'd heard of him, but I'd never actually met him. He didn't know me, but he called to me."

"He called your name?"

"No," he said. "He didn't call me Eamon."

I watched his face for an explanation.

"He called me by the nickname my mother had given me."

Eamon looked at me in amazement, "She called me Lion. At first, I thought I imagined it, but then I heard it again. It was coming from the alley. That's when I found him. I'm ashamed to say it wasn't his need for help that pulled me down that alley toward him. It was pure curiosity."

Eamon seemed embarrassed. "My whole life I'd been raised to puff my chest up and to intimidate and not be intimidated. But when James called me Lion, it reminded me of my mother, and something happened. He called something out of me."

"Why did she call you Lion?"

"She was from Nigeria. In Africa. Lions in Nigeria were extinct long before I was born, but she said I was born a lion."

"How did James know to call you that?"

Eamon looked at me again, "I don't know."

Eamon took a long stick from the ground in front of us and stoked the wood in the fire pit. The flames caught hold of new wood and reenergized.

"The book," Eamon said, "was on him when he was shot, but it didn't stop the bullet. It may have slowed the bullet down, which is why he was still alive when I found him. But it did hit his chest and within moments of calling to me, he was gone."

My face pinched as more tears trickled out. I hadn't considered what it would be like to know the details of his death. I wasn't prepared for the agony of knowing that someone had murdered him.

My mind sobered as darker thoughts clouded in around my sadness. "Who killed him?"

Eamon searched my face for a moment. He knew.

"Who?" I whispered.

"He was on a list."

A list of Storian.

Eamon slowly reached down and touched my ankle. At first, I didn't understand what that meant.

"May I?" he asked.

I nodded. Eamon pulled my pant leg up, revealing the gun holstered there. He pulled it out and handed it to me, turning it on its side.

The fire light barely illuminated the word on the side of the gun, but I didn't need to see it, I knew what was written there. *GUNNAR*

I dropped the gun on the ground as if it was a snake that just bit me. This whole time I'd carried the gun of the man who murdered my husband.

Francine. This may have been the gun that killed James.

"You and I have shared a similar enemy," Eamon said. "The same man that killed my sister, killed James. That's why I was surprised to see you holding this gun earlier," Eamon explained.

I cussed at Gunnar's memory. Then my mind shifted, and I relished that I had been there to witness his death. Cinder allowed the monitors to attack him, and I hadn't understood why. Maybe she sensed what he had done, or maybe she was protecting us from him. Either way, Buckley was the one that delivered the lethal gunshot to Gunnar's chest. In the same manner that Gunnar had killed James. Suddenly, I liked Buckley a lot more.

Eamon turned around to look at the farmhouse behind us. Seeing that no one was within earshot, he said, "I don't know how much more time he'll allow me to speak to you alone..."

He?

Allow?

Zale.

"But unfortunately, Britt, there's more that I need to tell you while I have the chance."

"I think I've heard enough for one day," I replied, exhausted. Eamon took a deep breath, like he was about to do something he didn't want to. "I know, but this is important."

"What?" I was concerned by his added seriousness.

"There are things you need to know before we go back in there." Eamon nodded his head toward the farmhouse. "Things that will be hard to hear."

"What?"

"Someone in there is working for the Underground."

"What?"

Eamon reached into his bag a second time and pulled something from it, his fist was clenched over the object.

"Today, back in the Outside, I left the door unlocked so Buckley could come in and help you and the others get out before things got worse. But I didn't expect them to let you go so easily. When they did, I didn't understand why," he added.

"So, why did they?"

"Because they already had what they wanted," Eamon unfolded his hand and showed me the half-full vial of Cinder's blood. "Someone handed it over while you were there."

"How did you get it?"

"My dad intercepted it before it got moved up the chain."

"Who gave it to them?"

"That's what I want to know. Someone handed it over," he said. "I was with you the whole time, so I know it wasn't you, which is why I'm asking. Who had the vial?"

"I don't know."

"Britt," he said. "I've been Storian since James passed away. No one knew, except my father, Buckley, and Maris. But now, they will. And they'll kill me if they find me." He scowled. "I just gave up everything to get this vial out of there because I know they want it for something that can be used against Storian. I can't go back now. Do you understand that? I gave up everything tonight, so that I could come here to warn you."

"Me?"

Eamon's eyes were heavy. "If it'd been anyone else, I don't know I would have been brave enough to do it. But you're in danger and if James were here, he would have—"

James.

Eamon is trying to warn me out of respect for James.

"Please think hard. Who had this vial last?" he asked. "We need to know who's against us."

I tried to remember. So much had happened in such a short time and my mind was exhausted. I couldn't think straight.

Maris is dead.

James is dead.

Forever.

Focus.

The vial.

I retraced the moments when we arrived back to the Outside.

"Fairchild had all of the vials," I retraced warily. "When we got back, she offered Cinder's blood to Buckley but---" I looked up at him. "Zale took it. He took it from Fairchild before Buckley had a chance to get it."

Eamon closed his eyes and sighed. "That's what we suspected. And it's a damn shame because Maris really hoped that he'd changed."

"But why would Zale--?" I asked aloud not expecting an answer.

"Even Maris didn't trust him, Britt. And Lucita, his own mother, disowned him."

I stared at Eamon, trying to decide if I believed what he was saying about Zale.

"Zale isn't what you think he is," I said. "Why would he give the Underground the vial of Cinder's blood. He thought they wanted Buckley to kill him. He isn't interested in helping them."

"I think you're underestimating his survival skills, Britt. He may have offered them the blood as a peace offering. He knows how to survive, even if it means turning over his friends. He'll do it. He did it to my sister."

I thought about my conversation with Zale while we waited at the rendezvous point. He wanted me to turn Cinder's blood over because he thought it would help us get in good with the Underground.

Maybe there is some truth to what Eamon was saying.

Eamon stared at me. "That's what kids from the Outside do. They learn to separate survival from emotion."

"You don't know him like I do," I said.

Eamon sighed. "Maris was worried about you getting too close with him. He was worried that Zale would charm you."

Charm. Had I been charmed?

My disappointment must have been very apparent.

"You're with him then?" Eamon studied my face.

"Excuse me?"

"You and Zale. You're together?"

"We're partners--" I started, but Eamon interrupted me.

"You don't have to lie, Britt."

I was quiet. I wondered if Eamon felt like I'd betrayed James by having a relationship with Zale before I knew for sure what'd happened to my missing husband.

"I was on the platform the day you found the tooth," he explained. "Remember? And after that, when you and Zale were in my father's office. I'm embarrassed to say it, but I—was the one that threw the tomato at the window when you and he were—"

"That was you? Why?"

Eamon seemed embarrassed.

"Zale has a checkered history in the Outside. I've seen what he does with women. He uses them for what he wants, gets whatever benefits he wants and then disposes of them. Like he did with Winnie. I know it's not my place, because you didn't even know me, but I felt like I owed it to James to try to..."

"Protect me?"

He nodded.

I took a deep breath.

"You're right, Eamon," I said. "that wasn't your place."

Eamon's face fell flat.

"I appreciate what you're trying to do here, and I can't tell you how much it means to me to know that you were with James in his last..." I swallowed, "...moments. And that you've held onto his book for all these years. And now you've risked bringing it to me. But, Eamon, I am so damn tired of men thinking that it is their job to protect me."

I stared at him.

"Do you know how I've survived without James? All these years, against the Guiding Authority, against my father's wishes for me? And out here? And in the Outside? By making mistakes. Not by depending on a man," I growled.

"Do you know why I was the first female farmer in the Outside? Against Maris' wishes? Because I was willing to die. Did you know that *I'm* the one that got Cinder's blood sample on the Blood Mission? Me. By myself. You know how I was able to do all of that? Because I was willing to die. I was willing to make mistakes. Because I didn't want to be told anymore that I can't do something just because I'm female. Today, when you and I were in the room in the Outside, did you know that I had Francine hidden on my lap and that I had made peace with the idea of killing you...if that's what it would have taken for me to get out so I could find Seph?"

Eamon's eyes widened.

"I think *you're* the one that has underestimated *my* survival skills!" I growled.

Eamon listened.

"I've made mistakes. A lot of them…"

Abigail.

"But they're *my* mistakes. And I don't need to be rescued from them."

He nodded, "Okay, I just—"

"I'm still talking. What's happened between me and Zale, is between me and Zale. I don't owe you an explanation for that. And maybe I'm about to find out that I'm not as good of a judge of character as I thought I was. Maybe this will be another mistake I've made that I will learn from, but you will not be rescuing me from him because I do not need you to rescue me. Do you understand?"

He nodded.

"Now, I will work with you to figure out what's happened. I want to understand all of this too. But you need to see me as your equal, not someone that you're responsible for saving. Can you do that?"

Eamon smiled.

"Can you?"

He nodded.

"You made choices in the Outside, to become Storian. You left tonight, of your own volition. You gave up everything because you chose to give everything up. I appreciate it, but let's be clear. I do not owe you anything because you did that."

Eamon laughed, condescendingly.

"Why are you laughing? I'm being serious."

"Because now I know why James stayed in the Ambit for you."

I retracted.

"You're as tough as they say you are."

They?

Tough?

"…and I now, I know why you didn't leave the Ambit…"

"The Ambit?" Zale's voice crept up behind us.

Eamon and I turned to find Zale behind us.

How long has he been there?

"You told him you're from the Ambit?" He seemed offended. "You trusted him with that?!"

268

Zale was threatened. It had taken me months to tell him where I was from. It appeared that it'd only taken me moments to open up to Eamon.

I didn't know how to answer.

How do I explain how Eamon knows where I'm from without explaining how? Without telling him everything?

"We're having a private conversation, Zale," Eamon said, standing up.

I remained seated, trying to find a way to explain.

"Are you okay?" Zale ignored Eamon.

I looked up.

"I'm fine."

"Are you sure? Is he bothering you?"

"Bothering me?"

Zale stepped closer to Eamon, "What'd you say to her?"

"Zale!"

Zale was focused on Eamon. "You need to leave her alone, she doesn't want you here!"

"Excuse me," I said. "I never said that. What makes you think you get to speak on my behalf!" I stood up. "You two seem to have some unfinished business to discuss. I'm not interested in being in the middle of it. So, leave me out of it."

I handed Eamon his handkerchief back.

"What'd you say to her?" Zale asked Eamon. "Are you down here filling her head with lies?"

"Filling my head?!" I spun around. "Is my head so easy to fill, Zale?!"

He didn't answer.

"Some stupid Ambit girl, doesn't know anything. Needs to be told what to think! Is that what you think I am?" I scowled. "Zale, did you really think it was your place to come down here to make sure I wasn't being brainwashed?" I asked.

"That's not what I said," Zale rebutted.

I shook my head. "I'm going to bed."

I bent over and picked James' book up from the log.

"What's that?" Zale asked.

"It's a book, Zale!" I yelled, exhausted. "Eamon gave me a book. A book. It's my book! Is that okay?!"

I felt a lump creep into my throat again.

Don't cry.

Don't let them see you cry!

KJ. SPENCER

Crying does something to men. It disarms them when it's directed at them and infuriates them when it's directed at another man. And no matter the reason, or how justified the tears may be, after they've fallen, it solidifies the man's idea that women need to be treated as some soft and delicate thing.

But they're the delicate ones. They can't handle my emotions and see me as anything but a wilted flower.

Tears aren't the evidence of weakness, but of fierceness that can no longer be contained.

Zale and Eamon looked at each other.

My chest heaved with anger and exhaustion.

"I'm going to bed now," I said. "Don't worry, I think I can get all the way back to the farmhouse in the dark without anyone to protect me!"

Neither of them said anything.

I stormed away from them.

My emotions were all over the place. I wanted to scream.

Zale doesn't know that I just learned of my husband's murder.

Zale doesn't know that Eamon just cast a shadow over everything I feel for him.

Zale doesn't know that I'm torn over him and that I'm grieving the loss of my last love at the same time.

Zale doesn't know.

He can't know.

I stopped on the porch of the farmhouse and sobbed silently in the shadows. I pulled James' book to my chest and squeezed it. His precious words were hidden under the pages splattered in blood and I was the protector of them now.

Were they Storian secrets?

Too much.

Too many secrets.

Can no one be trusted?

I took a deep breath and calmed my nerves. I shook my hands, trying to quell the shake in them. I was exhausted and while I knew my emotions were real and valid, I also knew I desperately needed sleep to think clearly.

I found my way into the farmhouse. Seph and Nanny were curled up in the corner by the fire, sleeping side by side. I made a bed near them. Before I settled in, I tucked James' book under my shirt. I wasn't going to leave it anywhere anyone could find it.

Laying next to Seph, I studied his face and thought of what his last two days were like. Immense gratitude filled me as the realization sunk in that I'd almost lost him too.

Too close.

Tomorrow. I thought. *Tomorrow I will find the truth.*

Then, I concluded.

Then I'm going to the Ambit to get my daughter back.

19
THREE DAYS

I woke to Nanny standing over me. She stared down at me, like she was trying to decide if I was food.

I reached up and patted the top of her head which she seemed to enjoy. She knelt on her bent legs and with a thud she tipped over on her side. She was trying to cuddle with me.

I rolled onto my side and allowed her to nest next to my stomach. I patted the wiry dry hair on her head and back. She didn't allow me to stop; each time I tried to pull my hand away she would nudge me with her stubby horn buds. She never seemed to care about me before, only Seph. But I guess over time, she began to trust me, finding me a suitable substitute in his absence.

Seph was across the room sitting at the table with Zale and Fairchild. They were eating. I didn't say anything to them; instead, I listened while I patted Nanny's back.

"Then what happened?" Seph asked. He was smitten with Zale and Fairchild, who I assumed were sharing stories of the Blood Mission with him.

"Then she screamed at her," Zale recounted. "And Cinder backed off."

Fairchild looked at me with a smile. "She saved my life," she said with gratitude.

Seph glanced at me and pressed his lips together. It was nice to see him smile. He seemed to be feeling better.

Zale and I stared at each other. The story they told of our time together on the mission, reminded me of my feelings for him. We'd nearly died, and, in those moments, we'd looked out for each other.

If he really is up to something, like Eamon said he was, wouldn't it have shown in those moments? Wouldn't those be the times that he would have abandoned me, if it was all an act?

Zale looked away from me and I felt something was lost between us.

Trust.

I remembered him standing in front of me while Cinder beared down on me. He didn't budge.

Was it possible that he could do both? Could he care for me and betray me at the same time?

Eamon said survival was in his nature. *Could he care for me and then, without telling me, turn the blood over to the Underground, to win himself some redemption or protection?*

The answer was obvious but painful.

Yes. He could do both. He could be both.

The question then was what would I choose to do with that?

I thought of James and *his* secrets.

I've been down this road before.

Was I really willing to go down that road again? I waited for years to understand James' secrets, and now I wondered if I'd ever really known him at all.

I twisted the wedding ring on my finger.

Why didn't he tell me?

He was a part of something he never told me about.

Or had he? Did he try to tell me? Did I miss it?

Either way, I should have known. I was his wife.

I pinched my eyes shut.

Was.

He's dead. I reminded myself.

Now I know for sure.

I felt for his book under the cover of my shirt.

Bullet hole, blood splatter and secrets.

I was tired of secrets.

"Where's Eamon?" I asked Fairchild. I wanted to tell him of my intentions to go back to the Ambit for Isla.

Zale stared at me, obviously annoyed that I was asking for Eamon. He picked up his things from the table and left without a word.

"They went for a walk," Fairchild said. She stood from the table, and I noticed she was wearing Eamon's yellow t-shirt with nothing on her legs. The shirt was oversized on her, like a nightgown, but short enough to see her bare thighs and pale skin.

I watched Seph's face as she passed him. He seemed to be trying not to look.

"Seph, can you come get Nanny?" I asked, to distract him.

"Sure," he said. He did as I asked.

"Why don't you let her down outside? There's lots of grass for her here."

He smiled and nodded.

As he left with the goat, I looked at Fairchild. She was adjusting her clothes on a clothesline above the fireplace.

"You washed your clothes?" I asked. It was obvious that she'd bathed too. She looked fresh and radiant.

She sat down on the floor next to me.

"Yeah," she replied. "I couldn't stand it. I needed to wash the last couple of days off me."

I nodded.

"There's a well outside," she said. "And a pot, if you want to do the same?"

She reached into her bag and pulled a bar of soap from it, "You can use my soap," she offered.

"Thanks."

I stood up from my bed on the floor and stretched. I was careful to keep the book under my shirt and tucked into my pants so it wouldn't fall out.

I made my way outside and found the pot and water pump where Fairchild said it was. I filled the pot and took it to the fire pit that Eamon and I had sat at the night before.

As I was rekindling the fire embers, Seph came to sit with me.

"Nanny doesn't know what to do with all this grass," he said, watching his goat hustle from spot to spot. She busied herself rushing from one green plot of grass to the next greener plot.

"She's happy here," he said.

I watched the goat. She was happy and safe.

Seph smiled.

He may not have been happy but at least he was safe.

"This place reminds me of the Ambit," he said, looking over the tall grassy fields surrounding the farmhouse.

"Me too," I said, placing the water pot into the embers of the fire.

"Do you think we will ever go back to the Outside?"

I shook my head, "I don't think we can."

"Then can we go back to the Ambit? To see Isla?"

I watched his face. I didn't want to get his hopes up until I spoke with Eamon. The truth was, without Maris, I wasn't sure I could find my way back to the Ambit.

"I don't know if we can go back there either," I said.

"Then where can we go?"

"Honestly, Seph, I don't know," I thought for a moment. "There's a place called the Collective..."

Seph scowled at me. "They only accept children."

"I know," I said, watching his face for understanding.

His eyes searched mine. I could read the disappointment in them.

"It wouldn't be forever," I said. "You'd age out in a few years, but by then I'd have all of this figured out. I just need some time to find a place where we —"

Seph shook his head, "No."

I exhaled.

We both sat in the quiet. A breeze swept over us, and I inhaled the smells of the fresh air. I watched Nanny continue to graze on the abundant grass around the firepit.

I moved over on the log next to Seph to sit closer to him. We stared at the fire.

"If there were other animals here, and you knew Nanny was going to be safe, and fed and taken care of at this farmhouse. Wouldn't you consider leaving her here? To keep her safe?"

Seph shook his head. "It's not the same."

"Seph, if I had known what the Outside was going to be like, I wouldn't have allowed you to come with me," I said. "The things that happened there, to you and to me, they're going to haunt us for a long time. You shouldn't have to carry that because you were being loyal to me."

I put my hand over his on his knee.

"If Eamon hadn't hid you in that closet," my eyes welled with emotion, "they could have hurt you while I was gone, and I never would have been able to forgive myself."

Seph was quiet.

"I'm not sure what will come next, but I can't take the chance that you get hurt because of my decisions again. I can't—"

"It's not *your* decision," Seph said, looking at me. His jaw tightened. "I know that you feel responsible for me. You took me in when I didn't have any other options in the Ambit…"

Abigail.

I am responsible for Abigail. He can never know that.

Seph continued, "—but we aren't in the Ambit anymore."

"I know, but there are people that want to hurt us. There are so many things happening out here that we knew nothing about. It's dangerous and unpredictable…"

I looked up and saw Zale walking in from the field. I watched him as he made his way back to the farmhouse.

"…and I don't know who I can trust."

"That's exactly why we need to stay together," Seph said. "You can trust *me*."

I looked at him. He was right. I'd overlooked it but he was the only person I knew, beyond a doubt, that I could trust.

"I'm young, but I'm not helpless. I'm not a child that needs you to protect me, not anymore. Not like when I was in the Ambit. The things we went through in the Outside, like it or not, it's changed us. We need to stick together now more than ever because of it. "

I was quiet, watching his face. The independence he was displaying reminded me of my own plea the night before. He didn't want me trying to protect him anymore than I wanted Zale or Eamon trying to protect me.

"Then its settled," he said after a quiet moment. "I'm not going to the Collective."

"So, what do we do then?"

Seph looked nervous, "I've been thinking about it," he said. "I think James may have been Storian."

I nodded.

"I know," I said. "I think you're right."

"He brought the Bible for Isla and all the books in the Ambit's library. He was responsible for most of those," Seph said.

"I know."

"Britt," Seph said.

I looked at him.

"I want to be like James."

James is dead.

I didn't have the heart to tell Seph yet. I wasn't sure that I could utter the words.

"What does that mean?"

"My whole life, in the Ambit, my mother would tell me of places beyond the borders. I knew one day that I would leave the Ambit. That's why, when they banished you, I didn't hesitate. My mother wanted me to be an explorer like James."

When Seph spoke about his mother, his hand found its way to the fish charm necklace. I thought about the charm and what Eamon said it represented.

"Do you think your mom knew about the things that the Bible talks about?" I asked him. "Do you think she wore that necklace because she believed in God, like they said?"

"I've been wondering that," he smiled. "Wouldn't that be something? If she knew what this meant?" He looked down at the charm.

"Maybe she was Storian too," I smiled. "I like the idea of there being Storian in the Ambit."

Seph beamed at the thought.

"If she was, then I want to follow in her footsteps," he said.

"You want to teach?"

"How could we not want that?"

"It's dangerous."

"It's more dangerous not to," he shrugged.

"What would you teach?"

Seph smiled again. It was refreshing how easy the curls were finding the corners of his mouth.

"Do you still have Isla's book?" he asked.

"The Bible? Of course."

"May I see it?"

I pulled the leather book from my satchel and handed it to him. He flipped through the pages.

"I think I'd like to teach about this," he said. "The history of God."

"What's that?" I said. I spotted something written on the inside of the book.

"What?"

"There," I said. "I've never noticed that before."

I pointed to the inside cover of the book. There was a small list of names written on the corner of the page. Previous owners. The first name was written in cursive, it belonged to a woman.

"Margaret Fields?" Seph said. "Who's that?"

I shrugged, "I don't know."

The next name wasn't in cursive but in a boy's handwriting. "Oliver Zale?"

Zale.

Seph and I looked at each other.

"Didn't Zale say last night that Maris named him after someone?" Seph asked.

"He did." I looked at the list. There were only two names left. The last one was Isla's. The one before hers was written in bold black letters and I couldn't believe that I'd never noticed it before.

"Joshua Maris."

"Maris?!" Seph cried.

Seph lowered the book to his lap in shock.

"How did Isla end up with Maris' Bible?" I asked. "Did Maris know you had this?"

Seph's face was frozen in thought. Then he smiled and inhaled a breath. "Thank you," he said. His eyes were glowing, like he'd just had a realization.

"For what?"

He was still too deep in thought to respond.

"Seph?"

His eyes finally registered that I was talking to him.

"Thank you," he said again.

"For what?"

Then he started laughing. He stood up and scooped Nanny up in his arms. He swung around in a circle and then kissed the top of her head.

"Are you okay?" I asked, laughing at his sudden burst of energy.

He stopped. "I'm more than okay," he said.

Then he stepped forward and gestured to the Bible. "Can I have this back?"

"Sure," I laughed. "Why?"

He sat Nanny back on the ground and patted the top of her head. Then he took the book from my hand.

"Because I've got some reading to do."

"Oh, okay," I started to say, but before I could finish, he was bounding toward the farmhouse with Nanny at his heels.

I smiled.

I turned my attention back to the water pot in the fire. I used the wood stick that Eamon had as a fire poker the night before, to remove the pot from the flames.

As I worked Fairchild's soap into a lather on my hands, I thought about what Maris' name being written on the inside cover of the Bible meant. The night before, Zale said that his father had a soft spot for outcasts.

Was James an outcast?

Did Maris teach James?

Did he give the Bible to James?

I remembered that James came to the Ambit looking for his father. It made sense to me that he could have been one of Maris' outcasts.

While I pondered their connection, I peeled off the layers of dirty clothes I had on and shook them out, hoping to loosen the ash and dirt from them. Then I folded James' bloodied red book inside of my jacket and laid it aside so that I could clean my skin and hair. I did this quickly, knowing I wasn't yet ready to see the blood stain and bullet hole by daylight.

I massaged the middle of the back of my head, where my ponytail had been for days. My scalp ached. When I'd finished washing it, I pulled my hair around to the side and braided it into a long braid, which I tossed back over my shoulder to hang down the middle of my back. A few curls escaped the bindings, but I didn't fuss to fix them.

My boots felt stuck to my feet when I removed them, as though the dried mud had molded my boot and foot together. I rubbed the arches of my feet, taking note of several large bulging blisters that had worn on my heels and toes. After knocking the dried mud off, I slid my boots on and laced them tight, hoping to squeeze the life out of my swollen blisters.

Finally, my hands warmed by the fire while I sat deep in thought. The red book was next to me, but I refused to acknowledge it. It beckoned me to open it, but I fought hard to ignore the urge I had to feed my curiosity.

"Maris *was* Storian," I whispered to no one as I washed my arms and face. "He was a teacher and James was his student. And then James was the teacher and Isla was *his* student."

I remembered the moment he gave her the Bible.

I remembered the red and yellow cars he'd gifted Seph.

I rinsed my hands and then pulled the cars from the pocket of my satchel.

As I rolled the red car with the squeaky wheel on my leg, it all came flooding back.

Pieces of the puzzle of my life were falling into place.

I took a deep breath and then reached under my jacket on the log. I retrieved the red book and pulled it into view. In the light of day, it was even more shocking. The red of the cover with the brown crisp splatters of his blood.

It hurt to hold.

Quickly, I tucked it back under my jacket.

A breeze came and dried my eyes. I closed them and inhaled. The fire's smoke filled my nostrils forcing me to tip my head back for fresh air.

I stared at the blue sky as the white clouds rolled slowly by. They seemed unchanged by the events on the surface below them. I began to wonder if they had always looked like they did now.

Dropping my head back down, I scanned my surroundings and felt inspired for a moment. The world's beauty was endless, yet there was so much ugly that had distracted me from it.

Monsters, murderers, and disease had plagued the face of the earth forever, and today was no different, yet this world was beautiful. With a renewed perspective, I looked again at the sky and clouds.

I thought of Seph and how he was a perfect example of goodness in this world. Without his loyalty, I would have shriveled up and died at the Ambit Crossing. Without his faithfulness, I wouldn't have had anyone I could trust.

Faithfulness.

Faithful.

Full of faith.
What is it to be full of faith?
What is it to be full of faith in God?
The character?
No, the person…
No, the presence, from Isla's book.
Presence. The being.
I inhaled through my nose.
Was it possible that there was some sort of presence that Elles knew of?
That Maris experienced? That Margaret Fields and Oliver Zale understood?
Does Isla know him? Is God even a 'him'?
I dropped my head back down.
I wasn't sure what I was trying to understand.
The untold story.
Seph had called it an untold story.
At the Ambit Crossing, after our banishment, while I grappled with Chasen's death, I remembered him saying, "I like to think that maybe there's an untold story inside of us, that can't be touched by all this pain. That maybe we are born knowing there's something more, and even in the worst of moments, and on the worst of days, we keep looking for it, because it's the only thing that doesn't change."
I looked up at the sky above me again. The sun was at its highest point of the day. I closed my eyes and welcomed its warmth on my freshly cleaned skin.
The sun was beautiful and dependable.
The sun was faithful to us, wasn't it?
I knew it would disappear at the end of the day. I knew there would be times that it would hide behind clouds and storms. I knew that somedays it would feel warmer depending on how close I was to it and other days it would be warm but feel distant.
But beyond all of that, the thing I knew best was that it would always be there. Even when I was below the ground of the Outside city, or in the hospital with the holes in the ceiling, or in the hammock of the Shelter Tree or in my cottage in the Ambit. I could look up and know the sun was always somewhere above me. It was unchanging.
Is that how it felt to believe in God?
Is God unchanging like the sun?
The sun would rise in the morning and set in the evening.

I could count on it.

A question popped into my head that I'd never entertained before. I didn't know where it came from.

Who hung the sun in my sky?

The answer came as easily as the question.

The presence.

The lack of absence.

God?

Could it be?

Do you exist?

If you do, do you know me?

Have you been watching?

Have you been watching us?

Have you been watching Isla?

Is she okay?

I looked down. This was silly. I was talking to the sky. How would the sky know if Isla was okay?

Or could it?

Wasn't this the same sky that covered all of us?

I closed my eyes.

Can you tell her that I miss her?

Could you do that for me?

Can you ease her pain?

Can you ease mine?

As I thought it, the pain hidden in my chest swelled. I'd given it recognition and suddenly, it filled me. It wanted to topple me, to consume me. Deep unacknowledged grief welled up and started bursting from my lips. The question I'd been asking came forth with one word.

"Why?" I whispered.

Who are you?

Who am I to you?

Why am I here?
Why am I here and James isn't...?
What happened to Chasen, my sweet boy?
Why was I his mother?
Why am I still here when he is gone?
James is gone.
Elles is gone.
Weren't they better than me?
More deserving of life than me?
Who am I?
Who am I to be worthy of being here?
How can I carry all of this?
Who am I to carry all of this?

I gasped for air between cries.

Why in this time?
Why am I here to see these events?
Why me?
James would know what to do. He knew how to help Chasen.
But... "...you!"

I was screaming now. I was yelling at the sky. I didn't care who heard me, I just wanted to scream at whatever was out there. I unloaded my emotions on the clouds and the sky and the beauty around me. I felt guilt for being there to see the world's beauty when James and Chasen were dead. I fell to my knees and screamed at the ground, pounding on it with my fists.

"I hate you! You don't deserve to be here!"

I felt a hand on my back. The warmth of it sent chills to my spine. A body covered mine and held me. He blanketed me with his body and rocked me. I sobbed and sobbed, until I was sure I was out of tears. Then heat consumed me.

More warmth and weight fell onto my back. Another body covered me. Two people now enveloped me while I wailed, but I didn't stop screaming and crying, I didn't have any control. I had years of tears and pain that flowed from the deepest parts of me.

"Get her away from it!" I heard one of the voices yell.

"She's burnt!" The other said.

I was delirious. I was out of sorts, confused and lost in my emotions. Under me, I felt arms cradle me. Someone lifted me. I felt weak. Daylight went in and out and my mind raced.

"Lay her down here," a female voice said, and Zale lowered me to the porch. I could sense that it was him.

"Britt!" I could hear Seph's voice, as he knelt next to me. I couldn't open my eyes to see him. I couldn't answer even though I wanted to.

"What happened!?" someone asked. Eamon.

"She fell in the fire," Fairchild said. I could feel her hands on my body. She removed my clothing and pulled off my boots and socks. "Her feet are bleeding."

"Seph, get some water!" Zale ordered.

Seph's feet pattered down the wood steps of the porch. Zale leaned over and opened my eyelids to look at my eyes. He snapped his fingers in front of my face. Then everything went dark.

Voices.

What are they saying? Why can't I understand them?

Talking turned to silence and the voices disappeared. I felt like I was floating in my mind, fighting to regain consciousness.

Wake up! Help! I can't wake up.

Move. Why can't I move?

Then the voices returned. I could hear them again. I could sense the warmth of their presence. At first, they sounded soft and calm, but then they turned fearful and scared. I could feel my heart racing.

Why do they sound scared? Am I dying?

Why are they screaming at me?

Silence.
The ground shook under me.
Hot air covered me.
Then warmth.
Liquid warmth.
Cinder.

20
NEW FRIENDS

I awoke to laughter.

Reaching up to rub my eyes, I found my hands were bandaged. In a panic, I sprang up out of the bed and inspected my body. My hands and feet were covered in white wraps, and my clothes had been changed. My head pounded as I tried desperately to recall what had happened.

Again, I heard laughter. I recognized that I was still in the farmhouse, but I was in one of its back bedrooms in a bed that someone had made for me on the floor. I was alone.

A cracked mirror sat leaning up against the wall. I shuffled toward it. The cold of the hardwood floor sent a shiver up my back as I got down on my knees in front of the mirror.

I wasn't wearing pants, just an oversized shirt. I rolled my eyes, thinking of how I was dressed like Fairchild as she flaunted herself earlier that day. Or at least I thought it was earlier that day.

In the mirror, I studied my face for injuries. I couldn't quite remember what happened to me, so I wasn't sure where else I might have wounds.

There were no visible wounds besides my bandaged hands and feet. Normally I would have found that odd, but I had been here before. I had stared at myself on other occasions, thinking about missing wounds and blood that didn't belong to me. I knew what had happened.

Cinder was back.

Buckley's bombs didn't kill her as we thought.

I used my teeth and began unraveling the wrappings on my right hand. Once I removed it, I unraveled the other. My skin was pink and fleshy, lighter than it had been before. I had scars on both hands, but no visible wounds.

I leaned back and sat on my rear end, so that I could reach my feet. I unraveled each of them one at a time, expecting to see more scars like the ones on my hands, but to my surprise, they looked almost exactly as they always had.

As I stood up, the cracked mirror flashed my underwear. I cursed my bare legs. Even though I knew I was alone, and no one had seen, I turned red thinking that someone had undressed me after the accident. And with my lack of options, I hoped it was Zale or Fairchild, not Buckley or Eamon.

Laughter erupted again.

I fashioned a cover for my legs out of the blanket I had been covered with, and then stepped out into the breezy hallway. At the end of the hall, a room opened into the area with the fireplace and table, where I had slept next to Seph and Nanny. No one was there.

I pulled my pants from the clothesline over the fireplace and slipped them on.

Sunshine beamed through the windows, and I could smell something cooking. I peered out the window and saw the group sitting on the ground on a blanket eating: Seph, Eamon, Buckley, Fairchild, and Zale. My heart leapt at the sight of hot food.

It wasn't until I got to the porch that I realized what they were laughing at. It was Nanny. She was fearlessly charging and wrestling with the enormous creature that grossly outsized and outweighed her. Cinder.

She is still alive! She survived Buckley's bombs.

The two creatures were like dogs, trying to learn how to play together for the first time. Everyone watched as they engaged in their game.

For the first time, I was seeing Cinder's full body in the light of day. She was magnificent. Her movements were graceful and smooth. She didn't stomp around, she glided. She had brilliant control over every part of her body, including her long thick tail and her feet that were the size of tree trunks.

One wrong move and she could have easily crushed Nanny, but she was gentle and careful. Cinder was showing us a completely different side to her. I couldn't take my eyes off the two of them.

Cinder was teasing Nanny with something. Every time she would tease her, Nanny would bear down and run at Cinder butting her head as hard as she could on the dragon's scaly foot.

Cinder was so solid that Nanny would bounce back, knocking herself on her rear and then shake her head in frustration. It was the funniest thing I think I have ever seen.

Every now and then, Cinder would raise her enormous foot to reveal a lovely green plant, and as soon as Nanny would go toward it to eat, Cinder would cover it again. Nanny would then grunt and again, she would run at the foot with all her might, in the hopes that she might be able to get to the food. I laughed so hard; I thought my sides were going to split.

"Look who's up!" Fairchild exclaimed, when she noticed me on the porch.

Seph smiled. "How are you feeling?"

"I feel good." I said, stepping down from the porch. I lifted my hands to show them the scars and then added, "I think I feel a lot better than I should."

"You must be hungry." Seph extended his open arm toward the food on the blanket. "I went fishing."

"One moment," I said, staring up at Cinder.

She shifted the weight of her body so she could turn to see me directly. When she did this, her foot moved and much to Nanny's delight the green plant appeared. Nanny wasted no time devouring it while she had the chance.

I stood face to face with Cinder. Her blackish purple skin glistened in the light of the sun. She lowered her head down to my level. She inhaled and exhaled softly, and I slowed my breathing to match hers. In so many ways, I felt connected to her.

I extended my hand, and she lowered her head down further. I closed my eyes and touched her snout. A current moved from the surface of her skin through my fingertips. I opened my eyes.

Somehow, we understood each other.

Her nostrils moved as she breathed in and out and I breathed with her.

"You're alive," I whispered. Her yellow eyes were kinder than I expected. They were so big; I could see my reflection in them.

I felt her reflect my statement back to me.

"Yes," I whispered. "Thanks to you, I'm alive too."

Cinder pulled her head back up and then retreated to lie down in the brush field. She was lying on her side, like a cat in the sun.

"How long has she been here?" I asked, as I took a seat on the blanket next to Seph.

"Since yesterday," Buckley answered.

"Yesterday?" I repeated. "I was out that long?"

Eamon handed me a plate, with fish on it, which he had grilled over the fire pit. I was thrilled to see food that wasn't freeze dried.

Zale didn't say anything to me. He barely looked at me.

"I don't know what happened," I admitted, shoving food into my mouth.

"You passed out," Fairchild said.

"I did?"

"I saw it. One minute you were over there crying, and I just assumed you were having a mental breakdown. I get those too, so I figured I'd give you space. Then the next thing I knew, you'd fallen into the fire. You almost put your whole face in it."

My eyes widened.

"You must be dehydrated," Eamon suggested, handing me a water bottle to drink from. I thanked him.

"Your boots were tied so damn tight, you cut off your circulation," Zale growled. "That's why you passed out."

I stared at him. He was obviously still angry with me, but at least he was talking to me.

"My boots? Is that why I had bandages on my feet?"

"Yup." Fairchild shook her head. "Your feet were bleeding. I almost couldn't get your socks off."

I remembered that I had tied them extremely tight, because I was trying to keep my blisters from bleeding. I looked down at my bare feet. They were completely healed. I watched Cinder, who was sleeping in the sunlight. "She saved me," I said.

"Again," Buckley added.

I looked at him.

"Aren't you glad you didn't blow her up?" I asked.

He rolled his eyes, but we both knew he was. She was different than the other monitors.

"I wonder if she lost her eggs," Fairchild said.

"I'm surprised she came back to find us," I said. "How do you think she found us?"

Fairchild shrugged. "I have no idea."

"She's bigger than I imagined," Seph said, and I remembered that he hadn't seen a monitor yet. Other than the glimpse of one we got on our first day in the Outside.

"She's the biggest one," I said. "There's a male that's almost her size that we saw on the mission. He had two tails."

"What?" Eamon scowled. "Two tails?"

We all nodded.

"She doesn't seem to blend in with them though, does she?" I asked Fairchild.

"No, she's definitely different than the rest."

"She eats fish, like us," Seph said.

"Really?"

He nodded, "While I was fishing, she went into the pond and caught her own food."

"I guess that explains why she doesn't eat humans. She's not a meat eater," Fairchild shrugged.

"She must be from the Ambit like us too," Seph teased.

Buckley and Fairchild's faces went serious.

"The Ambit?" Buckley said.

Zale gave me a look.

"I guess you might as well know," I said.

"You're from the Ambit?!" Fairchild exclaimed.

I nodded.

She smiled, "That explains so much!"

"I didn't think the Ambit was a real place!" Buckley admitted.

"Where is it?" Fairchild asked.

"Actually," I said. "I'm not sure."

I looked at Seph. His eyes were disappointed.

"You don't know?" Fairchild said. "How do you not know where you came from?"

"Maris," I explained, "he's the one that took us to the Outside from the Ambit. I don't know where it is."

"I know how to find it," Eamon said.

I looked up, "What? You do?"

He nodded. "If you want to go back for Isla, I can get you there."

"Really?!"

289

Zale looked betrayed that Eamon knew about Isla too. He must think I opened up to Eamon faster than I did him.

"Wait, who's Isla?" Buckley asked.

"My daughter."

Fairchild's face read surprise.

"How do *you* know where the Ambit is?" Zale asked Eamon.

"There's a map," Eamon looked at me, "in a book that I used to own."

What book?

The book?

James' book!

I gasped.

Where is James' book?

I jumped up from the blanket and rushed to the fire pit. My clothes were gone. The book was gone.

"Sht, sht, sht." I panicked. I searched the area, behind the logs. Devastated, I got down into the fire pit and began sifting through the ashes. It was still hot from grilling the fish, but I didn't care.

"No, no, no!" I cried. In the ashes there was a red piece of paper. It was a piece of the book's cover.

"Britt?" Zale called to me, concerned.

"The book," I panicked. "It's gone."

"What book?"

"The one Eamon gave me," I cried.

"It's okay, I'm sure we can find another—"

"No!" I yelled, "You don't understand, I need that one. There isn't another one!'

"Britt, you're scaring me." He came to me and pulled me to look at him. "Talk to me. What kind of book was it?"

I stopped struggling against him and looked into his eyes. I couldn't explain it. I wanted to, but I didn't know if I could trust him. If he was from the Underground, then James' book might be of interest to him because James was Storian. After what he did to Winnie, I couldn't be sure.

"Britt?" Zale said softly. "Talk to me. What's going on with you?"

"I –"

Zale waited.

I started crying.

He pulled me into him, and I buried my face in his chest.

"I can't go get Isla without the book."

"What?" Zale pulled away. "The map to the Ambit was in that book?"

I nodded, sobbing. "I need it back, but it burned."

"Come with me," Zale said. He took my hand and pulled me with him.

"Eamon!"

Eamon got off the blanket where he was sitting with the others. "What's wrong?"

"The book?" Zale said. "The one with the map to the Ambit? The one you gave her. Do you have it?"

Eamon looked at me.

"No! I gave it to you."

"It's gone," I cried. "When I fell into the fire, it must have fallen in." I extended my hand to show him the sliver of the book cover that I'd retrieved from the ashes.

It's my fault.

I'd lost the book.

He understood what a great loss it was to me. I understood what a great loss it was to him.

"Do you have it memorized?" Zale repeated. "Can you get her to the Ambit without it?"

Eamon looked at me. He nodded.

"Yes, I can," he said. "I can get you back to Isla."

21
RETURN TO THE AMBIT

"This is it?" Zale said. "We drove two hours for this?"

"No," I said, looking over the empty field. "I don't understand."

"Is the Ambit underground?" Fairchild asked.

"What? No," I said, frustrated.

"Where's the Shelter Tree?" Seph asked.

"Eamon?" I looked at him. "You said you knew where the Ambit was."

His face was calm. "I do."

"Then where is it?" I asked.

His eyes narrowed, looking at me. He seemed like he knew something that I didn't.

"It's right there, Britt," Eamon's eyes looked toward the field.

I scowled, waving my hand around. "No, it's not! That's not the Ambit, Eamon, it's an empty field."

Eamon laughed and turned to go back to his truck.

I followed behind him. "Eamon? This isn't right. This isn't the Ambit. The Ambit has people and cottages and farms…"

Eamon got to his truck and opened the tailgate. He started pulling things from it.

"What are you doing?"

He stopped at looked at me. "I'm setting up camp."

"Camp? Why?"

He looked at his watch. "Because I don't know how long this will take and the sun will be down soon."

"How long what will take?"

Then he looked behind us to where Cinder was. "You may want to do something about that."

"About what?" I looked at Cinder, she was sitting in the grassy field staring off into the distance.

"The dragon," Eamon said casually. "How do you think the people of the Ambit will feel when they see us here, with a dragon?"

"See us here?" I looked around. I was beginning to think Eamon was losing his mind. "We aren't here. We aren't anywhere near the Ambit!"

Eamon laughed, "Britt, can you just trust me?"

That was really the question wasn't it.

I stared at him.

"I will set up camp," he said. "While you figure out how to tell your pet dragon she needs to go."

I didn't know which part of his statement was more ridiculous. That he was setting up camp, thinking we are at the Ambit, which we clearly were not. Or the idea that I could communicate with the enormous dragon who had decided to escort us on the trip.

"So?" Zale came to the back of the vehicle. "What's the plan?"

"We're setting up camp," Eamon said.

Zale looked at me. "Here?"

"Yep," Eamon said, slamming the tailgate at the back of the truck closed. "Buckley," he yelled, "Come grab the tent and see if you and Fairchild can set it up."

Seph came up to me, confused. "We're staying here tonight?"

I sighed. "I guess," I shrugged. "Eamon seems convinced that we're at the Ambit."

Seph laughed. Then his eyes darted around, looking at the landscape surrounding us. "But this is a field."

"I know," I huffed.

"Britt!" Eamon yelled from a distance. I turned to him.

"The dragon!" he reminded me.

"Right," I said. Then I turned back to Seph. "Eamon wants me to see if I can get Cinder to leave or hide or something."

"Why?" Zale asked.

"Because he's afraid it's going to scare the Ambitors," I raised my eyebrows.

"Ohhkay," Zale laughed.

Zale and I walked toward Cinder. Before we got to her, I tripped over something hard and fell on the ground with a thud.

"You okay?" Zale asked.

"Yeah," I said. "There's something hard here."

Zale knelt next to me and pulled the brush back.

"They're tracks," he said.

"Tracks?"

He moved away from me, pulling at the long brush and grass. "Railroad tracks," he clarified. "They run from north," he pointed in one direction, "to south."

"See," I said, "the Ambit didn't have railroad tracks. I think Eamon has gotten us lost."

"Well, Eamon's lost something, that's for sure," Zale said, extending his hand to help me up from the ground.

When he helped me to my feet, we were within inches of each other again. I could smell him. I closed my eyes and inhaled.

I still had feelings for this man, but I didn't know if I could fully trust him.

"Britt?" he said my name softly.

I looked up.

Don't let him charm you. I told myself.

"Are we okay?" he asked.

We?

"I'm not sure," I said. "A lot has happened…"

He was quiet.

"Right now, I want to find the Ambit and Isla and…" I exhaled. "…then we can figure out where to go from there. Okay?"

He nodded. "Okay, as long as we're still in this mess together, right?"

Together.

I squinted at him.

He smiled at me, and I think I melted a little.

Dammit.

"Cinder?!" I called, trying to break up the obvious chemistry between us.

"I don't think she knows that we call her that," Zale teased.

"Oh, right," I said.

We approached the dragon cautiously.

"Hey," I called to her, as we stepped around the side of the dragon's massively long body. She didn't acknowledge us there. She was too busy staring intently toward the field.

"What's she looking at?"

I turned to look. "I don't know," I said. "The field?"

Zale scowled. "Do you think she sees the Ambit?"

"The Ambit?" I was confused. Did they not understand that the Ambit was a village? A town?

"The Ambit is a real place," I said. "It's not imaginary, you know that, right?"

Zale gave me a goofy look. "Obviously," he nodded.

"Is it obvious?" I asked. "Buckley didn't know it existed, and Eamon thinks it's a field." I pointed toward the vast nothingness.

Zale laughed and I couldn't help but laugh with him. The whole situation felt bizarre.

"Well, it's getting dark," Zale said.

"Yeah," I agreed. "Okay, so how do we tell her to leave?"

"Hell, if I know," Zale shrugged. "You're the one she likes."

"Me?"

"Yeah, she listened to you at the hospital, remember?"

That was true. Maybe she could understand me.

"Okay," I said, stepping around in front of the dragon. "Here goes nothing."

I stepped between Cinder and the grassy field she seemed to be obsessed with.

"Hey," I said. She glanced down at me and then back up again.

She swished the back of her body back and forth and then shuffled her feet. Her wings flapped behind her a few times and then folded back into place on her back. She was acting like she was anxious about something.

"What is it?" I asked her, feeling absurd.

She glanced down again and then back up.

"She's acting like she knows something is out there," I told Zale.

"Um, hey, girl," I said. "We need you to…disappear for a while….?"

Cinder looked down at me.

"Do you think she understood that?" I asked Zale.

He didn't answer.

"We need you to…." I tried again.

She exhaled through her nostrils at me, like she was frustrated.

"….can you hide or something?" I asked her.

She glanced up at the field and then back down to me.

Then she wiggled her body and then, starting at the tip of her tail and continuing to her head, she disappeared.

"What the--?" I stepped back.

She'd vanished.

"Sht!" Zale yelled. "Where'd she go?"

"I don't know," I exclaimed.

Then from the top of her head to her tail, she reappeared. She was in the same spot she was before. She hadn't moved. She'd vanished.

"She can disappear?!"

"Like, invisible?"

I looked behind her, the rest of our group hadn't even noticed.

"How'd you do that?" I asked Cinder.

She shuffled her feet again, then wiggled until she disappeared.

"I've never seen anything like that!" Zale said.

I felt my mouth gaping open. "Can you still hear me?" I asked the vacant space where she'd disappeared.

I felt a gust of warm breeze across my face. It smelled like fish.

I smiled at Zale. His eyes were wide and intrigued.

"No way!" he said. "That's the coolest thing I've ever seen."

I looked at Zale in amazement. I was blown away.

"So, she can fly, breathe fire…" I started.

"Her blood heals, and she can go invisible?!" Zale finished.

"Invisible?" I repeated. Then I turned around and looked at the field. Zale seemed to understand what I was thinking. "How could that be--?"

"Britt!" Eamon yelled. "Come here, quick!"

I ran to where Eamon was waiting for me. He stared at the sky. The sun was just beginning to set, and the sky was dark yellow.

"It only works on a clear night," he said. "We got lucky."

"With what?" I asked.

"See there?" He pointed to the sky.

I tried to see from his vantage point. "What?"

"Watch the sky over there."

Zale and I did as he suggested.

In the sky above the field, I could see a ripple in the yellow of the evening sky. The ripple darkened, as it was rising.

"What is that?" Zale asked.

"It looks like…" I said.

I could smell it now.

"…smoke?"

Below the darkening ripple, the field was empty.

"That's where we need to go," Eamon said.

I looked out of the side of my eye at Zale.

"Okay," I said.

"Buckley," Eamon called.

Buckley and Fairchild were still wrestling with the tent. The poles, stakes and large canvas cover were spread out all over the ground in front of them.

"Hold off on setting that up," Eamon finished.

"Thank you," Buckley sighed in relief.

"We're gonna move in a little closer and set it up over there," Eamon pointed toward the smoke plume that was hovering in the air above the empty field.

"Aw, man," Buckley said, realizing he was still going to have to set the tent up.

He and Fairchild began picking up the pieces. Seph and Zale stepped in to help them.

"Is that smoke coming from the Ambit?" I asked Eamon.

He nodded. "It shows up at night when they build fires in their fireplaces, but you can only see it when the night is clear."

"The Ambit's hidden?" I asked. "In the middle of that field?"

Eamon looked down at me and smiled. "There's a reason why no one knows how to find it."

"How'd you know this was the right field?"

Eamon pointed to two landmarks in the distance. One was a large plot of trees, and the other was a green hill that rolled over the horizon.

"The Ambit is directly north of Chicago," he explained. "Off a road called 41. Go 150 miles and then head east until you hit the railroad tracks."

The railroad tracks.

"But none of this looks familiar," I said. "I've spent most of my life in the Ambit looking at what was beyond its borders and this," I spun around looking at all the trees in the distance. "This isn't what I grew up looking at."

"Just wait," Eamon said. "You'll understand soon enough."

When the camping gear was loaded, Eamon said, "Okay, so when we breach the Ambit…we'll need to immediately shift into reverse and back out."

"How will we know when we've breached?" Buckley asked, as he was planning to drive the second vehicle.

"You'll know," Eamon said.

"We'll park the vehicles outside the Ambit so they can't see them, then we'll go in on foot. We'll take in what we can carry to set up camp for tonight. We won't be able to have a fire, so pack something warm."

"Why can't we have a fire?" Seph asked.

"We don't want them to know we're here yet," Eamon explained. "We're concealed by night right now, so that'll give us until morning to come up with our next move."

"What happens if they see us?" Fairchild asked. "Are we in danger?"

"No," I said. "The people from the Ambit aren't violent at all. There are no guns or anything. They're very peaceful. If they see us, a representative from the Guiding Authority will come out. If that happens, I'll handle it."

Eamon looked around. "Okay, Seph and Britt, you're with me. Fairchild, Buckley and Zale, you can follow us." Eamon looked at Nanny goat, who was next to Seph. "Remember, being quiet is of the utmost importance."

We nodded, then split to go to our assigned vehicles.

"Britt?" Seph asked me, once we were loaded into Eamon's truck. "If Eamon's right, if the Ambit is out there, that changes everything, doesn't it?"

"What do you mean?"

"Well, if the Ambit really is being hidden by some protective dome or something, then that means the Guiding Authority has been lying all this time."

I nodded. "Yeah, Seph, it does."

"And the people need to know that don't they?"

298

"Yes, they do."

"So, if we show them the truth, I guess that would make us Storian too, then, wouldn't it?"

I turned to look at him in the backseat. He looked at me with a smile on his face.

"I guess it would," I said.

Eamon climbed into the truck.

"You ready?"

I sighed. "As I'll ever be."

He looked forward and exhaled.

The truck crept toward the field, crossing over the railroad tracks and through the tall unkept grass.

Eamon kept his eye on the sky above the space in front of us. The dark cloud of smoke was hard to see, with the black night behind it.

"We just keep going this way," he told himself. "...and when we've gone far enough..."

In front of us, as though we'd passed over some imaginary barrier, the tippy top of the Shelter Tree started to appear. The closer we moved toward it, the more of its' silhouette we could make out in the distance.

I gasped.

"That's the Shelter Tree!" Seph leaned in between Eamon and I from the backseat and pointed. "See it?"

"How is this possible?"

As we approached the Shelter Tree, the dark outline of a tiny village came into view. The Ambit.

"It really *was* right there the whole time," I said, astonished with what I was seeing.

"Okay," Eamon halted the vehicle. "Now, you've seen it." He shifted the truck into reverse. Behind us, Buckley's jeep did the same. Slowly we reversed and watched as the Ambit and the Shelter Tree faded from view.

"There, that should be good." Eamon said, putting the vehicle in park just outside the barrier.

"They can't see us here?" Seph asked.

Eamon shook his head. "Nope. If we can't see them, they can't see us." Then he unbuckled his seat belt as Seph and I sat, staring at the reflection of an empty field in front of us.

"How is this possible?" I sat bewildered.

299

Eamon sighed. "I'm not sure," he said. "But if I had to guess, I'd say the Ambit has gotten their hands on some pretty stealthy technology."

Technology.

"The Ambit has technology?" Seph asked.

Eamon nodded.

"Fcking hypocrites," I whispered.

22
FLICKER

My finger traced the line of the bark running down the side of the Shelter Tree. I remembered standing at the Ambit Crossing as a young girl, staring at this massive landmark that stood alone on the horizon of the Ambit. I always wondered what it would feel like to touch it. I had wanted to climb it to see if I could see anything new from the top. Even at that age, I knew there must be more to see in the world.

There were trees within the Ambit, but none like this. I tilted my head back to look up at it. The mighty height and thickness was coated in woody scales, a rugged armor, and I knew the tree had stories to tell.

A gust of wind scooped my hair off my face and threw it backward. A few of the rustling leaves that still clung to the tips of the great tree, surrendered to the breeze.

"There's a storm coming," Zale warned me with a whisper.

He startled me, appearing from around the other side of the Shelter Tree, while I was deep in thought.

In the sky above, the darkness of the evening collected into thick clouds. Another gust whipped across the plains and more leaves gave into the wind's wishes and floated away with it.

There's a storm coming.

I remembered these words from the dream I'd had the night before Chasen died. I turned and searched the field between the Ambit and the tree. The tips of the grass bent in the wind, and I imagined James and I hidden in them.

"When it rains here," I whispered, "the sky flickers."

"Flickers?"

I looked upward.

"Growing up here, I thought it happened everywhere. But now," I felt anger rise in me, "now I know. It only happens here."

Zale was quiet.

"It's the barrier," I explained. "The rain hits the barrier that hides the Ambit, and each droplet creates a flickering light in the sky."

The smell of rain was upon us and then the smallest flicker speckled the sky above.

In the reflection of it, I could see Zale tip his head back, his jaw gaping open in amazement. "I see it!"

It was all so familiar.

The feeling of being in the Ambit, the flickering sky, the rain on our faces and the sting of betrayal.

"This is all a sham," I said. "All of it. All these years, the Ambit forbid us from using technology while they were using it to hide the whole damn society."

"Now we know why no one can find this place," Zale said. "This is why people say it doesn't exist."

"Maris knew," I said. "He knew how to find us, and he knew about the barrier, and he never told me."

Zale was quiet.

"Will anything ever be honest?" I asked.

I stepped away from the tree.

"Do you want to be alone?" Zale asked. I nodded.

I appreciated that about Zale. He knew when to give me space and didn't feel like it was his job to escort me or fix me.

I found the line of the Ambit Crossing. I paced back and forth, wondering what would happen when I stepped over it.

What will happen when I break their rules now?

They can't banish me again. They can't shame me anymore. Their power over me is gone. They don't want me here, but none of that matters anymore.

I spun in a circle and took it all in. From inside the invisible barrier, I could see the scenery I remembered. Flat fields without trees.

It was incredible. I'd seen with my own eyes what lay beyond the barrier. There were rolling hills and several thickets of trees.

There were railroad tracks that had moved trains at one time and roads that led to new places. But from where I stood now, none of that was visible. There was only a projection of some sort, cast by technology. Technology that we were told we weren't allowed to use. It was all false. It was an idea that we'd been tricked into accepting as our reality.

Yet, the conditioning I'd received all those years halted me before stepping back over the line. I stared at the ground and knew it was nothing more than a separation of surface. The grass within the Ambit was slightly longer and the grass outside the Ambit was slightly greener. But weren't they the same underneath? Didn't their roots share the same soil and water source. What made them appear different?

I wondered if the grass outside the Ambit's imaginary line knew it was free. Is that how it flourished and turned green? While the grass on the inside grew but appeared to be dead.

Dead growth. Is there such a thing?

The Guiding Authority had taught me that being within the Ambit was better, safer, and right. But they'd constructed my environment and within it I'd shriveled up and failed to thrive.

I'd grown dead.

Within the Ambit, I'd grown up dead.

Outside the Ambit, I was in a constant state of threat. From monitors or elements or broken humans or liars, but I was free.

Is there no place that is honest?

I wanted to march into the middle of the quiet society and scream. More than anything, I wanted to destroy all they knew to be real. I would unveil the lies that the Guiding Authority constructed. I will tear down the curtain and reveal the real world to the others. I will stop the flicker.

The Ambit is a cage. A bubble. An illusion.

What else had they lied about?

I remembered the night that Maris came to retrieve us. He didn't come until it was dark and now, I knew why. No one could find the Ambit in daylight. And it was because of the darkness that I didn't notice the difference when I'd left their manufactured manifestation of my reality.

Maris knew all along.

And James.

How did James find the Ambit in the first place?

Had Maris told him?

Neither of them told me.

Why?

That felt like betrayal too.

Now I understood why the Guiding Authority allowed James to stay in the Ambit. He hadn't just found their precious secret society; he'd broken into it.

Maybe he'd promised the Guiding Authority not to talk about the barrier, in exchange for being allowed to stay.

Maybe that's how James negotiated his place in the Ambit? How he got them to let him go on the journeys?

He knew something they didn't want him to share.

What if he had shared it?

Would it have made a difference to me?

Would I have wanted to leave with him then?

I didn't know the answer and it scared me. Was I so happy in my ignorance and bitterness that I wouldn't claim freedom for myself?

Freedom is a fragile and precarious thing.

As much as I wanted to march in and bring freedom to the rest of the people in the Ambit, I knew many of them would not want it. They would fight it. They'd be let off their leashes and then immediately return and buckle their shackles once more. Because being outside required courage that most wouldn't have.

I didn't have it.

I'd only learned to find it because I was forced out, because of the boy that I felt responsible for, and because of the words written on the inside of Isla's Bible.

Do not conform, transform.

I knew then, that as great and terrifying as it had been to walk away from the Ambit's control, it had saved my life.

And even if I knew that most wouldn't accept my offering of freedom, some would. And that was worth breaking rules. That was worth crossing lines.

I stepped over the line and planted my foot firmly on the other side. Then one foot in front of the other, I walked toward the interior of the Ambit.

Soon, my feet were moving so quickly that I was running.

Running toward my daughter and my father and all the others that were left behind. All the ones that were trapped, like I'd been. All the …

I fell. Hard.

My body collided with the earth, and I tasted the Ambit's dirt in my mouth. It'd happened so fast I didn't even remember the split seconds between being upright and running and being face down in the dirt. All I knew was that something had tripped me.

The rain came down harder and turned the dirt on my hands and face to mud. As the rainfall intensified, so did the flickering, until bright flashes of light would hold for seconds at a time before the next flash. I got to my knees and felt around in the darkness for the object that'd caused me to stumble.

In the bed of grass, I found something hard. A wide stone was half-buried into the earth. It was shaped into a perfect rectangle with a flat top. I knew it'd been placed there, because it was too evenly sculpted to be a product of nature. I smoothed my hand over the wet surface and felt that there were markings etched into it. Someone had painstakingly carved letters into the stone.

I pulled my flashlight from my belt and turned it on, centering it on the stone.

"Eamon!" I yelled, ignoring all his warnings about being quiet. "Eamon!" I screamed again.

He didn't yell back, but I could hear the movement through the grass and puddles, as he ran to find me.

The sky flickered.

"How?" I asked when he'd arrived in front of me, wet and winded. "How is this possible?"

I turned my flashlight onto the stone's face and revealed the carving on it. It was one word in thick unmistakable letters.

JAMES.

"James?" I pointed, trying to understand.

Eamon lowered to the ground and pulled the grass and weeds from the surface of the rock.

"Yes," he panted. "James."

"Yes?" I tried to find a reason in my mind, "Yes, what?"

Eamon stood back up and wiped his hands on his pant legs.

"This is where he is," he explained. "This is where I brought him to rest."

I melted into tears, which folded in with the raindrops streaming down my face. "What?" I asked. I fell to my knees and started pulling the weeds back to clear the stone. "*This* was where he was?"

"Yes," Eamon said.

"You buried him *here*?"

The sky flickered.

Eamon nodded.

"How long ago? How long has he been here?" I wept. "Right here, in the Ambit?"

"Since the day after," Eamon said.

I felt the earth under me. He was right here with me. I couldn't believe he'd been with us the whole time.

I stood up and hugged Eamon. "Thank you," I cried. "Thank you for bringing him home."

Eamon's face was touched with relief and pride.

We turned, hearing something approach.

Two sets of running feet, accompanied by two flashlight beams, found their way to us in the field of the Ambit.

"Are you okay?" Seph asked, wiping the pouring rain from his cheeks. "They said you were yelling."

"What's the matter?" Zale asked.

"I'm okay," I said. My mind was spinning, thinking of how this was the place that James and I had once laid in the field in daylight under the flickering sky and now, in an odd way, Eamon had restored that moment to me. I threw my head backward and let the rain wash the tears from my cheeks. I took a deep breath as I watched the flickering sky. I could feel James in that moment.

I wondered if there was more to my dream than I'd realized. James and I laying in the field. The flickering sky.

There's a storm coming.

Was it a coincidence that all of that collided with this moment or was it intentional? Was it a warning?

Was something beyond us present in this moment?

Seph allowed the beam of light from his flashlight to land on the stone that Eamon and I were standing over.

He saw the name and then looked up at me, understanding all that I did about its significance.

"Is that a gravestone?" Zale asked.

Eamon nodded, "It is."

306

Zale looked up. "That's odd."

"What is?"

"The name," Zale replied. "James."

He looked at me in confusion and then clarified.

"My brother's name was James."

23

THE REUNION

My feet were planted firmly on the ground, but the world seemed to spin around me. I felt like I could fall over at any minute, like I had been hit by something and was thrown for miles. I was dizzy from Zale's words.

Could it be the same James?

"What?!" I whispered. "Your brother?"

Zale stared at me, then at Eamon.

"Your brother?" I yelled over the thunder rumbling overhead. The sky flickered.

I could tell Zale was working it out in his memory too. He was looking at Eamon for clarification. I joined him. Eamon didn't seem surprised at all by Zale's comment.

"You never told me you had a brother?" I repeated. "Where is he now?"

Zale's eyebrows turned down toward the grave. "He died, why?"

My heart felt like it was going to explode. My hands began to shake. I looked at Eamon.

"Eamon?" I asked with desperation for him to clear up the misunderstanding, but he was quiet.

"When did he die?" I asked Zale.

"Years ago," he said. "In the Outside. He was murdered."

"How?" I looked at Eamon. "Why—?"

"Is this *him*?" Zale asked Eamon. The emotion on his face mixed with rainwater and flickering.

Eamon nodded.

"What--?" Zale started, "Why is he buried in the Ambit?"

Zale looked back and forth from Eamon to me to Seph. None of us answered.

"Did—" Zale was looking at me. "Did you know him?"

I felt my mouth hanging open.

"Who is he to you?" he asked me.

I stared at him. None of us were prepared for the answer to his question, but still it had to be said.

At a loss for words, I lifted my left hand up and reminded him of my wedding band. The one that he'd asked about on the Blood Mission. I'd told him that I would never take it off but that the man who'd given it to me was not coming back. I didn't know then that that man was his brother.

Now Zale knew too. His face expressed his understanding as he looked back and forth between my face and the ring.

"Your husband—?" he said softly. "—was James?"

He looked as devastated and confused as I felt.

Then he closed his mouth, as the rain trickled down his face. His jaw clenched.

"Did you tell her?" he growled at Eamon.

Eamon was staring at him.

"Tell me what?"

Zale repeated, "Is that why you wanted to talk to her at the fire that night? To tell her?"

"Tell me what?"

Zale rushed at Eamon and shoved him, "You were poisoning her against me! Was my mother not enough?!"

"I didn't have to tell her, Zale. You're revealing yourself right now!" Eamon growled.

"Stop!" I yelled, rushing to get in front of Zale before he could push Eamon again. I knew Eamon was restraining himself, but it wouldn't take much for him to respond to Zale's physical aggressions.

"He was giving me the book, Zale! He didn't tell me about you and James. I didn't know!"

Zale's eyes moved to me.

"What book?!"

"The book. The red book. The one that burned in the fire." I explained. "It belonged to James. It was on him when he was killed, and Eamon returned it to me."

Zale stepped back from Eamon. He kept stepping backward away from us.

"I didn't know -- Zale?" I said.

His eyes were wild with anger and something that I didn't recognize. There was darkness in them.

"Zale?" I asked again.

Then he turned around and walked away.

"Zale!" I yelled.

The rain slowed and the flicker faded. I could still see Zale as he made his way to the Crossing. Fairchild and Buckley were standing under the Shelter Tree, out of the rain, watching us. They said something to him as he passed, but I couldn't hear what it was. He didn't respond, he just kept walking.

"Where's he going?" Seph asked.

I looked at Eamon, "Why didn't you tell me?"

"I thought *he* knew. I thought *you* knew."

"Bullsht, Eamon!" I yelled. "You withheld the truth from me because you wanted this to happen!"

"Britt, I –"

"What?" I moved closer and stood in front of him, looking up.

"*You* said you didn't want to talk about you and Zale and I respected that. It's not my business."

"It wasn't your business when you threw the tomato, Eamon. Telling me that I was getting involved with my dead husband's brother, is different. You're supposed to be my friend!"

"Your *friend*?!" Eamon laughed, shaking his head.

I leaned back on my heels, thrown off by his comment.

Eamon tilted toward my face, "For five years, I've been looking for you, Britt. From a distance, I've learned to care about you. Don't you see that? I had this crazy idea that someday when we met and I returned James' book to you, that we'd be more than frien--"

"I didn't even know you existed, Eamon!" I shouted.

"Well, I did!" Eamon shouted back. "I – I was the one that sent Maris to get you after your banishment. Me! When you were in danger on the Rally platform, I was the one that protected you from that thug. Me!

I followed you around the Outside, looking out for you and Seph. I'm the one that held on to James' book and protected his secrets for you. Do you know how many nights it took to dig this grave in the dark, just so I could lay him to rest near you? I buried him here—"

"I didn't ask you to do any of that!" I screamed.

Then something he said caught up to me and I had a realization.

"Wait! *You* told Maris about my banishment?" I asked.

His face changed when he realized he'd let something slip.

"You?" I repeated. "How did *you* know I was being banished?"

He swallowed, then looked at Seph.

"Don't look at him!" I said. "Look at me! How did you know about my banishment?"

"How do you think?"

I narrowed my eyes. "My father? You know my father? You've spoken to him? He communicated with you?"

"Sort of."

"Sort of?!"

I looked down at the ground. My eyes settled over the gravestone at my feet.

"Does my father know that James is dead?"

Eamon was quiet.

"Did he know that you buried him here?"

Eamon's face was still.

"Answer me!"

The answer was obvious even though he didn't say it.

"You know what? I'll go ask him myself," I said. Then I turned and started marching toward the Mall.

"Britt!" Eamon yelled.

"Britt," Seph called, running up alongside of me.

"Go back, Seph," I growled.

"Maybe we should talk about this first," Seph said. "Isla—"

"Go back, Seph," I repeated.

"But—"

I whipped around, stopping in my tracks, "Seph!" I yelled. "You need to go back to the Shelter Tree right now. Stay with Nanny."

His face fell flat, and he pulled his chin back in disappointment.

"I understand you're angry," he started again, calmly, "But Isla is in there and she will be—"

"Seph," I growled.

"I just think that we should wait until –"

"Seph!" I shouted. "Go. Back!" I pointed. "This is between me and my father. I don't need you!"

Even though I couldn't see him, because the sky had stopped flickering and the rain had slowed to a mist, I knew he was hurt by my words. It was better that I couldn't see his face.

"Go back and go to bed." I ordered him. "I'll be back once I've figured this all out and we can talk in the morning."

Seph didn't raise any more objections. He was hurt. After another second of consideration, he did as I asked. He turned and started walking back to the Crossing. When he passed Eamon, I noticed Eamon was still staring at me.

Without another word, I turned around and stormed toward my father's cottage.

Eamon followed me. Several times, he tried to talk to me as we walked, but my anger made him impossible to hear.

When I reached my father's cottage, I stopped at the base of the porch steps.

There was light in the window. It was close to midnight, but someone was still awake.

Isla.

Maybe Isla is awake.

How would I explain my presence to her? How would I explain Eamon? Or my anger. How could I speak of her father's death without crushing her even more than she'd already been crushed?

My good sense returned. Seph was right. Maybe I should wait until I was calm, until I understood more.

I turned around. Eamon was there, staring at me.

"I'm sorry," he said.

I scowled at him. "How did my father communicate with you?"

"What?"

"He told you about my banishment. You told Maris to come get me...how--?" I turned my head to the side.

Suddenly, my senses were heightened. I could smell something. There was a familiar scent in the air. My memory worked to produce the source but, in the anger, and emotion, I couldn't place it.

It smelled like burning.

Like the fireplaces of the Ambit, but different.

Behind me I heard a creak.

I turned to find a woman standing in the doorway of my father's cottage.

"Britt?" she whispered.

She seemed familiar too, but I didn't know who she was. She wasn't from the Ambit.

"Who are you?" I asked her.

Her round brown eyes glowed with wetness.

"My name is Lucita."

24
THE SIX

"Lucita?"

Zale's mother.

Maris' wife.

James' mother?

The woman before me was small in stature. She had long black hair pulled into a braid that rested over her shoulder. Her eyes were dark and round. She was wearing a white sweater with blue jeans and boots.

"Hello, Eamon," she said, smiling at him.

Behind her in the door, my father appeared. He seemed relieved to see me.

"Britt?" he said with a sigh.

I turned to Eamon, wondering if he knew Lucita was in the Ambit. When I turned back, she'd opened the door the rest of the way for us.

"Please come in, Britt," she welcomed us. Lucita had an accent when she spoke. When she said my name, it rolled off her tongue in a way I'd never heard.

Cautiously, I followed the familiar scent of burning from the base of the porch, up the stairs and through the doorway.

Once I was inside, my memory caught up with me and I saw the old man sitting in the rocking chair, with the white stick hanging from his lips.

"Maris?"

"Hey there, Princess," he mumbled.

"What—How--?"

Next, I found Jonathon, seated at the table. He stood up and moved toward me with his arms open. He'd always been one of my favorite people, but I remembered the way he treated me at the Ruling on the day I was banished. He and my father had thrown me to the wolves.

"Bitty," he said. That was the name he'd called me since I was a child. He was the only one I ever allowed to use it. His gentle spirit made me want to hug him, but I was too angry and confused.

"Don't call me that," I said sternly, narrowing my eyes on him. Defeated, he dropped his arms.

Next, I looked at the man seated beside him at the table. Another familiar face. He had a glass of brown liquid in front of him.

Whiskey.

My stomach turned.

"Hello, Miss Britt," Rutherford's southern drawl pulled the words down and I wondered how many drinks he'd had.

Why is he in the Ambit?

I spun around. Eamon was behind me in the door. I continued to turn, taking each of them in. Eamon, Maris, Jonathon, Rutherford, Lucita, and my father were all there. Like they'd been waiting for me.

Eamon set me up.

He brought me back to the Ambit on purpose.

He used Isla as bait.

"What's going on? Where's Isla?" I asked.

My father stepped forward. "She's here," he said quietly. "Up there." He pointed to the loft overhead.

Without thinking, I moved beyond him and climbed the ladder. In the loft above, there was a lump in the bed. My feet carried me toward her.

"Isla," I whispered, reaching for her, but I pulled my hand back, afraid to wake her.

Would she want to see me?

This might be easier if she's asleep.

I knelt next to the bed and looked at her. Being beside her again, I felt like I was home. I wanted nothing more than to climb into the bed next to her to sleep.

315

I imagined how I would sweep the loose curls from her forehead and push them back. I closed my eyes and listened to her breathing. Calm. Her breathing was clear and steady. I thought of Chasen. Seeing her sleep alone in the bed, made my awareness of his absence ever more present. Thinking of him, remembering him as he was before, mixed with how he was in the end, made my stomach hurt. I fought back the urge to die, every time that feeling came. The feeling of regret and grief. How had I ever moved through it? How had she? As much as I missed him, I knew the pain his twin must feel. They'd shared so much.

I wanted to wake her then. I wanted her to gather her things so I could free her of the memories of all the places she'd shared with him. I wanted to tell her I'd come back for her and that somehow, we would find a way to live without him, forever changed but still alive. Together.

I leaned down and gently kissed her forehead.

"Soon," I whispered to her.

But first, I thought. *There's a room full of people that owe me answers.*

I found my way back down the ladder, stepping carefully. My senses were on full alert.

The whole group, except for Maris, who looked pale and awful, were seated around my father's circular dining table. Maris remained seated in the rocking chair with a blanket pulled up and his cigarette balanced in his lips.

My father nodded toward a spot at the table for me. He'd placed a towel on the chair.

"I made you some tea," he said, nodding toward the steaming cup on the table. "And there's a towel for you to dry off."

I scowled.

"What's going on?" I asked them.

Lucita looked around the table. When no one else spoke, she exhaled a burdened breath and then said, "We're here to warn you."

"Warn me? About what?"

Rutherford answered, "The Underground knows who you are."

I scowled. "That doesn't matter anymore," I said. "I'm not going back to the Outside."

"The Underground isn't just in the Outside," Rutherford said.

"It's not that you're from the Ambit, Britt," Lucita clarified, "It's who you are that they're interested in."

"Who I am?" I scoffed. "Who am I?"

Maris leaned forward, "Remember when I took you there, that I told you not to tell anyone where you were from?"

I nodded. "Yes, you said it would help us blend in."

"Well," Maris coughed from the cigarette. He winced from the pain. "That was true. But really, it's who you are that I didn't want you to accidentally reveal."

"Who I am?" I repeated. I looked at my father.

"You're shivering," my father said. "Can you please dry off?" He grabbed the towel from the chair and handed it to me.

I took it from him and squeezed the water from my hair.

"You're a Laden," my father said.

"A Laden? What does that mean?"

"Our last name is Laden," my father clarified.

I stopped drying my hair. "As in Alexander Laden?"

"You know who he is?"

I nodded, "He was one of the inventors of the MIL. We're related to him?"

My father confirmed, "Alex Laden was my father."

I felt my eyes widen.

"Your father?"

"Your grandfather," he said.

My grandfather?

Was my family responsible for the Crisis?

I shook my head, trying to focus.

"Okay? Why would that matter to the Underground?"

Rutherford answered, "After the Crisis, anyone associated with the vaccine was in danger. People were furious and wanted to take it out on anyone even remotely close to the creators."

"Us?"

My father nodded. "We came to the Ambit to hide, like a lot of others. Everyone that lives here, surrendered their last name when they came. So, no one asks questions about our pasts."

"It's been thirty years since then," I said.

"True," Rutherford agreed, "But they're still looking for your father."

"Why?"

"We don't know," he said. He took a sip of his whiskey and placed the glass back down on the table.

"We know they're up to something. Something that's been brewing for years. But the Underground is so damn slippery, we haven't been able to get a foothold to understand what they want or plan to do. Taking out Gunnar was…" he shook his head, "…the closest we've ever come to finding a crack to creep in. But now we've blown our cover, and our only shot at ever breaking in. Twenty years, I've worked for them. Kept my head down, did their dirty work, and now…" he shook his head, laughing. "…it's all gone."

He threw the glass backward and slurped down all the liquid.

"They're going to be coming for all of us. Now that they know that Eamon and Buckley and I are Storian, they will undoubtedly send an assassin for us," he explained.

"So, you're hiding here?"

"We all are," my father replied.

"Well, I'm not."

"Britt," my father argued.

Rutherford shook his head and scoffed.

"No," I said. "I came here to get Isla. I'm not staying."

My father looked around in a bit of panic, "Isla? You can't take her out of the Ambit. Britt, I need you to understand something…"

"No, I need *you* to understand something," I interrupted. "I'm not staying here, and neither is she."

"Britt," Maris sat forward carefully. "Slow down and hear us out. We know you're angry."

"Angry?" I laughed. "I'm not angry, I'm furious! We thought you were dead, Maris. We cried real tears over you," I growled.

"And I just found out that your son," I looked at Lucita and then back at Maris, "who I think I've fallen in love with, despite your warnings, is the brother of James."

I looked at my father. "Remember, James?! Your son-in-law? My husband? The father of your grandchildren. The one who was murdered in the Outside five years ago and buried right here in the Ambit?! Remember him?!

Or did you forget? Like you forgot to tell me that you knew all along what had happened to him! And then you…" I turned to Jonathon, "And you! The two of you helped the Guiding Authority banish me." My eyes burned at them.

318

"You accused me of killing Chasen," I shook my head. "You know damn well it wasn't true, but you told them I gave him the MIL vaccine. You let them believe that about me. You turned my daughter against me and sent me to the Outside."

I spoke to Rutherford next, "Which, by the way, is terrible and dirty and not at all outside. You know why? Do you know why it isn't outside?" I spun around to look at my father and Jonathon. "Because apparently, there are dragons in the Outside! Another thing no one bothered to mention." I looked back at Rutherford and Maris. "Dragons! Above the ground, hunting humans, real fcking dragons!"

"Britt," my father tried to say, but I wasn't having it. Because in all the confusion and chaos of the last few months, one thing perplexed and devastated me most and they had barely acknowledged it.

"I lost my son!" I slammed my hands down on the table.

They were all still. No one said a word.

"My son!" I yelled. "Chasen." I felt a lump swell in my throat, but I ignored it.

"My sweet and silly and sensitive boy," I growled at my father. "is gone because of the Ambit's stupid rules and your unwillingness to tell me the truth!"

If my tears came now, it would be justified but I was not going to let them silence me. "And I still don't understand what happened to him?! The condition of his body, it was--" my voice cracked. I turned to them. "I deserve answers!"

No one spoke.

"And I deserved your kind words and support that day," I cried. "The only person in the whole damn Ambit that cared about me was Seph. That thirteen-year-old child has more compassion and human decency than the lot of you!" I screamed at my father and Jonathon.

"So no, I don't want your tea!" I yelled, pointing to the cup on the table. "And I don't want your towel," I tossed the towel at my father. "I don't want or need anything from you. I came for Isla. She's the reason, I'm---"

"Mom?"

I looked up. Isla's face was at the top of the ladder in the loft. She was on her way down before I could utter her name. The lump in my throat held it hostage.

When she got to the bottom of the ladder, she stood there in her nightgown. She looked nervously at the rest of the group and then at me. "It was me," she said.

I scowled. "What?"

"Chasen," she explained. "It was me. It was my fault."

"What was?"

Her fault?

"How?"

She looked at her grandfather.

"Please sit," my father's voice was calming.

I looked at Isla. Her eyes settled on the chair at the table that they'd reserved for me.

I pulled it out and sunk down into it, but only because of her request.

Eamon stood from the table, so Isla could sit next to Lucita. He moved to the kitchen and leaned against the counter.

Isla put her hands on the table in front of her and pressed them together. "I was the one that—" she paused, " —it was my fault that Chasen died." She looked up at me carefully.

My pulse quickened.

"It was me," she said. Tears weighed her eyelids down. "I did something to him."

My chest hurt. "You--?"

Lucita took Isla's hand and held it. When she did this, Isla's eyes glanced upward and then back down. I remembered the day at the Ruling when she'd refused to look at me. Now I realized that it wasn't because she thought I was guilty; it was because she thought *she* was.

"She was trying to help him," my father clarified. "She didn't do it on purpose."

He didn't need to say that. I knew how much she loved her brother.

"Isla? What happened?" I asked.

Isla pinched her eyes shut and a tear slipped out. Lucita squeezed her hand.

"I tried to give him some of my blood," she said.

"What?! Why would you do that?"

Isla's face contorted.

"I thought it could heal him," she cried.

Heal him?

320

She thought her blood could heal him!?
There was only one kind of blood that I knew of that could heal.
How would Isla know about that?

"Why would you think that?!"

Isla looked up at her grandfather and said, "Papa?"

He took her cue and turned to me, "In order for you to understand what happened to Chasen, Britt, I need you to understand who *we* are," my father said.

"Who I am? You keep saying that," I replied. "You already told me. I'm a Laden."

My father exhaled nervously. "You mentioned the dragons," he said. "If I'd told you about them before you were banished, do you think you would have believed me?"

I scowled, not understanding.

"No, I don't think that I would have."

He continued, "Because sometimes you need to see something to believe it, right?"

I nodded.

My father took a deep breath and then rose from the table. He walked to the kitchen counter and took a knife from the drawer. He came back to the table and then he held the knife over the palm of his hand.

"Don't be afraid," he said. Then he dug the blade into the flesh of his skin. A red droplet of blood bubbled on the surface under the blade. He cut deeper into his hand, wincing from the pain. He slid the knife along the surface of his skin until he had a three-inch wound. Then he pulled the towel from the table and wrapped his hand in it.

"What are you doing!?" I exclaimed.

"I'm—healing."

"Healing?!" I scowled.

My father removed the towel from his hand. His blood stained the cloth, but the wound was already starting to heal.

I'd seen a wound like that before. I looked down at my own hands where I'd fallen into the fire. Then I remembered Fairchild's injuries when they were healed by the blood of...

"Cinder?" I whispered.

My father's eyes lit up.

"Exactly," he said.

"You know Cinder?" I asked.

He nodded. Then he said, "I don't just know her, Britt. Her blood runs through our veins."

I felt my mouth gape open. "What?" I looked him up and down, half expecting to find scales on his skin to prove it.

"Not just *my* veins, Britt," he said.

"Ours?"

He nodded.

"But I don't heal like that," I said.

"You don't," he agreed. "That's true, but you do have other qualities. Don't you?"

I scowled, looking around at the faces at the table. They were waiting for me to answer.

"I—" I started. "I'm not sure."

"Yes, you are. You've known it all along, Britt. It's okay to be honest about it now."

Be honest? Like I was honest about it when I was a child and he told me I was lying or imagining things?

I searched my father's face. Then I turned and found Isla's eyes were on me too. Her blue eye pierced me.

"Tell them about your pain tolerance," my father demanded.

Tolerance?

I remembered the wound I'd suffered in the farming field the night I found the tooth. I didn't know I was injured before Cinder healed me. I thought about the fire that I'd fallen in at the farmhouse and how I didn't know it until they'd pulled me from it.

I glared at my father.

All my life, he'd told me to suppress it. He told me never to talk about it.

"I—" I started. "I don't have a tolerance for pain," I said. "Because I don't feel it... I don't feel pain at all."

Lucita's eyes narrowed.

"You don't feel it?" she asked. "*Any* pain?"

"I feel emotional pain," I clarified. "I feel pressure and pulling. I can feel temperatures, like right now I'm cold because I'm wet. I can feel things on my skin, like a touch..."

I thought of Zale.

"...or the rain. I can feel sick to my stomach or when I have a headache. But pain - physical pain - I don't feel that."

"She doesn't feel it in the way that we do," my father clarified for them. "We suspected it when she was younger. She'd skin her knee and keep playing with blood dripping down her leg, like she didn't notice. She never cried like other kids. But it wasn't until she gave birth to the twins..." he looked at Isla, "...until you and Chasen were born, that we knew there was something very different about her pain tolerance."

I looked at Isla. "You never caused me pain," I said.

Her chin quivered.

"You and Chasen never brought me anything but joy," I added.

"You're a weirdling too?" she asked.

Wierdling?

I remembered Seph telling me that was the name that the kids at school called Isla and Chasen.

"I guess I am," I smiled.

"We all are," my father explained.

"Is that why you raised me in the Ambit? We were hiding because of our last name but also because of these abilities?" I glared at him. "Does the Underground know about the abilities?"

He looked at Rutherford.

Rutherford answered, "The Underground had no idea about you, while you lived there. It wasn't until after you left on the Blood Mission that they realized who you are."

"How?"

"We don't know."

"But *you* knew who I was?" I asked Rutherford.

He nodded, "I did."

"Then why did you send me on the Blood Mission?"

"You needed to get moved up in the Outside," Rutherford said. "You surviving that first farming mission made you a lot of enemies. You were getting a lot of attention and without that badge I gave you, we knew you and Seph would be targets. There are a lot of men that died trying to do what you did. And I know what men who are threatened by a woman will do to keep her in her place."

I scowled at him.

I thought of the man on the Rally platform that had chased me through the crowd.

I looked up at Eamon.

He was watching my face.

"I sent you on the mission because I was looking out for you and the kid."

"For the record," Maris told my father, "I thought it was a terrible idea."

Rutherford poured another glass of whiskey, "Eh, I knew she'd be fine," Rutherford flapped his hand at us. "Cinder wasn't gonna let anything happen to her."

"What makes you say that?" I asked.

"Because he knew she'd recognize you," my father said. "Since you're a part of her bloodline."

Recognize me?

That's why she felt so familiar to me. That was why she protected us from the monitors and Gunnar.

"Part of her bloodline? Is that why we have these abilities?"

He nodded.

"How do we have her blood in us?"

"When I was a boy," he explained. "I had a rare blood disorder. I was sick all the time."

"Like Chasen," Isla added.

"Yes, similar to Chasen," my father said. "Before he discovered the MIL, my father wasn't a scientist. He was a man of faith."

Faith.

"Religion?" I asked.

My father was surprised I knew that word. He bobbed his head, "Yes, he was very religious. He was a chaplain." He could tell that I didn't recognize that word. "He was a man of God?"

God.

"Do you know what I mean when I say that?"

I nodded, "You mean that he believed in God."

"Yes, and as a man of God, a chaplain, he accompanied doctors on missions to third-world countries, to provide medical and spiritual aid. While he was on a mission, he and some of the doctors he went with discovered...dragons." My father stared at me, waiting to see if I had any questions, then he continued. "They smuggled them back to the United States without anyone knowing. They wanted to study them, and that's when they discovered that their blood could heal."

He paused, then continued, "Now, my father, being a man of God, had a different perspective from his friends. While they were focused on understanding the science and evolution of the creatures, my father believed that the dragons were a miracle. A gift from God."

God.

"Together the six of them created the MIL vaccine from the blood of the dragons," he said.

I looked around, no one else at the table seemed surprised by that statement. I closed my mouth, trying not to give away how shocked I was.

"Motley Roberts," I said.

"Yes, she was one of the other inventors," Rutherford said. "She's the only one that survived the Crisis."

"She's still alive?!"

Rutherford nodded. "It's not common knowledge, but yes. She's in the Outside."

"So, she knew your father…" I said to my dad. "…worked with him? For BioRev? She knows about the dragons?"

"Yes."

I was quiet.

My father continued, "There were two dragons. One was red, the other was purple."

"Cinder?"

He nodded.

"Yes, except they called her Sangi, which was short for Sanguine. Sanguine means blood and it fit her personality."

"What happened to the other dragon? The red one?"

My father took a deep breath. "In the experimentation with developing the MIL vaccine, the doctors discovered that there was one significant difference between the blood of the two dragons. The red dragon's blood would heal without any manipulation. They could take the blood directly from the dragon and mass produce it in large quantities to develop the immunizations. All that was needed for each vaccine was less than a half a drop. Cinder's blood was different. Her blood kept failing in the drug trials."

"Why?"

"Because her blood didn't heal unless she volunteered it. She had to be willing to give it. When it was taken against her will, it did the opposite of what they wanted it to."

"It poisoned?"

He nodded.

"When it poisoned people, did they die from it?" I asked.

My father shook his head. "It never got that far. They couldn't get Cinder's blood approved for use, because the animals they tested it on kept dying."

"So that's what happened to the MIL vaccine in 2084? They used Cinder's blood to create it and it poisoned people?"

My father shook his head, "No, I don't know what caused the vaccine defect, but it wasn't Cinder."

"How do you know?"

"No one, besides my father and I, knew that Cinder was still alive in 2084."

I scowled at him, confused.

"When her blood didn't do what the inventors wanted it to, they decided she was of no use to them. They wanted to kill her and just use the red dragon's blood. They were worried that another pharmaceutical company might find out about how the MIL was created. So, the less evidence there was of dragons, the better. But my father was adamant that Cinder was a miracle sent from God, so he...took her and we hid her."

"Hid her? Like she was your pet or something?"

My father seemed embarrassed, "Sort of."

"How the hell did you have a forty-foot pet dragon without anyone noticing?" Rutherford asked.

"She can make herself vanish," I said.

My father turned to me, surprised. He nodded. "You're right, she can."

"Well, sht," Rutherford cussed. "No one told me that!"

"As time went on, and I got older," my father explained, "Cinder and I bonded, but I got sicker."

"She healed you, didn't she?" I jumped ahead. "Her blood healed you, didn't it?"

My father smiled, "It did."

"And it worked because she gave her blood to you willingly," I said. "She must have loved you."

That's how we have her blood in us.

I turned to Isla, "Did you know all of this?"

She nodded. "Chasen was getting worse," she said. "I'd been having dreams that he was going to—" she paused, and we all knew what she was going to say. "And they were scaring me."

"Why didn't you tell me?"

Her face was sad. "I knew you wouldn't believe me."

Just like my father didn't believe me when I told him I didn't feel pain.

"I told Papa and begged him to do something for Chasen. He told me about how Cinder's blood heals."

"And you thought maybe your blood would heal his?" I asked.

She nodded.

"We had the same blood," she said. "I thought maybe he just needed more dragon blood to heal, but instead...he...he started coughing..." she cried.

"She came to get me," my father said. "But by the time we got there, you'd already found him. And then Jebb—"

Jebb.

"He accused you of sneaking in medicine and we couldn't deny that it looked just like MIL disease, because it had the same effect on Chasen as the MIL had on people in 2084. But if we'd told them it was Isla...we would have lost them both."

"So, you told them it was me?"

I looked at Isla, then my father.

"We didn't tell them it was you; we just didn't tell them it wasn't," Jonathon said.

"Whatever helps you sleep at night, Jonathon," I said. "You could have told me. I would have agreed to it. You know I would have done anything to protect my children."

"I begged them not to tell you," Isla said.

"Why? I would have understood," I said.

"Because you trusted me to protect him. I was supposed to take care of him. I was his big sister," she cried.

"We could have left the Ambit together," I suggested. "We could have worked it out together."

"We couldn't take that risk," my father said, "Isla can't leave the Ambit."

"Why?"

"The Underground knows about her," Rutherford said. "They call her the girl with the one blue eye."

"How do they know about her?!"

"We don't know," Lucita said. "But James knew they were looking for her, he warned us not to let her leave."

"That's why he stopped going on the journeys," my father said. "He was worried they'd follow him and find her."

But then we decided he would go on one more to get medicine for Chasen.

I looked up, "What do they want with Isla?" I asked Rutherford.

"We don't know," he answered, "but I know someone who might."

"Who?" I looked around.

"The same one who turned the blood over to the Underground," Eamon said. He'd been silently listening. His arms were crossed over his chest as he leaned against the counter.

"Zale?"

"Yes," Eamon said.

"Why would he--?" I started.

"He isn't who you think he is," Rutherford interrupted. "He's Underground."

"What? No, he's not." I glared at him.

Rutherford said, "You think he's a victim of the Outside, a survivor, a loner. He's convinced you that he cares about you and that the two of you are partners."

Partners.

"We know that's how he operates. That's exactly how he earned Winnie's trust and convinced her."

"Convinced her? Of what?"

"To turn over the list of Storian," Eamon said.

"Turn it over?"

"He betrayed her," Lucita said softly. "Winnie had a thing for Zale since the moment she'd met him." Lucita looked at Maris. "He knew how to use that to his advantage."

"Winnie was smitten with him. She begged me to make him a Broker," Rutherford said. "Once I did, he got Gunnar's attention. He looked up to Gunnar, wanted to be just like him."

Gunnar. Murderer.

I felt rage grow in me.

"And when Winnie told Zale of her association with the Storian, he sold her out, to Gunnar," Eamon stated.

"He said that was an accident. He didn't know what would happen to her."

Lucita looked at Maris and then back at me. She exhaled. "You said you don't feel pain," she stated. "Physical pain. But you feel emotional pain, right?"

I nodded.

"Well, just like your parents knew there was something different about you when you were growing up, Maris and I knew there was something off with him."

"What do you mean 'off'?"

"He doesn't feel bad when he hurts people," she explained. "When he was little, he'd take what he wanted from others and show no remorse."

"It was like he was born without a conscience," Lucita added. "He uses people to get what he wants from them: power, position, glory, whatever he needs, then he disposes of them. "

"How can you say that about your own son?" I said, feeling frustrated.

"He doesn't feel emotional pain, Britt," she explained.

"He's a survivor," I said. "He's learned how to adapt to the Outside's environment."

"It's not adaptation, Britt," Lucita interrupted. "He doesn't feel emotional pain for the same reason you don't feel physical pain."

I was confused.

I turned my head to the side, trying to understand.

"You said I don't feel physical pain because of Cinder."

My father nodded.

"Then what are you saying? That he has Cinder's blood too?"

Is that why Cinder didn't hurt him? Why she'd protected him too?

Lucita's face was serious.

"Both of my boys did," she said.

"Both?!"

Zale and James both had dragon blood?

No wonder I was so drawn to them. I was rarely attracted to any others, but with them it was instant and now I knew why.

She looked at Maris and then back at me. "Did you know that I knew your father and Jonathon before the Crisis."

"Maris said you knew my parents."

"I did."

"How?"

"I was a patient of your father."

I looked at my father and Jonathon.

"What kind of patient?"

"We owned a fertility clinic," Jonathon said proudly.

Fertility. Babies.

That explains my dad's position at the Child Wellness Clinic.

"I was single at the time," she explained "but I desperately wanted a baby of my own. I didn't want to wait until I had a husband." She looked at Maris and said, "If I'd known I would only have to wait a few more months, I may have done it. But then I wouldn't have had James."

"I was a little preoccupied at the MCC at that time anyway," Maris winked at her.

"MCC?"

"Metropolitan Correctional Center," Rutherford slurred. "Federal prison."

"The building in the Outside, the one with the elevator," Maris clarified.

"The triangle building. That's a prison?"

"Not anymore," Rutherford said. His head dipped and his eyelids appeared to be getting heavy.

"Yes," Maris said. "Old Rutherford and I were cellmates at the MCC up until 2084."

"Why were you in prison?" I asked Maris.

He coughed, "Well, let's just say I wasn't the man then that I am now."

Lucita reached out and took his hand and they smiled at each other.

"After the Crisis," Eamon said, "The inmates were released because there was no one to keep them in."

"For a while there, we ran the city," Rutherford boasted. "We called it the Outside because when you're on the inside, all you care about is getting out."

Maris clarified, "In prison, we call the outside world, the Outside."

Suddenly it all made sense. The inmates named their society the Outside, not because it was outdoors but because it was not inside the prison.

That's why it's so violent there.

And I remembered the signs in the parking garage. They said MCC Guard. The prison guards. That was where they parked below the triangular building before they took the elevator above ground for work.

"You go ahead, honey," Maris said sweetly to Lucita. "Keep telling her about how you know Aldam and Jonathon."

He looked up at me, "I love this story."

She smiled at him and then turned back to me, "Where was I?"

I tried to remember.

"You wanted to have a baby, but you were single," I said.

"Yes, that's right. I saw every specialist on the west coast that I could. But none of them would work with me because I have a blood disorder that makes carrying a child full-term dangerous for me," she explained.

"But you had James and Zale?"

She smiled and then nodded toward my father and Jonathon. "I came all the way from Los Angeles," she stopped and corrected herself, "I mean Los Les."

"Los Les?"

I remembered Zale telling Fairchild that I was from a society by that name.

"Los Les," she explained "...was called Los Angeles before the Purge."

The Purge.

I remembered Eamon explaining that that was what they called the exclusion of some information from our culture after the Crisis.

"Angel," Lucita explained. "They took the word 'angel' out of Los Angeles. So now they call it Los Les."

"What's angel mean?"

Maris laughed, "That's a conversation for another time."

"Anyway," she explained. "The fertility treatment, that your father and Jonathon were experimenting with, worked."

"Experimenting?" I asked.

Jonathon nodded, "Does it really surprise you that your father, the son of Alexander Laden, MIL inventor and 'man of God'," Jonathon made air quotes when he said that last part, "tried some unconventional methods."

"What unconventional methods?" I asked.

"The same thing my father used to heal me," he said.

331

"Cinder's blood?"

My father nodded hesitantly.

"And you were okay with that?" I asked Lucita.

"Oh, I didn't know," she said. "Not until after…"

"After?"

"After the Crisis," she explained. "See, I didn't know I was pregnant and so when I got the MIL that year…"

"Wait, you got the MIL vaccine?!"

She nodded.

"In 2084?"

She nodded again.

"See!" Maris beamed. "I love this part."

"And you survived? Because of Cinder's blood?"

"They saved my life with that treatment," she said.

I sat back in my chair in amazement.

"How could I have been mad at them for that?" she asked. "Sure, it wasn't exactly ethical, but it saved my life. And then, after a few months, I discovered, it'd worked. I was pregnant."

"Of course, by then, she'd met me," Maris coughed.

"James was a part of the dragon's bloodline too," my father clarified.

Jonathon added, "He came to the Ambit all those years ago, to find us. He wanted to know who his father was."

He hadn't lied to me.

"Please tell me you weren't the sperm donor!" I said.

"No," my father shook his head, "there wasn't one. Cinder is asexual, she doesn't need sperm to reproduce. We were able to use Lucita's eggs and Cinder's blood to create the embryo."

"You mean James."

"James," my father corrected himself.

"How did James know where the Ambit was?"

"We knew how to get here," Maris said. "We'd come out a few times before they used the barrier to conceal it."

The barrier.

Technology.

"Did you use technology to communicate with them?" I asked my father. "How did Maris know I was going to be at the Ambit Crossing that night?"

My father looked down at his hands and sighed. "There's a man, in a mask…"

"War Storian," Eamon said.

I looked at my father, "He comes here?"

Rutherford, whose eyes were drooping with exhaustion and drunkenness, looked at his watch.

"It's almost two," he said. "Can we please get to the point here?"

"The point?" I repeated. "I thought this was the point."

"No," he stammered, "The point is…"

He looked around.

No one else responded.

"…now that Zale knows where the Ambit is…"

I looked at Eamon.

Rutherford continued, "…we have a problem on our hands."

"Where is he now?" my father asked.

"At the Crossing," Eamon said. "Buckley knows to keep an eye on him."

"Good," Rutherford said, "So…we need you to make sure he doesn't tell anyone where we are."

I nodded, "Okay, I'll talk to him."

"Talk to him?" Rutherford said.

I looked from one face to the next. "Yes, I'll talk with him. I need to talk to him anyway—"

"We don't want you to *talk* to him," Rutherford said.

I looked up.

"What?"

Rutherford stared at me.

"I'm not going to hurt him, if that's what you're asking."

"I'm not asking. I'm telling you what your part is in all this. To protect your daughter. You're the only one that he wouldn't see coming."

"See coming? You mean you want me to kill him?!"

Rutherford sat back in his chair with a casual ease. He seemed too comfortable asking me to kill someone I cared about. Then I remembered that someone had wanted Buckley to make sure Zale didn't return from the Blood Mission.

"It was you that told Buckley to kill him, wasn't it?"

I looked at Eamon.

"What?" Maris said. "You told Buckley to do what—?"

"--to make sure he didn't come back from the Blood Mission. Yes, I did that." Rutherford wasn't ashamed.

"You son-of-a-btch," Maris said, sitting forward in the rocker. He started coughing from the movement.

"Maris," Lucita put her hand out to stop him from getting up.

"What?" Rutherford said. He was clearly drunk. He stood from the table and swayed back and forth. "Yes, I did. I did what any good leader would do. We have to eliminate the threats. Zale is Underground, I'm sure of it."

"Good leader, my azz," Maris groaned. "If I wasn't half dead over here, I'd kick your azz for that."

"But you are half dead, old man," Rutherford taunted. "Have you asked yourself why that is?"

I scowled at Rutherford, not understanding his point.

"Who demanded the Lupio for you?" Rutherford asked. "No, let me restate my question, for the courts," Rutherford was swinging his glass around as he spoke. I think he was imagining that he was in a courtroom, making a case, like the attorneys I'd read about.

"Who was it that demanded the Lupio injections for you?" he didn't actually restate his question at all. "Why would Zale, who doesn't have the emotional capacity to care about other humans, make a demand like that?"

"Because he *does* have the capacity to care for others," I said to Maris. "I've seen it."

"Oh, she's *seen* it," Rutherford taunted.

I focused on Maris, "He knew you had the Crud, so he bargained for Lupio."

"But Lupio is impossible to come by," Rutherford rebutted. "What do you think Lucita's been out searching for?"

I looked at Lucita. She nodded. "It's impossible to find. I've traveled all over, looking for it."

"But then the Underground magically produced a case full of it and Zale didn't even question it," Rutherford said.

"You didn't question it either!" I scolded him. "None of us did. We believed you when you said it was Lupio! This is ridiculous!"

I turned to Lucita. "This is your son we're talking about here! Your flesh and blood," I turned to Maris. "There must be some part of you that wants to understand him…" I looked back at Lucita, "…you must want to forgive him."

"Blah, blah, blah…" Rutherford mocked me.

"This man is a drunk!" I pointed to Rutherford.

"Britt!" Eamon said.

"And he wants revenge for something that happened years ago. Zale said it was an accident and I believe him. He hates himself for his mistake with Winnie. As much as you all hate him for what he did, I guarantee he hates himself more!"

"His mistake with Winnie?" Lucita repeated.

I stared at her.

She scoffed, "What happened with Winnie was tragic, but Britt, that's not why I won't have anything to do with my son."

"Then why?" I asked, "What on earth could cause a mother to disown her child?"

"He's dangerous. To me and clearly, to Maris. I didn't disown him for what he did to Winnie, Britt. I disowned him for what he did to James."

My face fell flat.

"James?"

"Yes," she confirmed. Her round eyes focused. "He's the one that turned him in," she said. "Zale is the reason that James was killed."

25
THE COTTAGE

"That's not true," I said.

I looked at my father and then Eamon.

Zale was afraid that Eamon had told me something.

Was this it?

Once Zale knew I was the wife that James had left behind, did he know then that I was going to find out that he'd had something to do with his death? My husband's death? His brother's?

"When Winnie died," Eamon said, "She had a list on her. A list of names. The Storian."

"James was on it?" I guessed.

Lucita nodded.

"Did Zale know?" I asked.

"Of course, he did," Rutherford spewed.

"How can you be sure?"

"We can't be," Maris said.

"Which is why you didn't turn your back on him, when everyone else did?" I asked.

"He's my son," Maris said. "I thought there was still hope."

"But you don't now?"

Maris' eyes were heavy. "When a tiger shows you its stripes, you can't keep fooling yourself into believing it's a bunny."

I sat back in my chair.

"If everything you're saying is true, then I can see why you feel like he's a threat, but we don't have any concrete evidence that he's done any of these things."

"Are you serious?" Eamon asked.

"Deadly serious, Eamon," I said. "What if he *didn't* know that Gunnar was going to kill your sister, or that she had a list on her with James' name? What if he really believed Rutherford *could* get Lupio for Maris…"

"And what of the blood vial?" Eamon asked. "He turned it over to the Underground. You can't explain that away!"

"So, what? You want me to go there," I pointed toward the Shelter Tree, "right now and just kill him?"

Eamon's face answered me.

"And *you* agree with this?" I asked Lucita.

"Zale is not like us," she said. "He's a sociopath and he's convinced you that he's something that he's not."

"And you?" I asked Maris.

Maris looked away from me.

Then my eyes fell on Isla.

I thought of what she would think of me if I agreed to this.

"And what if you're wrong?" I asked them but no one answered.

"I'll talk to Zale, but no one is touching him until we know for sure what's happened here." I told them. I could guess that was not the answer they were expecting. I looked from one face to the next. All of them avoided eye contact with me. Isla was the only one that looked at me. She seemed surprised by what they were asking of me.

"I thought you were the good guys!" I said, standing up from the table.

"We are," Lucita said.

"Good guys don't kill innocent people."

"Exactly!" Rutherford yelled. "He isn't innocent!"

He slammed his hand on the table. "He isn't innocent. He's responsible for what happened to my daughter!"

Rutherford's eyes burned at me.

"Your grief is blinding you!" I yelled at Rutherford and Lucita. "Zale did not do what you're saying."

"Britt," Lucita said, "We're trying to stop the Underground from finding Isla and your father. They're sweeping our people. Good people. People who are trying to restore the things we played a part in eliminating with the Purge. We're trying to correct our mistakes--"

"Right! And Zale may be trying to correct his! You can still correct your mistakes, without murdering your son!" I was so disgusted with her for even being willing to entertain the idea.

"And I hate to tell you this, but you can't correct your mistakes by hiding under some invisible dome in a field," I said. "That's hiding from your mistakes, not correcting them."

I looked at Jonathon, "And the Ambit has technology?! Are you freaking kidding me with that? The hypocrisy here is comical!"

I looked at Isla. "I came here for you," I told her. "I didn't know any of this. I had hoped to find answers by coming back here, but more than anything, I came for you."

She smiled.

"The Ambit is your home," I said. "If you want to stay, then I will respect that because there was a time that I made that choice too. But if you want to leave, then come with me now."

"Where are you going to go?" my father asked.

"I don't know, dad," I said. "But I know that we can't stay here. There's a war brewing here that I want no part of."

Isla looked around the table at my father and Lucita.

"Isla?" I said.

Her eyes filled with tears, and she shook her head. "I need to stay."

My heart squeezed.

"You're sure?"

She nodded.

I moved toward her in her seat and scooped her into my arms. I leaned over her and kissed the top of her head repeatedly.

"I love you, Isla," I told her. Then I knelt in front of her and took her tear-stained face in my hands. "I love you more than anything, but I'm not going to kill for them. You understand that, right? They're good people, but they're wrong about this," I said.

She nodded her head.

"You have a choice to make," I told her. "And anytime someone tries to tell you it's only black or white, it's not. There's always a gray area. There's always a third choice, you just have to find it and be willing to stand in it."

I choked on my words.

"Even if that means you stand alone."

She started to cry, "I'm sorry for what I did to Chasen."

"It's all going to be okay," I told her, remembering Chasen's last words to me. I kissed her cheek. "Okay?"

She nodded as she sobbed.

Then I stood and pulled her toward me again. I hugged her and kissed the top of her head some more.

I forced myself to let go of her and stepped away. Then I gathered my emotions with a deep breath and headed for the door.

"Britt," Rutherford called to me. I twisted to look at him. "If you leave here, and go back to *him*," he said, "…we will have to assume you're with the Underground from here on out."

I looked at my father. Then Eamon. Neither of them objected to Rutherford's ultimatum.

I settled my eyes on Isla.

"I will never be part of the Underground, Isla. No matter what they say, do you hear me?"

She nodded.

Then I reminded her, "In an upside-down world, you stand upright on the Truth."

The middle ground.
Between left and right, black, and white.
There's always a space in between.
There's always a third option.
It's often lonely and misunderstood.
It can be barren and unjust.
It is the place between where truth waits, and grace resides.
It's in that tension that we choose love.

I stepped onto the porch and pulled the door closed behind me. My hand clasped over my mouth to conceal the whimper I made, as I broke into silent sobs.

Rejection.

Isla didn't want to come with me.

My father had betrayed me and now he agreed to view me as his enemy.

Maris, Eamon, Jonathon.

I'd trusted them all.

They all rejected me.

Reminders. I thought.

Look for reminders.

I looked up in the direction of the Mall. I remembered the times I'd walked down this same lane: in the snow, in the mud, in the sunshine.

I will never walk this lane again.

Reminders.

The Shelter Tree, I thought. I stepped off the porch and began the slow trek back toward the Crossing.

The Shelter Tree is tall. It has bark that feels like sandpaper.

Banished again.

Reminders.

The Shelter Tree stands at the Crossing between…

She rejected me.

Reminders.

…between the Ambit and the Outside.

Unworthy.

Reminders.

One foot in front of the other.

Alone.

Reminders…

Seph will be there waiting for me.

He is loyal and kind and I can trust him.

Reminders…

26
BROKEN GLASS

Trust can blind you.

When I got back to the Ambit Crossing, it was quiet. Two small red tents were assembled under the tree, and I could see a hammock hanging from it.

Hammock.

Zale.

I wondered which tent he was in. Seeing Nanny goat balled up at the bottom of the tree meant Seph was in the hammock.

I unzipped the first tent and found Fairchild and Buckley tucked in together. Zale must be in the other one.

I had to wake him and warn him. Rutherford and Eamon may come for him now because they believed he was from the Underground. Rutherford told me that they would assume I was too.

Rejection.

We needed to leave before Buckley woke.

I unzipped the tent.

"Zale?" I whispered.

There was no answer.

I crawled inside. It was empty. Not so much as a blanket had been arranged inside.

Where is he?

That was a painful thought.

Did he?

My pulse quickened.

I stepped out of the tent and looked around. There wasn't anything else in sight.

The vehicles. Maybe he is sleeping in one of the vehicles.

I ran toward where I knew the vehicles were parked. Once I moved beyond the barrier and the Ambit disappeared behind me, I found nothing but darkness.

"Sht," I said, fumbling with the flashlight from my belt.

I turned it on.

One of the vehicles was gone.

He left!?

"Cinder?!" I called, wondering if she was still there.

I spun in a circle. Maybe she'd gone with him.

A gust of hot air puffed at me from the darkness.

"Where are you, girl?"

She appeared in front of me.

"Where is he?"

Her yellow eyes stared down at me, unknowing and innocent.

Then I remembered what they'd told me about her. That she and I shared a connection. I put my hand on the side of her face and felt the brittle scales that were layered over her muscles and bones. She had permanent armor.

I wished I'd inherited that from her. What good did not feeling physical pain do me? It was the emotional pain that was going to do me in. I wished I'd had armor against that.

"He left us, didn't he?" I cried to her, like she could understand.

More rejection.

I'd just stood up for him, risked everything to give him the benefit of the doubt, to warn him. Now I had to ask the hard question of myself:

Was I wrong about him?

Then the ground under me rumbled and a horrible exploding sound filled the night. I spun around, but I didn't see anything because I was still outside the barrier.

Above the field in front of me, where I knew the Ambit to be, there was a plume of fire and smoke rising.

Without thinking, I ran toward it. Cinder followed me.

Within the Ambit, the sky was orange and red. An explosion in the Ambit lit up the sky. It looked like it was coming from the center of the Mall.

Fairchild and Buckley wrestled their way out of their tent.

"What happened?" Fairchild yelled.

"Britt?!" Seph hollered from the tree.

"Seph!" I ran to the tree. He was tangled in the hammock. In the confusion, he'd gotten stuck in the netting and was beginning to panic. I climbed up the tree and used his switchblade to help cut him loose.

Just as we climbed down from the tree, another explosion popped inside the Ambit.

"What's going on?" Buckley said. "Is that normal?"

Normal? Explosions are rarely normal.

"No," I yelled, "that's not normal!"

Another explosion. Soon fires were springing up across the Ambit and we could hear the screams of the Ambit citizens as they were waking to the chaos.

"We have to help them," Fairchild yelled.

We started running toward the Ambit.

"Wait," I said. "Fairchild, can you stay here with Seph? Please? I'm going to get my daughter. Take him and Nanny to the car and I'll be right back."

She nodded.

"Britt," Seph argued.

"Seph, trust me!" I yelled, "There's something going on here and I need to know you're not in the middle of it."

"Hey, where's Eamon?" Buckley search for his brother.

"In the Ambit," I said, "I was just with him."

Betrayal.

"Where's Zale?" Fairchild asked.

I stared at her.

"I don't know," I said.

"You don't know?" Buckley hollered.

"He's not here," I said. "I don't know where he is. He took one of the vehicles and left."

He left.

"He left?!" Buckley looked over the fires erupting in the Ambit and then yelled, "that son-of-a-btch did this!"

Did he?

Did he plan an attack on the innocent people of the Ambit?
Had I led him here?
Was this a distraction so he could leave to go back to the Underground to tell them where we were?

His eyes were dark.

Is he coming back for Isla?

Another explosion in the distance burst into the night. More screaming came from the Ambit.

Buckley growled and started running toward the fires.

"I can help," Seph yelled.

"No, Seph, stay here with Fairchild," I ordered. "Please," I said to them both. "Pack as much as you can up and be ready to leave as soon as we get back."

I looked at Seph, "I'm going to get Isla and then we are leaving."

I turned to go, but Fairchild yelled to me, "Britt? What if there are flame-throwers?" Her eyes were terrified. "What if those aren't explosions? What if it's a monitor?"

I hadn't thought of that.

"Cinder?" I looked up at her. She'd followed me through the barrier but had stopped at the Crossing.

"Cinder?" I called to her. "Come on," I waved at her. If there were monitors, she'd be able to help protect the Ambit.

She paced at the Crossing, like she couldn't step over the line.

"Come on!" I screamed, but she refused to cross.

Why won't she enter the Ambit?

Another explosion erupted and I turned. This one looked like it came from the schoolhouse at the end of the Mall. It was the tallest building in the Ambit. From this distance, I could see the flames rising from the peak.

In the sky there was a blue line that seemed to crack the space above the Ambit open. The barrier was breaking. It must have come from a signal in the peak of the schoolhouse building. When the building exploded, the signal broke and the barrier started falling.

I watched as the blue line slid down the outside of the barrier and revealed the real landscape around the Ambit.

"The barrier's down," I yelled. Then I spun in a circle. With the light of the fires, I could see the second vehicle and a thicket of trees in the distance.

"With the barrier down, no one is safe," I yelled. Then I turned and ran toward Isla and the others.

Six explosions.

I ran toward what remained of the schoolhouse where I could see that people were gathering. I knew that's where they would go to look to the Guiding Authority for guidance.

"Secure your livestock and make sure your loved ones are safe," Joylind was yelling to the crowds, "Bring anyone that's wounded here to the Mall. Then assist your neighbors."

Jonathon was there next to him, "Do not go into any buildings," he yelled. "Once your families are out, do not go back into your homes. Someone has planted explosive devices in our buildings, we don't know how many more might go off. Steer clear of them."

I looked around for Isla and my father. Instead, I found Jebb, who had a wooden trunk propped up on a wagon that he'd pulled into the courtyard in front of the schoolhouse. He used a metal crowbar to unlatch the locks on the trunk and flip the lid open.

From inside the trunk, he pulled weapons and started handing them to the citizens that were waiting there. He was arming them.

The Ambit has weapons?

I ran to Jonathon, "Where's Isla?"

He seemed nervous to talk to me.

"Jonathon!" I yelled, "Where's my daughter?!"

"In the bunker," he said. "Below the schoolhouse."

"What?" I said, looking beyond him, toward the schoolhouse, which was still on fire.

"She's safe," he assured me. "The bunker is fireproof. When the first explosion went off, she and your father and the others went there to hide."

"Where is it?"

Jonathon looked at me, then he pointed. "There's a set of doors, like a tornado shelter, on the other side of the school."

"No, there isn't," I scolded him. "I've lived here my whole life, Jonathon. There's no such thing."

"There is," he said. "Go look if you don't believe me, but it's there. It was just concealed."

More freaking technology.

I growled and ran toward the shelter.

"Britt," Buckley called to me. "I can't find Eamon."

"He's with my dad and Isla," I said. "In a bunker of some sort, follow me."

Buckley did as I suggested.

We ran around the exterior of the burning schoolhouse. Several of the Ambit citizens had started a bucket brigade from the lake. They were trying to extinguish the fire at the school. This was how we'd been taught to handle fires in the Ambit.

Along the end of the schoolhouse building, I found the set of doors that Jonathon described. When the barrier signal was destroyed, and revealed the Ambit to the Outside world, it must have taken down whatever was concealing the bunker doors too.

Together Buckley and I each grabbed a door to the bunker and pulled them open.

"Stop right there!" I heard Eamon's voice. He stepped into view with his gun drawn on us.

"Eamon?" Buckley yelled. "It's me!"

Eamon put his gun down. We shared a look.

He knew I wasn't a threat, even if Rutherford had made it seem like I was. All of that had to be set aside for the moment. There were much bigger issues at play.

Buckley stepped down the shelter stairs into the darkness.

I followed him.

Inside the bunker there were shelves of supplies and rations. The walls had hooks with weapons hanging on them. It wasn't just a bunker; it was an armory. For a split second, I was grateful to know that there had always been a plan to protect us. At least the Guiding Authority had enough sense to know not to leave us completely unarmed in a situation like this.

"Mom!" Isla said and ran to hug me around my middle.

They were all there. Everyone that had been at my father's cottage, except for Jonathon, was huddled into the bunker.

Lucita had made Maris a bed on some of the bags of grain.

"What the hell happened up there?" Rutherford asked. He'd clearly sobered up some since I'd last seen him.

"Explosions," Buckley said.

"How many?" Eamon asked.

"Six so far," Buckley told him. "It was Zale."

"Zale?" Lucita looked at me.

"That piece of –" Rutherford cussed.

"See!" Eamon growled at me. "I told you that he was Underground."

"I—" I wanted to defend him, but how could I?

He was gone and I was the one that looked like the fool now.

"You what?" Rutherford pressed me.

"Are there people who are injured up there?" my father stepped forward. "I can go help."

"No, Aldam, you need to stay put," Rutherford said. My father stepped back. "We don't know what's going on. Zale might still be up there."

"He's gone," I said. "I saw it with my own eyes. He took one of our vehicles. He must have rigged the explosives while I was with you," I said to Eamon.

"You were supposed to watch him," Rutherford growled at Buckley.

"I did!" he said. "But I thought that he went to bed, so I figured—"

"You didn't figure nothin'," Rutherford yelled at him. "You sht the bed again, Buck! You good for nothing, little—"

"Hey!" I yelled. "He didn't know Zale would do something like this."

Rutherford's eyes burned at me. "No, *you* didn't think he would. I knew the whole time what he was capable of." He turned back to Buckley, "Didn't I tell you?" He slapped Buckley upside the head.

"Dad!" Eamon yelled.

"Didn't I tell you to kill him while you had the chance?"

Rutherford shoved Buckley backward into a shelf.

I felt like I was getting a picture into why Rutherford may have been an inmate at the MCC. He was an abusive drunk.

"Stop pushing me around, dad," Buckley growled.

"Then stop being an idiot!" Rutherford said, closing in on him again. He raised his hand.

"That's enough!" Maris yelled. Eamon stepped in between his dad and brother.

"Leave the kid alone, Christopher!" Maris yelled.

Rutherford swirled around "Christopher? Are we first-naming each other now, Joshua?" Maris had sat himself up in the bed. He glared at Rutherford. "Whatever gets your attention," Maris growled. "Don't you hit that boy again. This ain't his fault."

"Buckley," Lucita moved toward him. "Are you okay?"
It was clear to all of us that Buckley's ego had been bruised by his father's words and actions.

Humiliated, he said, "Yeah, I'm okay."

"No, really?" she said. "Are you okay?" She pointed toward his chest. "You're bleeding."

"What?" he looked down. Sure enough, there was blood spreading on his jacket.

"I—" he reached up and felt for a wound underneath the jacket. "Ouch, sht!" he said retracting his hand. "What is this?"

He pulled a piece of glass from inside the coat.

"Why do you have glass in your jacket?" Eamon asked.

"It's not mine," Buckley said. "It's Zale's. I borrowed it last night when it got cold."

Zale's.

Jacket.

Glass.

Blood.

I gasped. "That's the vial!" I yelled, pointing to the blood on the jacket.

"What?" Eamon asked.

"The vial! The one you said that Zale turned over to the Underground. He didn't!" I exclaimed.

My mind was trying to work it out in my head faster than the words could come from my mouth.

"He put the vial that Fairchild gave him in his jacket pocket! It's still there! That's it right there!" I shrieked.

"So?"

"So, he didn't hand it over. He couldn't have!"

"Then who handed it over?"

I thought back to the Mission.

"Fairchild had the vials! She—" My eyes darted around the room. "She was the one that wanted the blood most. She's the one that tried to steal Cinder's egg. She's the one..."

Buckley's face was deep in thought.

"Wasn't she with you tonight, Buckley?" Eamon asked.

"Yeah, she was!" he said. "All night. She couldn't have set the explosives because I was sleeping right next to her. She couldn't have gone out without me knowing."

"Yes, she could have!" I yelled. "When we were at the hospital and you two were supposed to be keeping watch for monitors, I took your shotgun right out of your hand while you slept! Remember?"

I remembered how my satchel had swung down, off my shoulder, while I was trying to get the shotgun from his grip. It smacked him right in the face and he never woke up.

"This was Fairchild's doing!" I yelled.

"Where is she now?" Eamon asked.

I heard a screech pierce the air.

Cinder.

I felt panic surge through my body.

I gasped. "She's with Seph!"

Trust can blind you.

27
THE RED RAT

I watched what was left of his innocence slip away. Helpless, he could do nothing but watch as it all unfolded around him. While we were arguing in a bunker, she'd done this.

While I'd trusted her, she'd hurt him.

She'd deceived us all, but he'd paid the greatest price for it. And in this moment, there was no consolation for what she'd done to him. There was no amount of sugar-coating or optimism that could make him unsee the evil she'd brought to the Ambit. There was no way that any of us would ever be convinced that she was anything but what she was showing us now. Evil.

Fairchild is the red rat from my nightmare.

Tears streamed down Seph's face. He whimpered, trying to control his breathing and movements.

He swung ever so slightly.

He was in pain from his hands being bound so tightly behind his back. I knew without looking that they were the same raspberry red color as his face, because his circulation was being cut off.

"Seph," I uttered, agonizing at the sight of him hanging.

Only once did I see him glance to his right, toward the body of his beloved friend. After that he closed his eyes again, like he was wishing his surroundings away. Tears fell, drop after drop, but he knew better than to panic and let them flow uncontrolled. He knew to let the tears seep slowly, even if he couldn't make them stop coming.

I was as close to him, as she would let me get. Every time I tried to move forward, the gun she had pointed at me, would remind me to stay where I was.

Rutherford, Eamon, Buckley, and I had come to see if what I'd suggested was true. I was right but it was already too late. She'd made her move and it was clear that she had the upper hand now.

Above Seph's head, she'd lassoed a noose out of the hammock and tied it to one of the thick branches of the Shelter Tree. Below him, my eyes focused on the only thing that kept him from strangulation and certain death. Cinder.

Cinder balanced Seph's tip toes on her nose, keeping him from hanging completely. I scanned her body and found the source of the screech we'd heard in the bunker. A portion of her tail had been cut off. A pool of her blood and the detached piece of her body lay next to her with a bloodied axe.

I imagine what the moments prior had contained. As we bickered about Zale, foolishly overlooking the enemy in our midst, Fairchild had roped a child to the tree, severed the dragon's tail and…she'd killed our goat.

Other than Cinder under him, Seph was a mirrored image of Nanny's body on the other side of the tree. With nothing under her, to keep her alive, her lifeless body hung. I couldn't look at her for very long because hatred brought the vomit in my stomach to the brink of explosion.

What kind of a person would hang an animal from a tree like that? Not just an animal, but a pet, a family member. What kind of an evil monster was she that she could hang an innocent child from a tree?

Hate raged in my veins as I paced trying desperately to keep from running toward the tree that was threatening to kill Seph. I fumed at Fairchild as she smiled at me from the base of the tree. She had been there waiting for us, like she wanted us to see what she had done while we were gone, while we had trusted her.

My body forced me to breathe.

Reminders.

Seph is alive.

Fairchild won't be for much longer.

"Awe, come on now!" Fairchild taunted us. "You guys really seem surprised by this," she laughed.

Eamon lunged toward her. "Don't!" She yelled at him, pointing her handgun in his direction. Eamon stopped.

I recognized the handgun to be the one labeled *GUNNAR*. It seemed appropriate that she would have had it in her possession. I hadn't seen it since the night I learned its history. She must have picked it up from the fire pit, where I dropped it.

"All of your weapons…put them on the ground in front of you," she ordered. "Now!"

"Fair, what are you doing?" Buckley stepped forward. "This isn't like you."

She threw her head back, giggling at her own deception. "Like me? You don't even know me, Buckley! You really are as dumb as they say, aren't you?"

She pushed off the Shelter Tree, that she was leaned against. Then walking in front of us, she kicked the surrendered weapons away. She stopped in front of Buckley.

"Guess what, Buck?" she emphasized the 'ck' when she said his name. "I'm not as dumb as you." She smiled, extending her hand. He jumped as she touched his belt buckle.

"Settle down," she ordered. Then reaching down the front of his pants, she retrieved a tiny pistol that he had stored there.

Buckley's face turned red. She tossed the pistol to the side, then tilted her head and smiled slyly at him. "I'm gonna need this little one too."

She backed up a few feet.

"What do you want?" Rutherford demanded.

She turned to him. "Funny *you* should ask." She pointed her gun at him. "In fact, it's funny to see you here at all. Ya know, Gunnar had his suspicions about you, but I wasn't sure."

Rutherford didn't say anything.

"You *know* what I want," she said seriously. Then she nodded toward Cinder, "And I just got it. But I couldn't leave without saying good-bye."

"Then just go!" I screamed at her. "Leave!"

"I can't leave now," she said. "Not now that I know *you're* here." She said to Rutherford.

She didn't hesitate for even a second before she lifted her gun to Rutherford's forehead and pulled the trigger.

Time slowed, as the force of the bullet threw Rutherford's head backward. Bits of flesh and bone splattered on the faces of Buckley and Eamon, who stood closest to him.

Instinctively, I ducked down and covered my face. I had closed my eyes, but when I opened them, disbelief turned to terror. Rutherford's body tumbled to the ground. Buckley and Eamon both shrieked.

"Fairchild!" Buckley cried. He knelt next to his father's body.

She pointed the gun at Buckley. "Get up!" He took a long look at his father's body and then reluctantly rose.

"Might as well get it out of the way now," Fairchild shrugged. "They would have just sent me all the way back out here to do it anyway. It's the whole two birds, one stone thing."

Fairchild dabbed at her face with her free hand. Rutherford's blood had splattered on her. Even from this distance, I could see that she hadn't cleared it; she only smudged and streaked the red droplets. The red tarnish made her look even more insane.

Fairchild turned her attention to me. She patronized me. "Well, little Ambit girl, have you figured it all out yet?"

I didn't say anything.

"No?" she teased. "Well, let me explain something to you. In the Outside, everyone has secrets. Your secret is that you're from the Ambit. Rutherford's secret is that he was Storian. My secret is that I'm not some helpless little whiny girl."

"You're an assassin for the Underground," Eamon declared.

"See!" she pointed to him but looked at me. "He's the smart one here. I thought he was going to be a problem, that he'd be on to me in a heartbeat. But it turns out…"

She laughed. "…that he was so distracted with you and jealous of the thing you have with Zale, that he couldn't see past it."

She turned back to him and finished, "Couldn't see what was right in front of his nose because he wanted it to be Zale so badly."

She exhaled.

"All of you," she said, "it turns out were so distracted with each other, that I was able to slip under the radar." She looked at me. "I thought for sure that you all had me when I stole Cinders eggs. But no, you were more concerned with Buckley."

She laughed. "Word to the wise, Britt. Playing dumb and pretty and innocent and helpless always throws them off the scent. You know why?"

I glared at her.

"Because that's all they want us to be anyway. Men don't want women to be fighters. It's against their nature to see us as a threat. And the Underground knows that which is why they sent me."

She came closer to me. "But there's more to us, isn't there?" She seemed to be seriously asking me. I stared into her eyes. There was a genuine point there that she was trying to make.

Lights flashed across her face. Off in the distance, we could hear the engine of a vehicle approach. "Oh, and here comes lover boy now," she laughed.

"Zale?" I said without realizing.

"Of course!" she said, still smiling. "Who else?"

The vehicle came to a halt. The door flew open and Zale ran toward the tree. "Seph?" I heard the genuine concern in his voice. He hadn't yet noticed the rest of us.

Fairchild took aim with her gun.

"Zale!" I screamed.

Fairchild fired off a round toward Zale.

He stopped in his tracks. He looked around to see where the shot came from.

"Oh," Fairchild said, "You spoiled the surprise!"

"What the hell?" he asked, confused. His hands went up into the air. "Fairchild, what's going on?!"

She nodded for him to move away from the tree. Soon he was lined up with the rest of us. "You didn't find what you were looking for, did you?" she laughed.

I looked at Zale.

"C'mon now, tell her. It's too good."

"You want her to know something," he replied. "Tell her yourself."

"Okay," she smiled. "Zale was looking for your book or should I say James' book?" Then she laughed, "Actually, I should probably say that it's *my* book now."

"You took it?!" I moved closer.

"Ah, ah, ah…step back!" she growled.

"Zale thought he'd try to find it for you," she said, "isn't that sweet? And I…being the brilliant btch that I am…told him I saw it at the farmhouse." She laughed. "And he went all the way back to try to find it for you!" She chuckled, then she moved toward Zale.

"It was too perfect too," she told him. She laid her hand on his chest. "...because I really didn't want to have to kill you and hide your body in the trunk."

My blood boiled as she touched him.

"You and me, Zale," she proposed, "We're really not that different. Remember when you told Gunnar about Winnie? Remember all the fun it was to run the Storian off?"

She looked at me.

"Britt already thinks you're one of us," she leaned in close to him, while staring at me.

"And I heard a rumor...that the Caller position, just recently came available..." she laughed, nodding toward Rutherford's body.

Zale stared at him.

"I can put a good word in for you, if you're interested?" she asked him.

Zale looked at her out of the corner of his eye. "No, thanks. I'm good."

His eyes rose to meet mine and I knew he hadn't betrayed us. I was the one that had betrayed him because I believed what they said.

"What is it that you want?" Zale asked her.

"I got what I came for," Fairchild answered. "But you all have been so kind to give me more. Now I know where the Ambit is. And with the barrier down, it shouldn't be too hard to find my way back. And... if this is the Ambit, then I'm guessing there are a few people in there that the Underground will be pleased to know about."

I turned to Eamon. Fairchild was there for my father. She didn't know that I was his daughter.

"Mother?" a voice called from behind me, and Cinder screeched in response.

I turned; Isla was running toward me. My father chased behind her. Cinder squirmed and writhed, all while holding Seph up from underneath.

"Isla, no!" I screamed to her. "Go back!"

"Isla, wait!" my father hollered after her.

Isla stopped, scanning the area around us. When she saw Seph hanging from the tree, she started running toward him. "Seph!" she cried.

Fairchild pointed the gun at her. Before I could think, I darted in front of the weapon with my hands up. "No!"

Isla scurried behind me.

"Isn't that sweet?" Fairchild teased. "Your daughter came to join the fun."

"Mom?" Isla whimpered.

I twisted and pulled her around to my side. Then I leaned over and whispered, "Don't let her see your eyes," I said.

"What was that?" Fairchild asked.

We were quiet.

Fairchild gazed at Isla. Isla looked at the ground. The smile faded from Fairchild's face.

"Come here," Fairchild ordered her. "And look at me."

"No," I said, pushing Isla around behind me again.

"Stay where you are, Isla," I ordered.

"Move," Fairchild demanded again.

I gulped, swallowing my fear. "No," I said.

There was no way I was going to move.

Fairchild put the gun to my temple and screamed, "MOVE!"

"Britt!" Zale hollered.

"Mom?!" Isla squealed. Then she let go of me and stepped around my side. I froze; I could feel the barrel of the gun pressing into my temple.

"Keep your eyes closed," I muttered.

"Why?" Fairchild asked, "Are you afraid she'll see something you don't want her to?" Then realizing there might be a different reason, she quieted.

She looked down on Isla.

"Open your eyes," she said.

Isla stood with her eyes closed.

"Don't!" my father yelled to her.

"Papa?!" Isla cried.

"Shut up!" Fairchild yelled at my father, moving the gun from my head to point at him. Then Fairchild turned the barrel of the gun toward Isla and pressed the gun into her temple as she repeated herself, "Open your eyes!"

"Fairchild!" I shouted, seeing the gun pointed at my child.

Tears squeezed around the corners of Isla's eyelids. She could feel the cold metal of the barrel on her.

"Fine!" Fairchild said, "Then I'll just shoot your mom—"

"No!" Isla yelped, opening her eyes in response.

Fairchild watched her, studying her features. Then she smiled in delight, seeing what we were trying to keep hidden from her.

She looked at me in a knowing way.

"What pretty eyes you have," Fairchild told Isla, recognizing her one blue eye.

My stomach turned.

"So," Fairchild looked at me, "*this* is your daughter."

I scowled at her.

"And that is your father?" she said, gesturing toward where my father was standing in the field.

"Aldam Laden," she said. "You haven't aged a bit."

She recognizes him!

"You are quite the catch, aren't you?" she asked me.

"Okay, you can close your eyes again now, Isla," she said.

Isla looked up at Fairchild. Her eyes were wide and terrified.

"Why?" she asked.

"Close your eyes now, dear Isla," Fairchild said.

"Fairchild," I said, "Don't you dare hurt her." I inched closer.

"Hurt her?" Fairchild stopped and looked at me.

"I'm trying to protect her. No child should have to watch their loved ones die."

Before I could register what she'd said, Fairchild aimed at my father and pulled the trigger.

28
THE DEAL

The burst from the barrel of the gun rung in my ears, deafening me. Isla screamed.

I turned to look at my dad. She'd shot him in the chest, a spot of red instantly began pooling under his shirt. He fell to his knees and then onto his face.

Isla screamed again. By the time I turned, Fairchild had already begun pulling her away from me. She was moving toward the truck with Isla at gunpoint.

Terror rushed me, "Fairchild!" I screamed, moving toward her. I felt desperate angry tears flood my eyes and swell my throat.

I kept my hands up, but I charged toward them.

"Fair!" Buckley yelled, "Stop!"

"Shut up!" Fairchild shouted at him. Then she turned the gun back to me. "Stay where you are!"

I didn't listen. I slowed down but I kept advancing.

Fairchild reached the tree, still holding onto Isla. As they got closer to Cinder, the dragon began to squirm.

"Get her, Cinder," Seph was saying. "Help Isla!" He took a deep breath, "Let me fall, Cinder!" He was trying to kick Cinder away from him so she could go after Fairchild.

"No!" I put my hand up to Cinder. "Don't, Cinder, please stay!"

Fairchild and Isla inched toward the severed tail on the ground.

"Pick it up!" she ordered Isla.

Isla hesitated at first, but when Fairchild pointed the gun at me again, Isla did as she was told.

Once she had the tail in her possession, Fairchild grabbed her by the arm again and started pulling her toward the truck that Zale had returned in.

"Fairchild!" Zale screamed. "Let her go!"

"Fairchild, please?" I cried.

"Go get her, Cinder!" Seph begged.

Cinder squirmed.

I felt my blood rushing. Desperation was filling me. I knew that if Fairchild managed to make it to the truck with Isla, our chances of getting her back were slim.

"Mom!" Isla cried.

"Fairchild," I begged. "Please!"

They made it to the truck. Still keeping the gun trained on me, Fairchild told Isla to open the door of the truck and put the tail inside. Then she told her to get in, but Isla refused.

Something came over me. Words, thoughts, images of what would happen next if Fairchild wasn't stopped.

I knew the thoughts and words that were brewing inside me were not my own. They were emanating from somewhere deeper than my understanding.

I was still moving toward the vehicle.

"Stay back!" Fairchild screamed. She appeared to be panicking. Up until now, she'd been calm and collected. Something about me pressing toward her had her on edge.

"Britt!" she yelled. "I will kill you if you come one inch closer to me."

I stopped.

We stared at each other.

For some reason, she didn't move. She didn't rush off. I watched as her chest heaved with anxiety. It was like she wanted to hear what I had to say. She didn't want to shoot me.

I kept my hands visible.

"A lot has happened here," I said. The words were coming, but I wasn't sure where they were coming from.

"A lot has happened," I turned and nodded toward the field where Rutherford and my father were both laying. My eyes directed her toward the Ambit, where she'd blown up homes.

"And I don't know why," I said. "I don't know who you are working for, or why, but I do know that this is not what you want to do."

"You don't know anything about me!" she growled.

"I know more than you think," I said. "I know about the Ambiex."

Her eyes changed slightly.

"I know how Gunnar treated you," I said. "And I can only imagine all the things you've seen and all the wrongs that have been done against you. You said that day at the farmhouse that War Storian forgot about you. Forgot to rescue you. So, I know that whatever has happened to you. That it's been happening all your life."

Her chest heaved, but she didn't move. She stared at me, listening.

"I know that if you take my little girl back there, they will do the same things to her that were done to you!" I cried. "And I don't know why you think you have to do that, but you don't, Fairchild."

I shook my head. "No one will know that you found her," I motioned toward where she'd put the tail in the car. "You have Cinder's tail. You have her blood. That's what you came for, isn't it? No one will know the difference if you don't take her with you."

I closed my eyes and took a deep breath.

"A life for a life?" I asked.

I opened my eyes and looked at her.

"A life for a life?" I begged.

Fairchild's eyes were curious.

"You leave her here," I said, "And I will never come for you."

I cried. "And if I ever have the chance to repay you for leaving her behind, I will. I promise you."

Fairchild's face softened.

"I will see you, Fairchild," I yelled. "Not for what you've already done, but for what you choose to do in this moment. We can move forward from here. Just let her go and I will remember you in *this* moment, not the others."

Her face changed again. It contorted as though she was having a battle within herself.

Finally, her face was still, and she looked around at all of us, as though she was seeing us for the first time.

She looked down at Isla. She was holding her by the arm.

She pushed Isla toward me.

"Go," she whispered.

My heart thundered inside me.

Isla ran from her.

Fairchild moved around the vehicle and opened the door to the truck. Before she climbed in, she looked up at me.

I had Isla tucked into my arms.

Fairchild stared at us. She looked around at all the chaos that she'd created and then she said, "A life for a life."

Fairchild climbed into the vehicle and took off. Before the truck was even out of sight, we went to work. Zale and Eamon ran to the tree, climbing on top of Cinder to reach Seph. After cutting the rope that threatened him, Zale cradled the boy in his arms and helped him down to Eamon. Once Zale was off Cinder's back, she collapsed from exhaustion.

Buckley was laying over his father's body, sobbing. I looked for my own father. Isla was with him, trying to roll him over. Tears were streaming down her face.

"Papa?" she sobbed.

I ran to them. His breathing was labored, but he wasn't dead. Somehow, he wasn't dead.

He can heal.

"Dad?" I said. I got down and pressed my hands over the wound in his chest. "Dad?"

His face was pale, and his eyes were rolling back in his head. "Zale!" I screamed. "The medicine, from the pharmacy bag!"

Zale ran toward the other jeep for medicine. His breathing was slowing.

"Dad?" I cried. "Dad!"

I looked up at Isla. "He's supposed to heal, right? He can heal?"

She was sobbing. She shook her head, "Papa?!"

I turned to look at Cinder. Her blood could heal him. But she was too injured to move, and I couldn't take her blood against her will. They said it would poison him if I did.

I looked up at Isla.

"Isla?"

She looked at me.

"Can you—"

Her eyes cleared.

I started again, "Can your blood…heal him?"

She shook her head, "No….Chasen," she whispered.

"You thought you could heal him, and it didn't work, but you must have had a reason to think it would, right?"

I kept pressing my father's chest. My hands were covered in his blood.

"Isla," I said, "He's dying. Either way, he's dying."

She looked up, then back down at him.

"Please try," I choked.

She took a moment and closed her eyes and then she inhaled.

"I'll try," she said.

"Eamon!" I yelled.

He was behind me.

I ordered, "Give your knife to Isla! Quick!"

He pulled his pocketknife from his belt loop and switched it open.

"Cut your palm," I told her. "Just like you saw Papa do earlier. Not too deep, just until you bleed."

She pinched her eyes closed and pressed the blade into her hand until she let out a whimper.

"Good," I said, "that's enough. Now let it drip on him."

"Drip on him?" she asked.

"Yes, bleed on him!"

29
RIPPLE

The splash.
Circles spread.
Waves rolled and then the calm returned.

Seph was sitting at the edge of the water. He picked up a stone and tossed it. It skipped across the glassy surface and then disappeared below.

"Seph," I said softly, so that I didn't scare him. He turned to me, and I saw the bruise across the side of his face, his swollen eye, and the purple burn around his neck from the rope.

Rage.

I'd promised her a life for a life, but I would kill her if I had the chance. I already knew it was a lie, a promise that I was willing to break. I wanted to chase her down and hold my hands to her throat, until she felt the fear that Seph had. And then I would hold just a little longer, press a little deeper and let her feel her life leave her.

Fairchild had deceived us. And for what? For whom?

I didn't understand the kind of cruelty that she'd come from, to have been a victim to the things she had, but then to feel so afraid of them, that she'd still return. Still carry out their orders.

I looked behind me to where Isla was working alongside the others to clear the debris from the burned schoolhouse.

In the moments when I thought I'd lose her too, something had come over me. I'd made an offer to Fairchild, and it worked.

"A life for a life."

The offer haunted me, but it'd worked.

I took a seat next to Seph. He'd been deep in thought like this since we'd returned from the Ambit Crossing. Staring at the water, throwing stones, and watching them ripple. While he hadn't said much, I could feel the depth of his pain. He'd lost his mother, sister, father, Chasen, and now Nanny. He'd been beaten in the Ambit, stuffed in a closet for days, and hung from a tree.

And for what? To what end?

He'd been caught in the crosshairs of an adult world with selfish grownups who lied and stole and murdered.

Why had we done this to him?

For a child, I imagined it was hard to understand all the complex pieces to what could drive adults to such ugliness. But I knew them. All too well, I knew the pieces of my own life that had moved me to isolate, pretend, lash out, distrust, and rage.

Then an odd thought came to mind.

I thought of Gunnar and wondered what the pieces of his life were like. What was he like as a child? I imagined him in the arms of a mother and wondered how he had been moved to murder?

I thought of the Underground, the puppeteers, whoever they were, and what their stories were. I thought of War Storian and Fairchild and Coya and James and Elles and Rutherford. I closed my eyes and knew that we were all once children. Like Seph, we were all born hopeful and unaware of what made adults angry and mean to each other.

Maybe the Collective is on to something, I thought.

Maybe a society run by children was better than leaving it to jaded adults to try to decide the future of our world.

I turned to Seph and forced myself to see his face and neck. He was looking ahead at the water. He knew I was studying him, that I could see all that she'd done to him, but he chose not to look at me. He didn't want to see my reaction. This allowed me to respond honestly, without pretending.

It was horrifying. His lips were cut, cracked, and swollen. His eyes were bloodshot from the lack of oxygen. His fingernails were broken, and his wrists had burns from the rope that matched his throat.

I exhaled, allowing the knowledge of what'd happened to him to sink in. I didn't want to shy away from the thoughts, as painful as they were, because I wanted to share them with him, so he would know he wasn't alone.

The bruises and burns would heal, but the scars from the trauma of what and who had caused them, would never go away. Not for him and not for me.

What should I say in this moment?

As a good guardian, shouldn't I tell him it will all be okay? Shouldn't I remind him that Fairchild hasn't been loved well and so she acts this way because she doesn't know any better?

I didn't want to say either of those things. One felt untrue and the other felt too graceful. Instead, I wanted to offer him something that was in the middle. Something that wouldn't undermine his raw real emotions but would still offer him hope that was based on truth, not idealism.

"Remember the untold story?" I asked him.

He looked down at his hands. He was fiddling with a flat rock with a jagged edge. He was running his finger along the jagged edge. I wondered if the pain from the edge of the stone offered him some release for the pain he had welled up inside. He pushed the stone into his finger until a bubble of blood appeared and I knew it represented the pain he didn't know how to release. The pain he didn't know what to do with.

Then he looked up at me.

"You said, the untold story was inside us and that it feels like it's the only thing that all this pain and cruelty can't touch. Do you remember?"

He let his head nod ever so slightly. He rubbed the jagged stone against his finger again, pressing it harder this time. He was angry and didn't know how to let it out in a healthy way.

"It's the only thing that doesn't change," I reminded him.

He stared at me.

"This pain ends, Seph. I know it must. Not just the pain you feel on your skin and in your muscles," I reached across and laid my hand over his to stop him from pressing the sharp point into his skin any further.

"…but the pain that is deeper than that. The pain that has reached the insides of your mind and broken your heart. That pain will end. Maybe not in this life, but it will end someday because one thing we know for sure in all of this is that it ends. Pain doesn't get to hold us forever."

His eyes were heavy with wetness.

"But the untold story. I don't think it ends. I don't think it goes away. I think this is just the beginning of it actually. Listening to the untold story, allowing it to tell you about itself, I think that's the beginning of something."

I looked out over the water in front of us. Beyond the edge of the Ambit's lake, I could see subtle green hills framed by a line of red, yellow, and orange trees on the horizon. The fall had touched the leaves in the most beautiful way. With the Ambit's barrier gone, we could all see what was beyond. Our vision of the great unknown had been restored.

"I think the untold story might be our creation," I said. "I think it might be the tale of how a human came and walked the earth. How love was born. How grief was what happened when love continued after death. I think the untold story is where we've come from and where we go to…" I took his hand. "…when the pain ends."

He squeezed my hand.

"This hurts," I said. "It hurts really bad, but this isn't it for us. We just need a moment to let it hurt. We need some time to let the parts that can heal, heal. And we need to keep reminding each other that pain has an end."

He looked at me and a raspy voice, from the damage to his vocal cords, he said, "But the untold story doesn't."

Then my heart fluttered as he painfully pressed his lips together and let the curl in his lip appear. His Seph smile.

I nodded. Then I sat with him in silence and let the space between us be grief.

I sat and watched the calm ripple across the water. The reflection of rolling clouds danced on the surface. I looked up into them.

I remembered the day at the farmhouse when I'd recognized the landscape and how beautifully it was painted.

Who painted it?

In the sunshine, as a breeze swept across the water, I closed my eyes and remember that I was a part of the scenery too. I was a part of this creation, just as the clouds and yellow leaves and rippling water droplets were. We were all a part of it, yet humans and nature seemed to be at odds with one another.

Humans destroyed the beauty around them, or at the very least, they forgot about it. They ignored it or allowed themselves to be distracted from it.

How often had I walked the lanes of the Ambit in my life and stared at the ground? At the heavy snow or the muddy puddles. Even though there was an invisible dome over my head all those years, it never blocked out the sun. I just forgot to look up.

I was reminded of the unchanging nature of the sun.

What curse was upon me that I could keep forgetting its faithfulness? What weapon was used against me to deceive and distract me from what was real and tangible and gloriously placed right in front of my face?

Why are humans the only ones fated to feel that tension? What makes us different from the trees in the distance or the fish under the surface of the water in front of me? They don't war with each other.

So why are *we* doomed to despair?

The truth of the tangible things in front of me, were evidence of the thing that I could not see. Because the presence of the creator was in everything around me. Like he'd put pieces of himself into his creation. And wouldn't that mean that he'd also put a piece of himself into me?

That piece felt like a promise that I'd never realized was there. A promise for more, the untold yet known promise for something more complete than this war and hunger and loss?

The survivors of the Crisis tried to purge the afterworld of a presence known as God because they felt that if God was real, then he wouldn't have allowed the Crisis to happen. But what if, the Crisis happened despite God, because of us? Because it was what we chose? Because we were broken?

Would God let us choose? Wouldn't expecting him to stop the Crisis be expecting him to control us?

I didn't want to be controlled. Being controlled meant bending to the will of another. Was God in control, or were we?

If I'm a part of the creation that I see around me, and if I was beautiful in my innocence as a child, then wasn't it the mistakes, and jagged edges, of adults that marred me. Like the jagged edge of Seph's stone cut his finger? Didn't I collect my hurts and pass them on to others? To my children?

If God is in the presence of creation around me, then hasn't God been with us through it all? Quiet but complete. Forgotten but faithful. Unwavering but untold.

If He is presence, then even in their attempts to purge him, He never left us. He was never gone, only untold.

Somehow, I knew it to be true, looking out over the creation too beautiful to attribute to any other.

Didn't I know that humans were too flawed to create these hills and the clouds in the sky? Then I must know they were too flawed to understand the creator that did?

If I'm a part of creation, then there is a Creator.

The Creator is the untold story. Inside me there was a piece of Him, waiting to be discovered. I'd been separated from him. But not because he had ceased to exist, but because I didn't know to feel him. I didn't know how to name him.

He was just as much a part of me, as sight, and breath, and like those senses, I'd sensed Him. I just didn't know what he was.

He is the untold story.

He is the story.

He is history.

They weren't trying to purge history.

They were trying to purge His story.

I gasped and tears sprang from my eyes. This felt like a moment of realization, set in time, specifically for me. I twisted around and looked at the people around me. They busied themselves with the rubble from the fires and rebuilding. They were already set about their next distraction, while I sat at the edge of the lake aghast with realization.

The freedom I'd longed for was never about being in or out of the Ambit. I didn't need to be freed from the Ambit, I needed to be freed from the *fear* of the Ambit.

And if I was no longer afraid, then I could be released to press for change. I could be empowered to ask for something different for the future generations. I could move about. I could cross lines. I could learn. I could teach.

I turned to Seph. Hadn't he felt the earth shatter with that realization?

No.

Because somewhere I knew it was just for me. Just what I needed. It was my moment.

For a moment, it was like taking a breath of fresh air. I could feel it fill my lungs and flutter around inside of me. Just as the Ambit barrier had been broken to reveal new territory. So had the barrier in my mind.

I was no longer within the ambit of my mind.

With new-found perspective, I stood up.

I turned and found Zale working with the others. I watched him help them clear the debris.

After he finished moving a large cement block from the interior of the schoolhouse, he stood in the sun for a moment. He closed his eyes and let it warm him. Seeing him in the natural sunlight, without the distraction of farming or running for our lives, softened me to him. He knew how to appreciate the sunlight after so many years in the dark.

I drew closer to him.

When I settled in front of him, I blurted, "I believed what they said about you, because I don't know how to trust you."

His face was surprised but serious.

"The person I trusted most in the world, only ever shared half of himself with me," I said.

"I—" he started.

"I loved your brother more than I've ever loved anyone. So much that I overlooked the secrets and half-truths he told me. I didn't even know he had a brother," I said, smiling at how absurd it felt to be standing in front of James' brother now.

"I didn't know about the monitors or Storian. And I'm trying to understand why he would have shared the Bible and other parts of our history with our daughter, with Isla, but not with me."

It felt vulnerable to say all of it.

"I may never know why, and I'll probably spend the rest of my life wondering if it was just that I wasn't enough for him? Or if he tried to tell me and I didn't hear him? Or if he just didn't get the chance because he thought he'd have more time...?"

I took in a big breath. "But none of that is your fault. And when I reflect on every adult that's ever lied to me, the only person I come back to that told me the truth about absolutely everything, even when I didn't want to hear it..."

I looked at him, "...was you."

"And the only person that saw through all of my lies," I laughed, "from the beginning, was you."

His eyes softened.

"I'm beginning to wonder if anyone in the world has ever seen me the way you do, and I—"

"Britt," Zale started.

"Your mom told me that you don't feel emotions like I do," I continued, without giving him a moment to rebut what I needed to say. "She said you don't feel emotionally connected to others and I was thinking that maybe that's a good thing. Because then, you and I can still be partners but not anything else. That maybe..."

"I don't feel fear, Britt. That's all," he said. "I know it sounds crazy, but I don't." He looked at me, "But I do feel *everything* else."

I stopped talking and looked at him, in confusion.

"I don't feel fear the same way others do," he said. "That's why I was so good at farming. Why I was a good Broker. Why I stood in front of you when Cinder wanted me to move. Because I lack the good sense to run for my life," he laughed. "Remember I said to you once, you either run toward danger or you run from it?"

I nodded.

"I'm someone that will always run toward danger, because my brain processes the danger differently, but emotion..."

His eyes were tender as he shook his head back and forth, "I feel all of that. Like...the deep regret I feel for what happened to Winnie because of me. And for what happened to the other people on that list. I never meant for any of them to get killed."

He looked down at his hands and then back up, "And James." He exhaled. "He and I were never on the same page. I didn't even know he was back in the Outside at the time. He'd disappeared and I was…" he shook his head, "…I was happy he wasn't down there because he always had a way of, overshadowing everything I ever did. Especially when it came to mom."

I smiled. I could imagine that being true.

"James was my mother's greatest achievement, I could never live up to her expectations after having a son like him," he smirked. "Until last night, I didn't understand why, but now…" he laughed. "Knowing what we do about Cinder's blood running through our veins. It makes so much sense. He was her miracle…and I was…well, I was the product of Maris."

He looked toward Maris, who was seated in a rocker on the stoop of the clothier's shop, a cigarette clung to his lips.

"Don't get me wrong, I'm damn proud to be the son of that man, but I'm made different from James." he explained, "I'll never be him and my mother is never going to forgive me for my part in his death."

He stared at me.

"And I'll never be able to live up to whatever he was to you. And that scares me," he laughed. "Isn't that funny? I don't fear for my life when I'm faced with dragons, but you terrify me."

He stepped back from me.

"Zale?"

His eyes cleared and his jaw tensed.

"I'm going to be right here," he said. "Whatever comes next, I'm going to stay close by, if that's okay?"

I was confused. I didn't want him to just stay close by. I wanted him to be closer than that.

"But… you and I…" he said. "what we feel is because our blood is similar. It attracts us to each other, but you are my brother's wife and I'm the uncle to your daughter…"

"I'm not his wife, Zale. I'm his widow."

I stepped forward, but he stepped back.

"That's not how I want this to be," I said. "I was falling for you long before I knew you were his brother. Knowing who you are doesn't change things for me."

371

"But knowing who *you* are changes things for *me*," he said coldly. "I lived my whole life in his shadow," Zale said. "I can't spend the rest of my life wondering if I'm still in it."

His eyes were clear and decisive.

"Oh," I said, looking down.

Rejection.

"What all of this has taught me, Britt, is how much we really don't know about each other. You had secrets and so did I. And I know why we kept them, I know we were both afraid of getting hurt or being betrayed. What matters most to me right now is that you and I learn to trust each other. Completely. We're going to need to have each other's backs if we're going to go after Fairchild."

I looked up at him.

"You're right," I said. "It's better not to get distracted."

He turned his head to the side, recognizing that I was trying to recover from the humiliation of rejection.

He moved toward me and pulled me into him, which I allowed only because I really wanted to be close to him.

"I'm not going anywhere," he said. "I just think that a lot has happened and its gotten messy and…"

"And we got ourselves into this mess together."

"So we should probably stay in it together," he added.

Together.

"…as partners," he clarified.

30
LEADER

I found Eamon sitting in the field of the Ambit on the way to the Crossing. At his feet there were two mounds of fresh dirt. Next to them, was the stone with James' name on it. Eamon had created a graveyard.

I sat down next to him.

"Where's Buckley?" I asked.

"I'm not sure," he said. "After we buried them, he took the other vehicle and left."

"Do you think he's going after her?"

Eamon shook his head.

"I don't know. He hasn't said a word since..."

Eamon wiped the sweat from his forehead with the back of his hand. He hadn't left the field since the events of the early morning, and I knew he was exhausted. He and Buckley stayed behind to bury our dead. Later that day, we planned to have a ceremony for them.

I noticed that Rutherford's dried blood was still on Eamon's face and the collar of his shirt.

"I don't think he'd know what to do if he caught up with her," Eamon was talking about Buckley. "He thinks he loves her."

I shook my head.

"I should have seen it," Eamon growled. "She was right there, under our noses and I should have seen what she was doing, but I—"

His jaw clenched and he shook his head out of frustration again. "She was right," he admitted. "And that kills me."

"Right about what?"

"Every damn thing she said," he scoffed. "She was right. We underestimated her because she was young and sweet. We thought she needed us to save her, and the Underground knew that's how we'd see her. They played us right from the start."

In front of him there were several long sticks and his pocketknife. He picked one stick and the pocketknife up and began running the blade down the branch to remove the bark. I noticed there were several other sticks in front of him that he'd already stripped.

"And what she said, about me not suspecting her because I wanted it to be Zale," he lowered his hands again. "She was right about that too," he growled. "I hate that she was right about that."

Eamon looked at me, "I can admit to you that I was wrong about him. On this. I was wrong about him and I'm truly sorry for the pressure I put on you to believe me."

He turned back to the project in his hands. "I can admit that to you, but I don't know if I can ever say that to Zale."

"I think he knows, Eamon," I said. "I think he understands. He blames himself for Winnie too. And James. I think he's carried it for years and so he understands why you hate him..."

Eamon kept his head down.

"I think the question is, can you trust him moving forward?"

Eamon looked up.

"Moving forward?"

"Look," I said. "We're all in the same boat here. The Ambit isn't going to be home for us. They don't want us here anymore than we want to be here. And once word gets back to the Underground that Isla is here..."

"...they'll have someone here within a week," Eamon speculated.

"So, we can't hunker down here," I said. "The Guiding Authority has offered to send us with some supplies from the bunker: food, ammo and weapons. They just want us to leave. I'm not sure yet, but there's talk of some of the Ambitors wanting to come with us. Many of them feel betrayed by the Guiding Authority and I can't blame them."

"So where will we go?" he asked.

"I'm not sure. We can't go back to the farmhouse because Fairchild will know to look for us there. Lucita said she knows of a place on the other side of the great lake. It will take a long time to get there, especially with a large group, but it's something to aim for. I thought maybe, if she'll let me, we could build a harness and Cinder could take me there to scout it out. I know how to ride a horse. How different can she be from that?"

He looked at me in amazement.

"What?"

He shook his head.

Does he think I'm crazy for thinking I can ride on a dragon?

"I know there will be some differences in opinion, but we're all on the same side now, aren't we? We have a common enemy, and that makes us…"

"…allies," he said.

"I want to know what the Underground is up to. They're after my daughter. They've killed my husband, and your sister, and many others. Once we get set up somewhere and Isla and Seph are safe, I have every intention of breaking my promise to Fairchild."

Eamon smiled, "Good."

"I think we all have a vested interest in figuring out what she's planning, what the Underground wants with Isla. You know more about the Underground than any of us. And Zale is fearless…literally. Cinder can protect us from monitors. Jonathon has medical knowledge. Lucita has connections with other societies. Buckley's a good shot. Maris knows people in the Outside that can keep us informed and I…?"

Eamon looked at me.

What is my part?

"You?" Eamon waited.

What is my part? Besides protecting Isla.

"I—I'm sure I can be helpful in some way too," I laughed nervously.

Eamon didn't laugh. His face was serious.

"It's not obvious to you, but I see it."

"See what?"

"Who you are?"

"Who I am?"

Who am I?

"You're the leader."

Leader?

"You're the common link between all of us, and frankly, you're the one person I think we can all agree to trust."

"Me? I'm not a leader."

He nodded, then smiled. "You have great instincts, Britt. You don't see yourself that way, but it's true. A good leader will stand for what's right, like you did in the cottage last night. And a good leader can always see the strength of the individual members and their potential to be successful. But a great leader…is hesitant to lead. Because they don't want control as much as they want unity."

I stared at him.

"Even Cinder follows your lead," he said. "Even she can see it. You're the only one that hasn't noticed."

Noticed? He said it so casually, as though it was obvious.

"Noticed what?"

"That you're already leading. And if you're leading, then I'm coming with you," he said nonchalantly. Then he turned back to his task. He said that last part like it was already decided.

Was it? Would the others agree? Was I to be their leader?

Eamon turned back to the wooden pieces in front of him. He was tying them together to form three cross shaped creations. He turned one over and I saw a name etched in the side of it.

James Maris.

James had been raised by Maris. He was the only father James ever knew. I felt sure that James would have agreed with that last name.

The second creation said Christopher Rutherford and I noticed that Eamon took extra time tying the string. He was quiet, remembering his father. The man that was flawed but intended to do better. He shed a tear for his father.

The third creation had Nanny's name on it. The goat. Our small and stable friend. She'd made us smile at the Shelter Tree on the worst night of my life. She'd been Seph's companion during the darkest days in the city under the ground.

I thought of how my father's name might have been on a fourth creation, but it wasn't. Isla's blood had healed him. That was something I was still trying to understand. But it made me even more sure of our need to band together and move on from the Ambit.

"Have you seen my father?" I asked.

Eamon looked up and nodded toward the Shelter Tree. I stood and searched the line for a sign of my father. I spotted a set of booted feet reclined behind the tree.

"Is Cinder with him?" I asked, wondering if she'd healed and left, or if she was with him but not visible.

Eamon stood up next to me.

"I don't know where she went," he said.

Then he held one of his creations in his hand like a sword.

"They're swords," I stated, suddenly recognizing the shape he'd formed them into.

He stabbed each wooden creation into the ground by the graves and stepped back to look at them.

"I've seen pictures in books of battlefields that were covered in graves like this. Each with a sword handle above it." He explained. "It only seemed fitting to give them the same honor because like it or not, it feels like we are at war."

"Eamon?" I asked. "Is everything a battlefield now?"

He looked at me and exhaled.

"Yeah, I think it is. I think this war has gone on a lot longer than any of us realized. And now we're in it but I'm not sure what side we're on."

"That's because we aren't on a side," I admitted. "I think we're in the middle of it."

31
NEW TERRITORY

My father was asleep at the Ambit Crossing.

I kicked his boot.

"You dead, old man?" I joked.

He opened his eyes and I smiled.

"Apparently not," he admitted.

I sat down next to him and leaned against the tree.

"How are you feeling?" I asked.

He pulled his shirt to the side and showed me the wound where the bullet had gone into his chest. "I have a bullet in me somewhere," he said. "But I'm alive."

"How come you never told me?" I asked.

He looked at me out of the corner of his eye.

"About the dragon's blood?"

"About all of it," I said. "The dragons, the blood, James, the fact that you can heal?"

"Will any answer I give be enough?"

"No," I said. "It'll never be enough, but I'd still like to hear the truth."

His brow angled down as he thought about how to answer.

"I wanted to forget."

"Forget what?"

"All of it," he said. "What my father was a part of, what he'd put into my blood, what I'd passed on to you and to Isla. I wanted to forget the dragons and the MIL and the death that I'd caused."

"You caused?" I asked. "You weren't responsible for the MIL."

"Not directly, you're right. I wasn't. But I was a doctor, and I administered it. I supported it. I pushed it on people that didn't want it. I put my faith in medicine and when it failed, I felt responsible for the ones I'd misled. When I came to the Ambit, I was happy to let nature take its course without medicine. I didn't want to cure people or save them, in fact, when we lost people in the Ambit, I was jealous of them."

"Jealous of them?"

"Healing is something I've been able to do since I was ten years old." He fidgeted with his hand, and I noticed that the wound from the night before had almost completely disappeared. His skin had regenerated.

"Since then, I've wondered what it would take for me to die." He pulled up his sleeve and revealed the scars on his shoulder. He put his finger over one of his MIL scars. "This is where my immunization was that year. In 2084. I was supposed to die like all the rest. But instead...I was a witness to it. My blood had been tampered with. It was unnatural. We messed with the natural order of things and now I've lived a lifetime being reminded of it."

"Reminded of what?"

"Reminded that death is the unfortunate ending to every story...except mine." He laughed slightly.

"I seem—" he said, "—to be cursed to live it out."

"Live what out?"

"Last night, as I was laying there," he nodded toward the spot where he'd been shot. "I thought maybe that was it. Maybe I would finally be released from this hell I've been living and reliving. And then my granddaughter. My sweet little girl, who carries the same curse I do, she healed me."

My heart sunk.

"It's not a curse, father."

"It is, Britt. You just don't know it yet. Think about it. Chasen is dead because of it and so are billions of others. Because we messed with nature." He laughed. "We tampered with the natural evolution of life and tried to create medicine that reversed the order of things. Life and death. That's the natural order and we couldn't just leave it alone."

379

"My father accidentally cursed me, and I've accidentally cursed you," he said. He looked at me with heavy eyelids full of tears, "I'm so sorry, I just wanted you to be normal, to have a normal life. I didn't want you to know what we are."

"Normal?"

I laughed a little. Then I laughed a little louder and harder. Then I was laughing hysterically.

"What's so funny?"

"No one is normal," I said. "We're all just really good at pretending!"

I laughed again.

"We're all just trying to be normal because that's what we think everyone else is. What if no one is normal? What if we're ruining our weirdness by hiding these amazing qualities that Cinder's blood has afforded us? Wouldn't that be a shame?"

I looked around.

Cinder was there. I could feel her.

"Cinder!" I called. "Can you show yourself?"

Within seconds, she appeared. To my surprise, she'd regrown her tail.

"Look at her!" I said to my father. He was looking down at his hands. "Dad, look at her!"

He looked up.

"She's regrown her tail! There's nothing normal about that. That's incredible!" I laughed. Then I stood up and opened my arms. "Wouldn't it be a shame if Cinder thought she was a regular monitor like the others? If she refused to fly even though she has wings? Refused to breathe fire to protect herself? Wouldn't it be a shame if she believed she was nothing more than a bird?"

My father's face opened into a reluctant grin.

"She's a dragon!" I yelled. "She's a dragon! She's fierce and protective and loyal and powerful and she's the only one of her kind. Just like me, and you and Isla! Just like every person ever, regardless of whether they have Cinder's blood or not, every person has something that's wonderfully weird about them. We're so busy trying to be normal, we've forgotten how wonderfully weird we were created to be!"

"What if being weird isn't a curse, it's a gift? What if the fact that you can heal equips you for something incredible that no one else can do."

He stared at me.

"Last night, a woman came to our borders and murdered people. Doesn't that make you angry? Doesn't it make you want to do something? Fight back?"

"I'm too old to fight back," he said.

"No, you're too old to be feeling so sorry for yourself!"

I squatted in front of him and put my hands on his knees. "You're only a victim to all of this," I said looking up at the Ambit, "if you choose to stay a victim to it. And if that's what you want, then so be it. But if you could just see what I see...have vision, then maybe you will get to die!"

He looked up and gave me a smirk that said he knew I was teasing him.

"You still have time to die doing something great."

In the distance, I could see Isla walking toward the Crossing.

"Isla's coming," I said.

I stood up.

The sight of her sobered me and I pictured Fairchild pulling her away from me.

"The Underground will be coming for her, dad. Like it or not, she has to leave the Ambit now."

He stood up next to me. We watched her in the field coming toward us.

Behind us Cinder started stomping and dancing in circles.

My father exhaled.

"James said they're scared of her."

"Why? She's just a child."

Cinder moved to the Ambit Crossing and waited anxiously for Isla to get to her.

What is Cinder doing?

"I don't know why they'd fear a little girl," he said, "but I have noticed something in the last few months that you should know about."

I turned to him. "What?"

"She's having dreams," he said. "She's seeing things that I can't explain."

"Is it an ability?" I asked, "Like how her blood can heal?"

He shrugged, "I don't know but the worse they get the more she seems to be affected. She's started to see things while she's awake."

"What kind of things?"

"Sometimes it's people," he said. "Sometimes it's animals. She talks to them."

"What?" I scowled. "Is she okay? Should we be concerned?"

He looked down at his hands again. "To be honest, I don't know. It could be a mental disorder or dementia of some sort. She could have something going on neurologically. It's hard to say."

My eyes filled with tears at the thought of her being sick. I thought of Chasen, and my heart hurt.

We watched as Isla drew closer to the Crossing.

Cinder pranced back and forth, waiting patiently for her to step over the line. When she finally did, Cinder's body calmed, and she backed up.

"What's she doing?" I asked my father.

Isla's eyes were focused on Cinder as she stepped closer and closer to her. She was fearless.

To my amazement, as Isla got close to Cinder, Cinder lowered her body to the ground. She stretched out her two front legs, raising her tail end in the air, which lowered her head down further.

"Is...she...?"

My father gasped. "It looks like she's bowing."

"Bowing?"

Isla reached out and touched the top of Cinder's head. Cinder raised herself back up from the ground and nudged Isla's chest. Isla let out a guttural laugh.

"Dragons are territorial," my father said.

I remembered the two-tailed fire-breather at the hospital and how he hadn't entered the building because it was Cinder's nest.

Is that why Cinder wouldn't go in the Ambit?

Because she thought it was a nest?

Isla's nest?

Suddenly, the pieces began coming together in my head.

Isla ran back toward the Ambit and Cinder followed.

Isla hadn't come to the Crossing to see her grandfather or me. She came out for Cinder. To welcome her.

Did Isla know that Cinder was waiting for her permission to enter? Is Isla somehow an alpha to her, as Cinder had been to the other monitors?

Is that why the Underground is afraid of her?

Because she's an alpha?

My mind spun with questions. Thousands of them. But they all funneled down to this one.

"Dad?"

He watched silently next to me.

"If James and I both have dragon's blood, then what does that make Isla?"

I watched the two of them play in the field of the Ambit.

"Dad, what *is* Isla?"

END OF PART TWO

BONUS CHAPTER
MR. & MRS. WARDEN

The platform was quiet and dark, until the hum of the ramp broke the silence. The darkness dispersed as the headlights of the vehicle filled the damp hollowness of the cement parking structure. The truck pulled into the parking spot labeled *MCC: Guard 44*.

The engine's purr died and the door creaked open. A woman took her exit. Other than the splash of red that was splattered on it, her face was pale and colorless. She quickly tucked the keys to the vehicle in her pocket and then leaned back into the door to retrieve a long-handled bag. She strapped it over her shoulder and across her chest.

Again, she returned through the vehicle door, this time to retrieve a bigger object, which was wrapped in a blanket. The blanket was a dark green color, other than the blood that was seeping from one end of it. The blood dripped slowly onto the platform's cement. The woman didn't care if it was visible, she continued about her business anyway.

She stowed the blanketed object under her arm and with a mighty force, slammed the car door shut. The crashing metal echoed throughout the empty garage.

Next the woman sauntered to the end of the dark platform and through the door that overlooked the Floor of the Outside. Colorful lights flickered on and off. She stood for a moment, taking it in. Even as the liveliness of the lights reflected off her skin, her expression didn't change. From the outside, she appeared stone cold and emotionless. But on the inside, her mind twisted and writhed wanting to break free from the robotic movements her body executed.

"A life for a life."

She turned and made her way to the stairwell.

The blood-stained woman paid no mind to the attention that her appearance and cargo earned her, as she navigated the Floor. Swarms of people parted in her presence, as though they knew her and the importance of the bounty tucked under her arm. She didn't hesitate when some unknowing passer-by stepped into her path; she just shoved him out of her way. She told herself that he should have known better than to step in her way. He should recognize who she is. She didn't walk fast and she didn't walk slow, she just walked. And they just watched.

At the other end of the Floor, she found the elevator shaft. A small cluster of people were gathered there, waiting for a turn to elevate above ground or waiting for someone to return below it. She made no excuses or apologies as she forced her way to the front of the line and punched the button to call the elevator.

The others watched from a distance, whispering quietly to one another about her bloody garments and the strange object under her arm. One man was even brave enough to scoff at her rudeness. When she heard this, she turned and stared him down and said, "You don't like it, then do something about it." The man's mouth dropped open in disbelief. The woman held him locked in her view, like she had locked him in the scope of her gun. The man diverted his eyes away from her and disappeared in the crowd.

She waited only briefly for the elevator to ring and invite her aboard through metal doors. Without thought or hesitation, she stepped aboard. Once inside, she turned and faced the crowd.

Someone else followed her onto the elevator. But before he could get beyond the doors, she reached out her hand to hold him off.

"Take the next one," she snarled at him.

The man backed up, confused. She glared at him until the doors closed and broke her line of vision. The elevator rang.

Inside the woman hurried to set down the bloody object. Lifting her left foot from the ground, she removed her boot. From a thin crack, in the side of the black-soled boot, she retrieved a golden key.

She fit it into the keyhole in the elevator, and with the turn of her wrist, the digital number window displayed: *Floor 12*. With that, she started to ascend. The woman quickly replaced her boot and picked up her bloody cargo. She took in a nervous breath as she waited for the doors to separate again.

When they did, she found what was in front of her was not the dark, dingy underworld of the Outside. Before her was the bright, clean, and rich world of the twelfth floor. She was temporarily blinded by the intense yellow daylight that poured in from the windows that lined the outer walls. Once her vision normalized, she stepped off the elevator and made her way down the corridor.

The middle of the hall was adorned with a gold framed mirror. She paused for a moment and reached up to pat her hair and wipe her face. When she noticed the dried crusts of blood that blemished her complexion, she pulled up the corner of her stained shirt and attempted to wipe her face with it.

"Fairchild?" a woman's voice found her rubbing her face furiously, trying to make it clean. She jumped at the sound of her own name.

Fairchild whipped around to see an older woman standing feet from her. She wondered how they knew she was there, then she remembered the cameras that had probably followed her since her vehicle landed in its parking spot. Fairchild cleared her throat. "Oh, hi," she sputtered nervously.

Fairchild reminded herself to appear confident, to not let them see how afraid she really was. Britt's words echoed in her mind, "A life for a life."

The woman in front of her was more refined than Fairchild. Only in her fifties, the woman looked much older. She kept her hair long to remind herself of her youthful days, when her locks were once auburn instead of white. She was average height and carried more weight around her midsection than most women in the Outside could afford.

Fairchild's stomach rumbled.

The woman's eyes dropped down and stared at Fairchild's midsection and Fairchild wished that her stomach knew who it was in front of.

The woman's face was pointed and poised, but she could look kind when she wanted to. Fairchild had seen the woman's face change in an instant in the past. She hoped that the face she wore now, with a pair of blue jeans and an orange sweatshirt, would stay present. She had on gardening gloves, with one hand holding a bunch of fresh flowers, while the other grasped a pair of gardening sheers. Fairchild tried not to stare at the sheers.

"You're back," the woman said kindly.

Fairchild nodded. The woman studied the object under Fairchild's arm, which caused her smile to appear and her wrinkles to disappear.

"You poor thing, look at you. You're a mess."

Fairchild didn't bother to look down at her clothes; she knew the state of her appearance.

The woman waited, as though she expected Fairchild to respond. When she didn't, the woman added, "I'll go tell Oz you're back." She disappeared through a door off the hallway.

As Fairchild waited patiently for the woman to return, she found a window to look out. Stories below where she stood, she saw the basic outline of the city that once existed there, remnants of streets and cars, now overgrown with vegetation. The words came to her again, "A life for a life."

"Fairchild," the woman's voice crept into her ears, like the long, wet tongue of a snake.

"Yes?"

"Oz wants to see you," the woman waved for Fairchild to follow her.

The young woman complied with the request and followed the older woman down another hallway to a heavy metal door. She opened the door and held it for Fairchild to walk through. It was a stairwell, they climbed upward.

Another heavy door pushed open and introduced them to an outdoor area on the roof of the building. The weather was just as beautiful and delightful to Fairchild's skin, as the hall windows had promised.

On the far side of the roof, a man stood looking over the edge. She knew him as Oz.

On the other far corner of the roof was a beautiful lush garden, with vegetables and trees weighed down with fruit. Fairchild's mouth watered at the mere sight of it. She remembered a time in her youth when the trees bountiful fruits were her rewards.

Do this, get an apple.

Do that, get a cherry.

Just the memory of the sweet juices on her lips reminded her of the training she'd been forced to endure for all these years. Her stomach turned a little in confusion. The beauty and guaranteed deliciousness of the fruit did not justify the actions she would take to earn them. She knew that, but what choice did she have? For the first time that she could remember, she hated the sight of the fruit and the memory it produced. She forced herself to look away from the garden.

The woman with the gardening gloves disappeared behind a line of bushes lush with blueberries.

Fairchild cautiously made her way across the rooftop toward the man. When she was only feet from him, she stood still and waited for him to acknowledge her.

After a few moments, the man turned and studied her, "Simza said you were a mess." He smiled cruelly, "She was right."

Fairchild forced a smile. "I know. I apologize that I didn't clean up first, but I have something for you, and I didn't want to take any chances. I knew you would want to see it as soon as possible."

The man smiled again and looked down at the item under her arm. "Very well, would you like a piece of fruit, my dear?" he asked politely, opening his arm toward the garden.

Fairchild avoided following his gesture toward the green. "No, thank you." Oz's eyes narrowed on her. She hadn't refused him in years and wondered if she'd made a mistake doing it now. It was the way that the fruit repulsed her that made her decline so quickly. She regretted it, thinking it would have been safer to just accept the offer.

"A drink then?" he asked.

Sure not to turn him down a second time, Fairchild nodded without hesitation.

He walked past her to a table with two chairs. On the table was a pitcher of yellow liquid, a bucket and four glasses. From the bucket, the man pulled a few cubes of ice and placed them in the glasses. He began pouring a beverage for each of them.

"Simza!" the man yelled to the woman in the garden. She looked up from her rosebush, "Care for some lemonade, Darling?"

Simza wiped her forehead with the back of her gloved hand. "Oh, yes, Dear Boy, that sounds lovely," she said sweetly.

She crossed the rooftop to join her husband and Fairchild at the table. The man pulled the chair out for his wife and then sat in the second chair. Fairchild stood, holding her glass of lemonade in one hand and the bloody blanket in the other.

The man handed a glass to his wife and suggested, "A toast?"

She nodded, "To our Fairest Child?"

The two of them clanked their glasses together, neither of them offering to do the same with Fairchild's glass.

"Okay, Fairchild, tell us…" the man said. "What have you brought for us?"

Fairchild sat her glass of lemonade down on the table. She managed to avoid drinking from it without seeming ungrateful. Then carefully, she sat the blanket down on the rooftop and folded back the corners.

Simza's eyes widened, and she gasped, and then a long slender smile slithered across her lips.

"Is that what I think it is, my child?" the man asked Fairchild.

Fairchild nodded, letting a cordial smile find her face for the first time since returning to the Outside. "It's her tail."

The man knelt on the ground next to the dragon's appendage. He reached out to touch the severed end and retracted a bloody finger. He held his finger close to his face, studying it.

"Well done, child," he finally said. "Well done."

Fairchild reluctantly relished in her father's approval.

"Is that all?" Simza asked.

Fairchild thought for a moment. She wondered if somehow word of what else she had brought for them had traveled ahead of her. It's true that she had considered keeping it for herself, reading it in private.

Simza and Oz both stared at her, trying to read her expression.

Fairchild knew she could not risk keeping it for herself. Somehow, they would know, they always knew.

"I almost forgot," Fairchild lied. She dug into her bag and pulled out the red book with the bullet hole and blood splatter.

Simza's eyes lit up at the sight of it. She recognized it. She was so elated to have it back in her possession, that she almost felt forgiving of Fairchild's obvious disloyalty in that moment.

Fairchild placed the book onto the table. When she reached out, Simza took hold of her arm. "What's happened here?" she asked, gesturing to the scar on the young woman's upper arm.

Fairchild retracted her arm hastily. She hadn't meant for them to see the place where her limb had almost been completely severed on the Blood Mission.

Simza seemed put off by Fairchild's sudden movement. "Let me see it, child," she ordered.

Fairchild swallowed hard, and then rolled up her sleeve so that her parents could examine her scar.

"Such a shame," Simza observed. "Your skin was so perfect."

"What happened?" Oz asked.

"It's okay, really. The monitors got too close, and I got hurt, but it's okay. I'm okay," Fairchild reassured them, pulling her sleeve back down over her fleshy pink skin.

Simza stared at Oz. He watched Fairchild, staring at her. Fairchild tried not to look at either of them.

"Well," Simza finally broke the awkwardness after a moment, "*this* is good to see." She picked up the red book and flipped through the pages.

"Ah," Oz said, taking the book from the hands of his wife. "Now we have everything we need to resume our work."

END OF BOOK ONE of THE KHIMAIRA CHAIN

For more Khimaira Chain products visit:
www.TheKhimairaChain.com
THIRD EDITION

What happened to Coya, Jordan, and Conrad?

the
WIND FARM
MYSTERY

a Khimaira Chain
Murder Mystery
by KJ Spencer

www.thekhimairachain.com/product-page/the-wind-farm-mystery

Made in the USA
Columbia, SC
13 February 2023

11829142R00240